ARX

CITY OF BROKEN MINDS

EDMUND HURST

BARB ICAN PRESS

Published by Barbican Press, Los Angeles and London

Copyright © Edmund Hurst, 2024

Registered UK office: 1 Ashenden Road, London E5 0DP

US office: 1032 19th Street, Unit 2, Santa Monica CA90403

www.barbicanpress.com

@barbicanpress1

A CIP catalogue for this book is available from the British Library

Distributed in North America by Publishers Group West

ISBN: 978-1-909954-87-8

Ebook ISBN: 978-1-909954-97-7

For Biss, Nyx & Pickle

When we tell a story.
We are living
Memory.
- Amanda Gorman

Memories rust.

Sharp edges dull. Passions smoulder. Dreams disappear.

The past is quenched by the passage of time

and the truth is lost in the fog.

To return, we must forget.

Forget the chains of reality. Recall those dreams of

chaos. Look beyond the smoke and sweat, the mist

and dirt. Discover a city where truth dies.

Arx.

PART 1

AUDEAMUS

CHAPTER 1

Caelan splayed his hand, palm up, across the bench. Sat huddled in the alley, he stabbed the space between his fingers with a needle-tip knife. Five jabs. For the five memories he still had.

Blue fire.
Smoke in his mouth.
The twilight sky.
A knife against his throat.
Violet eyes.

Habit is not memory. Caelan didn't know how long he'd been slicing his fingers, though the heavy scars around his fingertips gave some indication. He just let his body do its thing, whilst his mind dug through the futile mists of the last six months. Anything before that was like trying to picture the inside of the womb. Or the taste of grave dirt. Dark and soggy.

Same as the sky. Dawn bled through ashen clouds stained by a caustic wind that tasted of rust. Arx's breath. Like tongue-kissing a chimney.

The knife jumped between his fingers, made a satisfying *clunk* each time it pierced the wood. Eight-inches of iron, it was his only relic of an existence before this one.

Blue fire blazing chains of flame around his wrist.
Smoke in his mouth, cloying sweet in his lungs.
The twilight sky void of all stars.
A knife against his throat, cold blood dripping down his neck.
Violet eyes in a grinning skull.

Faster now, his knife-hand blurring, breath panted out. There was something about the threat, the danger, that made the memories sharper.

Kept them in focus. Some mornings he woke in a sweat, heart grinding into his lungs because one more moment might have faded. One more fragment of his existence lost. That panic haunted the emptiness of his sleep. The place dreams were supposed to be.

Everyone does their best to ignore madmen in their midst, and the people of Rotheart were experts. Scarred and scared as he was, they pushed through the alleyway without speaking. Hot breath against his ears, the coin-bitter stink of unwashed wounds.

And so many eyes pocked with whirling blue cataracts. A legacy of broken minds, of memories sacrificed. But they had nothing on him.

As his knife leapt from the scored tabletop, his own eyes flashed back at him from a shard of sunlight caught in the burnished metal. Beyond mere cataracts, the sapphire blizzard in his skull swallowed his sclera, iris, pupils. Blue as frozen fire trapped in glass.

Blue fire blazing chains of flame around his wrist, boiling his bloody-tipped fingers.

Smoke in his mouth, cloying sweet in his lungs as another memory suffocates.

The twilight sky void of all stars, pierced by a spear of blue-silver.

A knife against his throat, cold blood dripping down his neck and a silken voice whispering survival in his ear.

Violet eyes in a grinning skull of the man who stole his mind, who incinerated his past, who looked at him empty and sobbing and said… and said…

'Aaagh!' Caelan slammed the knife into his little finger. Tears spit in his eyes and he sucked a breath through his teeth. He squeezed the wound with white-knuckled fingers. Blood oozed through the creases on his palm.

'I haven't seen you bleed in weeks.'

Caelan spun around. Kuyt had found him. The only man in Arx who still wandered down dirty alleyways looking out for those everyone else had forgotten. A halo of white hair puffed around his shoulders, caught in the cold cloud of his breath.

'I've forgotten. I've forgotten what he said to me, that first day I woke up. When he ripped my past out of my head, I looked at him and he said something and I can't remember it.'

The old man wrinkled his moustache and took Caelan's bloody hand in his own. 'You're obsessing again. What about your breathing?'

'Fuck my breathing.'

'I've never heard of a lungjob before. Sounds awfully stuffy.' He wound a scrap of bandage tight around the split fingertip. 'What do you remember from today? Talk me through your morning.'

'Waking up before the sun. The taste of salt from the washbasin. Addie's snoring.'

'That's three memories right there. So you lost one and gained three. You're still at a net positive.'

Caelan shook his head, hair whipping around his shoulders. 'Those aren't memories. Just experience. Memory is what we preserve, the moments we wind into stories that define us. I haven't had any of those since my first day.' He splayed his newly bandaged hand, pulse throbbing in his ear. 'Five memories. All connected. I'm still stuck on Day One. And it's starting to fade.'

'Only because you're afraid.'

Caelan barked a humourless laugh. 'Of course I'm afraid. Reality hurts the first time around. That's why infants wail their tiny lungs out. And if it hurts too much, I know what I'll do. If I forget again… emptiness is all that's left.'

'Memories make the man. Is this who you want to be?'

'Better than being no-one.' Caelan was silent for a while. 'Sometimes I fantasise about dying slowly. They say your life flashes before your eyes. I wonder what I'd see.'

'Who cares? You'd be dead.' Kuyt flicked Caelan's bandaged finger. Pink blood seeped through the gauze. 'At least this way you're still here, to bleed and cry and piss yourself in fear. Memories fade. That's why we make new ones.' He glanced skyward, frowned, then stood up. 'The execution starts soon. Come with me and I'll show you what you're so afraid of.'

Caelan looked at him. 'Why?'

'Because the alternative is to sit here obsessing over fragments until they fade and you lose your eyes. So come with me. And start Day Two.'

Caelan paused. 'Is Day Two a nice memory?'

'No. You'll hate it. But you'll survive. I'll make sure of that.'

Caelan wiped his knife on his trousers. 'A bastard of an assumption to bet my life on.' He stood up. 'Lead the way.'

Together they made for the square. Rotheart was well named. Narrow alleyways of shapeless concrete and cobblestone clustered into thick streets, all leading towards the rancid core.

A knot of Walkers forced past a group of kids, snarling and snapping. Black cloaks and scarred leather, their vow to keep Arx peaceful was a sharp contrast to the copper blades glittering at their waists. A single blue fleck swam in every eye.

'Remember the boot on your neck, because the boot itself sure doesn't,' Kuyt growled when they were safely out of earshot.

Cramped buildings and winding streets gave way to an open square, broken stone and old wood barricades clustered the edges like a chest cavity cracked open.

The scaffold throbbed in the centre beneath the clomping boots of Walkers.

Green with decay and rusted nails, it groaned beneath the force of the wind. Half-cleaned stains and splintered stairs were the scars of its own history.

Not much of a crowd. Twelve, thirteen people huddled together. The air thick with silence. An ex-foundryman, forge-burns gnawing across his chest, ran his nails down the flaking skin on his forearms. A lass in an apron clenched and unclenched her fists. Veins stood out on her arms like ropes.

'So few even bother to watch anymore.' Kuyt's eyes burned vicious.

A thump clanged against metal, a snotty sob, some bark of sour laughter broke between the bars of the holding pen. Six, seven prisoners dressed in sackcloth. Each with a black hood cinched around their necks.

'These executions have happened once a week, give or take, for the last forty years.' Kuyt's voice was oddly calm.

'Why are you telling me?'

'Because there are things that all of us should remember.'

The first of the condemned was led to the scaffold. Walkers locked his manacled feet into a metal loop, then tore the hood from his head.

The man blinked into the pale sunlight. He didn't look angry. He looked tired. Caelan found his eyes, forest green beneath thick eyebrows. Twin cataracts drizzled through his pupils.

Kuyt fished a small book and a charcoal pencil from inside his coat.

'What are you doing?' Caelan asked.

'Remembering him. Because he won't.' Kuyt sketched quickly, the bloke's face forming on the parchment. High cheekbones, a half-day of stubble. 'I started this when the scaffold was first built. Back when these executions were for rebels. My friends. The Austelli, that's what we used to call ourselves before they took that as well. Crowds so thick they spilled into alleyways and over rooftops.'

'What changed?'

'I already told you. Eventually, all memories fade. Or are taken from us.'

Something stirred in the smog. A shadow that broke the mist.

Heavy footsteps splintered the ground beneath an armoured giant. Blue-silver steel glimmered like a midnight sky set alight. Its scarlet cloak wrapped around the hilt of an enormous axe. It lifted its head.

Empty onyx eyes set in a screaming, metal mask. The void where a soul should be. Caelan knew what it was to have eyes like that.

'The Sightless,' Kuyt breathed. He tucked his sketchbook back beneath his coat.

A scrawny bloke scrambled to the front of the platform and cleared his throat. 'Voters of Rotheart! By the authority of Viceroy DeSüle, Mistress of the Ropes, these criminals are brought here to receive justice. As they forget their crimes, so too does the city absolve them of their responsibility and gift them their lives.'

The condemned man took a shaking breath of cold air. Caelan felt something oily squirm around his heart.

'Arthur Colis, guilty of trespass and acts of murderous intent towards Viceroy Jace DeSané, Minister of Commerce.' The scrawny bloke shouted.

'Murderous intent is it? We didn't have a blade between us. Couldn't have afforded one even if we wanted. No Salt Ponies means no food down here. Winter is on the way and we can't eat metal.' The prisoner shivered.

Without warning, Kuyt grabbed Caelan's collar.

Caelan struggled, but the old man was merciless. He dragged him through the meagre crowd and threw him to the ground before the scaffold.

The Sightless drew its axe. Blue-silver, same as its armour. A curved moon edge, sharp enough to slice through the morning smog. The prisoner fell to his knees. He didn't scream. Maybe that was brave.

Anticipation pounded in Caelan's ears. He locked eyes with the condemned man.

In that instant they were connected. Knelt together at the precipice.

'Don't let them do it.' The words burst through Arthus Colis' lips. 'I'd rather die. Rather a corpse than-'

A Walker forced a gag between the man's lips. The cloth muted his words, but he still sobbed. He still screamed.

The axe fell.

It slid through the prisoner's neck without resistance. Without... anything. No blood. No crunch of bone. The axe sliced through, but the head remained in place. Untouched.

And Arthur Colis' eyes boiled from his face. Replaced by a dense, blue fog.

Eyeless, the man once called Arthur Colis stood up. Breath filled his lungs by instinct. Without thoughts. Without memories. Hollow.

Caelan's heartbeat caught on the ragged edges of his throat.

Kuyt bent to whisper in his ear. 'You are not empty.'

Overhead, the clouds burst with cold rain.

CHAPTER 2

Samantha Acarris swung the clay crucible into the heart of her forge-fire. The basement shimmered with heat. White-gold flames curled through the coals and sparks flickered in the air like lost stars. On the roof of her mouth, the soot was sweet.

The molten mixture wound in syrupy threads in the crucible. Carbon, sand, glass, ash, bone, coke and just a fragment of precious iron. She wedged a forge-gloved hand down the front of her shirt and scratched her pits like a mongrel trying to dislodge a tick. Or like a guilty blacksmith trying to pretend she hadn't gambled her future on resurrecting the long-dead corpse of a myth.

'Figured you'd be at this again.' Forgemaster Jak Mendy shuffled down the stairs. Almost smacked his head on a low beam. The man was a colossus. 'How long you been up?'

Sam ran a gloved hand through her close-cropped hair. It squelched. 'Longer than you. We don't pay you to work mornings anymore?'

'Sun isn't even up yet.' He threw on an apron and made a pointed effort not to look at her. Or her forge. 'This don't look like horseshoes.'

'Horseshoes don't exactly get a girl out of bed.'

'Work is work.' Jak ran his stubby finger down the list pinned to the wall. 'Can't see any orders for a bankrupting lump of slag no idiot would call Callisteel.'

She might have blushed, if her cheeks weren't already glowing. 'I'm so close Jak.'

'How many years you been saying that now?' Jak lit his oven. 'You're wasting your Da's money, my time, and your life. Let it go lass.' He hefted his hammer down from the wall.

'Let it go.' Sam drew herself to her full height. She was no Jak Mendy, but most people lived in her shadow. 'Like you did?'

'Aye. Like I did.' Jak's eyes darted, as they so often did, to the metal rod that hung on the wall between their forges. It measured from her wrist to the tip of her middle finger. Black iron, beyond expensive. A double-edged blade wound into a funnel of overlapping feathers, inlaid with impossible spiral carvings. 'When I found my Father eyeless and drooling with that thing driven through his chest. When they took the last of his mind in payment for some more smoke and ash and empty promises. His heart stopped a week later, but the man himself was gone years before. Do you still call him 'Da' when he doesn't remember you're his son?'

'But Callisteel is...'

'Callisteel was a weapon.' Another man might have shouted that. Jak was soft. 'It died and was forgotten. Or perhaps we forgot it so it could die.'

'It's only a weapon when it's shaped that way. Callisteel could be so much more than just another way to die.'

'If you saw the Sightless swing its axe, you'd change your tone. It doesn't kill you. It's far worse than that. Be thankful that is the only blade that survived.'

'That isn't all that survived.'

'Aye, we also have that metal carcass the pierces the Midnight Chamber. For all the good it does anyone. That and a half-filled bucket of dead-men's gossip.'

Sam duly counted the rumours off on her fingers. 'Callisteel is made from unmined iron. Callisteel is tempered in a heat beyond fire. Callisteel can only be quenched in blood.'

'All bollocks,' Jak grunted. 'Iron comes from the ground, fire is as hot as we're getting and bloodquench is just water and acid. You can mix the same in a barrel without murdering anyone.'

'No one says it has to be human blood...'

'Sam. Listen to me.' Jak clamped his hands on her shoulders. Felt like a house was leaning on her. 'You can't waste this time. The era of the blacksmith ended when those foundries sprung up and mass produced our lives' work in an afternoon. Only reason we're still here is 'cause the iron mines ran dry. We can't go back to that. So we gotta figure out what happens next. Before someone else does our figuring for us.'

Sam felt the heat wash down her throat. 'Why do you think I'm doing this? Callisteel is Arx's legacy. You can't mass produce a legend.'

Jak glanced at her crucible. 'Only because there isn't any iron left. How much went into that? Your Pa is gonna kill me one day.'

'Unless I succeed.'

'"Unless." That was one of Da's favourite words as well.' Jak took the lancet from the hook, almost reverently. Then he flung it at her like the sting of an armoured hornet.

Sam juggled the razor edge, just about kept her fingertips attached. 'Luckily a blacksmith doesn't need her hands...'

'As your dutiful Forgemaster, I am honour-bound to tell you that your waste-of-time alloy is ready.'

Sam spun back to the crucible. He was right. The mixture glowed, a beautiful sunset heat that boiled her heart with expectation. Her forge-muscled arms slammed the lancet into the side of the crucible. The bladed edge slid through without resistance. Molten liquid metal flowed through the channel, igniting the spiral inlay like alien letters wrought in gold. The ingot mould beneath filled without a wasted drop.

Now the bit she was worst at. Being patient.

Luckily, the worst possible distraction arrived in a flounce of skirts and a tsunami of perfume. The door at the top of the stairs flung open.

'Samantha, you best be down here.' Vicky flowed down the stairs, every step taken with an irritating grace like the world was her dance-floor. Searing alabaster dress and ink-black hair, she sucked the colour from the world around her.

'What do you want?'

Vicky scanned the note in her hand with theatrical eyebrows. 'It would appear our material spend is far over what was budgeted.' Her eyes snapped up to Sam. 'Do you know why that is?'

'Do we have to do this every time?'

'There shouldn't be an *every time*.' Vicky's indignation rent her lips like a hammerblow through a wedding cake. 'We don't work with iron, because it's too expensive to waste.'

'It isn't a waste,' Sam snarled.

Vicky sidled past, and tapped the ingot mould with a manicured fingernail. 'Who's taking bets?'

With a flick, she tipped a lifetime of work over.

Shards of misshapen metal spilled out onto the floor, sliding from each other as the alloy separated. Brittle pieces of ruined iron. Same as every other effort.

Sam felt her failure like a weight on her ribcage. Her eyes flickered to the notebook on her workbench. The final page was filled with scribbled-out annotations. End of the list. That had been her last hope.

'Clean this up.' Vicky's voice was flat. 'Do you have any idea what this does to Father? Would you care if you did?'

The door shut behind her with a click.

Sam's arm cramped with the force of her grip on her hammer.

'Seen that look before.' Jak tossed a short bar of false-cast into the furnace. 'Hurry up, or you'll be useless for the rest of the day. And leave your hammer there.'

Sam gritted her teeth, but he was still the Forgemaster.

'If you want someone dead, you make the weapon yourself.' Jak's mantra was familiar, but it did nothing for the spike of rage still drilling into her eyes. 'Go grab the tongs.'

Sam scowled and set to work. She pumped the bellows, raked the coals, prepared the anvil. When she swung, the clang was deafening. With the endless iron shortage, false-cast 'iron' was the best they had and it was a bitch to work with. Old, stubborn and surprisingly brittle. Too firm and it would shatter, too light and it just wouldn't shape. Especially with such a small piece. The constant flicker between forge and anvil was exhausting. Still, under her Master's watchful eye, she shaped the blade, indented the tang, flattened the bevels, sanded the spine and whet the edge until it was sharp.

Sam collapsed in the corner and smeared the dirt on her forehead with a grubby sleeve.

'Still want to go stab your baby sister?'

'Baby my arse, she's eighteen.'

'Sam?'

'...Not until I get my breath back.'

He laughed at that and picked up her knife-blade to examine it. 'Ugly little thing. Anything made in anger is ugly. I reckon your Father musta been furious the night you were squirted into being.'

'Jak!'

'Proper metalwork needs a clear...'

'...clear head and a calm mind.' Sam finished for him. 'I'm not a child anymore Jak.'

'More's the pity, you used to listen to me.' He tossed her knife-blade to join the countless others she'd made over the years, then stalked over to her now-ruined crucible. Strong hands yanked the lancet free. He flipped it over and offered it – thankfully hilt-first this time.

'Take it.'

'Jak...'

'What? Callisteel might be dead, but that doesn't mean you have to widdle out all your ambition. Besides, not like we can afford any more iron. So you can take this as a reminder that maybe there might be something out there still worth discovering. Or I can keep it as a memento of my Da's obsession and end up chucking it in the river. Same place his bones ended up.'

Sam winced as she took the lancet and strapped it, carefully, beneath the band of her trousers.

'Good. Now, go clean the chimney.'

Sam grinned. Clean the chimney was one of Jak's favourite chores. He never seemed to mind that it managed to remain mysteriously soot-stained no matter how often he gave the order. She ducked her head in mock curtsey, mock because the last time she tried a real one she'd smacked her elbow on the forge and swore so loud Vicky came down to see if she'd been stabbed, and made for the metal-bracketed flume that burrowed through the walls. She gripped the thick rungs carved on the inside, slick with soot.

The chimney scaled the side of the house she shared with Father, Vicky and Jak. Sometimes she felt like a rat, crawling through the walls in the hopes that no-one would notice.

Sam poked her head out of the chimney and into a drizzling sky. Hefted herself on to the lip and let the warm smoke cook her backside. She didn't look down. The city and its people held no interest.

But the Iactura, shining like a bridge to the home of some long-forgotten gods, that drew her. The metal tower rose from the heart of Arx's citadel to break the skyline and pierce the heavy clouds. Soft silver burnished blue by the reflection of unshed lightning. No seams, no joins, no lines. Everything she knew about metalwork said that it should not exist. And yet there it was. An impossibility anchored in reality.

Callisteel.

Soot-stained rain dribbled down her face, but Sam bared her teeth. She gripped the lancet at her waist with white-knuckled fingers. What threat was a little rain to a blazing fire?

CHAPTER 3

Ruairi lobbed the crab pots out, long before dawn were a glimmer on the thumb-smudge horizon. Nowt to do now 'til low tide upped sticks and white-crested waves set the buoys to dancing between the rockpools. Then he'd see if here were smarter than a cast of crabs come slack water around high tide. Didn't fancy his chances.

The salty spray made him dither. Each twitch came with a little spasm that creaked down his spine. The Kink were a great place for crabbing. A clump of trees back near shore shaded the outcropping, like a little pier of rocks and seaweed direct into the Saltiron Sea. Ruairi had named the Kink hisself, on account of the crooked path of rockpools reminded him of the fist-sized knot in his spine that made his walking all skewiff. Twisted his body like a stubborn wine-cork and made tossing out the pots an exercise in broken-clay bones.

He turned back to the beach. Mistake. He knew it the sod-buggering instant his toes touched the seaweed and his arms gave it the pinwheels, cracked like shelling nuts down his arse. He walloped face-first into a rockpool, mouth full of salt and shame.

Roll over. Roll over you basket-bollocked pillock. 'Cept it were hardly that easy. The twist in his back kept him pinned like a spear through the shoulders. Blinked his eyes past the spray, snorted saltwater up his aching nose. Let the tears mingle in the tidepool. By all the bastard fishes, he were not gonna drown in three inches of water!

Sommat like a big hand wrapped its terrifying fingers around his chest. Little dark spots stabbed through his soaking eyes. He twitched his jelly-fingers, searching for sommat, anything to give him a little purchase. The rampant grind of bone in his back felt like he were being twisted in a fruit press.

Involuntary breath. Throat scraped by bitter seawater. Panic red over his eyes.

Come on you bastard, get those fingers tight. Bit of weed, but it were better'n nothing. Ruairi took hold and dragged. Inch by sodden inch. Scraped his face across the barnacles, a warm trickle of salt to join the cold.

He burst outta the tiny pool in a welter of bubbles. Spat-vomited his first few breaths, then filled his lungs like there weren't gonna be another chance.

By his reckoning, it took about eight tries before he finally levered hisself onto his back. Then a good half-morning before he made it back to his feet.

'Stay on the beach, use your chair,' Ruairi muttered, his Pa's words, a bitter curse. The chair itself were special made. Pa had it commissioned in Arx for his seventeenth, three winters ago. Extra-wide seat, short legs and a little holder for a fishing pole. And he'd rather drown than plonk his arse in it. Evi-bloody-dently. 'Cause when your Daddy's a fisherman, spending a whole day catching a couple of blinky-eyes don't change nothing.

So he'd settled on crabbing instead. Took patience that, and Pa were enamoured with the scuttling things. If you let him, he'd go on and on about the little fins on the back two legs, which is what made it a *Saltiron* crab. Sovereign to these waters, he said, like eating a piece of your heritage.

The day dragged on. Eventually, Ruairi managed to catch his breath and stop the snotty tears. For now, at least. Were extra careful as he yanked the pots in. Placed his feet all delicate like. Got the crabs back to shore, let them nibble at his raw scraped knuckles.

He were so focused on the scuttling things, he didn't see the big beastie sneaking up on him 'til it whickered right by his ear.

Despite his instincts, Ruairi made sure he turned around nice and slow. A horse. It snorted at the sand like an insult. Almost twice his size and beautiful as a painting. Soft brown coat with white socks. Saddlebags hung down the flanks. Not wild then. So where did it come from?

'Get back here Ro!'

Some bloke came crashing through the pools. His fancy boots were soaked and his clinging shirt hung on stocky muscles. Broad shouldered like a farmer, he panted up a storm.

'Scared me fit to death pissing off like that!' He flung his arms around the creature's neck.

'You two alright?' Ruairi shouted.

'Slap my bollocks lad, you could have said something! Bloody thing.' He nodded at his horse. 'Let her walk for a bit without my arse in the saddle and she bolts. That's gratitude for you.'

The man darted across the pools, leaping between the rocks.

'Hold on now, the things are right slippy, you'll hurt...'

Too late. Just like Ruairi, the bald fellow slipped and careened into one of the deeper pools. 'Course, unlike Ruairi he splashed right back to his feet and squelched over like nothing had happened.

Just then, Ruairi hated him.

The bloke held out a meaty palm, water running down the deep age lines around his eyes. 'Names Fetch.'

Let it go. Can't blame all folk that walk right just 'cause you can't. 'Ruairi,' he managed through clamped gnashers. The bloke's powerful grip sent a needle of pain all the way up his arm to lodge in his shoulder.

'You're wetter than a lass tucked up in my bunk. Been cavorting with your mates?' Fetch peered into the net then made a show of retching. 'Poor boy, did Mama not teach you proper? Never eat any animal that has eyes. That's advice you can keep.'

'What kind of animal don't have eyes?'

'Like a steak. Or bacon. If it can see me, I'm not about to chow down.' Fetch cracked his shoulders. 'Long day! You know the way out of that forest? City boy me, can't tell my cock from a carrot when the trees start getting taller than I am.'

Ruairi grinned. Forest? The trees around the Kink were sparse as the bloke's hairline. 'Aye.' He pointed to a little patch where the beach gave way to grass. 'Where you headed, down Vos?' The little fishing hamlet was the closest thing to a village they had. Pa went every other week to buy his beer.

'Aye, Vos, then Char, and all the homes in between. I lucked mesself into being the bloke that gets all the bad news. I'll be up and down the coast talking farmers and fisherfolk outta murdering me all week I reckon.'

'Why?'

Fetch wiped the water from his face, then reached into one of his panniers. Rummaged past some balled-up black cloak for a scrap of paper. 'Uh, the Salt Ponies have gone under.'

Ruairi winced. The Salt Ponies were the set of horse-and-cart teams that did the rounds for all the local homesteads. Purchased their catch, sold it on. 'Gone under?'

'One fella got himself knifed in a bar fight.' A shadow on his face at that. 'Two others got locked up for breaking contract prices. O'course, when Arx is the only place you can sell to then the Viceroys can set whatever pittance they like and you gotta take it or die. Point is! They won't be coming 'round anymore. Despite the best efforts of some angry fools who got all pissy up at the DeSané's house just so Rotheart got another show.'

Ruairi just stood there. 'But what are we supposed to do with a shedload of fish and no money?'

'What do I look like, a man with ideas?' Fetch mounted his horse. He tugged an imaginary forelock. 'Sorry I've bollixed your day.' He tossed a salute and put spurs to his horse. The mare kicked off and the pair lurched across the sand.

Ruairi just stood, numb as the showery rain that blew in across the ocean and slalomed itself down the crack of his arse. He should feel panic. Alarm. This were their way of life, slowly drowning in three inches of water. But instead of all that, he just watched some bloke riding some horse to somewhere new and wished beyond all reason that he could do the same.

CHAPTER 4

Caelan pushed his newly-scabbed pinkie finger against the tip of his knife. Two days since the execution. Maybe. Time was tricky. Hard to follow when memory is porous. He forced himself to look up from his feet. Mid-afternoon and the sun had broken through the smog enough that it was almost warm. Little foot-traffic on the dirty street. Of course. There was nowhere to go.

Maybe that's why he liked it. A lonely walk through the smog. Let him avoid thinking.

'Forget about us, did you?' A familiar voice. In itself a rarity.

'If fucking only.' Caelan tried for a grin, but Addie looked in no mood to mirror it. Just charged up the dusty street like a bear with bees up its arse. A spiderweb of scars bit her cheek and she topped him by at least a head. The other one of Kuyt's projects. He was the man without a mind and she was the 'actress-in-training.' Except her costume was scored battle-leathers and the ice-sharp hatchets at her hips were anything but props. You didn't get scars like hers from the stage. Addie was ex-Walker.

'Well?' she demanded.

'I'm sorry, what was the question?'

'Don't play the prick with me. Do you know how difficult it was to find you? Arx is bloody huge.'

Caelan shrugged. 'I couldn't sleep.'

'Kuyt said he hasn't seen you all day.'

'It's been a long walk.'

Addie rubbed the bridge of her nose with a gauntleted hand. 'Do me a favour and go shove your thumbs up your arse.'

'Only if you go first.'

'Why, can't find it? Makes sense. All your shit usually comes out of your mouth. Come on. I'm taking you back.'

'Didn't realise you were Kuyt's bounty hunter. You going to drag me back, pissing and screaming?'

'It's kicking and screaming, you idiot.'

'Not when I do it.'

Addie knuckled her eyes. 'You're lucky I'm being nice. Because you don't enjoy making the old man worry by running away from home. Because somewhere in that tattered soul of yours, there has got to be a shred of gratitude for everything he has done for you.'

Caelan rubbed the ropey scar across his neck. A pink line where his beard didn't grow. 'I didn't run away from home. I went for a walk.'

Addie gripped his shoulder and steered him into a nearby alleyway. 'Then you'll have no problem walking back. Do you even know where you ended up? We're in pissing Southbrace, right by the wall. It's going to take ages to get back Ferriway.'

'Well, you know what they say. It's not the journey, but the company.'

Addie looked at him. 'Gonna take fucking ages.'

Caelan followed her through the alley. Sure, he could have tried to run but Addie would have him trussed and over her shoulder before he'd even manage to piss himself in fear. There was more dignity in pretending it was his choice.

'So how was it?' Addie scraped oil-slick dirt from the side of a nearby building with her shoulder.

'The walk? Soulful.'

'The execution, dipshit. Did you cry?'

'No.'

'I did. Big slobbery ones.' Addie ran a finger over the scars on her cheeks. 'Second time too, thought I was going to choke on the snot. Got it under control by the third though.'

'Under control?' They turned down a split path. 'Kuyt said it isn't supposed to get easier.'

'He would. It doesn't get easier. But...' Addie shrugged. 'Maybe we become worse.'

'Oh I look forward to that then.'

'No chance. You're softer than he is.'

'Bullshit. I didn't even cry.' Caelan scrambled over a pile of metal scraps.

'Nothing soft about crying. You'd know that, if you weren't so soft.' Addie led him around another twist.

'I'm harder than a fucking priapism.' Caelan took the corner and almost tripped over a bloke slumped against the wall. He stumbled and whirled on his heel.

Everything went cold.

The face from Kuyt's sketchpad. The man with an executed mind. Blue vapour swirled in the empty sockets.

Fog-Eye.

Almost everyone in Arx had sacrificed a memory. Or two. Or entire fucking years. But it was a slow process. Memories are built from connections. Slice out too many, too quickly, and the whole thing falls apart. That Sightless' blade carved them all out in an instant. A blank mind with just enough instinct to breathe. The Fog-Eyed didn't last long.

'Caelan come on.' Addie's face was uncomfortable. 'Leave the thing alone. It's got to be in enough pain as it is without looking at you.'

'Is it pain if you don't remember it?' Caelan knelt beside the poor bloke. Sandy hair, the salt-and-pepper stubble had grown out a little. He put his hand on the thing's shoulder. 'I remember your name. Arthur Colis.'

The Fog-Eye blinked. Once. Then lashed out and fastened its fingers around Caelan's throat.

Caelan ripped at the hand, his nails dug out chunks of flesh but it didn't loosen. Light popped through his vision, a ring of gold around smoke-stolen eyes.

'Fucking soft!' Addie grunted and slammed a hatchet through the Fog-Eye's arm with a pop and a soggy crunch.

Caelan gasped a desperate breath and hurled the stub of an arm away. The thing didn't react. Those empty eyes swirled. The wound oozed. Not blood. Mist.

A whisper through his mind, insistent as ice cracking beneath his feet. '*Reality burns. Inhale the memory.*'

Fog boiled down Caelan's throat. Panic dripped with the bitterness of molten metal. The taste of magic. It soaked the alleyway, devoured slanted walls and broken stone. The world faded into a blizzard of featureless white. The sky warped into ethereal twilight, endless and vast. Addie vanished like a popping soap bubble.

The Fog-Eye stood up, feet planted on the mist like it was solid. A shadow crawled out behind it, thick as tar. Eyeless body shimmered, rocks beneath the sun. Then the shadow rose to consume it. First feet, then its ankles drowned in the gluey ooze. Darkness crept up the chest, crawled down the throat and licked deep into those empty eye sockets.

A woman broke free from the impossible silhouette. Shoulders thick with corded muscle, one arm covered in spiral tattoos the colour of cut grass and old rain, the other heavy with a forge hammer slung over her shoulders. Black hair tied back with delicate iron chains.

Caelan couldn't blink. 'Mindbreaker.'

She twisted her head. A gilded censer swung from her neck, a coal smouldering inside. '*You know what I am.*' Her mouth moved as she spoke, but it felt like her words formed directly inside his skull.

Caelan's fingertips twitched. 'Trained to cut away memories like a scalpel through flesh. I… knew one of you, once.' Though her eyes were thankfully grey. Violet and he wouldn't have been able to still his knife so easily.

'*Eyes like yours, I'm not shocked.*'

The mist spun between Caelan's feet, a whirlpool of featureless fog. There was something hidden beneath, something…

Everything shuddered and Caelan was flung to his knees. A blue-silver pillar burst from the fog and broke through the endless twilight sky.

The Iactura. Fragment of a broken memory lodged inside his skull.

It spread out before him, impossibly wide and endlessly tall. A blazing mirror, liquid smooth. Caelan lifted his hand. The scab had opened again. He reached for his own reflection, bloody fingertip touching the Iactura from within, and without.

Sensation. Like a spool of wire unwinding from inside his ear, two flat blades sharpening behind his eyes. Silver stars budded from the metal spire overhead, impossibly bright. A handful of them, so small in the darkness.

The sky pulsed, vibrated. Tendrils of shadow writhed between the stars, reaching and pulling others closer, trembling like a string pulled taut. A net of connections, impossibly complex.

'I don't want to forget.'

'*You can't lie to me here. Memoria. The mists of memory flow through the cracks in your mind. I can see your thoughts, Caelan.*'

'Then take a big fucking gander at this one, Mindbreaker.'

She snorted a mist-soaked laugh and opened her palm. '*He named me Ferra.*' One of the silver stars floated to hang over her palm, a perfect sphere. '*Manifest memories. The moments by which we are defined. I have never seen someone with so few.*' She dismissed the orb, sent it back to the sky.

The mist gathered around Caelan's feet. Shadows flickered behind the ethereal curtain that hung from his shoulders. 'My past was stolen from me. Everything before the last six months. I should be mindless as a Fog-Eye.'

'*Would you prefer that?*'

Caelan chewed his lip. 'No.'

Ferra laughed. Her hammer made lazy circles through the fog. '*Not right now. But on those nights, when you lie awake and sweat and gnaw the scars open on your fingertips, just praying that Adira doesn't wake up and see you smeared in blood and weeping. Those nights, perhaps you feel differently.*'

The silver orbs resolved slowly overhead, a mocking confirmation.

'Why are you doing this to me?'

'*I want to know how you survived.*'

'Get in fucking line.'

'*Perhaps I can help.*' Ferra reached towards Caelan's reflection. To his shadow. She pinched her fingers like ripping the wings from an insect. Her hand twitched.

An image flickered in the Iactura. Caelan's reflection warped into another. A man, with a cruel smile and a crooked nose. Blue eyes, though he at least had pupils. It was a dizzying sensation. Like seeing double.

Within the Iactura the figure raised his arms, face creased with effort. The web of shadow began at his fingertips. It kept the stars from drifting. Caelan understood like someone whispered it in his ear. The silver memories were so close to breaking free, from fading into the darkness. And yet the web, thin and stretched almost to breaking, held them in place.

He blinked and the figure vanished.

'*This is well beyond memory,*' Ferra said, almost to herself.

'Who was that? Is that me, is that who I was before?' The questions bubbled from his lips.

'*I have no idea.*'

'Bullshit!' Caelan yanked himself back. Ripped his fingers from the pillar. His bloody fingerprint sank into the metal, cauterised scar closed the wound. Overhead, the stars vanished.

'*Believe as you wish. That is the point, after all, of forgetting.*' Ferra slammed her fist against the Iactura and the metal pillar burst with silver. Countless memories clustered for space in the sky, achingly infinite.

Ferra drew one of the silver orbs from the sky. '*When the Sightless breaks a mind, there are still pieces of the person trapped beneath. Fog-Eyes cannot see, but those of us who walk with them can. I see you, Caelan.*'

Caelan was reflected in the silver surface. On his knees, Kuyt imperious at his side, locking eyes with a condemned man as the axe fell to break his mind.

Wishing, just in that instance, that their places were reversed.

Caelan squeezed his eyes shut. A future locked in the empty darkness. It was terrifying. How much easier would it be to forget that fear? One more memory lost for a moment of peace before the maelstrom of reality flung him into the void.

Paralysed by shame, he barely noticed as Ferra swept the knife from his belt.

'*Inhale the memory. Exhale the truth.*' She pierced each of her fingertips on her left hand and blew a soot-soaked breath through the gilded chain around her neck.

The coal around her neck spat, roared in a gout of brilliant flame. Fire burned blue, seared through the twilight. Sweat trickled down Caelan's face. Real hunger ripped down his neck. So close. Watching was agony. But he couldn't move. Couldn't beg.

Wouldn't.

The silver orb pressed against the back of her hand. Blood beaded on her fingertips. Ferra took a slow, deep breath. Smoke from the coal around her throat poured into her mouth. She clenched her fist. Steam boiled around her knuckles like tar, hissing like rain on hot metal. A blue speck swept through her grey eyes.

She opened bloodless fingers to reveal a chunk of metal. It looked like iron ore, threaded with razor-lines of jasper.

The manifest memory was gone. Forgotten.

'*The iron in human blood, excised. Memory given form. Bloodmetal is what remains when we forget.*' Ferra threw the lump of metal at him.

Caelan caught it. 'Why are you giving this to me?'

Her smile was crooked. '*It is your pain. It belongs to you. But pain alone cannot fill that vacuum in your head, Caelan. Come find me when you realise that.*'

Caelan blinked. And she vanished.

The alleyway re-appeared in a dump of heat and colour and noise. A hand grabbed his shoulder.

'Caelan you slobbering dipshit, say something!' Addie knelt beside him, pulled up his eyelid.

'Get off me. I'm fine, I'm...' He chewed his words like fatty meat, the ragged ache in his throat bursting through his voice.

Before Addie could notice, he shoved the bloodmetal deep into his pocket.

'And what about him?'

Who? Oh. Caelan glanced down at the Fog-Eye. Motionless once more, and now with a bubbling brook of blood leaking from its severed arm.

'Never seen a Fog-Eye do that before.' Addie narrowed her eyes.

'Me neither. That was a fun surprise.'

'What are we going to do about it?'

'Kill it.'

Addie raised an eyebrow. 'I'm not your butcher.'

'It's not butchery. It's mercy. If you won't do it, I will.' With trembling fingers, Caelan reached for his knife. 'And I want a promise from you. If I ever get this empty, I want you to do the same thing to me.'

Addie looked at him for a long time. Then nodded. She hefted her hatchet at the Fog-Eye's throat. 'Deal.'

CHAPTER 5

Sam hefted her wooden crate of metalwork into Father's ribs. 'I'm letting go.'

'Hold on...' Father said around the cigarette clamped between his teeth. Sam let go all the same, and he almost toppled forwards in a clatter of loose metal. 'Feh, that is heavy.' He took another drag. 'Sammy?'

She took the cigarette from his mouth and, in gratitude, he blew a cloud of smoke in her face. Sam chucked the cigarette on the ground and stomped it out. 'At least a forge fire burns clean. What's wrong with you?'

'Ingrate.' He balanced the crate on his knee, took another sheaf from his breast pocket and lit up from a nearby brazier.

'You better finish that before we get inside.' Vicky curled her legs beneath a marble bench. 'It spoils our professional image.'

'I am a professional.' A drop of sweat rolled down Father's greying temple. 'All the Councillors do it. It's a stressful occupation. Especially with that mob we faced down the other week. I'd think my daughters would be a little more sympathetic.'

'I heard they didn't make it past the driveway.' Vicky smoothed her skirt across her lap. 'Each Viceroy can choose between ten and fifteen councillors to support them, and each councillor is entitled to a Walker escort. You outnumbered them more than three-to-one.'

'An army of men like Father responsible for keeping us fed, watered and breathing. Iron save us all,' Sam muttered.

Father's face flushed. 'Children, the pair of you. No idea how the world really works. Can we get on with this before my back gives out?'

'Lift with your legs,' Sam offered. 'Or let me carry it.'

'Oh Sam just be quiet. They are just looking for an excuse to under-pay, this is all barter.' Vicky tossed her hair across the powdered top of her cleavage.

'So I see.'

'Yes. And the longer they spend drooling over my tits, the bet-ter price we'll get and the more iron you can afford to waste. Is that a problem?'

'My work is good enough with or without your tits getting involved.'

'You would certainly think that would be the case by now. That hammer has cost you everything else.' Vicky took the cigarette from Father's lips and crushed it out against the gates. 'Ready?'

'I was,' Father sulked.

'Sam, go wait by the coach until we're back.' Vicky touched Father's shoulder and steered him through, up to the market so she could give away Sam's hard work for pittance and complain that it was everyone else's fault.

Sam kicked a pebble down the road and walked right by the pad-dock of picketed horses and rented carriages. Sod Vicky if she thought she could order her around. She made her way towards the clay-baked field just south. The Iron Market. A legacy name, it was decades since they last sold iron there, but blacksmiths were not always the most imag-inative lot. Tents clustered together like mushrooms after a rain. Open-air forges sprayed sparks. She leant on a fencepost and just breathed it in, bitter and rich and hot.

A familiar *fizz*, with the agonising sound of splintering ice just beneath. Sam winced. Nearby, an apprentice stepped back from his quenching barrel. An enormous length of bronze rings spilled from the banded wood. Chains for the river barges. Lucrative work. Jak had grumped like thunder for a week when they didn't get the contract.

He took his shirt off to wipe his face. Moron. There was a reason for the aprons. Stand too close to the forge and that appalling trail of chest hair would go up like dry grass.

'You've ruined that.' She couldn't help herself.

'Mm?' The apprentice looked up, ran a hand through his curling hair.

'Didn't you hear the crack?' Sam gestured at the half-submerged U.

He drew it from the barrel and, sure enough, a fissure speared down the outside, a good finger-width thick. 'Shit, not again!' He glanced over his shoulder to a pile of the things. 'Master Llian's going to hammer my hands into paste. What do I do?'

'Well for starters, put your bloody shirt back on.' Sam spat in the dust. 'The heat is too high, bronze is a poor replacement for iron even if it is the best we've got. Didn't you think something needed to change after you butchered the first one?'

The boy made no move to pick his shirt from the grass. 'The heat treatment is supposed to make it last.'

'Does it also incinerate your clothes? Heat treatment is a controlled process, you don't just try it as hot as you can and see what happens'

'Now someone tells me... where were you this morning?' The apprentice took a deep breath, looked up at her. 'I know you. You're the Acarris girl. Vicky's sister.'

Vicky's sister. 'Journeyman to Jak Mendy.'

'Now *that's* a name. He knows what he's doing.'

Sam could have chewed off her own tongue. 'Yes. Jak also has a name.'

The boy stumbled towards her, grabbed her hands. 'Get him to help me. Please.'

'Get off me.'

He didn't listen. Instead, his thumb began to circle the veins on the back of her hand. He held his palm against hers and snorted a weak laugh. 'Your hands are bigger than mine.'

'Get. Off.'

Finally, he let her go. He rubbed the back of his neck. 'Sorry. You know, I've heard about you. Vicky talks.'

'Oh I'm well aware.'

'I don't get it. The things she says about you...but you're not.' He bit a laugh. 'I admire any woman that could break my arm if I got out of line. Look, If Jak helps me, we could work together. The two of us. I wouldn't mind that. And then, maybe...'

It might have been funny. The first time. 'You'd bed me? Is that where this is going? And for the privilege, I don't even get to actually fix your mistake. You want Jak for that.'

His ears burned red. 'I thought maybe courting, not just...'

Sam sighed. She'd figured it out years ago. The concept of courtship, of kissing, nudity, sweating, touching, tasting. It made her feel ill. 'No.'

'You don't even know me.'

'You think if I did it would make your little nipples less repulsive?'

His face twisted. 'Right. "Lady Blacksmith" is it? Bet if my sister asked…'

Sam almost laughed, she really did. 'Oh yes, that has to be the reason doesn't it? You know, if you were a better listener, maybe your master's lessons on curing bronze would have gone in, so do try and hear me when I say I'd rather weld my cunt shut than mount you, your sister or any sod-bothering moron who won't leave me alone.'

Even the market felt a little quieter after that.

Sam barged past the misty-eyed idiot, took advantage of his gormless silence.

Dress in clothes that make you hate being naked, then grow out your hair and maybe you'll get some leeway. You can go be a Walker and die, or go pour tea for some government official who doesn't know your name. But don't pick up a hammer because that's not ladylike and you'll no longer suit your skirts – that you're not even wearing, because the forge would ignite those lace-confections like tinder in a blast furnace. Stop swearing, learn silence, smile. Have some babies, or teach some babies, or look after someone else's babies. Fuck someone. By the walls of a broken city, why was that always what it came down to?

Sam passed by a handful of tents. A pair of smiths laughed over something, a child smacked her friend with a stick until he cried. She licked sour lips. Back to the coach, wait for Father and Vicky, and then go pound some barge-chains with Jak. There was a market for the things now, after all.

Maybe if she made them rich, Vicky would stop spreading whispers that she was a half-rotted apple just waiting to be plucked. She wouldn't, but a bit of self-delusion every now and then never did any harm.

She pushed back into the slow traffic of the market. It was all the same. Copper and zinc and false-cast gutted from the old foundries. Nothing that had seen a mine this side of the century, nothing with any decent purity.

'Witness the rebirth of Arx's glory. Callisteel, back from the mists of memory and the realm of the dead.'

Sam caught her breath like a spark down her throat. She wasn't the only one. Heads rose, muttering broke from smithies as she joined the growing crowd outside a green-silver tent.

'Who is it?' One of the smiths near the edge asked. 'Can't see shit from here.'

A tall fellow, hair tied back from his face, answered. 'Jonas Karrin. Wouldn't stop banging on about his patronage last week. I guess now we know why Mistress Ignis was so interested.'

Mistress Ignis. Patron of the Blacksmiths. The Ballari cart axel, Sicaran copper blades now exclusive to the Walkers, she owned them all. Paid for time, not for product. There wasn't a blacksmith in Arx who would turn her down.

Well. Except Jak. He never spoke about it, but the whispers were insistent. The only man to deny Mistress Ignis. Other smiths spoke about him with a mixture of awe and disbelief.

Sam eased through the throng, dodged past sweaty elbows and curling arm hair.

'No way he's done it. Callisteel is dreams and dust.'

'What does it matter? Not enough iron to mass-produce the stuff. It's a curiosity at best.'

Sam found her way to the front. Jonas Karrin was a short man, weedy for a blacksmith but nothing too noticeable given he pirouetted on his anvil as he spoke. Thick hair hung down the side of his face and when he spoke, his tongue tasted his lips.

'Unmined iron, quenched in blood, your pathway to another world of steel!' His voice was pitched to carry.

'How much?' someone shouted.

'The price point is iron. I make no apologies!' he shouted over the muttering of the crowd. 'A legend for no less!' He exaggerated a bow towards the gilded blade rack. A single sword, double edged with a reverse grip, glimmered blue in the weak morning sunlight.

Sam flexed her leg against the lancet strapped to her thigh, the whisper of the metal feathers sharp against her skin. 'How?'

She didn't realise how loud her voice was. A couple of nearby smiths sniggered.

'My lady, a true blacksmith never reveals his secrets.'

'I'm nobody's lady.' Sam stepped free of the crowd. 'Nothing we have was made by one person. We build on what came before us. You already mentioned two of the big rumours. Unmined iron, quenched in blood. You certainly didn't invent those. What did you forge it in?'

'A furnace of my own creation, fuelled with coal from across the sea.' He said it like a brag, but more than one smith lifted an eyebrow.

'How did you get coal imported? Isn't the purpose of those big walls around the city to keep outsiders out? Besides, coal is about all we do have left under the soil. And it hardly makes a heat hotter than fire.' Sam pulled the crucible lancet from her belt and lent forwards. 'What's this for?'

'What is that, a lancet?' Jonas licked his lips. 'Of course! Some may use that for bloodletting, for the quench.'

'Right. Figured as much. You don't mind if I...' Sam walked past the scrawny smith and grabbed the hilt of the blade. Her shoulders were used to swinging hammers, but it was still surprisingly heavy. The blue colour ran deep throughout, like ocean rain.

She met his eyes, reversed her grip on the sword and swung it with everything she had at the anvil.

Sparks scraped the metal with a screeching *clang* and the shock-wave set Sam's arm shaking. She turned the blade, looked at the tip. Nicked. Of course.

'Potassium nitrate.' She jammed the end of the blade beneath his anvil. 'Sodium hydroxide.' Twisted the grip in her hand. 'And water. Gives you that lovely blue colour. A great rust treatment.' She stomped a heavy boot on the flat of the sword. It didn't shatter as she hoped, but it did bend with a satisfying creak. She pulled it free and held the r-shaped blade back to Jonas. He took it, wordless.

Noise bubbled up from the crowd, but Sam had stopped caring. She left him to whatever fate a bunch of mild-mannered blacksmiths could mete out.

'Callisteel my arse.'

CHAPTER 6

Worst part of being human, far as Ruairi reckoned, were pissing. He stood out on the Kink at the edge of the world, todger in one hand, trousers in the other, trying to add to the waves before some angry sturgeon decided the little pink worm overhead would be worth sinking its teeth into.

'Course, those kinds of thoughts were not exactly helping. He shuffled his feet to get the juices flowing, but the motion rammed a splintering stick into his back and threw some salt into his eyes for good measure. Tried just breathing through it, managed a few errant drops, called it a win. Lucky he didn't need a shit. He scrambled over the rocks, bit back on some weepy cries that wouldn't help no one, and made it back to camp.

Well, a firepit, two sleeping skins and a kettle that could manage tea-tasting-stew or stew-tasting-tea. Three days they'd been out there, Pa buzzing between campfire and cottage like a blue-arsed fly. Ma and baby Abi, fourteen now but she weren't never shaking the nickname, were salting and smoking like worker bees to get everything ready.

Pa's plan were a simple one. Salt Ponies being gone meant that there would be disruptions down the whole supply line. And disruptions meant those who made it through might be able to pick up a handful of extra coins for their trouble.

Get to Arx, take the money, bunker down. It were almost exciting. 'Cept crabs aren't' the kinda creature you can rush. Ruairi glanced over at the lines. It'd be near dark before they were ready. So he lit the fire, stuck on a pot of water to boil and sat counting his toes.

Pa's skiff made it back with a soft *thump* into the beach. He dragged the bulging net up through the sand, left it hanging in one of the deeper rockpools. Best way to keep the things fresh.

'Reckon that's about it.' Pa splashed his face, drops splattering onto his shirt. 'These little beauties are as fat as they're getting, won't be long before migration starts and then we're looking at spring before they're homeward bound.'

'This it then? We done?'

'About as much.' Pa knelt beside the fire and set some tea to steep. 'We did good kid.' He slapped Ruairi's knee.

Ruairi wobbled so hard he almost went face first into the fire, sucked up a breath through a closing throat. Pa didn't notice. Well, he must have, you don't miss your son wiggling around on the sand like a carp out of water, but he pretended he didn't and that were all there were.

The leaves had barely touched the water before Pa was scooping them out again. He made two cups and gulped half of his in one go. Ruairi tried a sip and almost took off the roof of his mouth.

'Not that I'm looking forward to the next bit.' Pa eased to his feet and stretched out his legs. 'Arx ain't no place for proper folk. Not an honest person there. Can't be honest when you don't know your own mind.'

The familiar words rattled like rain. Pa used to live in Arx, Ma 'n all. They met there. Something about a river and some sewage and a quick wedding that Ma could never finish telling without misting up. Apparently, that were romantic. Not long after, they'd buggered off to build a shack in the middle of nowhere. Ma said that were romantic too.

'Not one?' Ruairi asked. It were bait, they both knew it.

Pa grinned. 'Oh aye, I suppose there might'a been one fella.' He eased hisself back to the sand. 'Though he weren't no ordinary person.'

'The Ant weren't a person? 'Cause this is a whole different story if the fellow was some massive bug.'

Pa grinned and went to swat at Ruairi's knee again, caught himself and jammed his fingers into the sand instead. The grin faded. 'Aye, the Ant were a man – Andross Gaya if you are one of those folk that speak proper. Or DeGaya now, I suppose. 'Course he weren't none of that when I met him. Must have been… forty years ago now. Long before you were a handful of wigglies baking inside Ma.'

'That's vile, Pa.'

'I were your age, I reckon. Maybe younger, how old are you now? Anyway, your Grandpappy had caught the lungrot on account of those bastard furnaces and I went down to his old foundry after we'd buried him.' Pa took a big swig of tea and cleared his throat. 'Offered to take his place. Ant were just a foreman then, but he weren't having none of it. Bollocked me until his ears were red, how'd I expect to go lifting iron and churning forges with arms like twigs and a runny nose? Smacked my face, shoved a bag of coins into my hands and told me to come back when I were old enough to shave.'

Ruairi scooched across the sand, ignored the protest from his arse. 'Never took his advice about the razor, eh?'

Pa ran a hand through his beard, smoothed it all the way to his chest. 'Boy asks for a story, then won't keep his gob shut. 'Course the problem were, day I sprouted whiskers we woke up to some massive earthquake and a big metal pillar cutting through the Citadel and doing its best to block out the sun.'

'The Iactura.'

'Aye, least that's what they call it now. Pure impossible, whacking metal spear growing from nothing overnight. Still, didn't bother me none. I went down the foundry, debt to repay and all. Cept it turned out, the Rustscrape Foundry weren't running no more. None of them were. Something about an iron shortage. Suddenly we had these packs of black-clad fellas patrolling the streets every hour, checking homes and making sure we weren't causing trouble.'

'Walkers.'

'So they said. And they were paying. What with all the foundries closed, enlisting were the only sensible option.'

'And they gave you a sword,' Ruairi snorted.

'For about two weeks.' Pa chuckled. 'Almost sliced my nads off with the thing.'

'Still can't imagine you in a fight.'

'Just go marching they told us, that's why you're Walkers and not Soldiers. Symbols of peace. Bollocks did they know. People were more'n angry. Iron shortage cut jobs and in response, they closed the ports. Shiny new wall goes up and killed trade overnight. Doesn't make a lick of sense. Us folks downriver weren't never rich, but there's a shitton of difference between having enough to get by and not. Does sommat to a person, that slow whittling away without any hope. 'Specially since the only escape comes from forgetting about it. But that lot in Arx were determined just to sit alone and get high off the fumes from their own burning memories.'

'What's that mean?' Ruairi cocked an eyebrow.

Pa just picked at the sand a bit. Shook his head. 'Anyhow, one afternoon, down by Patriae Common and suddenly the streets just *exploded* with Austelli.'

'The what?'

'Folks from the south-side of the river. Used to be what they called themselves, before all those districts got carved into some map I ain't never seen. All grubby faces and angry teeth.' Pa took to gnawing his moustache. 'Scariest moment o' my life.'

'I can imagine,' Ruairi said. 'Cept he couldn't. Scariest moments of his life were making it to the toilet and tackling a flight of stairs to get into bed.

'They told us "set down those weapons and no one gets hurt." Don't reckon they expected us to be so willing. We lobbed our blades into a pile sharpish, but that didn't sit right with this lot. Egging each other on, make an example of us. There were a bloke bearing down on me, thin as a rake with this great sharp dagger.' Pa held his fingers apart.

'This kind of size. You could tell in his eyes, this weren't about nothing but violence. Then, outta nowhere, comes this big booming voice. The Ant rushes over'n orders people to stand down, says we're all on the same side. Came and stood right in front of me.' Pa cleared his throat. 'Course, that stabby bugger weren't best pleased. Starts going on that he ain't foreman no more so he can shove his order up an orifice of his choosing. Lunged at him, but the Ant didn't draw to fight him. Just held his hand up and the blade squished through like gutting a carp. Bloke didn't even scream. Just looked at him.'

'What'd he say?'

'He says "Are you satisfied?" Fella let go of the knife, left it in the Ant's hand if you can believe that, then went off with his tail between his legs. Ant made sure the rest let us go free, hand still dripping. Next time I heard about him the whole rebellion were on his shoulders.'

'Not tempted to join him?'

'What, and get a knife in my own hand?'

'You could have stayed. Even without fighting.'

'Not back then I couldn't.' Pa scratched his beard, then sighed. 'After we got back to the barracks that night, they tell us we've got one bit of training left to do. All the Walkers gotta do it. Ushered us into a room with some lass, hair like coffee threaded with steel silk and this massive golden chain around her neck. Says that now we've got sommat worth forgetting, we can become Walkers proper. Or at least I think she said it…' He ground a finger in his ear. 'Heard it, anyhow. Tells us that any of us want to leave, now was the last chance. We just gotta give back our training. Sommat about not being turned against them. Then the candles start burning blue.'

'What did you do?'

'Whadda you think? Weren't too interested in getting a blade through the guts. I gave her a bow and a thank ye kindly, but I had no aspirations in sticking it out.' Pa rubbed his fingertips and frowned at them. Were those tiny scars? 'Don't rightly reckon I remember what she did next.' He blinked. Must'a caught the light sommat odd, cause it looked like a little blue fleck darted across his eyes. 'All I can recall is that when the fire died down, she looked at me and said her thanks. I buggered off sharpish. Soon after, we heard about the Supply Levy. Your Ma decided to make an honest man outta me and well…' He gestured at the nets and fishing poles. 'Then this. Paradise.'

'You ever miss it?'

'Arx? No. The place is built on corpses. When your Ma got in the family way with you, I swore I'd never go back. 'Course the Salt Ponies have iced that fire, but I won't be there for long.'

'I could go.' The words leapt out before he could stop them.

'What?'

'I…' How could he say it? 'I wanna be useful.'

Useful. Aye that might be the word. And he weren't getting it at home. Paradise, the old bugger called it. Probably bang on the money, 'cause everyone were agreed that paradise had to be the most boring place there were. No worries, no happenings. No life. Being alive had to be about more'n just existing. There had to be more to this whole thing than just hurting and hoping. Didn't there?

'Ah son, you are useful!' Pa patted the sand next to him. 'Want to prove it? Go get those pots in.'

Ruairi snorted. 'They've only been out since sunrise. It'll take the rest of the afternoon before the tide's ready to hand them back.'

'They'd be ready by now if you'd tossed them in last night like I said to.' Pa's voice cooled faster'n Ruairi's tea.

'It weren't low tide! And it were pitch black. You want me to break something?'

'Look son, I know it hurts sometimes…'

'It hurts *always* Pa.'

'Yeah well whinging about it does no one any good. Pull your socks up and go and get the pots!'

'They aren't ready.'

'Right! I guess I'll bloody go and do it then shall I? Don't you worry about it, you just stay here and tend the *bloody* fire.' Pa stomped off.

Ruairi ground his teeth until they hurt. Why'd he never listen? If Ma'd said the exact same thing there'd be no problem. If *Abi'd* said it then no one would question it. But Pa were on the warpath now. Marched across the rocks, splashing through tidepools and yanked the first pot to shore.

Six crabs. Tiddlers at best.

'What did you bait this with?' Pa shouted.

'Just leave 'em!' Ruairi scrabbled to his feet.

'Your attitude to everything.' Pa shuffled over to the next line and started heaving. The rope behind him got caught in the waves and curled around Pa's ankle. The old man didn't notice, he were too busy hauling the empty pots from the waves. Set his boots on a familiar rock. Slick with seaweed and three inches of deadly water.

Ruairi said nothing. Pa don't want to listen. He could mind hisself.

His old man turned to the next line, rope got caught between his legs and down he went with a wet *thwack*. Disappeared behind the rocks.

Ah shite. 'Pa, you alright?' Ruairi scrambled across the rocks, forced the acid bite between his shoulders out of mind.

He splashed down between two rocks near the ocean's edge and found Pa in a tangle of ropes and broken cages. His knee were ripped open, bold and bloody.

'Shit, my back, my *bloody* back!' Pa groaned.

'Let's get you up.' Ruairi squatted beside Pa, felt the *squeeze* clamp down his spine, then yanked him to his feet.

It were hard to tell who yelled louder.

Ruairi wedged hisself under Pa's armpit and they stumbled back to shore.

'Can you slow bloody down?' Pa growled through his teeth. 'I can't *bloody* walk.'

'We slow down we won't start back up again.' Ruairi blinked tears down his cheeks. 'Ma'll be back soon, just wait it out.'

'Sods law.' Pa slumped down to the sand by the fire. 'Can't send Abi and I know *exactly* what your Ma'll suggest.' He glared at Ruairi. 'Looks like you win, boy. Best pack your favourite blankie. Might snow out here, but Arx don't do winters kind.'

CHAPTER 7

Addie's hatchet thumped into his chest. Caelan lumped to his knees in a spray of spittle and tried to suck a breath into his lungs. The pulse of another bruise beat across his ribs.

He was really shit at this.

'Soft.' Addie's cloth-dulled hatchets thudded to the warehouse floor. She wasn't even winded.

'Advice?'

'You're hopeless.'

'Cracking tip that.' Caelan gasped another breath and rolled on to his back. His similarly-muted dagger felt just a pinch lighter than picking up the world beneath him. 'Why the fuck are we doing this?'

'Because next time some idiot wraps his fingers around your neck, you should at least have the decency to stab him yourself.' Kuyt perched on a rickety stool, wrapped in blankets like some ancient bird moments from flying to the rafters and shitting on them.

'You stabbed a lot of fellas have you old man?'

Kuyt glared at him. 'Again.'

Caelan sat up, tossed his sodden hair from his face. 'No more. Can't do it.'

'Addie?' Kuyt asked.

She marched over, hauled Caelan to his feet.

'Right, again is it? Just what I was hoping for.' Caelan took one of the stances Addie had been prattling on about. Left foot forwards, knees bent, arms loose. How he was supposed to remember any of this when a blade came for his face was anybody's guess. 'Aren't you going to…?' He gestured at Addie's discarded hatchets.

'Don't need them.'

Oh this was going to go well.

'Ready?' Addie asked.

'No.'

She launched herself forwards and smacked him in the stomach. Caelan doubled over, bruise on top of bruise, and clenched his jaw to keep from spraying her with vomit. Best he could do was an awkward swing of a tired fist. Untrained and ugly.

Addie kicked him in the knee, slammed his leg down. Caelan raised an arm and she twisted. Slapped him. Hard.

He stumbled at her, pain like a rushing tide, ripped out with his dagger. She leapt from his cut, launched herself at him. Arms around his waist, she threw him back and his head smacked the wooden floor. Black spots danced in his eyes.

'Up.'

'Fuck. Off!' Caelan leapt to his feet, lashed out, stabbing and slicing, muscles cracking and biting. But she just wasn't there. It was like trying to stab a waterfall. He ripped at her legs, overbalanced and stumbled.

Addie planted her hands on the floor. Her foot lashed at his face. *CRUNCH.*

Caelan staggered back with an agonised yelp. It was like being slammed face-first into an anvil. Blood streamed down over his lips.

'Addie!' Kuyt raced over.

'He didn't duck!' She opened her arms. 'I thought at the very least he'd step back. Who doesn't duck when someone kicks them in the face?'

Kuyt grabbed Caelan's hair and dragged his head back. 'Ah shit, I don't know if this is broken or not.' He took a handkerchief from his pocket and jabbed it at his nose.

A rusty spear being forced between his nostrils. 'Fugeenstop!' Caelan spluttered through the blood and pushed Kuyt away.

'He's right Kuyt, that's not how you set a broken nose. Caelan, get your arse over.'

'You know, I think I might just be safer all the way over here,' Caelan said. The wrappings on her foot were stained with his face-blood.

'I doubt that.'

Caelan stepped back, but Kuyt stuck out a leg and he tripped. The old bastard's smile was sympathetic as he pinned him down. The blood in his throat choked out in a spray of crimson.

Don't! The pain was like a razor against bone.

Addie straddled him.

'Get off.'

'Stop being such a baby.' She gripped his chin and tilted. 'Nice, clean break. Easy fix. Good job you can't get much uglier. Hold your breath and try not to shit yourself.'

'If you fuckin' dare...'

She gripped the bridge of his nose and, with a grunt, dragged it straight again.

Caelan screamed until his lungs burned. Light reversed into two black circles that swallowed his vision. He hung there, on the edge of unconsciousness, weeping and bleeding with a roaring, rushing sound scouring his mind.

'I thought it would hurt less, second time around.'

The voice rang inside his skull. Caelan's breath caught against a sudden boulder rammed down his throat. A face flickered into view behind his eyes. That cruel smile, sunken cheeks. A broken nose.

That shadow in the Iactura that kept him from becoming a Fog-Eye. Caelan's chest hurt, felt like his heart was trying to squeeze out between his ribs.

'Who are you?' he asked of the retreating shadow. But the sound of his voice squirmed him back into wakefulness. The shadow-face vanished in a blink.

Caelan woke to an odd, scratchy, snuffling noise in his ears. The sound of his own breathing. He sat up, cleared his throat, spat out black blood.

Kuyt waddled over. 'That stuff stains you know.'

'We doing jokes?' Caelan touched his nose. It was tender and swollen, but the worst of the pain had dulled to a throbbing beat inside his skull.

Kuyt huffed and sat beside him. 'How is it?'

'Terrific.'

'Sarcasm is the lowest form of wit.'

'No, breaking someone's nose is the lowest form of wit. Where is she anyway?'

'I figured you wouldn't want to see her right now. Come on, let's get some air.'

Kuyt struggled to his feet and reached to help Caelan up. They hobbled from the empty warehouse that served as home, hearth and bedroom for the three of them and walked down the bank of the Ferriway. Mid-afternoon sunlight glittered on the oily-slickness of the River Mucro. For a moment, Caelan was almost thankful for his broken nose. The fish-and-tar stink of the Ferriway was usually enough to set his eyes watering.

The bank was packed. Workers stacked boxes, lit torches, shovelled mud. Barely anyone spoke. No one begged. What was the point? There wasn't anything to spare.

Barges clanked across the river on chains. Some water-wheel mechanism ran the things, thick coils dug through the mud at their feet.

'I hate this place.'

Caelan turned. 'What, Ferriway? Then why the shit do we live here?'

'One street is much the same as another. Austellus died in a revolution forty years ago, and yet somehow my side of the river remains this city's unwashed arsehole.' Kuyt stopped beside a railing on the river's edge and leant on the splintered wood. 'Miserable place.'

'Then why stay?'

'I've thought about it. Left through the north gate once. Made it about a week hiking until the snowstorms hit. Mountains made of ice, I swear I could see the corpses of the idiots that came before me. Lost a toe and decided it was worth tucking the tail and coming back. Few years later I figured I'd go south.' He looked at his hands. 'Followed the road as far as it goes. There's a sheer cliff, a few grubby ports crammed with Walkers making sure no foreign ships dock. East or west you're just throwing yourself into the Saltiron, not like there is any reason for us to build boats anymore. We're isolated here kid. Idiots dying on an island.' He paused. 'And besides. It's my home. I can't just abandon it.'

'What, so just because some woman copped a squat and squeezed you out in the muck here, you have to stay?'

Kuyt's eyes flickered. 'That's my darling deceased mother you are talking about there.'

'Sorry. So just because your darling deceased mother copped a squat and squeezed you out in the muck down here you have to stay?'

Kuyt's lips moved from angry to amused then back again. 'I don't have to stay. I choose to. Austellus might be gone from the maps, but the Austelli aren't. I won't forget who I am.'

'Wouldn't recommend it.' Caelan winced at his own joke.

'I was convinced I was going to change all of this. Just a kid, lost in the rhetoric.' Kuyt looked over to one of the enormous chimneys that broke the skyline down the river. 'The Ant got me to march when I was a teenager. You should have heard him speak.'

'Addie says he still does speeches. Isn't he Governor of Rustscrape?'

'That's the problem. Andross DeGaya is a fine governor, but the Ant was bile in your blood, the endless promise of hope. Can't fix the system if you're a part of it. We were going to break it all open and start anew. We would have died for him.'

'Would you have preferred that?'

'Depends what day you ask me. The Ant kept our demands simple. Food on the table, no risk to the limbs for working, and a little control over our own lives. Still too much to ask. The Flame Protests were long and bloody and hungry and cold and... wrong.'

'Wrong how?'

Kuyt sucked his teeth, debating something. 'First time I ever saw a blue fire was the day after that Iactura broke the sky overnight. Mist that made wounds vanish like nothing. It was an endless war. The almost-dead standing up and fighting again with just a bit more of their minds lost. I watched the humanity burn from my friends' eyes.'

'How'd it end?'

'No idea. Just heard one day, the Ant'd been made Viceroy. He never told us why. Something to do with his number two. They told us that they'd heard us, gave us all a little square to put our mark in and called it voting. Elected representatives who'd get us what we wanted. That was enough for most to call it a win and go home, even though it didn't really change anything. But a man has to live for something. Else he's...'

'Empty?' Caelan offered. 'Addie tell you it was a Fog-Eye that tried to rip my throat out and feed it to me? That same Fog-Eye from the execution. Would have managed it too if she wasn't there.'

'She also told me you asked her to kill him.'

Caelan rubbed his thumb across the bloodmetal in his pocket. 'You've never killed, have you?'

'Never did do well with blood.' The old man's hands squirmed together. 'I can't even imagine how it feels.'

'Me neither,' Caelan whispered. 'But he had to die, Kuyt. Better dead than blue eyes and no memories.' He pulled his hand from his pocket and ran his thumb between the fingertips scabs 'You know, these are the only scars I have that I can remember. Well, these and…' He gestured to his neck. 'Anyway, I've got two on my ribs, look pretty shallow, but there's a big one half way down my side as well.'

'I'm not going to look at you naked.'

'That's your loss.' He sighed. 'I thought it'd be easier with new memories. And it is, some days. But I can't help but think what I *should* be remembering.'

'We can't go back, Caelan. We have to live with the choices we made. Grieve for your memories kid, but let them go.'

'And what if I can't?'

'Then I worry about the next time you find yourself alone on this riverbank.'

Caelan lifted his hand to his scarred neck, but there was nothing new to say. They just stood there in the cold. Together.

CHAPTER 8

'Getting fucked by one's government is supposed to be metaphorical. If I throw up, I'm doing it on your face.' Sam dabbed the corners of her mouth with a performative flourish.

'I love the time we spend together.' Mira, Sam's best and only friend, picked an invisible spec from her skirt.

The brothel, *Lupanar* was painted on the sign outside, smelled of sex. Thick as maggots clustering in her nose. She cleared her throat but the powder and perfume coated her tongue. Like eating a cremated daisy.

The others in the queue spoke softly, grumbled at the wait, chatted with the workers. One fellow off in front was eyes-deep down some girl's blouse. Rather, one eye was. The other was made of glass and peering somewhere off into a dusty corner.

'Voting doesn't start until mid-morning.' Mira straightened her blouse. White as an albino crow, she didn't allow a single crease to settle. Made her look like a sheet of paper.

Sam fingered a scorch-hole in her sleeve, knocked a bit of soot from her elbow. 'We didn't leave mine until after dawn. What exactly would you call now?'

'Early morning.' Mira folded her arms. 'It wouldn't be fair on the other districts if we started first.'

'No, what's not fair is that you were banging on the door before I even got the coals lit so I could participate in this fa...'

'Farce? Were you about to say farce?'

'I was about to say fair and equitable voting process.'

'My left titty were you.' Mira twisted one of her lengthy curls around the ear of her glasses, a sure-fire sign of pique. 'Fine. Then go home.'

'I'm here aren't I? Look at me, caring about all of this.'

A well-stocked bar crouched against the wall, a few thickset Johns with empty glasses. She was almost tempted to join them. If the thought of sitting beside them didn't make her skin want to crawl clean off her body and rumple into a pile on the floor.

The brothel was clean. At least there was that. She tried her best not to touch anything either way, but at least the place didn't look... sticky. That might have done her in.

One of the whores wandered past the queue, cigarette in hand. The oils layered between the creases of his lithe stomach made him look like someone had sneezed on him and his penis pendulumed between his thighs with little wet *smacks*.

Sam's arms crept around her shoulders. The taste of bile was barely an echo these days, but it never quite went away.

A hand on her shoulder. Sam whirled, but it was only Mira. Her glasses were practically steamed up, eyes glued to the starkers bloke's arse. 'Are you okay?'

'Until you drown me in your drool. Get off.' Sam shrugged her hand away. 'I can't believe I have to vote here.'

'DeMori ran on a ticket of legalised prostitution. Well, Councillor DeXahhn gave him the idea, but it's his name next to it. Our district is the only one where you can pay for it legally. And voting has to take place in a government building.'

'Vicky's friends vote in a chapel. They get tea and pastries.'

'There's tea here.' Mira nodded at a table off to the side. A cloud of steam clung close. Porcelain teacups, patterned in pink flowers. No, not flowers. What was...?

Oh. Charming. Bodies writhing together in some sort of pattern. Who would spend the time making a cup that had a man bent over on his knees like that? And was that his genitalia or a green bean on a trellis?

'I'd rather die of thirst.'

'And Jak says you can be overly dramatic.'

Sam made the adult decision to take a period for sulking. Mira sniffed at her silence but said nothing and it wasn't long before she was gazing, starry-eyed at the council table. All this voting nonsense, it got Mira randier than any number of greasy whores.

A miserable councillor sat behind a rickety counter taking votes. Half the morning he'd been flanked by a pair of Walkers, but they'd long since wandered off. Busy ejaculating their pay into some pillows no doubt. Sam winced but the image wouldn't fade and her stomach roiled. She burped acid.

'If you're going to vomit, do it outside.'

'Maybe some air, that'll…' Sam turned to the exit, but it slammed open before she could as much as swallow down half the rising chunks.

A man loomed in the doorway. White-crusted beard and wings at his temples aged him up past Father. Scraggly shirt and holey trousers. Eyes sharp as coal, he had a woollen cap tight to his scalp. Only one ear poked through the side. The other side was twisted in a thick scar.

'So this is where your lot do it.'

'Do it?' A nearby woman, no skirts and a corset that must have eaten a good few of her ribs, raised an eyebrow.

'Not that. That.' He jerked his thumb at the councillor and stomped over to the desk, no regard for proper queue etiquette. A few sniffed at him, but that didn't last long before the handkerchiefs came out. He had a unique odour. Like uncured fur that had been left sitting out in the sun.

'People have been waiting…' The councillor's voice was a squeak. Colour drained from his spotty face when he noticed his Walkers were absent.

'Aye they have. Tell you what, you find me someone whose paid more'n me and they can go first.'

'Elections are free and fair…'

The man burst into a storm of unfeigned laughter. 'Free and fair? Which of those would you call this?' He rummaged about in a pouch at his belt then tossed something on to the table. The councillor blanched. What was it? Looked like a large raisin with leathery bits.

Ah. The missing ear. Now, that was truly disgusting. But for some reason, she couldn't stop staring at it. Sam was struck by a desperate urge to lean down and whisper into the thing.

'Lost that when your Walkers decided that the best way to deal with the Nest was to burn us out.' He thumbed the scar on his face. 'According to your maps, I aren't able to call it the Nest no more. Apparently, I now live on the outside of Meadowside somewhere. I've come here to cast my mark.'

47

'I don't...' Mira's began, far, far too loudly.

Sam scowled at her, but she didn't look over.

'Whassat?' The man turned on Mira. The coals in his eyes sparked.

'Forgive me, but I don't think there is any need for the theatrics.' Mira cleared her throat. It was like watching a mouse standing up to a horse. 'Queuing can bring out the worst in all of us. Why don't you go next? Take my place and give your name.'

'Hm. Good then.' He actually seemed quite taken aback. 'Nice glasses. Aspectum lenses, right? Used to have a pair myself when I did gold chasing. Sold them when I couldn't keep 'em on anymore.' He poked at the rubbery skin around his missing ear.

'Speaking of...?' Mira gestured at the shrivelled lump of flesh.

'Fair. Wouldn't want to go forgetting that.' He almost laughed as he scooped the thing into his pouch. The glare returned when he turned on the councillor.

'Name?' he squeaked.

'Sy.'

'Second name?'

'Can't afford one.'

The functionary slid a sheet across the table. Three boxes for the governor of Meadowside Boulevard; Antonio DeMori, Francesca Capican, Quill. 'Ensure your mark is contained wholly within the square. If it leaves the highlighted area, your ballot will be spoiled. Ensure it soaks through the sheet. If not, your ballot will be spoiled. Do not spill on any candidate name. If it does...'

'You'll let me have another go?'

'Your ballot will be spoiled.'

'Fucking shocking.'

'Your finger. Please.'

The man, Sy, held out his hand. Didn't as much as flinch when the blade nipped his flesh. He looked down at the list of names and drew a scrap of paper out of his pocket.

The word 'Quill' was written in childishly large letters. He checked it against the list.

'What's that?' Sam asked Mira.

'How else do you know who to vote for when you can't read?'

He pressed his finger into the box. But it didn't really do all that much. Sam squinted over his shoulder. She wasn't the only one being nosy. The mark was almost invisible, colour closer to copper than red.

'Unfortunately, sir...' the councillor began.

'Don't you fucking start.'

'If your mark is not visible...'

'It will be.' The man gripped his finger tight and squeezed. The bead of blood barely welled.

'Iron deficiency,' Mira whispered to Sam. 'Mucks up the blood. It's a diet thing. Common across the river.'

Sy grimaced. He gripped the edges of the tiny cut with his fingernails and pulled. The cut opened wider until he had a fine trickle of blood dribbling down his palm. He jabbed his finger into the box.

Blood seeped out of the square.

'Thank you. We have registered your spoiled ballot. Your act of protest will be noted.' The councillor cast his eyes to the table.

'Like fuck. Give me another one.'

'One ballot per person, sir.'

'Give me another!' He slammed his bloody fist against the table.

'Sir, I...' The councillor's beady eyes darted around the room. They landed somewhere just beyond Sy's shoulders.

The two Walkers had returned from upstairs. One tucked her shirt back into her trousers. The other hid a sheaf of cigarettes in his pocket.

The councillor's face transformed. Spotty terror replaced by smothering arrogance. His lips curved into a snarl. 'Are you aware that it is illegal to threaten an elected councillor?'

'I don't give the tiniest shit.'

'Lars, Annie? Do you intend to do your jobs, or just stand there like recently-fucked lemons?'

The two Walkers marched forwards. The shorter one grabbed the fellow by the elbow.

The air in the room stilled. One of the working boys slid his oily legs behind the bar and cowered there. Everyone knew what people from that side of the river were like.

But it didn't happen. The violence. Sy just sighed. 'What do you think I am? Gonna kill you all just 'cause I talk different and don't wear a shirt.'

'That's a threat!' The councillor pointed a shaking finger.

The Walker at his elbow slammed the hilt of her blade into Sy's face. Something *popped* and blood sheeted down from his mouth. The fellow yowled.

'Another for the Sightless,' the councillor snarled.

Sy shook his head slowly. His eyes swam. 'Forty fucking years I've been bled by you lot. Nothing's changed.' He spat blood on to the floor.

'Would one of you shut him up?' the councillor mewled.

The Walkers gagged him. He struggled, but they had him out-matched. It didn't take long for them to drag him out. Sam watched silent at the speckling of blood that trailed after him, like rain on dust.

CHAPTER 9

Ruairi wiggled around on his belly like a worm with a knot tied in the middle, holding tight to what he'd call a gut snare if anyfolk were around to tell but what looked a lot more like a brittle loop of dry entrails. Hunting for his dinner. This were how the big boys did it. If they were addled morons.

He scratched his arse. Week of bumping around in the cart, every dip and divot scraping his bones together and he still weren't there. Camping out again tonight, he were determined to close his gums around sommat fresh.

Rabbit. Maybe, or a hare? No idea what the difference were. Point were some furry creature with big ears hopped across the clearing. Closer to the snare. Closer still. Nice thick drumstick leg just a whisper away... *now!*

He jerked the snare tight with both hands. It didn't close. Just scraped across the grass as the rabbit hopped off with nary a fuck given.

Crabbie, the ancient cart mule, blustered at his back.

'Oh aye, like you'd've done any better.' With some effort, Ruairi turned back over his shoulder. Crabbie gnawed on some nearby shrubs, smacking the straps of the cart with her swishing tail. 'You eat worse'n I do.' He took a strip of Pa's famous, vile, fish jerky from his pocket and shoved it between his molars.

Thudding. A whinny. Sounded like a shriek. The sound of a dying beast.

A horse thundered up the path towards him. Ruairi shrank in on hisself, for the first time glad he were making friends with the ants amongst the grass. The beast were black as pitch under the setting sun.

White froth speckled its front and as it got closer, it were obviously in trouble. Each step a limping effort. Ruairi recognised that pain.

Its rider hung on. The bloke were tall, shock of sunlight hair. He looked worse off than the horse. Eyes closed, cheeks sallow. Sommat black tumbled from his knee. Soot, maybe? His entire body jerked with every breath.

It happened like cut strings. The horse crumpled. Almost stately, the thing went down on its front legs. It didn't scream, just gave one final snort before that chest weren't moving no more. The rider slid from his seat, motionless. Lay in the dust of the road, barely breathing.

Ruairi crawled forwards on his elbows. 'Ey, you still alive?'

The fella's eyelids flickered.

'Taking that as a yes. Hope you don't mind a bit of manhandling. I've become the world's greatest expert in being helped up off my arse. Should take no time at all.' He gripped the bloke under the armpits and *heaved*.

Crawling were easier than walking, but it still felt like some rusty chain were being dug outta his spine. Before long, sweat pearled down his cheeks, mingled with the snot dribbling from his nose. Managed to get the bloke into the clearing by Crabbie before his arms gave out and he slumped to the dirt, shaky as a foal.

'Do you... have a fire?'

Ruairi jerked back at the sound of the rider's voice. Faint, insubstantial. Like he weren't sure about each of the words.

'Uh, can do.' Ruairi scrabbled a quick firepit and his flint quickly got a spark going. The bloke leant towards it.

'I haven't been warm in so long.' The rider fingered a gilded cage around his neck. It were shattered open, black flecks of dust clinging to the twisted bars. 'The arrow is still in there, isn't it?'

'Aye.' No sense lying to the poor bugger. Though it were powerful strange, a thick layer of soot coated the wooden arrow shaft that just looked to vanish where it pierced his trousers. Ruairi couldn't see any hint of the metal beneath. 'What did you do to get thumped with iron?' He were feeling a mite awkward about it all, now he had time to think. Normal folk didn't get arrows through the body for nothing.

'Iron? I wish.' The rider leant forwards. His eyes glittered in the firelight. Violet as the final gasp of light at sunset. Sparks swirled like fireflies being swallowed by the night sky. 'Draw it out.'

'What? No!' Even looking at it made Ruairi's stomach squiffy.

'Do you want me to die?' It weren't a question asked in anger. The rider almost sounded... curious.

Ruairi shook his head.

'Well. It won't fall out on its own.'

Ruairi licked his lips. 'Right. Fine. No skin off my bloody nose.' He choked down a couple of breaths, set his hands around the shaft of the arrow. 'What do I do when you start bleeding out?'

'You won't have to find out.' The rider winced, his face twisted. 'Ready?'

'Wait. First, tell me your name.'

'Ruairi.' Moment he said it, he felt wrong. Like he'd given away some great secret.

The rider nodded. 'I will remember you.' He gasped. 'Okay, do it. Do it now.'

Ruairi swallowed, gripped the arrow between his fingers. Pulled, hard as he could.

The rider screamed, loud and sharp enough to break the night open.

The hunk of metal began to smoke, thick white fog boiled from the bloke's knee. Little blue dots swam through the rider's eyes. Almost intense enough to drown the violet, until eventually the arrowhead came free.

Beneath it, the bloke's knee was unmarked.

'So many gaps.' The rider's head slumped to his chest. 'I can't lose my eyes. Not now.' A faint blue steam rose from the inside of his left eyelid. 'But there is no smog beyond the city walls, so far away from the Iactura. Unless...'

He looked up at Ruairi. Blue-violet eyes cut like a razor.

'Reality burns. This,' he said, 'is a very bad idea.'

He took a knife from his belt and pierced each of his fingertips. Then he yanked the arrow from the grass and slammed it into the back of his hand. He spat a tiny breath into the fire.

It roared and, in an instant, the clean orange flame burned blue.

Ruairi scrabbled backwards, heedless of the spiking pain in his back, just desperate to get away. The flames rose like eels, twined around the clearing, spat out white smoke and the smell of rust.

The arrowhead glowed in the back of the rider's hand. Pierced fingertips leaked blood in thick ropes. The rider held out his hand, puppet-master over a marionette. The lines of blood curled and crushed together, some metal chunk forming in their bloody net.

Smoke rose from the metal. When Ruairi sucked in a desperate, hot breath, it seared down his throat.

He blinked. And the world were different.

The clearing were gone, rider too if his eyes were to be believed. Instead he were suddenly stood in some grubby fishing village, a dark rain spattering against some cloak he'd never worn before.

He didn't hurt.

The ceaseless weight, heavier with each passing year, and all at once it were gone. Were this what others felt like, all of the time? He coulda wept. He went to move, to jump into the goddamn air and holler his lungs out.

But he couldn't. Tried to blink. Couldn't manage that neither. His hand lifted on its own, palm out against the rain. This weren't his body. Somehow, he were just a passenger, peering outta some other bloke's eyes.

He found hisself staring at the blue-silver arrow. A Walker, black cloak streaming in the wind, bowstring drawn back towards his ear. Some woman with steel-grey curls shouted sommat, lost in the wind. A coal flickered to life around her neck and the Walker fired. The arrow slammed into his knee. Ruairi screamed with some other man's throat.

He coughed out the smoke, found hisself back in the clearing, lungs afire. This weren't right. Ruairi's heart battered itself into a bloody mess inside his chest. 'This isn't possible.'

'Exactly.' The rider's eyes were blue now, glowing like the light of twin stars trapped inside his skull. Tears sizzled down his face as a lump of black-red metal fell from his fingertips. He gripped his wrist, blue-silver arrowhead still rammed into the back of his hand. His fingertips dripped again. No longer blood. Now they dripped that terrible blue fire. It ate through the grass, through the soil, burning a spiral around the rider's feet.

'Stop it.'

'Do you regret saving me?' The rider stood up, leg outstretched. 'So many others do.'

'Stop it!' Ruairi shouted. 'You'll cremate us both!'

Without thinking, he lurched forwards and ripped the arrow outta the bloke's hand.

The fire burst outwards in a deluge of heat and smoke, forced Ruairi to the edge of the clearing. The rider was swallowed by the smoke. All he could see through the haze were those glowing eyes. A voice spoke inside his head.

'I will remember you.'

Ruairi fled back to the road like a kid running to Ma. Felt like his whole body were being scraped up and down a washboard, but bugger that. This were madness. Blue fire, other folk's memories. He hoped the wet in his trousers were just sweat. He flung hisself on Crabbie's back. A mule were a mule, but he jammed his feet in hard to get her going.

An axel from the bloody cart caught a rock. The wheel went splintering and the cart crashed outta the harness. Crabbie jerked sharp as the leather straps split and Ruairi yowled at the spike of pain. He turned back to the broken cart, leaking ice and fish liver into the road. Behind it, blue fire wound around the trees, burning like a beacon.

In that instant, he could see it. Blue flames burning through the cottage back home. Pa's body broken as those branches, Ma's hair ablaze, little Abi choking with smoke.

I will remember you. No. He couldn't lead that thing right back.

Only one other place for him. Arx. Hide behind that massive stone wall. Find some of Pa's old Walker mates and beg for their help. Slim hope, but what else were there for fighting fire-demons from his nightmares?

Ruairi left the cart in the dust and rode on through the night.

CHAPTER 10

'I know you're there.'

Perhaps not the most natural thing, talking to himself, but Caelan was sat outside a Sootheel pub. Talking to himself was probably the height of manners here.

He sniffled against the cold and winced. Most of the swelling had gone down, ditto the bruises, but his nose was still tender. Best that could be said was that he no longer looked like a man who had lost a fight with an angry stone wall. The worst part was that he hadn't seen Addie since. Made it very difficult to be condescendingly magnanimous as he accepted her apology.

'I'm not doing this all day.' He rubbed his thumb against Ferra's bloodmetal in his pocket. Ever since his nose broke, he'd felt something. That face between the shadows in his mind. It was tempting to believe he had imagined the whole thing, but it was one of the few memories he had. That made it easier to keep track.

'Waste of bloody time.' Caelan tilted the whisky down in a single swallow. Blackened stars! He coughed the liquid back up. What *was* that? Why would anyone drink something so *bitter*? He could *feel* it settle in his stomach. For a moment, he was almost tempted to laugh. Six months old and already drinking. Mama and Papa would be so proud.

Whoever they were.

Caelan gritted his teeth and wiped a sleeve across his mouth. It was difficult. For the most part, he did what he could to not think about what was lost. But sometimes, it was impossible. Family. Friends. Childhood. They hit like hammer blows. It wasn't fair. How could he miss something he no longer remembered?

Caelan scrubbed his face with his palms. He could be maudlin later. Endless reams of time to sit about and feel sorry for himself. Today, he had a focus. He was going to talk to himself.

Sootheel was a busy place. Gaggle of young blokes fell about pissing themselves on the corner, two older lasses chucked knives towards a target outlined in the dust. But there was an edge to it. Something missing. No one really looked at each other. False laughter shattered like glass.

The Walkers saw to that. Black-and-gold shadows ever-present, dogging footsteps. A visible threat, though a threat against *what* it was hard to tell.

Something pulsed in the back of Caelan's head. Felt like… anger?

Caelan blinked. That was new. Chase it.

He made for a nearby alleyway. It bordered a home with a collapsed roof, filled with metal girders, soot-stained bricks and shards of ceramic. One pile was high enough that he could find some purchase. A quick scramble later and he made it to the rooftops. Broken roof beams and shattered tiles. He took it slowly.

'If I fall, do you die too?' he asked himself. The wailing wind was his only reply.

Even so, there was something about being up so high. Something comforting. Caelan walked with arms outstretched, the bloodmetal gripped tight in his fist, trailing the Walkers. He leapt over a short gap towards a cluster of abandoned workhouses, skidded on a tile and sent a shower of dust raining down.

One of the Walkers looked up. Caelan swallowed and ducked out of sight. Perhaps some distance. He made for an old factory, used the collapsed chimney as handholds and scrabbled up to the top of the roof, high over the city. Sat down and swung his legs over the edge.

Arx spread out below him.

Intermeshing gears twisted into the isthmus of a peninsula whose name everyone in the city had long since forgotten. The jagged teeth of fractured outer walls bit into the chalky rock. Ocean spray sluiced oil from the black-stained bricks.

Streets wound like sprocket chains, interlinked and lined with metal. No iron. Copper lintels, zinc window-bars, corroded lead roofs of sheet metal shacks and abandoned factories.

Arx was designed to move. The twist of drills tearing iron from the ground, ore clanking through foundries in Rustscrape, Southbrace, Sootheel, pumping into Rotheart and out through the Mucro.

Before the Iactura ground Arx to a halt.

An unbroken pillar of metal through the spokes of the city, it pierced through reality and into the mists of Memoria. A symbol of hatred for everyone this side of the river. Whispered rumours claimed it was the source of the smog. Sure, Arx was an industrial city. It still had blacksmiths and furnaces. But it had been forty years since the Flame Protests, since the foundries had last belched their poisons into the sky, and still the smoke remained. So thick it blackened the stars.

Caelan bit back the shards of a laugh. At least, so Kuyt said. Not like he fucking remembered. He drew the knife from his belt, held it beside the Iactura. An iron replica. His fingers scratched across the tip without drawing blood. Cold wind toyed with his hair. 'It's a long way down.'

He sat there for a long time. Alone. Dots moved through the streets. Ate. Drank. Pissed. Survived. Nothing more. Far enough away that he could disassociate. Forget they were individuals.

He was surprised to find how easy it was.

'They still stick around. Despite it all. I guess it's hard to leave something so familiar. Even if you can't remember it.'

He watched the figures. Tried to picture the lives of those so far away, but it was impossible. Not a surprise. He barely had enough patchwork to keep his own life in mind, let alone any others.

Except for one. A figure, a woman. Something about the way she moved, like an errant drop of water that flowed up the falls rather than down. She held something close to her chest.

Curiosity is disturbingly powerful. Caelan scrabbled down from the factory roof and crawled closer to the square. She ducked into an alleyway, glanced behind and unwrapped the bundle.

A baby.

It started screaming. Caelan almost fell from the roof. The thing was shoestring thin. How could it still make such a noise?

'Shut up. Shut up,' the woman hissed. She fished a handkerchief from her pocket and dipped it in a nearby rain barrel. It came out grey, filthy as rain. She squeezed the liquid into the child's mouth.

Oily water splashed across the infant's face, across its tongue. It made a motion. Almost a swallow. Then coughed.

Blood splattered down its shroud, bright as buttons. One rattling breath. Then silence.

The young mother was still for a moment. She blinked. With impossible gentleness she set the child on the floor and wiped the water, the blood, from its face.

Her single sob came as a tremor. A shudder that wracked her tiny frame. So violent, like her bones had snapped.

'Infanticide is still a crime, miss.'

Caelan jerked from his perch atop the nearby roof. A Walker, bearded and heavy, stood in the mouth of the alleyway.

The woman ducked her head, tried to scuttle away, but he blocked her in.

'Even if it isn't your fault.'

The woman opened her mouth, but nothing escaped.

'We'll do it right. Get you through quickly. Bugger me, after what you've just been through you might even welcome it. Can't imagine any-one would want to remember this.' Resignation. Maybe even regret. His thick fingers tightened around her pale arm.

'*Do something.*'

The whisper was like footsteps across his mind. Caelan blinked. 'What?'

'*Stop this.*'

'Why?' Sweat trickled down the side of his face. He caught a glimpse of a face when he blinked.

'*People like her shouldn't suffer because of people like him.*'

The Walker dragged the woman towards the end of the alleyway. The sword at his hip shone in the weak sunlight.

'Ah, come on!' The words burst from Caelan's mouth, coarse and painful. He leapt from the rooftop, landed in the alleyway. Almost slipped and fell flat on his arse, but a quick pinwheeling of his arms kept him upright.

The Walker raised a meaty eyebrow.

'She didn't kill the thing. It just... went.'

'This isn't worth it kid. Walk away.'

'I know it isn't,' Caelan said. The woman hung from the Walker's grip. Her eyes were empty. He drew the knife from his belt. 'But I can't do that.' His legs began to shake. 'I'd remember if I did.'

'You see who you're doing this for?' The Walker groaned and scratched his shoulder. 'Look at her. Mind's gone already and taken her voice with it. She wouldn't lose much.'

'No, I'm the one whose mind has gone. She's just grieving. Let her go.'

'Please tell me that's not a threat.'

'Oh fuck off, of course it is.'

The Walker sighed. 'Alright then.' He released her arm and let her from the alley.

She glanced back over his shoulder. Her eyes locked with Caelan's. Then she fled.

'You feel good about that?' the Walker asked.

'Not really.'

'Figured. Imbecile.'

The Walker charged.

Caelan barely had time to get his guard up before that enormous blade clashed into his dagger. The impact stunned him. Felt like his arms were frozen. The Walker brought his heavy boot around and slammed it into his stomach.

Caelan fell back, coughing.

The Walker came again. Caelan leapt aside. He tossed out a slash, once, twice, but the Walker turned his thrusts and parried with vicious, sweeping cuts of his own.

Caelan slammed into the wall.

'You're really shit at this, aren't you?' The Walker advanced like Addie did. Aware. Ready. Prepared

Caelan didn't respond. His bravado was gone. Swallowed by the gulf between idiot and soldier. How could he possibly have convinced himself this was a good idea? Or maybe that was it. Maybe he knew how it would end all along.

Kuyt was right. If he had nothing to live for, maybe he was just looking to die.

The Walker's blade crashed down, slammed Caelan's knife aside and sent him sprawling in the muck. The blackcloak's boot pinned his wrist to the floor.

'I hate that you made me do this to you. At least with the Sightless I can pretend it wasn't my fault.' He lifted his sword.

Caelan cowered. Pathetic. Was this the end? Six months of suffering, just to go out like a melted snowflake in some filthy alleyway?

At least he saved that woman. That was something, at least.

'Not enough.'

A burning, boiling sensation burst from his fingertips. The voice blasted through his skull and with it came... clarity. A deluge of emotion, of rage. And something else. A rush of mental sensation slammed into him. Not memory.

Experience.

Caelan rolled as the Walker's blade smashed into the sludge behind him and danced to his feet. A lifetime of experience, tamed in an instant, raged inside his chest. His knife, suddenly so familiar, leapt between his fingers.

The Walker swung. Wide and ugly. Was this what he'd been so afraid of? Caelan slipped between the blows, jabbed his blade just beneath the Walker's armpit.

The copper sword fell from nerveless fingers. The artery was open. Blood sprayed across Caelan's face, his hands, his chest. The Walker grunted. Slumped to the slime.

Caelan's breath came in white clouds. A grin ripped across his lips. Survival. The face in his mind reappeared. It mirrored his smile.

'*This is a reality worth remembering.*'

Caelan blinked. And the weight of what had just happened tore the breath from his lungs.

'Help me.' The Walker clamped a hand over the wound, but rich blood squeezed crimson between his fingers.

'I don't...' Caelan knelt beside the Walker. Adrenaline thumped behind his eyes, bile bubbled down his throat. 'I can't.' He crumpled to the floor. Wet blood soaked into the seat of his trousers. 'I think I've killed you.'

'I didn't let my guard down. It's not fair. Captain says... you only die when you get cocky.'

Caelan shuddered. He nicked his finger on the bloody edge of his knife. 'Have… you killed before?'

The Walker nodded. His face was pale.

'How many?'

'They tell us not to keep count. Six. Or seven.'

'Don't you remember them?'

The Walker coughed again. The blood was black. 'They make you forget your first. Cut the connection, so she says. Keeps us from getting used to it. It's supposed to hurt but we do it anyway and when it gets too much that blue fire is waiting. She let me keep just enough of each death so that I can hate myself. But rather that… than this.'

'You're my first.'

'Bully for me,' he rasped. 'Fuck I'm thirsty.'

Caelan pushed himself up, cupped his hands and dipped them in the rain barrel. He brought the water to the Walker's chin, but his hands were shaking so hard he splattered the liquid down the man's chest.

'My throat… is so sore.' A tear leaked down his crooked nose.

'I'll remember you,' Caelan said.

'Lot of good… that'll do…' the Walker sobbed.

'What's your name?' Caelan asked.

But the man was dead.

CHAPTER 11

Sam slammed her hammer against the final chain link, heating and working it against the anvil horn over and over until the edges closed into a solid oval. 'Reckon that's it about done.'

Jak looked up. 'Aye, that oughta do it. A good twenty foot each. Job's a good'un.' He slapped Sam on the back.

She leant back and let her hammer clatter to the floor. Usually, she'd treat it better, but after a good week in the forge her arms felt like they were ready to fall off. She wiped the sweat from her top lip on to the collar of her shirt. 'You sure they'll pay?'

'No doubt. Good call on the Llian contract. They were behind anyway.' He cleared his throat. 'Got a man coming 'round later to pick them up for us. Might not be glamourous, but Acarris Chains will span the Mucro for months. Maybe more, if we did a good job. And we did.'

'Careful Jak, you're almost sounding content.'

'I've heard it happens in the autumn years. Don't get too smug, you'll be back down here tonight helping me load these things. Until then, well I don't know about you but I could go for a wash and a bite.'

Sam nodded. Exhaustion was lapping at her ears. 'And a nap.'

'You don't nap after a hard week's work. You pub.'

'*You* pub. I sleep.' Sam yawned.

The door bounced open and Vicky, right on schedule, poked her head through.

'It's all done!' Sam opened her arms towards the lengths of chain before Vicky could speak. 'Look, see? Done *before* time, so make sure you negotiate a bonus.'

'There is someone here to see you.' Vicky scratched her nose, wiping a thumbs-worth of powder from her face.

'All okay up there ma'am?' Jak asked.

She didn't reply.

'Well who is it?' Sam asked. Mira wasn't due for another couple of days. She'd been… off, since the incident at the brothel. The bloke they'd arrested, that Sy fellow, she'd been chewing his name all week.

'Now Sam,' Vicky said and disappeared back upstairs.

'Any idea what that's about?' Jak wiped his hands on a rag and set his hammer back in the rack.

'Not a clue. You coming?' Sam splashed her face from the saltwater quench.

Almost the instant they left the forge, Father was on them. 'Sam, there is someone to see you.'

'I know I don't get a lot of visitors but I didn't realise it was a family event.'

Father leant close, his lips twisting around an invisible cigarette. 'What have you done?' He didn't seem angry. But he definitely wasn't pleased.

'That's both of you pissed with me now, one of you should have the good grace to tell me what I've done. Who is it?'

Father ignored her, just took her hand and placed it on his arm. 'We won't be keeping her waiting.'

He escorted, and dragged, her into the living room. A fire crackled in the hearth. Shadows danced across the curtains. A decanter of whisky rested on the table, a glass poured for the single occupant.

'Uh, may I present my daughter Samantha Acarris,' Father said. 'Oh, and our Forgemaster, Jak Mendy.'

'Thank you, Councilman DeAcarris.' The stranger stood up, and before she was fully on her feet Father had scuttled from the room. A gilded cage swung around her neck, a black lump of coal held inside a golden frame. Half-shaved head, covered in a spiral pattern of tattoos and eyes the same crimson as her dress. 'It is your pleasure, I'm sure. I am Mistress Ignis.'

The anxious beating of Sam's heart made her feel ill. 'Mistress Ignis.' Instinct dragged her legs down in, what was that a curtsey? It was sodding difficult in trousers too so she stumbled a little. 'Jak.' She elbowed him in the stomach. It was like striking a concrete wall. He didn't even look at her.

'Why are you here?' Jak asked.

'Jak!'

'Jak Mendy. Sootheel blacksmith. Son of Carl Mendy who, official records state, died in the Flame Protests.'

'Aye, except he didn't, did he? He died because of your poison between his ears. He died because you demanded a legend and he failed at finding it. He *died* because you took his eyes and left him...'

'He died with your hands around his throat until his heart ceased.' Mistress Ignis' words cut across Jak. She held out a hand. 'Or have you forgotten him already?'

'Jak?' Sam's voice was small. 'What is she saying?'

'That... *thing* weren't Pa.' Jak didn't look at her. He clenched his fists and snarled at Mistress Ignis. 'Just some breathing husk you left me with.'

'Are you going to hit me, Jak Mendy?' Mistress Ignis approached him, set her hand on his chest. 'Would that satisfy you?'

Jak's face flashed and for all of a moment, Sam was convinced he was about to take a swing. Instead, he took a deep breath. 'Sorry Sammy.' He marched off and slammed the door behind him. It rattled against the hinges, but Jak had made them himself so they held strong.

'Now that the pantomime is over, let us discuss business. Come. Sit.'

It wasn't a question. Sam plopped down into the armchair opposite Mistress Ignis. Her mind felt raw. Jak's hands tight around his own father's throat... 'Mind if I drink?'

'I'd be offended if you didn't.' Mistress Ignis sat back and held her whisky up to the faint sunlight.

Sam poured herself one and knocked it back. Much like forge work, Jak had taught her drinking. She poured another, this one to nurse. 'I'm sure you're busy,' she mumbled.

'Very. So let us begin.' Mistress Ignis' face was unreadable.

She reached into a pouch at her waist and drew out a lump of metal. Sam squinted. What *was* that? Looked like iron, but with a... what, jasper imperfection? It glittered like a slit throat.

'I have come to expect that everyone facing accusation begins with a lie. So I prefer expediency.' Mistress Ignis closed her eyes. She held a breath between her lips, then blew it out slowly. The coal around her throat burst into flame. Blue flame. Like a copper chloride burn, but much brighter. A line of smoke curled from the flame and touched the metal on Mistress Ignis' palm.

'Reality burns. Inhale the memory.'

It sounded like Mistress Ignis' voice was coming from inside her skull. Sam shoved a finger in her ear, took a breath.

Two figures formed in the smoke on her palm. Miniature sized and impossibly detailed. One short, long haired and dancing over an anvil. The other...

It was her.

Sam's stomach rebelled. What was happening? Like a puppet-show, she watched the smoke figures play out that day in the Iron Market. Fake-Callisteel clanging against the anvil, bending beneath her mist-wreathed boot.

She blinked again. And the image was gone, along with the fire around Mistress Ignis' throat.

'What was that?' Sam swallowed.

'A memory. Of you, humiliating Jonas Karrin. From the mind of the man himself. And believe me, I was very thorough in its excavation. This is your only chance to apologise.' Mistress Ignis knit her fingers together.

'I'm sorry,' Sam said. Jak had always told her that it was easier to bow the head. But then, Jak had also just disappeared in a smog-thick cloud of simmering rage. 'Though I stand by what I said. It wasn't Callisteel.'

'It wasn't. And for that he has been punished.' Mistress Ignis spoke smoothly.

'You disciplined him?'

'No. Punished. Disciplined implies that he is able to learn from his mistakes.'

Sam took another sip of her whisky. The glass rattled against her teeth. 'That memory stuff, huh.'

'You are experienced?'

'No. But it's not like you can escape it in this place. Mir... My friend tells me that the Viceroys and their Governors do it at the fancy parties. Some drink, some whore and some forget.'

For an instant, a dark look shattered Mistress Ignis' careful façade. 'A dangerous rumour.'

'Right.' Sam swirled the last of her drink. 'Well, as I said. I am very sorry. So, if that is everything?'

'How did you know that it wasn't Callisteel?' Mistress Ignis' smile didn't reach her eyes.

'Aside from how shoddy the blade was? He had no idea. Heat hotter than fire. Unmined iron. Quenched in blood. He'd done none of that.'

'Quenched in blood?' Ignis' eyes glittered. 'What does that mean?'

Sam chewed her lips. She was suddenly very aware of the lancet hidden beneath her trousers.

'Uh, well, you know the rumours. Or, well, myths by now. It's been a long time…' she trailed off into her whisky.

'Have you ever tried to forge it yourself?'

The next attempt at a laugh was even stranger, high and sharp. 'You think if I could make Callisteel I'd have spent the last week smashing together chains for the Mucro?'

'I will ask you once more. Have you ever tried to forge it?'

Sam licked her lips. Mistress Ignis' red eyes burned through her. 'Yes.'

'And?'

'And nothing. I failed. Several times. I don't even know *why* I failed. But Jak says its natural. Says all blacksmiths try it once. But no one can make Callisteel anymore. Best forgotten.'

Mistress Ignis stood up. 'I know all the metalwork contracts out at the moment. Your family has none for chain work, especially of the size the Mucro requires.'

Sam felt something sink into her stomach.

'Why have you been working on this?'

'The Llian contract, we figured… …'

'Of course. The apprentice, the delays… How very rapacious of you. It speaks to me of a woman with ambitions. Just as I am.'

'And what is your ambition?' Sam asked.

'The same as yours. Power. Women like us, women who don't fit the mould, must be powerful. Else the pressure would attempt to crush us. And there is nothing more powerful than Callisteel.' Mistress Ignis stood up. 'I will see to it that your barge chains are paid in full. And you will receive a similar payment, every month, from here until the end of our acquaintance.'

Sam felt her eyes widen. That kind of money... 'Why?'

'Because there is another defaulted contract I will place in your hands. One recently ripped from an ex-smith with ambitions beyond his skill. You will work for me, Samantha Acarris. And together we will bring Callisteel back to this world.'

CHAPTER 12

Ruairi shuddered the last steps of the long, winding road to Arx on foot. His whole body felt stretched to breaking. Days of riding Crabbie bareback and he were spent. The ancient mule weren't doing much better. Still panting, wind gone.

He grit his teeth. Even that hurt. How were his jaw connected to his back? It weren't fair. 'You did good, girl.' Ruairi rubbed her neck and unclasped the bridle, let the worn saddle slide off into the dust of the road. 'But I don't reckon you're coming with me.'

He held a hand against her neck and she spat frothing slaver down his shirt for good measure.

'Aye, I'm gonna miss you too. But you've been doing this long enough now. Reckon you know the way back on your own.' He gave her a little shove. It did bugger all.

Crabbie just looked at him, white eyelashes framing her black eyes.

'Now don't you be giving it all that. City ain't no place for a mule and I can't afford to stable you. Just think of your nice warm shed back home eh?' Ruairi weren't sure who he were trying to convince. 'No wolves in these parts, so you'll be fine as long as you take it slow.'

Crabbie blinked again.

'Go on now. Get going.' Ruairi summoned the last of his energy and clapped his hands a couple of time, wet driblets peeking down the corner of his eyes at the effort.

Crabbie snorted, but at least she half-turned. Walked a little, turned back, then kept on going.

She limped on home. Ruairi limped on forwards.

The wall that swallowed Arx were much less spectacular than Pa made it sound. He'd expected patterned stone, carved brick. What he got were cracks and crumbles, filth and bird shit. Like a fist of stone, he could see between the gaps of the fingers.

And rising, right above it all, were the Iactura. Ruairi couldn't help hisself. He looked up, tried to spy the tip and got his gaze caught in the clouds.

Its shadow fell on him. Ice cold.

Ruairi struggled another step. This close to the city he could taste the smog. But suddenly, his legs wouldn't move.

Sommat heavy on his shoulders. Like a giant fist trying to force him to his knees. The blue-silver pillar grew in his eyes. The blade of an axe, hanging high over him ready to fall. Breath slapped in and out of his lungs. He scrabbled at his throat with his fingers.

'Ey, what else can you see?'

Ruairi blinked. Some lad, fourteen summers at most with a shock of white right over his eyebrow, poked him in the elbow. He dragged a stack of firewood on a sling over his shoulders, axe strapped down his side.

'What?'

'Look about. What else is there, 'sides that big silver cock?'

'Uh.' Ruairi cricked his neck. 'Black stone walls. Clay-baked road. Massive gates. Coupl'a houses. Pile of horseshit you've just walked through.'

'Ah shit a brick.' The kid kicked his feet on the dusty road. 'Gonna be smelling that all day. How's your breath coming now?'

His what? Ruairi cleared his throat. Iactura felt all sorts of far away again. He sniffled. 'Better. Thanks.'

The lad gave him a mock salute, and they walked the last coupla steps up to the gates in silence. The enormous bronze bars were open and unmanned.

'No guards?' Ruairi asked.

The kid laughed, but it were a bitter rind. 'Where else would we go?' He jerked his head and darted through the gates. Instantly, he were gone. Vanished into Arx proper.

Ruairi followed slow. People. Like crabs in a bucket. Kiddies scuffled and screamed. Some woman ripped the wall from a house with a prybar. Man next to her took a big swig from some flask and belched.

And the smell. Offal stinks, manure stinks, but there is sommat natural about them. Arx reeked of ash and scabby wounds and that frothy scum that gathered on oil slick ocean currents.

He leant on the wall to catch his breath. Spat it back out again. Bugger it, even the wind were dirty. A great black mist that weighed heavily on his shoulders and dulled the sun to a spark.

Bunch'a folks were drifting the same way, so Ruairi hitched into the crowd and followed right along. Kept looking over his shoulder, despite the twinge in his neck. Didn't much enjoy the experience, so many people up so close to him. Like he were trapped in some big box buried deep under the earth.

Still, somewhere to hide. That blue-fire nightmare'd have a job tracking him down here. He ducked his head and walked on.

Some big platform opened up at the end of one of the roads, and a bloke stood in the middle talking to a crowd. White hair, creased eyes. He gestured when he spoke, and flashed a scar on his palm. Ruairi recognised him like a legend come to life.

The Ant.

'... and your votes have revolutionised laws on personal liberties. Division in Arx has been consigned to the mists of memory as we come together to...'

Whatever else he'd tried saying were lost in a wave of boos.

'You didn't give a shit about that when we came out fighting with you. What have you done 'cept bow to that lot since? Where's our work? Bring us iron!'

The crowd took up the chant.

'Bring us iron! Bring us iron! Bring us iron!'

The Ant held up his hands. 'The mines are exhausted, you know that. It's been four decades, it isn't coming back. But we still work metals here. I was a Foundryman, and I'm proud that we make more copper blades in Rustscrape than any other district!'

'Forging the blades that gut us. Next you'll have us making the boots we'll be licking.'

'The Nest fought for you!' Some bloke snarled up at the Ant. 'And what do we get? Sy's up for execution, just for trying to bleed his mark. Your pet Walkers'll be marching him to the axe themselves. You used to be one of us, *Ant!*'

The anger were raw, like the hungry stare of a wounded predator. Ruairi almost jumped clean outta his skin when some hand fell on his shoulder.

'Move along lad.'

Ruairi groaned as some Walker dragged him outta the crowd, no care about the grinding around his neck. 'I were just listening.'

'Aye, but when they start fighting they'll set on the easy target first. And I'd rather not be dragging your corpse out of here later.' He shoved Ruairi towards a nearby alleyway. Some bloke were sleeping half-way down, nestled in a bank of old metal and rags.

'Hold on! You're a Walker right, I gotta tell you something.'

The bloke drew his sword. 'It's really worth keeping it to yourself. Go drink yourself senseless and leave the violence to those who can handle it. Down the alley, two roads over to the east. *The Broken Hook.* Serves you lot.'

'Us lot?' Ruairi asked, but the Walker were already gone back into the crowd.

Ruairi licked his lips. The light were already fading, and he weren't too curious to see what the city did to lads with squiffy spines come nightfall. It weren't the worst advice. A meal and a bed would do him wonders.

Down the alley. Two roads over to the east. *The Broken Hook.* At least, that's what he figured it said, found words tricky sometimes, but the picture of a shattered metal crook made for easy reading. He hobbled on inside.

Warmth like Ma's treacle tart got soaking through him. Plenty of tables, not too many folks. Perfect. He stumped over to the counter.

'Y'alright love, what you want?' The woman set down a glass with her single arm. The other sleeve of her jacket were tied up around her torso.

'Uh, I guess a bed. And a bath if you have 'em. Any food going? I'm famished.'

She laughed and set her ringlet hair dancing. 'I'm sure we can sort something. Want a drink?'

Ruairi touched his purse. 'Prob'ly not. How much?'

She shook her head. 'We'll settle up later. But the first one's free.'

'You sure?' Ruairi blinked. 'Cheap here.'

'Cheap for people like us. What did you in?' She nodded at his legs.

'Oh. Uh. Birth, I guess.'

She had a pretty smile. 'Poor sod. Still, 'least you remember what happened. Better'n most.'

'What do you mean?'

She wiggled her stump. 'No memory of where I lost her. Keeps me up some nights. I just hope the middle finger was up.' She tugged at her knotted sleeve. 'Anyway, you take a seat, I'll send Carl around with your meal as soon as.'

'Cheers, Miss…?'

'Miss nothing. It's Lucy.'

It really were a pretty smile.

Ruairi took hisself over to a nearby booth and slumped down to the chair. It hit him instantly. The exhaustion, the pain, like some cruel god were stacking boulders on his back until they finally squished him flat. He blinked against the urge to set his head on the table and drift off to the land of nod.

'This'll wake you up.' A man, Carl he reckoned, came stumping over with his own limp. 'Course his was on account of the metal plug he had instead of a foot. It clicked every time it hit the floor. He set a short glass and a steaming bowl down on the table. 'Get your gums around this.'

For all of a heartbeat Ruairi reckoned he were too tired to eat, then the watery smell of twice-boiled beef caught his nostrils and he fell to it with a will. Scraped the bowl with his fingers and all, didn't waste a drop. Probably shouldn't have necked the beer just as quick, but a bloke got thirsty.

The door banged open and bodies started pouring in, a cloud of noise and bickering. Figured he recognised a few from the crowd earlier. Some of the ones who'd been shouting at least. And leading the charge were Fetch's familiar, shiny head.

'Here Luce, a round for all my mates,' Fetch shouted to a muted cheer, and chucked a purse over the bar. 'Nothing better after dodging the axe than a good beer. Since you ain't got any of that, we'll have what's on tap.'

'Dodging the axe?' Lucy started pouring pints.

'Aye, the blackcloaks get antsy when we're too loud.' Fetch went marching around the pub, waving his hand. "Course, I were all for fighting, but some of these wussbags are… ere, hopalong!' He stopped at Ruairi's table. 'What you doing in my city? Not been peddling those nasty insects have you?'

'They ain't insects.'

'Sure, sure, tell you what why don't you sit yourself with us and get a drink down you? That'll push the smacked arse look off your face and down to the seat of the chair where it belongs, eh?'

Fetch didn't give much of a choice, so they waddled over to the big table in the middle of the room. 'Bloody blackcloaks,' one of the lasses grumbled. 'They recruit from down here. How'd they turn so easy?'

'I hear they do something to their minds. Break 'em, just a little. Blue fire and what else,' Fetch said.

Blue fire. Ruairi shuddered.

'Whassay, kid? You given yourself the willies?'

Ruairi nodded. He slipped his hand into his pocket and drew out that arrowhead of blue-silver steel. A part of him couldn't believe he'd kept it, but he couldn't bring hisself to just leave it lying in the road. 'Aye. Had my own taste of blue fire on the way in. Wouldn't mind if I never heard of that stuff ever again.'

A candle flickered in the centre of the table. Without thinking, Ruairi touched the flame with the tip of the arrowhead.

A tiny curl of smoke. A spark of azure fire burst from the arrow-head in a blast of light.

Ruairi dragged the arrowhead back and blinked his eyes clear.

Everyone at the table were staring at him. And their look were no longer friendly.

'Where'd you get that?' the lass asked.

'Some bloke on the road. Violet eyes-'

Fetch gave a big, forced laugh. He snatched the arrowhead from Ruairi's fingers and jumped to his feet. 'Pay him no mind Annie, he's just making it up so he can wank over you.' He gripped Ruairi's collar and hoisted him up. 'Come on, I need a smoke.'

Fetch dragged him outside, heedless of how much he scrabbled and groaned at the squeeze in his spine.

Six figures waited in the darkness outside. Cloaks as black as the smog-soaked sky.

A blade nestled between Ruairi's shoulder blades. He froze.

'Fetch. Talk.'

'The Ant's lost it.' Fetch's voice changed. 'Who'd have thought the best way to deal with the most dangerous man in the city was to give him a title? The citadel business has buried him.'

'What else?'

Fetch scratched his head. 'You lot need to cool it.'

'Us lot?'

Fetch sighed. 'We. The temperature is rising. People are talking about the executions again. That bloke from the Nest dies tomorrow. Flame Protest veteran. People knew him, it's sparks on dry wood.'

'Agitator. Isn't your job to set them off where we can do something about it?'

Fetch chewed his words. 'My job used to be to keep the people of this city alive. It's handled. I spoke to Quill. He was pissing blood about it, no surprise, but we talked him down. He's now Governor of the Nest in all but name. Some of his lot will be at the execution. But it's a show of force, he's promised no killing. Unless we start it.'

'DeMori won the election,' the Walker spat. 'I didn't realise we sold pieces of Arx for threats.'

'DeMori didn't even realise his constituency spread that far. He agreed to this. Besides, the Nest is a maze. The Flame Protests were fought hottest there, it's little more than a ruin that spans half the river. Far as I'm concerned, they're welcome to it.'

'It is still cheap. One life for all of that.'

'Tell that to Sy. Would you feel the same if it was you instead?'

The Walkers were quiet for a moment.

'And who's your armrest?' The blade at Ruairi's back jabbed him.

'Did find you something. This one met someone on the road. Someone with violet eyes.'

'Dirk,' the Walker hissed.

'You know any other? By the sounds of things, the man survived DeSüle's ambush. Figured she'd have questions for the last bloke to see him. And she'll definitely want this.' Just like Ruairi had, Fetch touched the arrowhead to a nearby torch.

The light turned blue, thick enough to drown under. Ruairi felt himself go very cold. A pair of manacles clicked hard around his wrists.

Fetch sighed. 'Sorry kid. Shoulda kept quiet. This is Arx. No-one remembers anything.'

CHAPTER 13

The crowd by the scaffold was bigger today. Thirty, forty people maybe? Louder too. Something about an earless man drifted through the smoggy wind. Twice the Walkers from last time. Tense and bitter as unshed violence. Caelan huddled in his coat and waited for it to start.

'You sure you should be here?' Addie asked.

'Where else? The whole city used to turn out for this.' Kuyt thumbed through his sketchpad.

'We belong here.' The voice in Caelan's head was sharp. Ever since that Walker, it'd gotten stronger.

'Least we can do is remember them.' Caelan squeezed the blood-metal in his pocket.

Kuyt looked over. The old man had been cold with him all week, ever since he came home covered in Walker blood. Addie's grin had been wolfish, but Kuyt just looked… guilty? Hadn't said much since.

A Walker stomped past, made for the holding pen. Eleven at last count. One, a suspiciously small body, kicked out against the bars. The tolling thud echoed across the square, until the back of a blackcloak's hand sent them careening towards the dusty floor.

'Addie, how many people have you killed?' Caelan asked.

She looked up from chewing a fingernail. Raised an eyebrow. Shrugged. 'Twelve.'

'So thirteen, including the one they make you forget?'

'Twelve. I never finished training. Blue fire never scoured the first from me.' Addie cracked her knuckle so violently it sounded like she'd actually broken the thing.

'Do we have to talk about this now?' Kuyt asked.

Caelan drew the knife from his belt. Sent it spinning over his fingers, skilled and precise. The knowledge of how to hurt, to injure, to kill. He drew on that feeling, the experience fresh inside his head.

It didn't come alone. The shadow inside Caelan's mind grinned. With experience came anger. Came rage.

'Put that away,' Kuyt whispered. 'There are Walkers everywhere.'

Caelan flipped the blade over. 'At what point do you stop being a killer? I could forget what I've done, but that won't stop the Walker from being dead.'

The memory was fresh. The blood beneath his fingernails. The scrape down his elbow from smashing into the wall. The baby. Dead and cold, staring sightless at an uncaring sky.

The crunch of armoured boots crashed against the cobblestones as the Sightless arrived. The air, the smog, felt thicker. A pair of braziers by the stage puffed out smoke from flaming coals.

'Why does it hit so hard? Why can't I sleep because of him?' Caelan's fist tightened around the hilt of his dagger. He watched the Walkers patrol the crowd. They were jumpy. Some had their blades out already, others barked orders. One found a weeping couple and shoved them apart. Just because he could.

Caelan took in the faces nearby. A young woman chewing her hair. A child sucking its thumb. Two blokes, white knuckle grip around each other's hand.

An old man with kind eyes. A woman with a scarred face.

'You don't notice a callus forming. It's protection for something you do over and over. But a scar.' Caelan stared at the starburst skin on his fingertips. 'A scar is mortality. A reminder that just beneath the skin is raging, frothing blood.'

'*And it is time they remembered,*' the voice said.

Caelan took a moment. A cold breath of air. A Walker passed close by.

Viper-quick, he slammed his knife into her throat. She crumpled.

People turned. Voices broke the silence. The crowd began to swell.

A nearby Walker twisted, bellowed at Caelan. His blade swung. Addie's hatchet crunched into his nose and he flew back in a gurgling spray of gore.

'What have you done?' Kuyt's horror cut the wind. Shouting, screaming broke the sky. People rushed towards the scaffold. Bodies rocked and shifted.

Sanity snapped. The riot hit like a fist.

A Walker bellowed from a knot of fighting nearby. The blackcloak attacked and two men fell with open throats. His blade spat blood as he swung it at Caelan.

Instinct kicked like a horse and Caelan ducked, rolled beneath the cut. Experience flowed through him, each movement terrifyingly familiar. Almost without thinking, he struck out and warmth drenched his arm. The Walker grunted. Red blood splattered on black mud.

Caelan leapt up. A shadow flickered in the corner of his eye. He threw himself out of the way. Another Walker. The man's beard was knotted with blood.

The Walker's blade flashed. Caelan dodged, slipped, went down. Concrete leapt to smack him. Mud splattered his face. Blood-beard roared and raised his sword high overhead.

Idiot. Caelan lashed out, drove his knife into the Walker's side. Right in the kidney. The blackcloak fell, mouth open in a silent scream.

Some bloke rushed a Walker nearby. Swung and missed with a three-fingered fist. The copper blade darted at his throat. Caelan grabbed the bloke by the hair, dragged him back. He lashed out with his boot and sank the tip in the Walker's groin.

A lass nearby leapt on the blackcloak, drove a sharpened corkscrew into his throat. Blood gobbed down the Walker's neck.

'Cheers,' the bloke said. 'For Sy and the Nest!'

Caelan turned. What was that about?

A thud from the scaffold. The Sightless slipped its axe from the throat of the last condemned. It hadn't stopped. And as the final man lost his eyes, a nearby Walker leapt in to slice his throat for real. A pile of eleven eyeless corpses piled at its feet. The most recent, a bloke with one ear, rolled into the filth beneath the wood.

Rage like a rope of golden fire tightened around Caelan's heart.

He forced his way through the crush of bodies. A woman drew three inches of metal from a Walker's chest. Another blackcloak swung and she fell with her throat cut.

So much screaming. It pounded inside his skull. Caelan burst from the crowd before the scaffold. The Sightless hefted its axe.

Caelan leapt to meet the giant. His feet hit the scaffold with a crunch. Rotten planks cracked and splintered under his boots. The creature was enormous. A beast of steel. It glowed in the sunlight, a ripple of cobalt blue shimmered across the armour. The scaffold creaked under its weight.

Caelan charged. Right then, the world shrank down to the size of a single armoured figure. He drew on every sensation, every *feeling* that his shattered mind could provide.

He attacked. A whirlwind of blade and fury. His knife pinged and clanged and clashed with that armour.

With a sudden burst of speed, the hilt of the Sightless' axe rose to smash into Caelan's cheek.

Spots exploded in his eyes. Groggy, he lashed out. His blade, right between the Sightless' eyes. It didn't so much as scratch that blue-silver mask.

The Sightless sank a fist into Caelan's chest.

Agony slammed his ribcage and Caelan was thrown backwards. Breath whistled from his lungs.

The Sightless stepped closer.

Tears leaked from Caelan's eyes. He had to get up. To move. But he could no easier leap to his feet than he could take the sun in his hands. Blood was thick in the back of his throat. Something smelled like burning. The planks beneath his hands were hot.

'Don't just lie there!'

'I'm. Trying.' Caelan lifted his knife. Blackened stars, it was heavy. Smoke whispered through the wood at his feet. Sweat drizzled through his hair.

The Sightless stood over him. 'It has been twenty-six years since someone last raised their blade to me.' Its voice was like a mountain of ice breaking the earth beneath their feet. 'Who are you?'

'No one,' Caelan managed.

'I see your eyes.'

'And I see yours, *Sightless*. How many people have you killed?' Caelan spat blood.

'I do not kill those who do not know the mists. They pay for their crimes with their mind. It appears by your eyes that you have done the same.'

'My name is…'

'Unimportant. You will soon forget it.'

That terrible axe rose once more. Caelan could feel the bloodmetal from that first execution weigh heavily in his pocket. The shame. Pain alone was not enough to fill the void. But what else was there? Oblivion awaited at the feet of the Sightless.

He saw his own face reflected in that gleaming blue-silver axe. His mortality. And for the first time he realised that he wanted it. The breath in his lungs, the scrape of his knuckles, the taste of ash and the smell of smoke.

He wanted this life. The memories, so few and so precious. They were his.

But his body wouldn't listen. All he could do was kneel there.

And wait for the end.

A keening shriek. Addie raced from the smog, slammed a hatchet into the Sightless' mask. A tiny chip in the gemstone eye.

The Sightless backhanded her and Addie fell back on to her arse, hatchet rolling from her grip and slamming into the wood of the scaffold. Her eyes rolled back, just for a moment, before she wobbled to her feet. She kicked out at one of the nearby braziers and sent glowing coals scattering across the wood. Blood stained her grinning teeth, coated her remaining hatchet. 'Let's burn together. Kuyt, do it!'

Fire roared between their feet. A plank fell from the scaffold. Beneath, the remaining braziers had been forced below the shallow platform. Flames licked across the oily planks. Kuyt's pinched and weeping face peered between the slats for an instant before he ran clear.

A spark licked the Sightless' foot. Touched the blue-silver armour. The air fell still for a heartbeat.

The clap of a silent explosion. And the wind caught fire.

A pillar of blue flame roared around the Sightless, incinerated planks and flash-dried pools of blood. Addie threw herself at Caelan, arms around his waist she flung them both from the scaffold, smacking into the ground below.

'Addie, I…!'

'Later!'

They leapt to their feet as the scaffold collapsed in a crash of wood and coals. Stinging ash blasted across Caelan's face, he held up a hand and closed his eyes.

When he opened them, the Sightless was stood amidst the flames. A maelstrom of suffocating fire with that screaming face at its heart. In its hand, it held Addie's dropped hatchet.

With a silent step, it flung the hatchet at her. Blue flames caught that wicked, cutting edge of her blade.

'Addie, move!' Caelan shoved her aside as something *swicked* through the air behind them.

A thud in the small of his back. The world burst into a dark star of agony. Blood dripped down his hips, thick enough to drown in.

'Caelan!' Kuyt burst from the smoke with shuddering steps. He grabbed Caelan's coat, blood-slick cloth slipped between his fingers. The old man's eyes were dark and wet.

Something flickered. The sound of burning. The smell of iron.

Caelan fell into the choking darkness.

CHAPTER 14

If this was death, why did it hurt so much? And why was he naked? Caelan groaned. Sweaty chest hair stuck to the metal slab. He tried to ease up on to his elbows.

Mistake.

A spasm wracked him from neck to arse. Snot burbled across his cheek, darkness punched his eyes like a fist to the face. A river of ooze slurped down his sides.

Breathe. Just breathe. Moments passed like days, measured by each agonising gulp. Tears dried in his beard long before he could open his eyes again. He daren't move any more than his eyelids.

Footsteps. Cold sweat beaded on his forehead. Something rattled behind him. A door? The air changed when they entered the room.

Addie quirked an eyebrow. 'You look like shit.'

'Let's see how pretty you are with your back sliced open.' Fuck it was embarrassing how good it was to see her. 'How is it?'

'Bad.' She walked around the table.

'You're limping.'

'Burned my ankles something bastard fierce.' She winced. 'Though I'm surprised you're in any state to speak to me at all. Even Master Sarrk didn't think you were coming back.'

'Sarrk?'

'Surgeon. Up from that temple in Dreamscale. Supposed to be brilliant, but it didn't take him long to run out of ideas for you.'

'You got me a doctor from across the river?'

Addie shrugged. 'Figured you'd rather one of those than some braindead dog leech who thinks that feeding you your own blood mixed with citrus oil is the way to get you back on your feet. Told his guards I had a message for him. When we were alone, I balanced an axe between his legs and told him I'd cut it off and feed it to him if he didn't come with me.'

'Classy.'

Addie nodded. 'Figured I owed you. That hatchet was mine. You shoved me out of the way.' She awkwardly shuffled the reclaimed blade at her hip and then found a sudden interest in the wall.

Caelan flicked his eyes towards Kuyt. The old man's hands were coated in thick bandages. The burn spiralled out from beneath the glove and half-way towards his elbow.

'Eleven people were scheduled for execution yesterday. Not only did each of them fall to that monster's axe and those Walker blades, more than double the bodies were left for the corpse carts by the time they got the fire under control. What were you thinking?'

'I had to do something.'

Kuyt's honest face twisted. 'There is enough suffering here. Without you making things worse.'

'I...' Caelan shuddered. Something warm and wet burst down his side. 'Damn it, can we talk about this when I've cleaned the blood out of my arse crack? I'd like to focus on not dying, you know, just for now.'

Kuyt didn't respond. He looked at Addie.

She laid her hand on his arm. 'Goodbye Caelan.' Her voice was devoid of the usual mockery. She almost sounded sincere. The door clicked shut behind her.

'What was that?' Caelan asked.

Kuyt shook his head. 'I'll come see you when the doctor is back.'

'Wait, Kuyt!' Caelan shouted, but it was useless.

The old man was already gone.

Caelan woke to the feeling of something tingling and a slow, yellow warmth washing around him. Ah. He'd pissed himself. Hadn't even noticed.

'Still alive?' Kuyt again.

'Barely. Though I seem to have-'

'It is unimportant.' A new voice, accompanied by firm fingers. 'Brace yourself.'

A spike of pain rammed into his back as Caelan was lifted an inch from the metal. Towels mopped underneath him.

'You're the surgeon, right?' Caelan asked.

'Lincento Sarrk. At your service by threat of castration.' A short, fat man sporting a beard the size of an overgrown rat carefully wouldn't meet his eyes as he wiped the worst of the piss from the metal slab. A wet stripe cooled down Caelan's side.

'Where's Addie?' Caelan asked.

'Out.' Kuyt folded his arms.

'Well, I'll have to go find her when this is all over. Spot her a meal or something, she did save me from immolation. Thanks for that by the way.'

'I didn't have a lot of other options.'

'Don't suppose... that fire didn't *kill* the thing, did you?'

Kuyt's snort was like a gale. 'It was back out before we'd finished dragging you away, so I'm guessing not.'

'A pity.' Caelan braced himself for an echo of that unbidden rage that the Sightless brought out. But it never came. He just felt tired. 'You, surgeon, how are you going to heal me?'

Sarrk made a noise and looked away.

'Tell him,' Kuyt demanded.

'You can't feel this, can you?' Sarrk asked.

'Can't feel what?'

'Caelan, your foot is bleeding,' Kuyt offered.

'What?'

'More accurately, your foot is bleeding because I stabbed it.' The surgeon flashed a bloody-tipped knife under Caelan's nose. 'And you can't feel it, because that blow has severed your spine.'

'I... what does that mean?' Hot, close air stuffed his lungs. 'I can't walk?'

'That would be bad news. What I have for you is worse. Yes, your legs no longer connect properly to your body. Which means you won't be getting up from this slab. However, the axe that hit you... I don't know what makes that fire burn blue, but it burns hot. The blow itself is half-cauterised.'

'Okay. Then how *can* you heal this?'

Sarrk just shook his head. 'There are important veins near the spine and they are still bleeding beneath the burn. If I cut open the scar, you'll bleed out before we can get them shut. If I try to cauterise again, I'm just burning burnt flesh. If I leave you as you are... that is the slowest way. Gives you the most time.'

Icy fear drilled into Caelan's heart. 'I'm going to die?'

The surgeon nodded. There was no sorrow in his eyes. Just cold competence. 'Despite your lady friend's best efforts, it does me no joy to see a man die. I will stay close. When the end comes, I will help you take that path without lingering. That is all I can offer.' Sarrk turned and left, the door clicking closed behind him.

'Kuyt. We need another doctor.' The rage came now. Caelan's shoulders twitched, shuddered. Blood dribbled down his back. He barely noticed.

The old man took a seat on a stool beside the metal slab. 'Relax kid. Take a breath. You can't see the cut. It's just not the type of injury you survive. It was obvious the moment we got your coat off.'

Caelan's anger drained like wine from a shattered bottle. 'Then why are you here?'

'Because no one should die alone. And Addie asked me to.' Kuyt gripped Caelan's wrist. 'You did good, son.'

'I failed.'

'No. You didn't. We've been under the boot for as long as I can remember. You shouldn't have done it. But the Ant would have done the same. Before they called him DeGaya and stole his anger. This is how change starts. The match that lights the flame doesn't burn until the end. I forgive you.'

'Don't!' Caelan snarled through a wet mist in his eyes. 'Don't you *dare* forgive me.'

Kuyt just looked at him. 'Get some rest. I'll be back to check on you later.'

The old man left and for a long time, everything was quiet.

Caelan didn't blink. Maybe the tears would re-absorb.

'Pathetic. Die with dignity. I did.'

The voice was back. Caelan sucked up half a breath, tainted by the smoke of a nearby candle. Something flashed. He blinked and everything reversed. Light flickered and he was falling…

Caelan sat on the edge of the scaffold. Black rain fell from a smog-soaked sky. Immediately, he tried to stand up, to call out, but nothing happened. It wasn't him at all.

He was trapped in someone else's memory.

His fingers picked at the edge of the platform. Where were the splinters? The moss? Rotheart plaza looked odd. Clean, wooden buildings. Glass windows that glittered like diamonds. How long ago was this?

His stomach was warm. Caelan glanced down. Blood poured between his fingers. The body was dying.

'Reilo.' A voice from the darkness.

Caelan recognised the name he'd never heard before. Clarity came in a burst. Reilo Sandrasova. The voice inside his head.

A woman walked through the rain. The gilded chain around her neck held a lit coal. Thick curls stuck to her scalp, brown going to grey. Her skirt wisped around her legs. Spiral tattoos curled against her thigh, darting like blackbirds and crows mid-flight.

Mindbreaker.

'Aer. Here to make sure I go out?' Caelan felt his lips move as Reilo spoke.

'Unfortunately.' Aer sighed. 'Dirk does this to people, you know. You weren't the first he taught.'

'Oh he told me all about you.'

'We shouldn't exist. This magic… it's a cancer. A tumour, spreading through anything healthy. We were healers first, even if he doesn't remember that anymore. When you find a cancer, you cut it out. I'm sorry you have to die.'

'Not a fair fight. I'd have killed any mortal you sent after me. I'd have killed *you*.'

'You would. That is why Lucianus made this sacrifice. They call him Sightless now but he saw the future better than either of us. And he loves us despite all of that. This wasn't supposed to be what happened.' Tears prickled in her amber eyes.

'You know this doesn't end things. The Flame Protests will continue. People are going to die.'

Aer sat beside him. She sighed. 'Did he ever tell you that it was our fault? When the Iactura awakened, it drew out iron from beneath our feet. Fed on it. We killed industry that night. Arx won't survive this. How can it, when it's beating heart is pierced by that thing?'

'The Iactura isn't the blade in Arx's heart. It *is* the heart. And Callisteel is its will.' Caelan felt Reilo's lips curl into a snarl.

Aer looked out over the city. 'The Walkers are taking the foundries tonight. Forgemasters will submit and lose their eyes, or resist and die. If Dirk shows his face again, Lucianus will have his head. We learnt from your survival. He needs more than a mortal weapon. His axe is the last piece of Callisteel we will ever forge. After tonight, it will be nothing more than a memory.'

'You can't kill a memory.'

Aer laughed, long and loud. 'What exactly do you think it is we do?'

She lunged. A knife punctured Caelan's neck. A spear of ice sent blood into his throat.

He grunted. Blood ran down his chest. His senses began to fade. Cold. Then hot. Then numb. Light faded into the void.

He didn't die straight away. The cut was not clean. Instead, he lingered. Lingered until the edges of his vision began to fade into the dark sky. He held a hand in front of his eyes.

'Master,' he whispered. 'I'm ready.'

He drew the familiar needle-knife from his belt and pierced his fingertips. A tiny blue flame danced on his palm. And the sky broke open to a pair of violet eyes.

Caelan blinked again. The memory faded and he was standing in the endless mists of Memoria. A field of white-grey beneath his feet, shadows darting around the translucent curtain on the edges of his vision. Light dribbled between the smoke overhead.

He grabbed at his stomach, his throat, but Reilo's wounds were gone. He turned his head. His back was smooth. Unbroken. But he could still feel it. An echo. Even here, he could not escape the inevitable.

'*It finds us all. Eventually.*'

Caelan spun. A figure in the mist. Familiar. Sunken cheeks. A once-broken nose. Blue eyes over thin lips.

Reilo.

'You're dead.'

'*I was.*' His thoughts were vicious. '*You saw my memory, after all. You're welcome to it. To learn the price of failure.*'

'I don't want your past.'

'*You weren't complaining before. When I taught you how to fight. I spent my life in blade work so I could kill those blackcloaks. You were gifted that in an afternoon. And you have no qualms carrying my knife.*'

'That wasn't all you gave me.' Caelan clenched a fist. 'I survived this long without your anger.'

'*True. I could never separate experience from rage. Anger has such power. Just look what you accomplished.*'

'Then… it was you! By the scaffold. All that death.'

'*Those decisions were yours. I simply gave you the means. I know how empty you are. You'll use anything to fill that darkness. Even blood. I cannot take your body. Not whilst you still remember it is yours.*'

Reality pierced the mist. Agony. Caelan was dying. He could feel it.

Reilo's lips cracked in a terrible smile. '*Oblivion is freedom. Forget yourself.*'

A pool of darkness spread from Reilo's feet. Mist fell into the void. And Caelan's pain lessened.

'*Just let go.*'

It was tempting. So tempting. Mist wisped between Caelan's lips. He closed his eyes. Images flickered. Kuyt's face. Addie.

'*It'll only hurt whilst they remember you. That will fade. In time.*'

Caelan's eyes snapped open. 'I saw this. In the axe.' It came out sharp. 'I know what it is to forget people. I know what it is to forget *everyone*. I wouldn't wish that on anyone.' His voice rose. 'This is my life. Those two idiots… they are the only reason *I* don't forget who I am. I can't… I can't throw that away on someone like you.'

The light overhead broke through the mist. Shards pierced the shadow around Reilo. He shrank back.

'I don't remember who I was. But thanks to them, I know who I am now.' Caelan lifted his head.

Reilo flickered beneath the pouring light. His teeth set in a snarl. *'You are weaker than you know. We are all forgotten in the end.'* He held on for all of a heartbeat.

Then vanished.

Back on the table, Caelan opened his eyes.

Existence was fire. Breath crackled in his lungs. He tore his lips open to the taste of blood. It was like being trapped in a corpse. Everything was tinged in white and gold.

'Kuyt?' Speaking hurt, like gravel in his throat. Hopefully the old man was still around. Hopefully he hadn't given up.

'How are you still conscious kid?'

Thank fuck. 'You were right, Kuyt. The memory makes the man. But it's not just my memories that matter. Yours. Addie's. How you see me... it becomes a part of who I am. I can't just die and be forgotten. I need... people to remember me. I owe you that much.'

'Bollocks to that kid, this is hardly the time!'

'You're right. Go. Find a... Mindbreaker.'

Kuyt's eyes bored into Caelan. 'Why?'

'I need to survive. To make things right.'

'By forgetting what has happened here today?'

'I'll forget my death. But I won't forget the ones I killed. I won't forget those who died because of me. That's why I have to live through this. Who else would remember them?'

The old man looked down. Eternity passed under his consideration. He left without a word.

Caelan fought to stay alive. Blood pooled under his tongue. Sweat dripped into his eyes. Darkness crept into the edge of his vision and dread, real as gold, flickered through his veins.

His eyes rolled shut. Maybe it was already too late.

'Breathe. Don't forget to breathe. Come on, stay with us.' Kuyt's voice. 'You need to wake up!'

'Shh.' New voice. Female. Shattering steel. The fall of a chain-link waterfall. A hammer broken by the wind. The taste of smoke on his lips as a voice spoke inside his head.

'Reality burns. Inhale the memory.'

Caelan drew a deep breath. His mind opened. A bridge of blue fire spread out before him. He crossed over and the pain vanished.

The mists of Memoria returned to surround him but this time it was no longer featureless. It wisped and rose to form that single, unbroken pillar.

The Iactura. The spire glittered blue-silver.

'Caelan.' A figure materialised beside him. Ferra walked through the mist, queen in her domain.

'Kuyt found you,' Caelan projected. Talking was as simple as thinking the words and willing them out.

'I found him. A shame you left it so long. You already look like a corpse.'

'Help me to forget.' Caelan touched the Iactura. Manifest memories swarmed the sky. A handful more than before, but still so few. A familiar shadow darted between the silver orbs. Reilo vanished almost as fast as he appeared.

'You won't survive. We relive memories as they are forgotten. You'd be trapped inside it whilst I cut and with a mind like yours...' She trailed off.

Caelan forced himself to focus on the pain in his back. The weeping, jagged, ripping numbness that bit through his spine. The memory. As it danced through his mind, a silver orb slammed into the mist between them. Such was the strength of the memory it contained. The flying axe.

Caelan shuddered. How long would it take her to get a clean cut? No matter how skilled she was it would not be quick.

'There is no other choice. I don't want to die.'

'And how will you pay for it?'

'What do you want?'

'The name,' Ferra thought, *'of your shadow.'*

'That easy?' Caelan let go of a breath he forgot he was holding. *'It's Reilo. Why?'*

She paused. *'Dirk never speaks of our predecessors.'*

Dirk. The man who had taken his memories from him. The mist reacted to his name. White became black, fog boiled like water and silver memory orbs resolved as red. Hatred, thick as bile, drenched his mind.

Caelan took a deep breath. The white fog began to return. Slowly.

'*Keep breathing. I'll be back.*' Ferra's presence vanished.

Caelan let a little reality seep back in. Just voices.

'So you can save him?' The hope in Kuyt's voice hurt. 'Close the wound, repair the spine?'

'Repair? Not a chance. But he is insistent. And there is metal in blood.' Ferra said. 'Go get the doctor.'

Caelan watched the memory orb spin slowly in the mist. Fear bubbled in his chest. Not because of the pain. Not because he might die. Not even because he could lose his mind.

Back in his body, Caelan's fingers crept down his side. Into his pocket. Fished the bloodmetal into his fingers.

No, he was terrified of just how easy the decision was. To fall back into the mists that had already taken so much from him.

Ferra appeared beside him once more. She gripped her hammer in those massive hands and glanced at the manifest memory. '*Ready*?'

Was he?

AD INTERIM

ONE

KUYT

'Firewhisky, Paul.'

Kuyt slumped into the stool and leant his elbows on the bar. He was getting old.

It wasn't time's biggest surprise. He'd known it was coming. When the colour in his hair had gone. When the pain in his knees didn't. When it got more difficult to piss, and wasn't that just the cruellest one? As a young man, he could have out-widdled a prime stallion, but now a couple of drops were a moderate success. Still, despite all of that, in all of his sixty-odd years he'd never *felt* old. Until now.

Paul, Bill and Mari's boy with his Mama's green eyes and his Papa's height, slid the glass down the bar. Or tried to. It got caught in a divot about halfway down, wobbled and stopped.

'I'll get it.' Kuyt waved the lad away. The pub was as miserable as he felt. The seats were half-kindling at this point, and a cruel wind blew in from the shattered holes in the once-glass windows. It had not brought the warm feeling of nostalgia he'd hoped for. The place was empty, apart from Paul, the two lasses he poured beer for, and some bald bloke sat opposite who was... staring at him.

Kuyt squinted, just a little, eyes weren't as bright as they once had been. A handsome fellow, the shaved head suited him remarkably well and it was no question which of them wore their age better. Laughter lines traced the corners of his lips. He hadn't the energy for much more, but a fellow could look with no harm caused.

Eye contact, and the bloke stood up. Kuyt almost blushed, had it really been that long? Yes. Still, there was no time for it and he was shaking his head before the fellow even spoke.

'Elucid.'

Kuyt blinked. The ancient name picked at something buried deep in the back of his mind. 'Pardon me?'

'Elucid, in *Of Broken Measures*. I knew I recognised you!'

Kuyt found a smile peering beneath his moustache. 'Recognised? I wouldn't know myself from that long ago.'

The bloke grinned back and pulled out one of the stools. 'It's the way you sit. Pinch my arse, you made me laugh my bollocks off back then. I'm a eunuch now because of you. Spot you a drink?' He held up his hand to Paul before Kuyt could so much as nod.

'I haven't run those lines in decades...' He lifted his glass. '"To those we owe and those we pay."'

The bloke chuckled. He held his glass to the mote of sunlight breaking through the open window. 'Can't believe he's practically giving this stuff away. Liquor from the desert across the Saltiron Sea. What was that city called, Na... something?'

'Narisé.' Kuyt surprised even himself with that memory.

'That's the one! Fuck my ear, no one's mentioned Narisé since I was a teenager.'

'Well we haven't traded with them since the wall came up,' Kuyt said. 'Though I'd sacrifice the liquor for the food. I can't remember the last time I ate something that wasn't fish, beef or beans.' They hadn't traded with anyone since back then. At the apex of the Flame Protests. When all the iron was gone, and something far worse had taken its place. Build a wall. To keep their secrets. And their shame.

'Now that's not fair. I once ate a potato. Horrible thing.' A faraway smile toyed with his lips. He took a sip of his drink and sighed. 'Aged Narisian firewhisky. Honestly, kids these days don't know what they're missing.' He grimaced. 'I never wanted to become a "kids these days" kind of guy.'

'If they don't know how to drink, clearly we didn't teach them well.' Kuyt blinked past the sudden image of blue fire and a blood-soaked back. 'Not that they'd remember if we did.'

'Naïve bastards.' The bald fellow gripped his glass with white knuckles. 'First thing I learned is to keep my mouth shut. Not to stick my barely working feet right into the middle of things first chance I got! What, consequences don't exist anymore?'

'There are consequences. We burned their city down after all, didn't call it the Flame Protests for nothing. What else is there when you inherit ashes?'

'We?' The bald man's eyes gleamed.

'Our generation,' Kuyt corrected. 'I didn't kill anyone.' Easier to keep things straight if it wasn't a lie.

'I did,' the bloke almost whispered. 'My Pa always used to say, leave things better than you found them. Well I bollixed that up right good.'

'Me too,' Kuyt sighed. 'But maybe that's... okay.' He frowned into his glass. 'Maybe it's good we buggered it all up. So we can teach them not to be as colossal fuckups as we were.'

'You think it's that easy?'

'Not at all. But at my age, just getting to sleep at night is hard enough. A man needs something to believe, even if it is bollocks.'

The bloke raised his glass. 'To believing bollocks. And not following the wrong man.'

Kuyt mirrored the gesture. 'To knowing who you are. And who you fight for.'

Their glasses clicked together.

MIRA

Mira didn't sneak well. Ordinarily, she would cite that as a distinct positive. No one could sneak well unless they were practised, so her inability must stem from the upright honesty with which she lived each day. The problem was, now she was really quite desperate to sneak and finding it obnoxiously difficult.

Not that she didn't enjoy breaking the law! Quite the opposite, the adrenaline was most welcome. And really, everyone should break a law at least once in their lives. No, the problem was that the warren of tunnels beneath the Citadel that made up the Arxian Archives were a sprawling mess of caved-in passages and water-damaged staircases.

And it didn't help that they were crawling with Walkers.

A torch bobbed into view and Mira pressed herself against a crack in the stone wall. Not that she got very far, a few toes and maybe an eighth of her knee disappeared into the shadow. If the Walkers turned they'd see a very frightened, very pale woman attempting to fornicate with a block of dank stone.

The Walkers hove into view and suddenly it wasn't nearly so funny. Mira's tongue stuck to the roof of her mouth, the only thing that kept her from vomiting out her racing heart into a crack in the wall that was far too small for her. She crept backwards, praying that the darkness hid her shadow. The way back sprawled out behind her, but off to the side was another passage with a familiar crest carved into the stone. Election records. She just had to hope that it was not the Walkers' destination as well. Trespassing down here was good for a decade or two in chains. Maybe even the scaffold if DeSüle got involved.

Still, she'd come this far.

Mira took the passage, stepped on the hem of her skirt and almost went cartwheeling down a staircase hidden in the gloom. Walls tight to her elbows and no handrail. It would be a miracle if she avoided breaking her neck. Not to mention the spiderwebs festooning every crevice in the ceiling. Arxian flatfoot spiders weren't poisonous, but they grew to about the size of a woman's hand and if one fell on her shoulder then there was a good chance her spirit would simply exit her body and leave her bones for... well, for the spiders.

Something creaked behind her and Mira held her breath. Voices, somewhere close. Down the stairs or past the Walkers?

She took the stairs two at a time. She owed it to Sy. She'd found his name on the board of executions. His words echoed incessantly in the back of her mind. *Nothing's changed.*

The shadow floor beyond the staircase reached out for her ankles and she stumbled down the final step. The underground hall was almost as dark as the midnight sky she'd left outside. A few candles, drowning in their own wax, gave her just enough light to see by.

Dust danced through the gloom, speckled on her glasses. Beautiful stuff, dust. A marker for the passage of time. You could look at a person and depending on their diet, their ancestors, their occupation and a whole host of other factors, you'd never be able to guess how old they were. But a layer of dust was like a signature. Proof positive of undisturbed age.

The Library of Records was enormous. Dug into the stone beneath the Hall of Laws, it was a repository for the city's history. Documents festooned the shelves, parchment, vellum. It smelled like an old book, of storage herbs and camphor.

'Oh now that is something,' she breathed. On the wall over the entrance, a document was framed and hung against the stone. She recognised it like a favourite child.

The Ashen Accords. The *original* Ashen Accords. The armistice agreement signed to end the Flame Protests. The single most important document in Arxian history. It was this that split the city into constituencies, this that gave each citizen a vote.

And that was the problem.

At the back of the room, she found what she was looking for. Mira ran her finger across the bottom shelf.

Countless wooden lockboxes dotted across the walls. Stacked and ordered, each one a square in the dust. Even on her tip-toes, she couldn't get close to the top shelf. Forty years of voting records. For a moment, she just stood there and looked at it.

The shelves were labelled, names carved into the wood, so it didn't take long for her fingers to find it. Last week's election, Meadowside Boulevard. The thick lock rattled as she brought the box down to the floor.

Mira might not sneak well, but she was an exceptional lockpick. Another positive of her character, really. Honest people had nothing to hide, so her ability to remove the shadow that a lock provided was clear certainty that she was an upright member of society. Dad had taught her when she was little.

The picks flickered in her hands. The lock was weighty, but simple. She swapped out her pick for a rake and twisted the tension wrench.

The click was so loud she was certain they must have heard it upstairs. She caught her breath and counted to ten. Were those footsteps getting closer?

She had to hurry.

Mira lifted the lid. A tidy stack of ballots nestled inside. With trembling fingers, she drew them out. The official count was listed on the top. Fifty-six for DeMori. Eighteen for Francesca. One spoiled ballot.

She flicked through the papers, sorted them into piles. It didn't take long to come across Sy's ballot. The blood oozed out of the square, covered the LL in Quill. Someone had scrawled a thick S over the top. Spoiled.

But the rest were just fine.

Mira sat back, wiped her hand down the back of her neck. Surprised to find it was so sweaty. She let a smile flicker across her lips. What had she been so worried about? Even if they'd counted Sy's vote, Quill was so far behind it wouldn't have made any difference.

Relief thundered like a waterfall through her. Mira stuffed the ballots back into their box and pushed it back on to the shelf.

A flutter of paper fell from beneath where the ballot box had been left.

She pulled it to her nose.

Wealthy district. Keep the houses north of the riverbank, six-tenths of the walkways south of the park. Can afford three, possibly four, ex-Nest. They keep breeding, re-draw for next cycle. (N.B – after winter, see how many the cold kills off.)

What? Mira peered closer. Beneath the scratchy writing… was that a map? A sketch, but it looked off. It wasn't a square, or even segmented into any measurements she could see. A hastily drawn blotting of a few houses, curled like a half-shed snake. She could just about recognise it. The Lupanar. Her house. What was this?

Meadowside Boulevard – Registered Voting District (Reballoting)

Mira scanned the drawing. This wasn't right. The districts were supposed to be drawn out in full, each slice of Arx equidistant and measured from all the others. This was some cruel mockery.

Mira slumped to her backside. She'd come down that day looking for an easy answer. A miscount, or faked ballots or even just some good old-fashioned incompetence. But this was so much more. Arx had been carved into tiny fiefdoms. Votes meant nothing when they could just re-draw the election map and put your X wherever it wouldn't be heard.

Was this really what she had spent her life defending?

Anger, like a storm breaking through a river dam, surged in her veins. She launched to her feet and hurled the ballot box with everything she had. It clattered into the stone wall with an almighty *smash*.

'Someone down here?'

Oh tits. Mira shoved the document down her shirt and glanced back towards the staircase.

A pair of Walkers stumbled down, torches picking her out like a child caught with sticky hands in someone's orchard.

'Ma'am? Who the fuck are you?'

Good lord they were bigger this close. Mira stumbled back towards the ballot boxes. 'I'm a historian. A scholar. I'm here to study…'

'Why the fuck is this one open?' The other Walker held her discarded ballot box with pinched fingers.

'Now, there is a very good reason for that.' Mira bumped into the wall.

'Which is?'

'I'll tell you.' She grit her teeth, hands sweeping across lids from years and years of show-elections. Dust mounded against her palm. 'As soon as I think of it…'

'This isn't funny.' The nearby Walker, black-haired and hook-nosed, reached out and grabbed her arm.

'Get off me!' Mira flung a hand at his face, the dust from a thousand forgotten elections leaping from her fingers and grinding right into his eyes.

'Ahh!' The Walker dropped her arm and pawed at his face.

Bless the beautiful dust! Mira sprinted up towards the stairs. She couldn't let herself get captured. Not now.

There was so much more she had to do.

ADDIE

Addie sat on the stone floor and sharpened her hatchets. She'd been at it all morning and her arse was numb. A puddle of dirty water soaked into her thighs like she'd pissed herself, except without the warmth. The whetstone dripped into the bucket between her knees.

She scraped her hatchet across the coarse side of the stone. Had to get the right rhythm. Smooth, like oil on leather. *Whisk-whisk-whisk,* one hundred stokes. Time each breath, that was the trick. *Whisk-whisk-whisk.*

Besides, there was bugger all else to do. Kuyt had ordered her to keep a low profile, ever since the Sightless. It was cute that the old bastard thought he could order her to do anything, but good advice was good advice. Not that he kept his mopey arse around to see to it.

Whisk-whisk-Krr. Addie growled as the grind sliced her ears. Just bollocks, she'd be feeling that down the sharp edge of her tailbone all day. She washed the whetstone in the bucket, jammed it between her knees again.

The door opened. Sod's bloody law, she was never going to get to the end of this. The smell of unwashed flesh and peppery blood filled the corridor.

'So how is the little twat?' she asked.

'You could always go in and see for yourself.'

It was not the voice she'd expected. Female, blunt. Addie flicked her eyes up.

Ferra twisted her head and slung that fuckoff hammer over her shoulders. A coal smouldered in the golden cage beneath her chin.

Addie yawned to her feet like she'd been about to get up anyway. Bit back on the wince as a blister burst on her burned ankle. 'Didn't know you were back. Isn't your mindfuckery over with? Concerns of the flesh are best left to that arsehole doctor.'

'But concerns of metal are mine.' The iron-chains in her hair chimed when she shook her head.

Addie tried to loosen her sudden deathgrip on the hilt of her hatchet, but somehow, she just managed to squeeze the fucking thing tighter. 'If you've done anything you shouldn't have...'

'I did exactly what he asked of me. Perhaps Ignis could have worked with the cauterisation, but we all work to our strengths.' Ferra shrugged her hammer off her shoulders and it clashed against the floor. 'But the man who is just about breathing back there is not the Caelan you knew, not anymore. A hairsbreadth of difference, but every memory sacrificed changes us. The Walkers know this well. I am told that they all forget their first kill as part of their training.'

Addie forced a grin. 'Her name was Zee. My first patrol near Sullenwards and she tried to disembowel me with a combat knife.' She slapped her stomach. 'Didn't even get close.'

'I am well aware that yours was different. You never finished training, after all.' The coal around Ferra's throat sparked blue. 'Shall I remind you what was taken when we two walked the mists of Memoria together?'

Addie ripped her thumb away from her cheek. Keep it up and she'd rub the skin right off.

'Knowledge and memory are two very different things. You can't trust anyone who doesn't know their own mind.'

'Don't start.' Addie narrowed her eyes. 'You were a last resort. Kuyt might not agree, but I do; he's better alive than dead, even if he pays for it.'

'Memory is connection. No one recalls with objectivity. We make mistakes and accept the lies we tell one another until they become a part of us. When memory is lost, it's those connections that fade.'

'I know what a Fog-Eye is.'

'I'm not talking extremes. Why do you think Aer puts all the Walkers through it? Even one connection severed makes it harder to connect, to re-join the rest of us. It's what makes them such effective killers.'

'What are you, a recruiter? I did my stint in black, didn't find it to my liking.'

'I don't work with the Walkers. They'd kill me just as fast as you.'

'And don't you sound pleased by that. Is it lonely to be the only one so hated?'

Ferra's laugh was brittle. 'Of course I'm lonely. Who else do I talk to? There are four Mindbreakers left.' She glanced over her shoulder, towards the door. 'And one of them is trying so very desperately to have me killed. I too cut my connections. Sacrificed them for blue fire, if not blue eyes.'

'Caelan isn't like you.'

'Not yet. But you haven't heard the voice inside his head. Reilo Sandrasova, now that's a man who should have stayed dead. One day, Caelan is going to reach for that maniac instead of reaching for you and you'll realise the kind of man you have bound yourself to. And you will come to me and beg for my help to put him down.'

'Then why the fuck did you do that to him? Why save him at all?'

Ferra snorted. 'He fought the Sightless once. I figured I'd try to even out the playing field.' She buggered off up the stairs and vanished.

Addie growled like a wounded fucking animal. Fuck Caelan. Fuck Kuyt. And fuck the Mindbreakers, the lot of them could take turns shoving that hammer up their arse and swivelling. She hadn't set herself on fire just so that blue-eyed prick could piss it all away. No fucking chance.

Addie darted upstairs, threw open the doors to the warehouse and stalked out on to Ferriway. As usual, the smell was like having two tiny shits nestled in each nostril. She snorted a cloud of breath, eased her shoulders. Needed to go and hit someone, but Kuyt was old and Caelan was basically dead, so she'd settle for straw.

She raced down the bottom of Ferriway, until the sludge beneath her boots shifted into packed clay. Way back when, according to Kuyt's cobwebby memories, they used to host fistfights there. But no one had used it in decades, so she'd commandeered it and set up a handful of training dummies. At least they didn't blubber when she kicked them in the face.

She shrugged out her shoulders, stretched the muscles down her back. Took a deep breath.

Attacked.

She whirled between the dummies, axes slashing, biting, ripping through with a satisfying *thunk*.

Faster.

She threw herself between the mannequins. Her blades flashed, flickered, a whirlpool of deadly metal. Muscles cracked, clouds of breath panting from the animal of her body. This was what Kuyt never understood. Fighting wasn't about killing. It was about existence, life as something physical. Something those blue-fire addled Walkers could never understand.

A shadow darted from a nearby alleyway. Hooded beneath a grey dustcloak. Watching her.

Nice fucking try. Addie ducked her shoulder, swept beneath the stick-arm of the nearest dummy, beheaded it for good measure, and spun towards the figure on the edge of the dirt. Her hatchet quivered inches from the hooded face.

'Adira Signasti?' the figure asked.

She didn't answer. Just peeled the hood down with the blade of her hatchet. A woman peered out, blinked mismatched eyes. One green and one red.

Beneath the dustcloak, she wore a familiar set of leather armour. Black cloak tucked tight to her back.

'This was not your smartest idea.' Addie set the blade of her hatchet against the woman's collarbone.

'We're not here to fight.'

We? Addie glanced over her shoulder. Shite. Down the Ferriway, a pack of shadows moved towards her. She leapt aside, back pressed to the wall, hatchets ready. This was probably why Kuyt had told her to keep her head down. Oh fuck it, if she died *and* he was right, that really would be a shitting awful day.

The woman stepped closer, carefully out of range. 'You used to be a Walker.'

'I was a trainee.'

'You killed your Captain.'

'He tried to kill me first.' The scars webbing Addie's face felt like they were burning.

'And now you've attacked the Sightless.'

'I've attacked a lot of people.'

The woman had a crooked smile. 'It is you.'

One by one the others closed towards her, hooded faces and the glitter of concealed weapons.

Addie bit down on a breath, heart bouncing across her ribcage. 'If you say so. Does it matter? The names of the dead are soon forgot.'

'That is why we are here.' The woman held out a palm, scored with calluses. 'The Walkers have forgotten too much, but I choose to remember who I am. We're here to fight with you.'

PART 2

DEFICERE

CHAPTER 15

'Get up.'

Caelan opened his eyes. Didn't sleep much anymore. Just skirted unconsciousness until Reilo decided to skewer his mind and drag him back. The bastard was louder in the dark.

'Get up.'

Two weeks since Ferra, but the shadow that shared his skull still wouldn't shut up. It felt like a thought. It felt like *his* thoughts. Caelan dug into the soft part of his ear, found a hair.

'One time, I'm going to catch your foot,' Caelan pinched the hair and pulled, felt the whole of his ear go with it, grunted, 'and I'm going to drag you out of my head. Then I'll piss in your mouth.' He yanked it out. Tried to chuck it on the floor, but it wafted down like a feather in a light breeze. Didn't help. And now his ear hurt.

'Get up.'

'Fuck off, I was up anyway.' Caelan eased himself to the edge of the slab. Stood up. It was that easy.

A single candle flickered in the corner of the room, spilled off-yellow light over the basement floor. Lit up the mirror.

His spine was exposed. From the base of his neck, all the way to his tailbone. A new spine, made from bloodmetal. It fused to his flesh, pulled the edges of the skin tight. Metallic vertebrae clicked when he rolled his shoulders.

Ferra had kept him alive. But it had not come without a price.

'Listen.'

The door creaked open. Just enough for an old actor with privacy issues to peer in. Caelan made sure to stare right about where he figured Kuyt's eyes were. Gave a little wave.

'You're up.' Kuyt shuffled in.

'I missed you too.'

'I've been busy.' He scratched his stubble. 'How do you feel?'

Caelan snorted. 'How do you think I feel?'

'Angry. Miserable. Depressed.'

'Is that why you've been avoiding me?'

'I told you, I've...'

'Been so busy that you can hand-deliver meals but can't say hello, yes I heard. I'm not miserable. Not angry or depressed either. I'm ambivalent. Fuck it. I might go as far as cheery. Kuyt, I survived. I was dying. Dead, even. But I don't remember why and because of that I'm still breathing.'

Something changed in Kuyt's eyes. 'That Sightless cut your spine like puppet strings. Doesn't that bother you?'

'I'm not going to pretend to give a shit about something just so you feel better. I don't remember. So it didn't happen.' He bent to touch his toes, felt his new spine ripple. 'Far more interested in the metal she welded into me. Never seen them do something like this. Leave a scar sure, but... how'd she manage this?'

'She whispered in your ear. Candles burned blue and lines of your blood lashed between the edges of the cut, like lacing a boot. The flesh sort of... quivered, like it wanted to pull together but couldn't. Blood became solid, became metal and Sarrk vomited.'

'I hope he turned his head. Rather that wasn't melted into my back as well.' Caelan crawled his fingers up his back. 'A bloodmetal connection from the base of my skull down my spine... I know who I'd blame.' He went fishing for another ear-hair but couldn't find any.

'We are all forgotten in the end.' Reilo's voice scraped a needle down his spine.

'A metal backbone is something memorable.' Caelan didn't know which of them he was speaking to.

'Letting the Sightless hack at you isn't the most forgettable thing either.'

Caelan snorted. 'Speak for yourself.' An odd sensation, that lurch in his chest at the lost memory. Like running a tongue over the gap where a tooth should be.

Kuyt threw a shirt at him. 'The day I start speaking for you is the day I rip off my own lips. Now get dressed.'

'I wondered why you decided to grace me with your presence. I'm assuming my recuperation is over?' The feeling of cloth on his spine made him shiver.

'The Walkers are looking for you. Sarrk vanished yesterday. He'll point the way as soon as they ask, even as he pisses himself.'

'I'd have cut out his tongue, but I was a little preoccupied fucking shadows. Where have you and Addie found to hide?'

'It's not just us.' Kuyt flickered a faint smile. 'I'll show you.'

Rustscrape was a graveyard, the rotting soul of industry. Stank like it too. Smoke, lead and corpses. All of which Caelan could have just about dealt with. But Kuyt's reverence might be what pushed him over the edge.

The old actor ran his hand across a metal housing beam like he was caressing some lover's cheek. Orange flecks flaked off around his fingers. 'Forty years ago, this was the heart of Arx. Beating with fire and iron. Forges burned through the night and our metalwork was legendary. Traders from across the continent came to us for our steel.'

'I can... imagine.' A flash of cognition. Reilo allowed him to feel the edges of a memory. Rustscrape, glowing with life. The shock of metal quenched in unexpected laughter. He blinked and the soot-soaked spectres vanished.

'But nothing lasts forever. Not least of all iron. We were overflowing with the stuff, up until the day we weren't,' Kuyt said.

'The Iactura.'

'Mm. It rose one night in a burst of cobalt flame. A silver fang that pierced our city. The next morning the mines were drained. Like the hand of some vengeful god had scooped the stuff out. Without iron, industry died. We suffocated in the smog of our empty forges. Until the Ant took charge.'

'Kuyt, look around you. He's been Viceroy ever since and Rustscrape is a wasteland.'

'I know.' Kuyt sighed. 'It's a cruel game we old men play. What if the Ant never accepted peace on their terms? What if the fires of protest never went out? But nothing changes. With the scaffold under repairs the executions are on pause. And yet I've seen more corpses in the last two weeks than even at the bloodiest edge of our failed rebellion.'

'The Walkers?' Caelan scraped his fingernail down the edge of his knife.

'No. The Walkers are an enemy you can fight. You can't fight starvation. Rations have been hoarded across the river. For safekeeping, so they say. Because of what happened with the Sightless. All those dead.'

'*This is your fault.*' Reilo's voice ripped like claws behind Caelan's eyes.

Caelan spat, forced a grin that he hoped Reilo could feel. 'This isn't our fault, Kuyt. They were just looking for an excuse.'

'I know. It's always been this way. We never broke our chains. We just hid them long enough that we forgot they were there.'

'Then what are we left with?'

'This.' Kuyt mimed pulling back a curtain.

They turned a corner and a trench swallowed the ground. The cobbles surrounding the lip were melted like wax. Caelan could barely see the other side. Smog rose from the darkness, thick and heavy, wreathing the broken stone staircase cut spiral into the rocks.

Kuyt grinned like a child. 'There used to be a warehouse over the top, the stairs led down to the forge. Careful, it can get a little slippery.'

The old man started down like it was nothing. Caelan felt a bead of sweat slalom down the back of his neck. Not even a Mindbreaker could save him from *that* fall.

He placed a foot and immediately skidded. Fuck it. He'd have legged it in an instant if Kuyt wasn't beating him down. Rather swim arse-naked through the Mucro than let that decrepit old man put him to shame.

Caelan gripped his heart between his teeth and forced himself to match the old man step for step. Step for fucking step, desperately trying to ignore the swooping pain somewhere south of his stomach. Come on you old bastard, how long could one bloody staircase be? Each step was accompanied with the soft metallic click of his shiny new spine.

When he finally reached the bottom, Caelan slid to his knees. 'That was not fun.'

'You get used to it.' Kuyt drew a skin out of his coat. The old man was barely sweating. 'Drink? You're looking a little… moist.'

The water was gritty and warm. Caelan tossed the last mouthful over his head and let it run down his back.

'Better?'

'No.'

'Welcome to the Rustscrape Foundry. Or what's left of it.'

The cavern, dug deep into the rock, was speckled with mineral deposits. Slick, stone walls, with broken metal scattered over tables, old anvils, kilns, forges. Rust was ruler of it all.

A gout of orange steam burst from a hole in the middle of the floor. The source of the light, the heat. Caelan crept closer. Sweat swam in twin channels down the sides of metal in his back. He peered over the edge.

Liquid fire boiled black and orange. A bubble spat, flecks licked hungrily against the rock. The wave of heat dried Caelan's mouth and scorched his face.

'*Heartfire. Arx' molten blood. The drills spilled it when the Flame Protests began.*'

'Why?' Caelan managed through desiccated lips.

'*Fire is enough for iron. But Callisteel demands something stronger.*' The hunger in Reilo's voice crashed with the waves below.

'Kid, you alright? Wouldn't recommend a swim in that stuff.'

'Yeah. Yeah, I'm…' Caelan ran his hands through his hair. An ache in his chest. He tried to push it back, but that emptiness remained.

He stepped away from the heartfire. Laughter echoed in his head. He followed Kuyt.

'This is what we're left with.' Kuyt led Caelan over to a balcony overlooking a cavern below.

Wooden weapons clattered together in soot-coated hands. Thirty, forty were fighting. Addie held court in the middle, correcting stances and bollocking in equal measure.

'Who are these people?'

Kuyt scratched the back of his neck. 'The Austelli.'

'Again?'

'Memories can be powerful things.' The reprimands were getting even less subtle. 'Before they got the maps out and carved us into Rotheart and Southbrace and whatever else, there were just two. Malafide, across the river, and Austellus. Us lot. Easy to unify when you share a name. Harder, when invisible lines on a map say you don't. And there is power in reclaiming who you are.'

'I wouldn't know.' Caelan leant on the balcony. A sea of eyes turned to him, glittering in the light of the molten fires. 'They're looking at me. You told them I'd be here.'

Kuyt at least had the grace to look guilty. 'You're a symbol. The man who fought the Sightless and survived. I'm convinced half of them only showed up because they wanted to gawk at you.'

'Last time I tried to fight, I didn't do so well.' Caelan shifted, felt his new spine click.

'You survived.'

'But they won't. You keep telling me things have gotten worse since I attacked the Sightless. And I was just one angry idiot. How do you think they'll react when you lot show up, organised and demanding?'

'All change starts with one angry idiot.'

Caelan rubbed his eyes. 'You know what I kept thinking about, those two weeks sitting in the dark? That dead child, when I killed my first Walker. I keep picturing its face, those little eyelashes, the sound it made when it coughed its last. But even when I killed the Walker... *I wasn't angry.*'

'*But I was.*'

'I attacked the Sightless that day because I couldn't understand why I didn't care more that I'd killed someone. I'd ripped out a part of my soul but it didn't change anything. So I figured, kill the symbol of all those unnecessary deaths and I might feel better. About myself. The man I'm turning into. But I don't. So much of me is so... far away. I can't be the rebel you want, Kuyt. Even I wouldn't fight alongside me.'

'*If you won't fight, then loosen your grip on this miserable shared life and I will!*' Reilo's anger pounded through Caelan's skull like a searing migraine. He pressed a thumb into his eye to relieve the pressure and let the madman rage.

'I don't want you to fight. I want you to take your shirt off and turn around so that lot down there remember what they're up against,' Kuyt said.

Caelan picked splinters from the balcony. Below, Addie kicked someone's feet into position, then smacked the back of his head. Good to see she hadn't learned patience over the last few weeks.

'There's your rebel,' Caelan said. He sighed. 'I owe you. So I'll spar with them. That's it. And I'll take my shirt off. You old pervert. Easier ways to get me to undress without starting a rebellion.'

Kuyt barked a laugh. He gripped Caelan's wrist and looked him in the eye. 'Thank you.'

Caelan shook him off. 'Piss off. Save the sentiment for when one of us is dying.'

'You didn't want it then either!'

Off to the side of the balcony, a freight elevator swung from old chains. Kuyt yanked at one and flakes of rust showered them like dried blood. A screech of grating metal filled the cavern and the platform descended to the lower level.

Addie met them at the bottom. 'Caelan. Kuyt said you survived.'

'Addie. Missed me?'

'Like I'd miss rotting vulva.'

'Caelan's come to join you,' Kuyt cut them off. Over his shoulder, any pretence at sparring had been abandoned. They just stared at Caelan. At his eyes.

Addie cocked her head. 'Broke your nose last time. I can't wait to see what you do with a weapon.' She threw a wooden practice sword at him. 'Danni, stop walloping Mitch and get over here. You're sparring with Caelan. The rest of you, I didn't call a break so get back to it.'

The woman with the spear sauntered over, her weapon resting over her shoulders. Mismatched eyes, one red, one green. 'I didn't know your name before. Caelan?'

'Mm.' Caelan hefted his wooden blade. 'What do you say, first to three touches?'

'If you like.' She yawned. Then snapped into motion, launched herself back and flung her spear.

The cloth-muted spearhead slammed into his chest and sent Caelan frothing to his knees. Breath burst from his lips and he groaned.

'Pathetic.'

'One-nothing.' She flashed her teeth, scooped up her weapon.

Caelan laughed. Then coughed, surprised he wasn't spitting up blood. 'Danni, right?'

'Good memory.'

'Not what I'm usually known for. Why're you here?'

'You that desperate to catch your breath?'

Caelan charged. Reilo's training, years of combat, flowed into him. Danni jabbed with her spear, but he slammed her attack aside, forced his wooden blade up the spear-haft and jabbed her under the jaw.

'One-one.' He danced back, dodged her petulant stab at his retreating leg.

'I'm here because you are.'

'Bullshit, I didn't even know I'd be here until today.'

'I knew you'd come.' She was more cautious this time. Circled slowly, swept her spear at his ankles. Caelan leapt over, kicked the head away. She reversed her grip, brought the haft slamming at his shoulder. He caught her attack on his sword with a dull *clack*.

Danni grunted, tried to force her weapon down, but Caelan stepped back and brought his sword around with a flourish. Spearhead, shaft, wrist. Her spear fell from nerveless fingers.

'Two-one.' He gulped in air. All that recovery had stolen his stamina. 'How'd you know I'd be here? Aside from Kuyt telling you.'

'Kuyt told us.' That smile really was insufferable. 'Why'd you attack that Sightless?'

'I was bored and figured it was selfish to keep all my blood inside me.'

'Come on.'

Caelan braced his knees and held his sword in both hands. He raised an eyebrow.

Danni rushed him. Her spear flickered, so *fast*, he could barely knock it away. Every time he parried, she swept right back. He crunched into the wall.

She slammed her spear down, set her hands on the floor and lashed a kick at his face.

Caelan cowered back, held his sword to protect his nose. Weight slammed on top of his sword and a sharp scratch spread across his stomach.

'Two-two.'

Caelan blinked. Danni had one hand on the floor, both feet hooked over his weapon and a knife, real metal, in her other hand. The point of which had cut open his shirt and left a red line in his skin.

'Addie taught you that,' he said. 'This is why memories are worth ripping out. I wouldn't have winced. Besides, if this was a real sword then your tendons are sliced open.' He nodded at her feet before he pulled his weapon away.

She didn't fall over as he'd hoped, just sprang back and drew her spear up. 'My tendons? Feel fine to me.'

Caelan fingered the hole in his shirt. 'I don't have a spare one of these.' Still, it was a good excuse. He pulled his shirt over his head and tossed it aside. Pretended he didn't see the eager flicker of her eyes towards his spine. 'I attacked the Sightless because I thought it would make me feel better.'

'Did it?'

'No.'

'No one has attacked the Sightless in thirty years.'

'Twenty-six actually. It told me. Why do you want to play at rebellion, Danni?'

'I could ask you the same thing.' Danni's eyes narrowed, her hands tight around the spear.

They met in a thump of wood. Caelan swept his blade into her spear, she spun and came again. Swatted his blade aside, forced her spear at his chest.

Caelan turned his back. Caught her attack on his metal spine and sent it clashing away. Barely felt it. Smashed his sword at her. It bounced off her shoulder.

'Your spine was severed,' Danni said.

'My spine? Feels fine to me.' Caelan grinned. 'Three-two.'

'That's bollocks.' She folded her arms. 'Anyone else and their legs wouldn't work.'

'I'm not anyone else.'

'No, you're a cheater with a silver spine.'

'Silverspine? That's a name, Kuyt'd love that.' Caelan rubbed his chin.

She snapped her spear up to rest across her shoulders. 'The Flame Protests killed both my grandparents, but not before they infected my parents. Twenty years later, when I was a teenager, they came back to Arx and got themselves killed trying to set fire to a grain stockpile. I hated them for it. Orphaned by idiocy, I wanted to be a Walker. Figured if they put their foot down hard, there'd be a damn sight fewer pointless deaths. Did the training, even had a sponsor to get me across the river. They invited me to the execution. I was there. Same as you.'

'What changed your mind?'

'The Sightless. Even as chaos boiled around it, it just kept going. That axe, up and down like hewing wood. We aren't people to that thing, but the Sightless doesn't act alone. It's an enforcer for all those Viceroys so they can keep their hands clean. I hated it in that moment. Then you attacked the thing and all I wanted was to see it fall. When you fucked up, I killed my sponsor and went looking for you.'

'Why? Any Walker would have wanted me dead.'

'Because I was... sad.' She looked surprised to have said it, a soft crease between her eyebrows. 'These were my people. And they were dying.'

'Your people. Austelli then. Is it really that simple? United through knowledge of what side of the river you were born.'

Danni hawked and spat. 'Being Austelli has nothing to do with geography. I wasn't even born in Arx, Mama pushed me out in some hamlet down the coast long after 'Austellus' was redistricted. The name isn't important. It just means... we've figured out who *our* people are. The ones we'd fight for. The one's we'd come back for. You get it.'

'I do?'

'Knew it the moment I saw you suicide on the burning scaffold. Addie might be training us, but the cause is yours. It's not enough to just set some fires and kill some of my old colleagues. If things are going to change, it's going to take something big. And there's no bigger symbol of those bastards lording over us than the Sightless. We're here because of you.'

There was something honest in those mis-matched eyes. Sweat rolled down her freckled cheeks.

'My Austelli. Death itself could not keep me from you.'

A tiny ember sparked in Caelan's chest. It wasn't him. This rebellion, it wasn't his reality. It was Reilo and Addie and Kuyt and Danni, but… the ember held. Purpose. It had been a long time since he felt that warmth.

A wordless scream snapped like a whip from the platform above. Kuyt.

'Addie, who's with him?' Caelan ran over, throttling his practice sword.

'No one.' She jerked her head. 'Took the fucking platform up alone. Arnie get that thing down here!'

'No time.' Caelan gripped his fake-sword between his teeth and leapt up to the chains. Grunting, sweating, he dragged himself up. Felt like his arms were pulling from his chest, but he didn't stop.

He flung himself over the balcony. Someone had Kuyt by the throat. Big bastard, half a day of beard on his chin and a wicked knife inches from the old man's chest.

'Get away from him!' Caelan managed to shout, breath pounding.

The man spun, gripped Kuyt around the throat and held him like a shield. His dagger settled beside the old man's neck.

Tears dribbled down the attacker's cheeks. 'I knew you'd be here, I recognise those eyes. This is all your fault.' Spit flecked from his lips.

'Kuyt hasn't hurt anyone. Let him go. Before I hurt you.' Caelan gripped his sword until his hand cramped.

'I'm sorry, Caelan,' Kuyt's voice was soft.

The dagger jabbed into Kuyt's neck. Drew a bright, bloody bead. 'My daughter died because of you.'

'If she was a Walker, then…' Caelan began.

'She was on that scaffold! The Sightless executed her. She was in a bar fight. But because of people like *you*, they can't show leniency. Because of people like *you*, she had to die!'

Something pulsed in Caelan's head. Reilo. For the first time, their voices were united.

'I'm… sorry. But only that I wasn't quick enough to save her. She was dead the moment they took her.' Caelan walked towards the man, hand outstretched, sword behind him. 'What's your name?'

'Gaz.'

'Gaz. They don't need a reason to kill us. They've been doing it for forty years. It won't stop. Not unless we stop them.'

He was close enough to count Gaz's missing teeth. To see his blood-shot eyes. Caelan eased his hand under the blade of his knife, curled his knuckles loose around the cutting edge at Kuyt's throat.

Behind him, a rusty screech announced Addie's arrival. He waved his other hand at her. Stand down.

Gaz sniffled. 'You don't know… how it feels.'

'I had a daughter. She died in the Flame Protests. Just a child. They set her on fire.' Tears welled and Caelan's heart thumped his throat. 'Lara. Eyes so wide they could swallow the world.'

He caught himself too late. Reilo's memory cracked like an egg on concrete. A curl of sickness spat acid into his throat.

'That's impossible. You're not old enough.' Gaz's eyes were flint. 'You're lying. You killed my daughter and now you lie to me!'

He ripped the knife across and Caelan screamed. It sliced through the meat of his palm, the muscles of his fingers. Split skin and spat blood down his arm.

Half-mindless with pain, Caelan ducked his shoulder and barged Kuyt from Gaz's grip. He spun and slammed his practice sword into Gaz's stomach.

Gaz double over, scrabbled backwards until his heel caught the edge of the heartfire pit and he slipped. Slid down the edges, screamed as fingernails bent on slick stone. 'Help me!'

Caelan bared his teeth and reached down to Gaz with his bloody hand.

The bloke grabbed his fingers and Caelan screeched. Foaming crimson poured from the cut in his hand. The meat in his fingers tore.

And the ember in his chest ignited in flame.

'I'm slipping.'

Caelan flexed his hand. Felt his tendons snap. Black spots punched his eyes. Blood bubbled down his fingers. 'You threatened one of mine.'

Gaz fell from his grip and into the heartfire below.

Caelan threw his head aside, closed his eyes. But he still heard the screaming. Still smelled the cooked meat. A thin line of vomit dribbled from the side of his mouth.

'Caelan,' Kuyt breathed from behind him. 'You tried to save him. That's all you can do.'

'I...' Caelan blinked. 'He threatened you.'

Kuyt raised an eyebrow. 'He did, but what's that got to do with anything?'

Behind him, Addie's face was carefully neutral. Her eyes were heavy. She knew.

'I want to fight, Kuyt.' Caelan stared at his hand. The gushing blood that stained the old starburst scars on his fingertips. 'All I have left is this body. I'm going to use it to jam the gears that run this city until the whole operation shatters around me.'

'Why?'

'To keep you alive. Addie too. And all those idiots down there that thought following in the footsteps of a maniac like me was a good idea. My people.' He met Kuyt's painfully grateful eyes.

'Let's get someone to take a look at this hand first. You might not be *able* to fight anymore...'

'I'll sort it.'

'It'll take more than bandages.'

He touched his spine with a bloody hand. 'I know.'

Desire washed over him. He'd find Ferra. Lie before her and let her wipe the dirty corners of his mind clean. The shadow of a knife through his hand. And something else. Fear, maybe. She could cleanse him of that. He knew where to find her.

One final taste. That was all.

CHAPTER 16

Sam drew her cloak around her shoulders. Weak sunlight brightened the street and shutters banged against lead-lined windows. The signposts shuddered as the borough shivered.

'I still can't believe I have to waste the day with you.' Vicky, in a rare shift in demeanour, had decided once again to be petty.

'Being supervisor doesn't just mean shouting at me when you feel like it. There has to be some work involved.'

Vicky just scowled at her.

Steelhammer Row was oddly cold for the morning. Where was everyone? Smithing started early, leave it too late and you boiled yourself when the heat of the sun and the forge combined, but only a single tent at the bottom of the street was lit.

Beside the tent, a wooden plaque held a crest to the weak sunshine. The Iactura picked out in metal, cracks spidered down its burnished surface. This was the place. Everyone knew Mistress Ignis' sigil.

The heat of the tent was delicious. A proper forge burn, it made her skin prickle. A smiling blacksmith nodded over his Indentina hammer. 'Welcome. My name is Kyle Carosso.'

'Forgemaster Carosso.' Sam grinned. 'We use your anvil in our forge back home.'

The burly bloke bellowed a laugh. 'Aye, you and most of this city. Keeps me in luxury.' He gestured at his leather apron.

'Samantha. You are here.' Mistress Ignis stood from her stool at the back of the tent, a small book set down on the table before her. Her dress a midnight blue, a silver chain hung between her nose and ear. The coal around her throat glowed. 'Let us begin, Kyle?'

The blacksmith nodded and began working the bellows. It wasn't long before the air shimmered with the heat and sweat dripped from Vicky's nose. Sam's hair was soaked through and Kyle's beard dribbled.

Mistress Ignis was unaffected. 'Take this.' She handed Sam a lump of silver.

'What are we making?'

'A sign of patronage, forged by your own hand. You will have seen my crest outside.'

'That flat-stamped Iactura with cracks all over it? Easy enough, but that temperature is wrong for silver. And do you have a stamping hammer, a stylus?'

'The girl knows her stuff!' The blacksmith laughed.

Sam glared at him. The girl.

Ignis ignored them both. 'Forged by your own hand. Not by petty tools.' She took a deep breath and blew softly into the forge.

The flames dimmed. For a moment, the air was cool. Then the forge burst with blue fire. Sam sheltered her eyes. Phantom smoke filled the tent.

'Cut your hand and place the silver in the flames,' Ignis commanded. The coal around her throat blazed, so bright a blue it was almost white. She handed a copper knife over to Sam.

'This isn't... proper fire is it? Jak wouldn't like it if I...'

Ignis met Sam's eyes. 'Men without ambition are lodestones to women like us.' She shoved her hand into the fire, pulled a coal from the heart of the forge. It blazed like a miniature sun between her fingers. And yet her painted nails were not so much as chipped. 'You will not get another chance.' She tossed the coal in the mud at her feet. Instantly, it extinguished.

Sam looked around for support but Vicky just shrugged and gestured towards the fire. 'About time someone else was a weight around your shoulders, eh Sam?'

Sam gritted her teeth. The anger was useful. She barely felt it as she dragged a shallow gash in her palm. Before she could think any better of it, she thrust her hand into the flames.

It was warm. Like swishing her hand in a bath, though sweat still rolled down her face. Smoke tickled around her ears. She swallowed the soot, the grit.

'*Reality burns. Inhale the memory.*'

A voice spoke inside her head. Just like back home, the smoke marionettes in the living room. Sam blinked.

The forge grew. Like a mouth of some great beast, the black iron expanded until it was all she could see. Blue fire spread into the darkness. A pathway of flame.

Sam's heart squirmed into her mouth. She took a step across the pathway and white mist grew like tendrils of ivy from her feet. It spiralled out, expanded like an ever-growing blizzard until the darkness was coated in wisps of translucent smoke.

A person materialised beside her. Scalp tattoos, red eyes and a look of sneering superiority. Ignis raised a finger. She pointed into the mist.

A pillar of metal burst from the smoke beside Sam.

Sam cowered. The metal rose far higher than she could perceive. The Iactura. Real as life.

She turned to Ignis.

'*If you wish to speak, merely think the words. I will hear you.*'

Sam's thoughts bubbled up. '*Okay, then what in the name of my sweating arse is going on here? Where am I?*'

'*This is Memoria. A place where memories and thoughts are made manifest. Place your hand on the Iactura.*'

Sam stepped forwards, still surprised she wasn't just plunging through the mist to her death.

Ignis grabbed her wrist and placed her bloody palm on the pillar.

The dark sky shuddered and silver stars formed high overhead, budding from the Iactura like cherry blossoms. '*What are those?*'

'*Manifest memories. They are why we are here.*'

'*What?*'

'*It is a pity your Forgemaster is blinded by his hatred of me. He appeared to have some knowledge of what we were about. I would not have to explain myself so vigorously.*'

'*Oh, he, uh, was busy. Sends his apologies.*'

Almost as soon as she'd spoken, a silver orb slammed from the sky and into the mist beside her. Jak Mendy's voice broke from the silver.

'*...rather slit open me sack and pull my stones out with a pair of tongs than spend one moment with that woman. No. You go, it's your patronage, not mine. I'll piss off down Ferriway. Seein' as though you've got us both* *chained to rumour and bollocks, I'll go see if any of my old mates have resurfaced. See what they can tell us about Callisteel beyond "you're wasting your time…"'*

The memory faded, and Sam's cheeks burned.

Ignis ignored it. *'The silver will not wait.'*

'Then what are we doing?'

'I am a Mindbreaker. I remove memories and invest them in metal. I want you to bring forth your memories of Callisteel. I shall pare them from you and create bloodmetal, mixed with the molten silver in your palm.'

'I have no idea what you just said.'

'Come! The silver is beginning to form.'

'Uh…' Right. Memories of Callisteel. But what did she have? Memories of failing to make it, sure. Rumours she'd never been able to follow. But that can't be what Ignis meant. Did she… did she think Sam knew something? Was that why she was here? And if she found out that her mind was empty as Jonas Karrin, that was it. No patronage, no nothing.

Sam swallowed. There was only one tangible link she had to Callisteel. Her hand jerked towards the lancet beneath the waistband of her trousers, fingertips accidentally jabbed sharp against the razor edge.

The spirals that were carved into the filigree feather spout burst with light.

Agony like glass was ground into her eyes, up into her brain. She tried to scream, but her lungs didn't work. Silver orbs rained from the sky, round and huge reflecting… everything. She saw herself as a child, scabs like rubies on her cheeks. She saw herself as a teenager, shame flooding her face as she stumbled through that one-sided crush on Mira that had extinguished at the exact moment of their first kiss. She saw herself as an adult, fire burning at her elbows. Like a blacksmith's puzzle, the pieces of her life came loose.

'What have you done?' Ignis' voice slammed into her mind, fury writ large on her face.

'I…' And that was all. Who was she?

'Hold yourself.' Ignis held out a hand. A blue flame danced over her palm, roared, expanded, burned so bright it hurt to look at. Ignis' eyes blazed. *'Inhale the memory. Exhale the truth!'*

The silver orbs flew back at Sam, slamming into her. Memories. A lifetime. She could *see* it. She fell a thousand times. Mama was dying. In her mind, Mama had always been dying. A final breath that lasted forever. She had never managed to deal with it, not properly. How could she, when these were the only memories she had? Papa's eyes were cold. He loved Vicky still. What was wrong with her?

'*Don't make me go back,*' the body that was called Samantha thought as the memories passed through her.

And then there was a pair of arms. Enormous arms, comforting and Jak Mendy was by her side and he was holding her and he was soothing her and then he did the most amazing thing. He made her laugh. And suddenly the edge of pain was dulled, just a touch.

'*But he's not here. Gone over the river alone, because of my obsession.*' Silver tears fell from her eyes. '*Everyone disappears eventually.*'

'*Not if we remember them.*' Ignis' face was covered in sweat. A thin dribble of blood spotted from her nostril. '*But first we must remember ourselves. Samantha Acarris.*'

Her name was like a chain. It wrapped around her and held her, somewhere between existence and sorrow. The memories coalesced once more and this time, they slammed into her chest and stuck there, pounding through her body over and over and over until the pain and pleasure and loss and joy was all just too much.

Then everything was dark.

Sam opened her eyes. The forge was back and Vicky knelt over her.

'Samantha?'

She rubbed her eyes and sat up. 'Vicky. I...' She blinked, her tongue trying to find the right words as so many memories of their lives together bubbled up to the surface.

'Are you done?' Vicky cut her off.

'Clearly.' Ignis' voice was cold.

Sam looked down into her hand. The silver had melted into a shapeless lump and her hand bled sour around it. Not quite the sigil that Mistress Ignis had demanded.

'Good.' Vicky nodded. 'Congratulations Sam, I truly expected nothing else.' She turned on her heel and stalked from the tent.

'Wait! Vicky, I have to tell you…' Tell her what? That she loved her? That she hated her? Sam couldn't tell. A headache began behind her eyes. So strong. She could have wept, but she very much doubted she had any tears left in her.

Ignis reached down to help her up. The forge fire was out and the blacksmith was gone. How late was it? Ignis kept hold of her hand as she led them to a small table in the back of the tent. Wordlessly, she bandaged the slash in Sam's palm.

'What just happened to me?'

Ignis tied the bandage tight, then knit her fingers together. 'I am very rarely surprised, Samantha. To see a person's memories is to take their measure. And yet I would love to know how some girl, with no training, was able to shatter her own mind so successfully.'

'Shatter?'

'You were coming apart.' Ignis' voice was matter-of-fact. 'I slice a person's mind, a sharp knife to take a tiny fragment of memory and store it in metal. You… you managed to slam a hammer against your psyche and send every tiny particle of yourself to the corners of your mind. If I had been a moment slower…' she shook her head. Her eyes bored into Sam. 'Who *are* you?' Ignis' lips flattened into a firm line. She sniffed and a single drop of blood fell from her nose to splash against the table.

'I don't think it was me.' Sam pulled the lancet from beneath her trousers. Her heart hammered in her chest, but nothing happened. Nothing changed. She set it on the table.

When she looked up again, she could see the cold fury in Ignis' eyes. 'You never mentioned this.'

'In keeping secrets, it seems we're two of a kind. If you'd cut out my memories of Callisteel… I wouldn't have been able to remember them, would I?' Sam snatched the lancet from Ignis' clawed fingers. 'I wonder, just what did Jonas Karrin discover before you got to him?'

'I should kill you for that. I should take your eyes.'

'But you can't, can you? Because you have no idea just exactly what it is I know.' Sam could feel her pulse racing in her temples. A bluff, razor thin. It was the only thing keeping her mind her own.

'I could tear your memories from you without a thought.'

'Not without Callisteel you can't. And if you try, I'll shove this thing right through my heart and see what you're left with.' She flipped the lancet in her fingers.

'Do not tempt me.' Ignis spoke with the roar of fire. 'You will hear from me again. Until then, keep your forge cold. And remain silent.' The Mindbreaker marched from the tent and vanished.

Sam sat by herself for a long time, running her fingers through the spiral inlay of the lancet. When she finally left the tent, the streets were deserted. She walked home alone, through the quiet and the cold.

CHAPTER 17

'If I had to take a guess, I'd say it should be right around here.' Addie stumbled across a pile of broken bricks, scored a gash on her knee from a particularly vicious stone and growled at Caelan as if, like bloody everything, it was his fault.

'What should be?' Caelan asked.

'The place where we are brutally murdered.'

'Have faith woman. They won't kill us. We're here to recruit.' He said it confidently enough, but when the slow wind rolled through the alleyway he still shivered. The Nest was a claustrophobic nightmare.

There were two ways to cross the river and neither came without the threat of death or disembowelment. The first were the barges, six chain-powered flatboats that spanned from Ferriway to Highdock. Anyone could take the barges. So long as they had a permit. And, for some unfathomable reason, the folk on the Ferriway side found it remarkably difficult to track down Highdock Councillor DeNori and get his personal signature. Of course, even if you did manage to steal, forge or bribe one, you'd still have to deal with the Walkers. They clustered in the barges like flies on shit, a coin toss that they'd decide anyone sailing with them would look prettier under the Sightless' axe. That was, if they didn't decide to gut you there and then for the sport of it.

So, if that method of murder didn't suit your fancy, then the other choice of death was through the Nest. Not technically its name anymore, Kuyt loved to waffle on about the different districts, but Caelan had never managed to force himself to pretend to care long enough to take any of them in. The maze-like walkways rose in tight bridges to span the delta of the Mucro. Walkers avoided the Nest. Even the blackcloaks were too smart to fuck with it.

Buildings hung overhead, blocked the light and dipped the stone walkways in ink. Locked in twilight. It was like being trapped in the mists.

Caelan swallowed. He gripped the knife at his waist, felt his palm flex around his newest scar. The fingertip scabs throbbed, flecks of new blood staining his fingernails. A third piece of bloodmetal rattled in his pocket. Ferra had been as good as her word.

The wannabe rebels spoke about it. Talked with useless pride about how he'd saved Kuyt's life. The old man had even managed to develop the vastly irritating habit of not being able to look at him without his ancient eyes misting. Caelan had no memory of what happened after he climbed those chains.

Until Gaz's death.

Caelan clicked his jaw. That memory, he'd kept. The look in the man's bleeding, weeping eyes as he slid into the heartfire. The taste of the smoke from his flesh. That scream.

'He deserved to die.'

'No one deserves to die like that,' Caelan whispered. He turned over another thin bridge. The Mucro bubbled in darkness far below. A hollow rattle. He leant on the rusted railing and watched the water. Let himself feel the guilt that crept up his shoulders with shadowy fingers.

'He would feel none for you. Put it out of your mind. Literally, if you must.'

'He was grieving his daughter. There are some things we shouldn't forget.'

'You talking to yourself?' Addie's voice snapped Caelan out of his mind. 'It's irritating enough following you around, without having to listen to you mumble.' Her tone was insulting, no surprise there, but the look in her eyes. If she wouldn't have snapped his arm just for the thought, he might have called it concern.

'Just trying to figure out if there is enough time for a quick dip.' Caelan made a show of sniffing himself.

'Give you a shove if you like?'

'Maybe next time.'

Her smile was brief. She looked at him. 'Caelan, who's Lara?'

Something stirred in his head. 'Who?'

'You spoke of her, in the foundry, when that bloke threatened Kuyt.'

'She's dead. She's no one,' Caelan said. Reilo howled anger inside his head. 'Just a lie to try and keep Kuyt alive. For all the good it did.'

'I've heard you lie plenty of times, Caelan.' She met his eyes. Not many did. It was something he'd gotten used to, folk avoiding his glassy blue gaze. Even Kuyt had struggled, at the start. But Addie never had. 'That wasn't one. It's not too late to turn back.'

He gave her an awkward laugh. 'I don't have a choice.'

'There is always a choice.'

'We can't take on the Walkers with a handful of ill-trained civvies and some ex-blackcloaks that I'm half convinced intend to start cutting us down themselves the moment they get bored.'

'That's not what I mea... Caelan. Up there.' Addie nodded. A shadow, darting across the rooftops opposite. 'There too.' The alleyway. 'More coming, around the back-'

'Drop the hatchets, love.' A man emerged from the shadows behind Addie and levelled a blade between her shoulders. A thick, weeping scar stole his left eye and half his hairline.

'I stole the kidneys of the last bloke that called me "love".' She slipped the hatchets from her belt and placed them, gently, on the bridge.

'You too,' a voice grunted from behind Caelan. He turned to the lass, bright green eyes and a three-pronged spear levelled at his chest. 'Knife. Drop it.'

'*Don't you fucking dare.*'

Caelan's hand curled around the hilt of his blade. 'Why?'

'I'm not asking.'

Caelan drew the knife from his belt. He licked his lips. 'I can't.'

'Caelan, this is not the fucking time,' Addie hissed.

'I'm not trying to flash my bollocks here.' He strained his knuckles. 'I *can't.*'

Reilo's face flickered through his mind. Caelan could feel his influence, a vice inside his skin. Sweat poured from his temples.

'Give me a fucking break. This is still my body!' Caelan shook his hand, slammed his fingers against the railing until finally the knife sprang free and clattered against the stone. He panted like he'd been running.

'What the fuck was that?' Addie snarled at him.

'I'm not dead yet,' Caelan spat. The new scar on his palm burned.

133

'*The gaps in your mind are mine. And thanks to Ferra, you are ripping those wider.*'

'S'a nice knife. Iron and everything, but not worth dying over.' The trident girl scooped it up and slid it into her belt. 'Figured you were mad enough to talk to yourself, no one else would come wandering in here. Anything else?'

'Just these.' Caelan drew the three chunks of bloodmetal from his pocket.

The lass burst into laughter. 'Aye, you can keep those. Wouldn't do to take memories from a man.' She peered at his eyes. 'Especially a man like you. Quill told us to keep an eye out, but I wasn't thinking you were thick enough to hand-deliver yourself.'

'We're here to talk,' Caelan said.

'You're here to do whatever the fuck you are told. Else you'll die and we'll lob you into the river.' She glanced over her shoulder. Caelan followed her eyes to a line of archers crouched on a nearby rooftop. Eyes shone in the darkness behind. Countless others, hidden and waiting. 'Reckon he'd like a word. Zane, you get rid of her. I'll take him.'

'If you hurt her, I'll do something stupid,' Caelan said.

'Even if they don't the odds are pretty high,' Addie growled. There was an edge to it.

'I can be very irritating when I'm dying.'

The lass glowered at him. 'Zane. Escort her out. You can even have your weapons back, as soon as you've fucked off. Adira Signasti.'

'You know who I am,' she said.

'I know how many Walkers you've killed. This is us paying you back. It won't happen again.'

'I've killed Walkers too,' Caelan offered.

'Now would be a very good time for you to shut the fuck up.' The lass pushed her trident into his chest, sharp enough that he could feel the spikes against his ribcage.

'Caelan.' Addie looked over her shoulder at him, raised an eyebrow. 'Don't get killed.'

'Oh, well now you've said it...' Caelan said.

Addie stepped off the bridge. Zane snatched up her hatchets, pressed his blade against her shoulder and forced her back into the darkness.

The twilight swallowed her.

'Move your arse,' the lass ordered.

She put her trident up and Caelan followed her deeper into the Nest. Voices whispered from the alleyways. He brushed against the scorched walls and shattered glass crunched beneath his boots.

'What's your name?' Caelan asked.

'Speak again and I'll break your fucking jaw.'

This really had been one of his best ideas.

He followed her through the labyrinth. Tried to follow each turn and memorise the way back out. It didn't take long for that to become a waste of fucking time. He had no idea where he was. Only way out was if they let him.

She led him to a short, thick building. The wooden walls slanted, splintered across the walkway, but it was still standing and that made it unique. She posted herself outside the door, held her spear at rest.

'He's inside.' She jerked her head.

'Don't I need guarding still?'

She laughed, cruel and sharp. 'You wish.'

Caelan followed her imperious finger. Candles dotted the walls, the floor, spat greasy smoke into the air. The whole place stank of mould. Discarded plates cluttered around a single table, gouged and hacked.

Someone was chained to the back wall. Gagged. Blood oozed from his sides. Dripped into the black cloak that had been used to tie his ankles together.

A man stood before him, a three-lash whip spinning in his fingers. It gleamed sinuous leather, silver-spikes rattled at the tip of each knotted cord. Polished, they sparkled like coins.

'Caelan.' He didn't turn as he spoke. Instead, he sent the whip snapping out and drew a fine strip of skin from the bloke in chains.

Silent screams broke through the gag. Tears and blood dribbled down his chest.

'Quill, I figure? At least put the fucker out of his misery before you take his fucking skin.'

'You've got some weighty bollocks coming here after what you did.' He turned around. Short and stocky, blood dribbled from his silver-spiked whip.

The chained Walker's head fell to his chest, eyes rolled back.

'After... what?' Caelan asked.

'Rotheart. We were there.'

'I didn't figure you'd be the kind whose heart bled for the Walkers.' He nodded at the senseless bloke chained up. 'Or was he a special case?'

'He's one of the first. They always start with volunteers. That's when you can still make an example and try and scare them off. It's when they start forcing idiots through, that's when things get messy.' Quill walked towards Caelan, his whip dribbling a bloody trail into the floorboards behind him. 'We vowed there would be no violence during Sy's execution. I sacrificed a good friend for that peace. Until you fucked it up.'

'I have no clue what you are talking about.'

'Ignorance is no excuse.' He lashed out with his whip and left a stinging gash across Caelan's forearm.

Caelan groaned. 'Then what? We kill each other here?'

'I tie you up and send you off to the Walkers. They execute you and we get them to fuck off.'

Caelan blinked. 'I can't believe it. Kuyt was right. They really did win.'

'What the fuck are you talking about?'

'I came here today to try and ally with you arseholes. Everyone knows that the Nest never bent to the Walkers. I don't remember fucking anything, and even I know that. But it's all an act. You're just another little boy who does as he's told.'

'Careful,' Quill said.

'Or what? You'll tell your Mommy and Daddy Walkers on me? Give me a fucking break.' Caelan felt Reilo's anger in the back of his skull.

'It seems the Sightless won't get your head after all. Still, they'll recognise the eyes when I send them a nice soggy package.'

'Yeah, that's right. Kill me. Do their job for them. The Nest held against the Walkers even when they set it on fire and murdered anyone who fled the flames.' Caelan's voice was sharp. Reilo's memories flickered through his head. 'More Walkers died trying to storm this shithole than anywhere else in Arx.'

'We bled them here. Bones in the river. They never held the Nest.'

'Now the rest of us have finally caught up, finally started fighting back, and you've surrendered.' Fuck it but his heart was hammering now.

'Surrendered? You child. I would burn this city and everyone in it alive just to keep the last living person here free. That is all there is. Freedom or bondage, existence or extinction.' Quill's voice specked with froth. 'You said you're fighting back. You have no idea. We *have* been fighting the Walkers. And unlike naïve little shits like you, we know the cost. Skinning men and sending them back to the barracks keeps those fuckers afraid. And they should be. This is what they've done to me. To us. Death is easy. It's what they do to you living that's hard. So go play at rebellion. Go back to the idiots who would follow a man like you and die. Maybe you'll draw their attention long enough that we'll be able to take a fucking breath. Suzi. Suzi!'

The trident-woman poked her head through the door.

'Get him the fuck out of my sight.' Quill turned back to the Walker. Spun his whip.

Caelan was dragged out of the building, just as the bloke began to scream.

'Well. This was a waste of ti…' he started.

Suzi grabbed his collar and rammed the tip of her trident against his chin. 'One more fucking word, I swear.'

Maybe it was time he shut up.

She led him between the buildings. He peered up towards the sky, but the shadow and smog stole any sunlight. He had no idea what fucking time it was. It felt like an age before she finally shoved him out into the orange sun of late-afternoon.

'Where the fuck are we?' Caelan glanced around. The nearby buildings were painted, fresh brick and chased glass windows. A wide, open plaza. 'This is… across the river.' He reached for a knife that wasn't there, the iron winking at him from Suzi's belt. 'Your boss didn't tell you to bring me here.'

'You have no idea what her boss ordered her to do.'

That voice.

A blue fleck darted through Suzi's eyes. Caelan's mouth dried. His arms shuddered uncontrollably. He blinked. It felt like it took him a lifetime. He turned around. Slowly.

Tall. Blonde. With crushingly familiar violet eyes. The first thing Caelan could remember.

Dirk.

CHAPTER 18

Ruairi groaned from his pallet. Thing were about as comfy as a bed of porcupines and six blinks into waking his back were already kicking off about it. Morning were always the worst.

Two weeks locked in a cage with nothing but his aches and twinges for company. A chicken locked up like this would go feral before sunrise.

It took him three tries to stand. A tremor shot down his withered legs and he almost kicked over his piss pot.

Ruairi gasped and bent his knees. Should have known better. No. He had known better. Pa warned him often enough. Head down, get on with it. Turns out, what he'd heard was "take a massive shit and see who slips in it".

'Didn't realise you were a dancer, Hopalong.'

Ruairi twisted upright. First reckoned he'd been having some sort of hallucination, but there he were, poking his bald head through the bars of the cell with a shit-eating grin.

Ruairi limped over and grabbed for the bastard.

'Sweaty palms lad!' Fetch wiggled back outta reach. 'You know what they say about sweaty palms? Sweaty bollocks. When'd you last get your leg over?'

'You crabfucker!'

'Kids were much politer in my day.'

'I ain't playing Fetch. I'm in a cage 'cause of you.'

The grin faded. 'Aye and I'm sorry for that. But you haven't been executed either. That's also because of me, that's gotta win me a few points eh?'

'What? Why would they execute me?' Ruairi chewed up the side of his cheek. Worst he'd figured were a bit of time cooling his heels in a cell. Not... 'I didn't do nothing.'

Fetch made a show of looking for eavesdroppers. ''Cause of this.'

That damned arrowhead flickered across his fingers.

'You can keep it! I never met the bloke I took it from before. I just wanna go home.'

'His name is Dirk. Shite. Should I have told you that? Well, you know it now. It's... complicated.'

'Fetch. I need out.'

'I know. That's why I'm here.'

Ruairi leant close. 'You here to break me out?'

Fetch snorted. 'You're in a holding cell beneath the barracks on Highdock. I could get the door, locks aren't difficult, but we'd make it about six steps before copper blades were cutting us down.'

Ruairi sniffled. 'Why'd you do this to me Fetch? I thought you were a good guy.'

'I'm not. Worth remembering that. But I am here to help. I won't let you die. I promise.'

'Oh aye, 'course I'd trust that from you.'

'Looking around, I don't see any other options for you kid.'

Ruairi sucked in a slow breath. 'What.... what do I do?'

'Be honest. Tell them the truth. Everything you saw.'

'You told me no one remembers anything here.'

'I did. But you're about two weeks late for playing the moron. Trust me. This is the best choice you've got.' A bell clanged down the corridor and Fetch winced. 'Shit. I gotta go. Chin up kid!' He jogged away.

Ruairi leant his head against the bars and settled in to wait for his lunchtime slop.

Tell the truth. It were all he could do.

'Wake up.'

Ruairi's eyes snapped open. A woman looked down at him.

Steel-grey curls clung tight down her back, ashen dress swooping low in little ripples down her legs. Everything about her were immaculate. Little round half-moon nails clean as a coastline, clothes like they'd never been worn before. Ruairi felt grubby just being near her. Well, that and the fact he'd been sleeping in the same shirt for two weeks and they still ain't emptied his shit bucket. A small scar curled around her upper cheek and the lines on her face pegged her around Pa's age.

'Ma'am?' Ruairi cleared his throat, scooched to the edge of the bed. Sod bugger damnit but it hurt like someone were popping out the notches of his spine one by one. His eyes watered.

A Walker, so tall he were bent double just to fit inside, stood by the door. He pared his fingernails on a curved copper knife. 'It's "Viceroy", not Ma'am,' he rumbled.

'Be kind, Sebastian.' She turned her amber eyes on Ruairi. Even just looking she had him sweating. 'My name is Leanne DeSüle. Mistress of the Ropes.' She unfolded a small lap-desk between them. 'Place your hands over the desk.'

'My name's Ruairi.'

'Hands please.'

Ruairi laid his arms flat against the desk. The Walker barged in, God of the fields but it were getting cosy all of a sudden, and plucked each of his fingers. Checked his fingertips.

'Clean,' he murmured.

'Hardly his only method,' she said.

The Walker shrugged and clamped a pair of manacles around Ruairi's wrists.

Ruairi winced. Felt like a lobster had got hold of him. He opened his mouth to say sommat, but the ladylass just looked at him and he bolted his jaw sharpish.

'Tell me about Dirk. Start from the beginning.'

Ruairi swallowed. Felt like he'd tried to down his entire Adam's apple. Still, not much else he could do. He went into it. Started with the news of the Salt Ponies, got a frown when he mentioned Fetch's name, rushed through fishing with Pa and made it all the way to when Dirk's horse died.

'You helped him?' she asked, disapproval thick as toffee in his voice.

'I did. But I didn't know who he were.' Still didn't. 'I just saw some bloke dying in the road. I couldn't let someone die just 'cause.'

'You should have.'

'I figured he was gone anyhow. 'Til I got him to a fire...' Ruairi licked his lips. Still felt odd, saying it out loud. Like weeping to Ma about a nightmare. But he were in too deep to stop now. 'It burned blue. And the hole in his knee weren't there, and then some metal lump fell from his fingers.'

'Did it look like this?' She set a chunk on the desk. Black, with a bright red line down the middle.

'Yes! Exactly like that. What is it?' Ruairi asked.

'Bloodmetal. I never thought he'd head back to the city. Why now?' She shook her head, then snapped back to Ruairi. 'Why should he have had a hole in his knee?'

''Cause there were a whacking great arrow lodged in it. Blue-silver thing, right through his knee. He used it to make the smoke-show. When I left, I... took it from him.'

Her eyes glittered. 'Then, where is it now?'

'Fetch has it,' Ruairi said.

That glitter in her pupils turned into sommat like murder. 'Sebastian. Has it been logged and reported?'

'No Viceroy.'

'Go and find Fetch. Now.'

The massive Walker bumbled off with a nod that made it look like a mountain were bending. The lass turned back to Ruairi.

'That arrowhead was Callisteel. A weapon unlike any other. Did he cut you with it? Would you even remember if he did...?'

'That thing weren't exactly easy to forget, Ma'am Viceroy.'

'Callisteel cuts through memories. It is not a painless process. A Mindbreaker can, with your consent, excise a moment from your past. Callisteel would slice the connections between your memories in a heartbeat. And trust me when I say, Dirk himself is far, far worse. If he cut you, you would follow him without question. But even if all you did was speak... it may already be too late.'

'I swear, he didn't cut me. I just snatched it outta his hand before he burned the whole place down. Didn't even look at it again until Fetch took it from me.'

She tilted her head. 'When Fetch returns, your story will be easy to verify. If there is anything you haven't told me, now would be the time.'

Ruairi rubbed sweat into his eyebrows. 'It didn't cut no-one. Fetch saw it at the pub 'cause I couldn't believe what I'd seen... but I did, I swear it. When it touched the candle, that same fire...'

'You introduced Callisteel to fire. In front of others.'

'Aye, but it just made some fancy blue sparks. That's it, I didn't cut no-one.'

'You summoned the Flames of Remembrance.' She raised to her feet. Half his size and in a cell cramped as a donkey's arse, but she towered over him. 'There is no leniency for Mindbreakers. That is why Luc- that is why the Sightless made his sacrifice. To purge the city of all blue fire. Yours is a hand that had brought that fire into our reality. We cannot risk that memory surviving. Your journey ends at his axe.'

She gestured and the Walker released Ruairi's shackles.

Ruairi shook as his manacles were released. Clicks and cracks made their way up his spine, but he barely felt them. A rushing, pounding in his ears. 'I didn't do nothing.'

She turned her back on him. 'That you know of.'

The cell door crashed shut and Ruairi... fell. Went crashing to the concrete floor in a tangle of limbs. It hurt. The whole thing hurt. But he couldn't move. Couldn't blink. Just lay there and let the tears leak out.

CHAPTER 19

Caelan's fingertips burned. He couldn't look away. The cut of Dirk's sandy jaw, the close-cropped beard. Not a scrap of grey in his hair, but those violet eyes were ancient. Gilded chain around his throat, coal an ember inside. The scabs on his fingertips a mirror of his own.

Caelan's jaw clenched, tight enough to saw through his tongue and chew open his gums. This was the man who had stolen his memories. This was the man who knew who he really was. A man who deserved his rage.

'Suzi. Give Caelan his knife back.'

The sound of his voice skewered like a spear to the guts. Ageless, firm. Like every word was considered for a lifetime before it was offered.

Suzi snapped out her hand, proffered the blade to Caelan.

Caelan snatched the knife and Dirk waved her back into the Nest. 'Still can't let it go. Controlling people.'

'Control is needed. If people will not see what is best for them, then I will make them see. That or I will take their eyes. There are always those willing to let me in. The Nest. The Walkers. The Government. Even within the rebels heartsick enough to join a man like you there are those who answer to me. Though they might not remember it.'

'That a fact?' Caelan flipped the blade over.

Lashed out, vicious and sudden, picturing the squeeze of blood from Dirk's silent throat. Fuck how he'd dreamed of this moment.

But his strike was uncontrolled. Sloppy. Not even close to connecting, he skidded off balance and awkward.

'You think I would let you harm him?'

Caelan growled and threw himself forwards, whirled around with a big, ugly slash. He gripped the knife tighter, sliced the meat of his own thumb, stabbed at Dirk's heart.

And the knife swung wide and wild. Caelan overbalanced and slammed into the stone floor, smacked his cheek and blinked past sparks.

Cold, oozing sweat formed at the back of Caelan's neck. Reilo's scraping genuflection washed through his mind. He clung to a scrap of fury like self-immolation as ice water rushed through his veins.

Caelan stared at his palms, fastened to the ground like they were nailed there. He tried to rip them free, to leap to his feet and ram his knife through Dirk's crotch. But he couldn't move.

Reilo smirked inside his head.

Like a giant hand on the back of his neck. Caelan found himself bending. Bowing before Dirk. He strained, struggled, felt something pop in the back of his neck, but still he bent. His forehead touched the ground at Dirk's feet.

'Master.'

Caelan's lips squirmed as the word threatened to leap from his throat.

He ripped his knee across the stone floor. Sharp, scraping pain tore through his trousers and into his flesh. The shock snapped his jaw shut and he forced himself to unsteady feet. Reilo's grip on him faded. But the pressure on the back of his neck remained.

'Why…?' Caelan panted. 'Why do you worship him?'

'He gave me everything.'

'By taking it from me.'

'Are you finished?' Dirk raised an eyebrow.

'Why are you here?'

'Rebellion stirs in Austellus. Again. Last time, the Viceroy's got to win. But that didn't work. So this time, the Austelli get to win. And if that doesn't work…' His violet eyes drifted to the shadow of the Iactura on the horizon. He snapped back to himself with a bark of laughter. 'Though I did not expect to see you leading the charge. Why bleed for this place?'

Answers rattled through Caelan's mind. Because Kuyt wanted him to. Because Addie fought with him. Because Reilo poured obsession like poison into his ears. Because these were his people and he owed them his death.

And quietly. Lying on a slab. Dying, a forgotten man. A life was such a small price to pay to become a memory.

'None of your fucking business,' he snarled.

Dirk grinned. 'Fine, keep the why to yourself, I am far more interested in the how. I heard that you died.'

Caelan stood motionless as Dirk's fingers came for his neck. Not his flesh. Dirk gripped his collar and ripped open his shirt.

'Bloodmetal and flesh. Did Ferra know, I wonder?' Dirk asked. 'An honest attempt to keep you alive? Or a failed attempt to mimic Lucianus?'

Who?

'I have no idea why she melted metal into my back. But it was the only way I was surviving.'

Dirk wandered around Caelan, a curator admiring a particularly troublesome piece. 'Memory worn as armour. Aer managed it first, but she was working with an intact mind.'

'What the fuck are you on about?'

Dirk didn't even acknowledge him. He drew five pieces of bloodmetal from a pouch at his belt.

Five memories. From Day One.

'Are those mine?' Oh how Caelan reviled that desperation in his voice.

'Would you take them back if you could?' Dirk asked.

'... you can do that?'

'Oh yes. If you retain the bloodmetal, we can melt the memory back down and return it to the host. It's difficult, and gets harder with each other memory you lose, but it can be done.'

Caelan froze. If that was true... *would* he take them back? The memories of the man he was before all of this. Hope. He could have been someone so much better.

But then, he could've been so much worse.

'Of course, these don't belong to you.' Dirk smiled. The coal around his throat sparked into life, a wire-thread of azure flame. It leapt like fingers of a hand, five needles into the bloodmetal.

Despite himself, Caelan sucked down a lungful of smoke. The street wavered like a mirage. Hid the world in a curtain of ash.

'*Ever since the Flame Protests, Arx has been in the hands of elected councillors.*' Dirk's voice came from a long way away. '*Seventy-two of them at this very moment, to be precise. Once elected, they each cast their vote to elect the five Viceroys that sit in council over Arx.'*

A face formed in the smoke. Impossibly detailed. White hair and a grizzled jaw, the weight of a lifetime in his eyes.

'The Ant. Andross DeGaya. High Governor of Arx. A weightless title. Even those who vote for him could not tell you what he does. Earned his seat in the crucible of the Flame Protests.'

The face twisted, warped in on itself and resolved once again as... a Walker. Black cloak snapped in unfelt wind. He swung a blade at an invisible adversary.

'Var DeKeita. Head Captain of the Walkers.'

Another image. A mask. Onyx eyes. Caelan's metal spine throbbed.

'Leanne DeSüle. Mistress of the Ropes. In charge of executions. And the Sightless.'

A paper-thin blade of blue flame sliced through the mask. Replaced it with a pile of gold.

'Walter DeWhit. Lord Treasurer.'

The gold fell into the ground, each coin bursting into ash. The steam curled into the image of a horse-and-cart team, pounding across an open plain.

'And Jace DeSané. Minister of Commerce. Responsible for feeding the city.'

The smoke vanished. Caelan blinked grit from his eyes, wiped a hand down his face. Dirk emerged from the haze.

'The death of even one of those would cripple the government. It would demonstrate that you cannot be denied.'

'Five deaths does even more.'

Dirk chuckled. 'That will come, in time. But the Ant is a war hero. A fallen one, to be sure, but his death would not endear people to your cause. It was he who first united the Austelli. You have resurrected that term. His is a useful shadow.'

'Fine. I've heard of the Ant. But the others...'

'Var DeKeita spends his time in an office set above the main barracks, up in the Citadel. How many blackcloaks do you think you can cut through before they stop you? And DeSüle...' Dirk tapped a finger to his lips. 'The only time the Sightless leaves her side is for executions.

Which you have temporarily put a stop to. I hear your last attack on that creature was less than successful?'

Caelan blinked. He'd expected to feel... anger? But there wasn't anything there. The cost of his memory sacrifice. Just cold knowledge. 'No one is a match for that thing.'

'Thus, we are left with a toss-up. Walter DeWhit. Or Jace DeSané.'

Caelan very nearly shrugged. What did it matter? He'd never met either of them. But something stopped him. An execution. What felt like a lifetime ago. On his knees, watching the eyes boil from an innocent face. What had that scrawny bloke called their crime? Trespass and attempted murder. Of Jace DeSané.

'DeSané,' Caelan said. 'We're owed his blood.'

'And how such debts can grow. Very well, let me take you to him.'

'What, so you can stab me in the back as we go for a lovely stroll?' Caelan stood back.

'If I had wanted to kill you, I would have.'

'*You blame Dirk for taking who you were. Will your pride now prevent you from becoming who you wish to be?*'

Caelan squeezed the handle of his knife until his fingers ached. Relio's certainty was like a balm. To be so sure, so confident. For once, to not hate himself for second guessing. 'Then I want an answer. What do you get from this?'

'Access to the Iactura. It has been a long time. Your rebellion distracts the Viceroys, distracts the Sightless. That is enough, for now.'

'And after that?'

'I will give everyone in this city what I once gave to you. A new existence. Freed from painful memories.'

'Is that it?'

'It is all I ever wanted.'

Caelan hesitated, for all of a moment. Dirk was lying. Dirk was always lying.

But his reckoning would come one day. Just like he said. Debts of blood always grow.

'Then let's go kill a Viceroy.'

The pair of them made their way down the street. The afternoon gave way to night and the roads were silent but for the sound of their boots on the gravel. A chill wind blew across Caelan's naked shoulders and he shivered.

The street split into curated walkways and the size of the buildings increased. Some of the manors were incredible. Countless storeys of stained glass and gleaming latticework. It was a different world to the cramped shacks and broken stone of Rotheart.

'Built on corpses.' Reilo's voice ground like dirt in Caelan's ears.

They wound around an extensive row of hedges, breaking free as the sunlight finally lost its battle and dipped behind the clouds.

The skyline melted into firelight. Off in the distance the final gasp of the setting sun burned like fire across the Iactura.

Dirk stopped in its shadow. 'Can you hear it? In the mists, the Iactura makes our memories manifest. But in Arx... the Iactura is a repository for everything we've forgotten. Its terrible hunger is the source of our power.'

'I don't hear anything.'

'You will.'

Dirk led them up a gravel passageway towards a towering manse. Three storeys tall with a dozen real-glass windows, thick panels, white-washed brick and a huge chunk of bird shit right down the front window. Darkness held grip on all but one of the windows.

Two Walkers stood either side of the front door. One, bald as a lice-shaven child. The other, tall and slender. It didn't take them long to notice. Hands flickered to blades.

'Dirk, you're seeing what I'm...' Caelan began.

'Easy. What is it you said? I enjoy controlling people.' He jerked his head.

The bald Walker lunged, his blade plunging through his partner's shoulders. The blackcloak fell, that look of surprise never quite making it over his face.

The traitor Walker nodded to Dirk. Threw something to him, something metal. Dirk looked at it, a glimmer of blue-silver in the moonlight, then slipped it beneath his belt. Wordless, the fake Walker vanished into the night.

'Pity he couldn't get me a key. They lock from the inside, but we'll make do. It's something Ferra couldn't quite grasp, but Ignis took to it instantly. The fire we manipulate, it might release a memory – but it is still fire.'

Dirk whistled a breath between pursed lips and the coal around his neck sparked blue. He touched a finger to it, a flame flickering on his index, and he placed it inside the keyhole. The lock began to melt. Tears of metal rolled down to hiss against the wet shrubs. A formless chunk that had once been the lock fell from the door with a thud.

The door swung open.

Caelan followed Dirk inside.

'This is a Viceroy Manse. A gift from the city of Arx to allow them to comport business and to live in…'

'Luxury.' Caelan looked around. 'Look at this place.' The hallway broke out into separate corridors, each panel-lined and… what the fuck was that on the floor? Coloured wool? It squished under his boots.

'If you're finished? We are trespassing after all. The Viceroy's all have a security contingent on hand, I've only bought us a few moments.'

Caelan let Dirk lead him up a huge, curving staircase.

'They're working late tonight. Supplies are short and even the Walkers are getting antsy.' A set of dying candles flickered down the corridor, leading towards a single door on the right wall. 'The council chamber. This is the place the magic happens. And the reason why your little rebels can barely eat.' He pushed it open.

Caelan stumbled after him into a small antechamber. Most of the room was swamped by an enormous oak table, paper and glasses cluttered on the polished wood. Fourteen chairs, but only one held a person. An older bloke was almost asleep at the end, lit cigarette drooping between his fingers.

'Wha?' He rubbed his eyes, wiped his hands down his cheeks.

Dirk leapt across the table and curled his fingers around the man's throat. In his other hand, he drew something from his belt. Was that… an arrowhead? Lashed to a wooden handle, it made an odd approximation of a knife. He set it against the man's chest. 'Who are you?'

'C… Councilman Leonard DeAcarris.' The bloke's chin shuddered with his breath.

'Tell me Councilman DeAcarris, do you wish to live?'

'Yes! Yes, of course.'

Dirk tilted his head. 'Very well. Then I will save your life.'

He slid that blue-silver arrowhead into the councillor's heart. The man convulsed. His eyelids flickered and each breath came from his throat like it was being forced out.

Dirk twisted the shard of metal. Beneath him, the old man's eyes were gone. Blue fog boiling in their place. A mind lost in memory. A body left to breathe and rot.

'You should have killed him,' Caelan said. 'Fog-Eyes... its worse than death.'

'Let us compare.' Dirk pushed open the door on the other side of the room.

A small chamber sat inside. Desk, chair, candlelight flickering through an empty glass and a single occupant.

'Leonard? Leonard are you out there? Damnit man, have you seen the wine? My head is...' The bloke looked up. Middle-aged and fashionably dressed, black jacket and a tailored white shirt. His eyes took in Dirk, Caelan and the Fog-Eyed councilman in an instant. He leapt to his feet, dropped a hand to the rapier in his belt, slid half the blade free and got it caught beneath the table. He flushed, shook his head and dropped his hand. 'There were fencing lessons when I was little,' he offered.

Dirk turned his violet eyes on Caelan. He gestured at DeSané.

'You,' Caelan said. 'You are responsible for starving people over the river. My people. The Austelli.'

'I am.'

Caelan felt sweat dribble into his eyes. He wiped it away. Hadn't expected the bloke to admit it so readily. 'What?'

'But not through lack of trying! I bailed out the Salt Ponies three times until my own purse became too light and Walter decided he was too stingy to lend me anything. A fresh barge is sent over the river every month and local farmers were ordered to switch to beans and grains before winter strikes.' He rubbed his brow. 'I know the precise weight of food needed to keep a child alive. But what do you do when you just don't have enough?'

'Stop fucking lying!' Caelan darted forwards, leapt over the desk and sank his fist into DeSané's soft stomach. 'You think we haven't wept enough because of you?'

'No, no,' he gasped and slumped to his knees. 'No, I'm sure you have. But I don't want to die.' He looked up, grass-green eyes shining. 'I really don't want to.'

Pathetic. It was just so pathetic. Caelan drew his knife and placed it against DeSané's throat.

'Please,' the sobbing idiot whispered.

'Oh fuck me,' Caelan growled. 'I can't do this.'

'*Kill him!*'

'He's just an idiot in over his head.'

'*He is everything wrong with this city! The Austelli demand his blood.*'

'Well they won't be getting it from me.'

'*Oh yes they will.*'

Caelan blinked. Or tried to blink. His eyes were no longer his to control.

And his hand was moving.

Caelan watched, helpless, as the needle-blade disappeared into the soft spot just under DeSané's jaw.

Face pinched in terror, bright blood burbled down his rich shirt. Thick red, almost black. The knife slid free, and he toppled forwards. Dead.

CHAPTER 20

Caelan stared at the blood on his hands. He curled them into fists. They were his to control again.

'How?' Caelan asked Reilo, but the voice was silent. He could feel exhaustion pulse in his skull.

Reilo was fading. Exhausted from taking control. The shadow in Caelan's mind was barely a flicker of a flicker. And when his voice fell silent, it took his experience with it.

'A good question.' Concern laced Dirk's voice. 'I did not expect both personalities to remain. Physical instinct yes, but I had thought the dominant voice would seize control.'

'Oh it has.' Caelan turned his knife on Dirk. 'Your pet isn't here to stop me from killing you now.'

'Must we? Here?' Dirk eyed the body on the floor. 'I bought you a few moments for an assassination. I did not...'

The door to the outer room creaked open. A stocky Walker bumbled in, speaking to a bottle in his hands. 'Councillor? We found a Senei Red. Shoddy vintage, but it should shut the mewling Viceroy u...'

He looked up. The wine bottle fell and shattered against the floor.

'Captain Kairi!' he screamed and drew his blade.

Boots thudded in the corridor behind him.

'We need to go.' The blue flame around Dirk's throat flickered. A line of fire curled down his arm and he flung it against the window nearby. Flames ate through in an instant.

Dirk grabbed Caelan's arm and threw them both beyond the glass.

For a moment, high over the ground, Caelan felt like he was floating. Then his stomach tried to swap places with his bollocks and they were falling, crashing through vines and brickwork, crumpling to the shrubs outside.

Light flashed from inside the house. Shouting. Screaming. Buildings nearby began to flicker as the occupants woke.

Caelan managed to make it upright. Nothing broken, far as he could tell. Just a bruise the size of a barge on his arse.

'We need to leave. Now.' Dirk struggled to his feet, a gash in his elbow dripping blood down his shirt.

When he ran, Caelan was only too eager to follow.

They raced through pristine streets and limestone pathways. Caelan curled his fingers around his knife.

'Reilo? You there?' he whispered. As much as he hated him, as much as he despised the blood that had been forced onto his hands, he needed his skill. Without it, he was defenceless.

But the voice remained silent.

They turned a corner and a pair of Walkers emerged from the darkness.

'Stop fucking running!' A tall bloke with the hint of a dusty fringe left on his head levelled his blade.

'You would challenge me?' Dirk's voice boomed like thunder. 'Beneath the shadow of my power?' Fire raced from the coal around his neck. Wound like ribbons across Dirk's body. Smoke and steam poured into the street. The fire roared. A maelstrom, with him at its heart.

Dirk lifted his arrow-blade to the sky.

The fire burst from him. A column screeched, high enough to burn a hole in the clouds. Blinding, flashing light. Caelan covered his eyes.

The light faded. From the hole in the smog, a handful of stars glittered overhead. Dirk's arm was burnt.

Both Walkers sat slumped on the ground. Blue fog where their eyes should be.

'I can't do that again,' Dirk said. Sweat dripped down the sides of his face.

They ran.

The streets were alive around them. Voices, the scrape of blades on scabbards. Twice they changed direction as squads of Walkers boiled around corners, through gardens.

'Where are we going?' Caelan gasped. 'Back through the Nest? Get your minion to lead us through?'

'Too slow. They'd be on us before we got half-way. We're heading for Highdock. Take a barge across.'

'And what of the Walkers that infest those things?' Caelan asked.

'We will have to deal with them.' Dirk grabbed his sleeve and led him pelting out towards a familiar stink of ammonia and tar. Even on this side, the Mucro was filthy.

'Right, now just...' Dirk began. 'Fuck!'

Caelan followed his eyes. The barges were missing. All six across the river, docked on the Ferriway side.

Both ends of Highdock burst open to the slap of Walker boots. Faces, shouting. Hundreds of them.

'Shit. Shit, shit!' Dirk yanked Caelan back, closer to the river. Blue fire wound around his arm, blade gripped tightly in the other, but no matter how strong he was it was an impossible task.

'There are more coming.'

That voice. Caelan felt it before he heard it, the aching groan of a city reduced to rubble.

The Sightless.

It strode through the Walkers, blackcloaks making deferential way for the monster. It gestured with an armoured hand, Dirk's blue fire reflected in that metal like a dagger of ice, and pointed over the river.

A pair of barges began their slow way across the sludge.

'Lucianus.' Dirk's voice was odd. There was no anger there. It sounded almost... tender.

'I have not worn that name for a long time.'

'You still remember me,' Dirk said.

'That is my purpose.' It twisted its hands behind its back and brought out that terrible axe. 'I remember only those I am here to stop.'

'Is that really all you are now, Lucianus? Her enforcer?'

The Sightless turned its empty eyes on Dirk. 'I was yours once, too. Not all memories are so easy to burn.'

The Walkers bubbled close around the Sightless. Their numbers blotted the streets. And behind, the barges drew ever closer.

'Caelan, are you intending to fucking help me?' Dirk hissed. 'I hadn't planned to die in sewage!'

'I can't,' Caelan whispered. 'I can't hear him. Reilo's experience, it's… gone.'

'Then we are dead.' Dirk sounded tired.

The barges squelched into the muck of the bank behind them. Caelan turned, Dirk with him. Behind them, the Walkers closed in. And the booming footsteps of the Sightless drew closer. The ramp to the barge began to descend.

Knowledge of his imminent death swirled through Caelan's mind. He'd fought before, risked his life, even got as close to death as a human could go. But that had been with Reilo's experience. He never thought he was invincible, but he could have *done* something about it. Not now.

Now he was just another corpse in the river.

The ramp splashed into the mud of the Highdock bank. And a body slumped from the barge into the muck. A blackcloak captain. Dead. Behind him, Caelan was met with a familiar face.

'With me, Austelli!' Addie screamed and leapt over his head, her backhand slash crashing through a Walker's skull. Danni followed with a wordless roar, spear flashing.

The rebel Austelli poured out of the barges and into the Walkers.

Highdock became a bloodbath.

Caelan ducked under the Sightless' axe whipping over his head, threw himself into the muck as a Walker sword ripped at his side. The blackcloak fell with a thrown dagger buried in his throat.

'Reilo. Help!' Caelan swiped wildly with his knife, but he caught nothing but air. A boot slammed into his side and he groaned. The links in his back clicked.

Still the voice was silent.

'Forget me!' Dirk's voice boomed across Highdock, waves of azure flame flying from his fingertips. The Sightless was flung back before the onslaught as the Walkers nearby crumpled with misty eyes. A sphere of cobalt fire wrapped the metal giant. Held it. For now.

'Caelan!' Addie yanked him to his feet, cracked her hatchet into a Walker's mouth.

'Addie, where the fuck did you come from?' Caelan ducked around her as she decapitated some young Walker who'd tried to sneak up on her.

'I waited for you outside the Nest. What, you thought I'd just go home? When you didn't come back, and no one flung your head at me, I figured you'd be across the river. Then we saw that pillar of blue fucking fire. Knew it would be you in trouble. So I brought them with me.' She spun and hamstringed a Walker. 'We can talk later. This is a rescue, not a war.'

'They are dying for you.' Dirk was matter-of-fact as he drew a blade from the chest of a Walker. The man didn't bleed. Fog soaked his face. 'They are dying for you and you are letting them.'

'I can't do anything!' Caelan growled. He watched a young Austelli go down under a trio of Walker blades, hacking and grinding into unprotected flesh. The metal stink of blood, of rusty smog tore at his nose. Cold sweat shuddered down his naked back.

'Oh but you could.' The coal around Dirk's throat poured with smoke.

'We need to go!' Addie barrelled forwards, swept a Walker blade around and rammed the spike on the back of hatchet into his chest.

'Reilo is still there. But you cannot hear him. I could cut the gap between you.' The blue-steel arrowhead danced in his fingers. 'Open your memories to one another. Share this body you are both entombed in.'

'No!' Caelan said. He ducked as a Walker swung, but Dirk slammed fire into the attacker's face. He fell with a scream. 'I can't risk losing control. He would *know* me.'

'And you him. The blade-work he earned himself. But he did learn something from me.'

The blue fire around his throat glittered.

'He was a Mindbreaker...' Caelan whispered.

'Caelan, come on!' Addie tore the throat from a nearby Walker. Blood sheeted down her back, down her arms. When had she got cut?

Caelan watched the fight like it was underwater. Everything slowed. So much death. An Austelli went down to the fierce blows of a pair of Walkers. Danni leapt in, rammed her spear through the back of one. The other Walker caught her. Sword lashed out, blade through her throat and sent her slamming into the sludge. Her spear squeezed from her hands and she grabbed the gash in her neck and tried, desperately, futilely, to keep her lifeblood inside.

They had come to save him. And they were dying for it.

No more.

Caelan tore from Addie's grip. He slammed his palm down on Dirk's outstretched blade.

Reality froze. Blades poised mid-swing. Blood frozen in open wounds. One of the Austelli held out a hand, blade pinning his palm to his chest. The Walker's face was fixed in a snarl as he stabbed the weapon home.

All that moved was the blue flame. And the shadow of the Sightless caught inside.

Fog boiled around him. Rolled in waves across the docks, the water. Swallowed everything in a tsunami of white.

But as reality vanished, the Iactura remained.

It filled Caelan's eyes, growing larger and larger until it swallowed the world.

Reflected in that blue silver was Reilo. Broken nose and sunken cheeks. His shoulders were thick, hands delicate and those blue eyes shone with intelligence. Burned with anger. How could they do this to his city? Boots that blackened his streets. Their blades taking aim at his pride.

Caelan knew him. His shadow. No. More than that. Himself. A part, at least. Another man, another life and yet without each other they were both dead.

'*This is not your fight,*' Reilo said.

'But these are my people.'

'*I will not surrender to your control. You're weak.*'

'You can't take it without me. I know what DeSané cost you.'

'*I can wait.*'

'But the Austelli can't. Lend me your strength. And when I die, you can have this body.'

A pause. It felt like a lifetime. '*Then we will breathe together.*' Reilo's fingers reached from the Iactura. Scarred from fighting. A promise of violence. Of fire.

Of memories shared to mask the emptiness.

Caelan reached for him with the same hand pierced by Dirk's blade back in reality.

Reilo's face twisted. He brought his fingers together and stabbed them through Caelan's palm.

A hot knife through an infinitesimal thread. Something severed. And Reilo's experience began to flow into him once again. His skill with a blade seared through Caelan's tired body.

Reality returned screaming. But behind that came something else. Something much more powerful.

He could feel it. On the smog. The Iactura. Dirk had called it hunger, but that word was too small, too human. It wasn't hunger. It was emptiness. A feeling Caelan knew better than his own name.

The silver pillar shone in the moonlight and Caelan finally understood. Not an axe, or a knife. A bridge. Between body and mind, the mist and reality. He sucked down a breath of the smog. Breathe in to forget. Breathe out for remembrance. His lips moved, but he didn't speak the words.

Reality burns. Inhale the memory.

Blue fire burst from the coal around Dirk's throat and raced down Caelan's arm. A serpent of fire, he flung it at Danni.

She screamed so loud the battle dimmed. The coil of fire bit the wound in her throat. Steam and smoke boiled from the hole.

Danni opened her eyes. Gasped a breath. Touched unbroken skin.

A Walker saw her. Raised his blade.

Caelan threw himself at the blackcloak. Dagger slammed into his throat, once, twice, three times. The blood was hot and thick.

A smile curled his lips.

Behind him, Dirk laughed. 'Another Mindbreaker walks again in Arx. Untamed. Lucianus knows his duty. Try to stay alive as long as you can.'

Smoke boiled from the coal around his throat. It spread out behind him, thick as the night, pouring like a cloak from his shoulders.

He threw himself into the Walkers.

The blackcloaks turned, hacked at each other, but their blades found nothing.

In a burst of smoke, Dirk disappeared into the shadows.

And as he did, so too did the fire cage around the Sightless. The metal giant was free.

And its axe was pointed at Caelan.

A hand grabbed his shoulder. 'We're leaving. Now!' Addie screamed in his ear.

'Help me with her,' Caelan said.

'Retreat!' Addie shouted. 'All of you, back to the barge!'

Together, Caelan and Addie dragged Danni into the metal boat. Austelli leapt in beside them. Less than half of those who had come for him.

Addie kicked the mechanism and the barge began to move. A Walker leapt to grab the ramp, but Austelli blades rammed into his fingers and he plunged screaming into the Mucro.

The Sightless slogged through the sucking mud and blood back on shore. An injured Austelli mewled near his feet, until its axe silenced those cries for good.

Caelan met those onyx eyes until the ramp of the barge hid them from him.

The chain dragged them across the river.

'Caelan.' Addie's eyes were narrow, her blood-soaked face creased.

'You saved me.' Danni sat up. Dry blood crusted down her shirt. 'I was dead. And you saved me.' She grinned and wobbled to her feet. 'I am yours until my death. We are yours. Silverspine.' She turned to the Austelli, raised her fist. 'Silverspine!'

They roared with her. 'Silverspine! Silverspine!'

CHAPTER 21

'It was Callisteel.' Mistress Ignis sipped from her porcelain cup, tiny in the shadow of Sam's pint. 'The blade that cut your Father. That cracked his mind.'

'Don't.' Sam crammed her palms into her eyes.

The silence lapsed again. The café was almost empty. Most shops were, ever since the attack last week. The young lad serving had taken one look at the gilded chain around Ignis' neck and fled back inside to hide behind the counter. Sam hated it. Gave her time to think.

Fog in Father's eye sockets. Unspeaking. Eyelids drooping. She drew the lancet from her belt and set it on the table.

Ignis' eyes glittered hungrily.

'Jak was right. This thing is evil.' Her memory of that day was vague, like fingerprints on a dusty windowsill. She could remember the silver orbs, the fresh pain of a lifetime of memory. Ignis' rage. 'What happened to me... is that what Father went through?'

'No, his mind was touched by true Callisteel. He broke before he knew what was happening.'

Sam wrapped her arms around herself. 'Does it amuse you? To watch me stumble around when you already know more than I about that bloody metal?'

Ignis' eyes flashed. 'I do not know how to make it. I was never considered strong enough to be given the knowledge. What it can do is all I know.'

'And you kept it from me until it took my Father's eyes!'

'I can take that pain from you.' Ignis' face was blank. The coal around her neck sparked into life.

Sam paused. 'What do you mean?'

'Your memory. Of your Father. It can be excised, stored in metal.' Her eyes were deep, flaming pools. 'You could forget this ever happened.'

Forget. Like Father had.

'I have to remember this. Else I might do something stupid.'

'Such as?'

'Keep working on Callisteel.'

A breeze rattled the chain between Ignis' earlobe and nose. 'Excuse me?'

'It's better off dead.'

'This is not a time for absolutes. Besides, I have seen your notes. What was it that made Callisteel worth searching for all these years?'

Sam picked the soot from her nails. 'Money, at first. Figured a legendary metal would bring in some coins, make Father proud. That didn't last. He never forgave me for... whatever I'd done to be such a disappointment to him.' Strange. She'd never have an answer to that now. Had she expected one? 'Then it became about the challenge. Not for my ego, but for the metal itself. Unbreakable, eternal. It never had to be a blade...' She sighed. 'Better a childish dream than this reality.'

'You signed a contract Samantha.'

'You can't possibly expect me to keep going.' Sam pushed back from the table, her chair scraping across the concrete. 'Take it. Take the lancet. Do... whatever it is you want to do with it. Just leave me alone.'

Ignis blinked. Slowly, she reached out and took the lancet in her elegant fingers. It vanished swiftly from view. 'Your Father was not the only casualty last night. Jace DeSané had his throat cut. And twelve Walkers lost their lives on Highdock.'

'Silverspine,' Sam said. 'I've heard his name. The Walkers are telling stories of blue fire.'

'He is cruel, Samantha.'

'So are you. Perhaps it is a trait of you Mindbreakers.'

'Silverspine is no more Mindbreaker than a child in a black cloak is a Walker. I am nothing like him.'

'No. You don't leave the bodies behind, do you? A Mindbreaker stole my Father's eyes, and you tell me Silverspine is no such thing... You know who did this to Daddy, don't you?'

For the first time, Sam saw Ignis speechless.

She glared at Ignis' blood red eyes. 'You just want power. If you can't have it through contracts and money, you'll take it through Callisteel and fire and forcing folk to forget everything.'

Ignis' eyes sparked, for just a moment. 'Power exists only because there are those strong enough to wield it. You must be strong enough to break your chains. Else they simply tighten.' She drew a coin from her purse and spun it between her fingers. 'That is something your Forgemaster knew well.'

Sam felt a pulse of panic in her chest. It had been weeks since she'd heard from Jak. She'd just figured he'd been sulk-drinking himself stupid in the pubs south of the river. But now... 'What did you do to him?'

Ignis' smile was bitter. 'It is difficult to become a Forgemaster without hearing something of Callisteel.'

'What does that mean?'

'Have you visited the Iron Market recently? A graveyard. Apprentices and retirees trying to keep the fires burning. Their masters have all disappeared. Without word or warning.' She cocked her head, teeth clenched between her lips. 'Even poor master Carosso who stoked the fire for your test was taken. A pity, we'd worked together for decades. He was very good.'

Something cold coiled around Sam's bladder. 'What have you done to them?'

'We are just trying to see how much they've learned.'

Sam's jaw clicked. 'Can you say a single thing without trying to manipulate me?' She needed to find Mira. She'd know what to do. '

'I am not manipulating you, Samantha. I own you.'

Ignis flipped the coin on to the table. One side was stamped with the Iactura, cracked. Mistress Ignis' sigil.

Ignis gripped her wrist.

Sam squirmed against the nails digging into her skin. 'Get off me.'

Ignis twisted the coin on the back of Sam's hand and held it in place with her palm. The coal around her neck sparked blue and a sudden burst of heat rushed from the metal coin.

'Stop it!' Tears ran from Sam's eyes. The metal was burning, searing against her skin. The smell of cooking flesh, the throbbing skin. Black smoke.

'This is my power. Still think you can escape it?' Ignis blinked. Sweat beaded on her forehead, her eyes pinched.

'Let *go!*' Sam kicked back from the table, toppled her chair and went sprawling into the concrete. Clear liquid dripped down her wrist.

'We are bound, Samantha.' Ignis held up her hand, palm first. A circular brand stood red raw. An outline of her side of the coin, three knotted chains imprinted into her flesh.

Sam stared at the back of her own hand. The Iactura, cracked and broken, was stamped into her skin. Blisters swelled from the edges. She scrabbled to her feet. 'You're psychotic.'

'Consider it a gift. A thank you for your lancet. The only thing that made you worth my time. You will never see me again. But even then, you will remain mine. That brand will serve as a burning reminder that you were never strong.' Ignis finished her tea like it was a social call and left without looking back.

Sam kicked out at the table. Her pint glass shattered against the concrete. The morose server looked out from the window and held up his hands.

'Sorry.' Sam tossed a coin down and took off, the opposite direction from Ignis. She tried to stop from touching the edges of the burn. Felt the round pustules on the edge, pulled against the heat trapped under her skin.

CHAPTER 22

Caelan sat with Ferra on the lip of the smog-scarred wall surrounding Arx. The last two weeks had been… strange. Wonderful. Unnatural. Word about Highdock had spread like crabs in a brothel. For a while, it felt like the whole city was in mourning but then… people had begun to find him. Normal people. They'd not come to fight, not yet. But they'd buy him a drink. They'd toast his success. They'd chant his name.

Not Caelan. The mortal, the man, the fuckup. Silverspine. Something more.

Caelan leant on his elbows, looked out across the sea 'You ever wonder what's across there? Aside from drowning, I mean.'

Ferra nodded, eyes still closed and her hammer resting across her knees. 'Constantly. It's more tantalizing when you've glimpsed it. Old memories I've cut away are often tangled up with it, though I don't get a huge number of visitors that pre-date the Flame Protests. Food and drink are most common, the taste contains the memory. Even one ancient bloke who saw his Da take off in a boat loaded with steel and return home with silk and strawberries and a shipful of things I have no names for. The world is endlessly vast. But not for those who live behind these walls. And certainly not for us.'

'Us?' Caelan tilted his head.

'You can hear it now.' Ferra took a deep breath of the light morning smog and opened her eyes. The Iactura glittered over her shoulder in the distance.

'Faintly.' Like an echo of his own emptiness.

'We all learn how to tune it out. Else it becomes maddening.' She grimaced. 'Except Dirk. I don't think he can. Guess that's why he understands that pillar more than the rest of us. And why he could give you the Fires of Remembrance.'

'Is that what it's called?' Caelan lifted a nearby candle and blew. The wick spluttered and sparked blue.

'One of the great Mindbreaker secrets I suppose.' Ferra shrugged. 'And the chain that keeps us here. The Iactura draws us. Iron to a lodestone. You can stretch your collar, but it brings us all back eventually.'

'Is that how you knew Dirk would be coming back?'

'You are not as afraid of him as you should be.'

'What use is fear?' The blue flame grew, licked at his fingertips. The scars were barely scabbed over, so recently bloody.

'Arrogance. That scrap of power you're wielding, he gave it to you.' Ferra rolled her shoulders. 'You're a child trying to catch sparks from the grindwheel. He knows what it is to burn.'

'And yet still you follow him.'

'He saved me.'

'And made you a Mindbreaker.'

'Did the same to you, and you hate him for it.'

'I don't hate him for the fire. I hate him for slitting the connections in my head until I was barely fucking human.'

'Exactly.' Ferra rose to her feet. 'No one would choose a life lived alone.'

She turned and her clomping bootsteps clanged against the ladder pinned to the inside of the wall. Vanished off into Rustscrape.

Caelan counted for six heartbeats before he fumbled the bloodmetal from his waist again. Four glittering ores. He tossed one in the air, caught it. Threw another. Started juggling. A rather surprising addition from Reilo's skillset.

He licked the smog from his lips. Gently, so gently, he drew a thread of smoke from his blue-flame candle. It felt like breathing, a needle-thin stream of air. He whispered breath between his lips, touched the smoke to the bloodmetal. Felt the memories he'd lost. The strength that loss had brought him.

An eyeless man, looking down from the scaffold.

A hatchet through his spine.

A blade ripping against his palm.

The eyes of dying Austelli, reaching out for him.

He caught them, then slipped his hand beneath his shirt. Silverspine. The axe that metal scar contained.

Gritty wind swirled across the wall.

'*I won't help you kill him.*'

'I know. But that's the way this ends. I'll use Dirk. I'll use what he's given me. Us. But it ends in blood and fire. Just like everything else.'

'*You wanted this reality. To remember.*'

'I wanted to see if I could survive. And I have. Now… what else is there?'

'*Our people.*'

'The Austelli. That heat… it's not me, is it? You love this place like I never could, and yet when I think of them now…'

'*They have become yours.*'

'How much of me is you, now? The fighting, the juggling, the way I kill… Caelan was never that. Now the rebellion, that desperate, slavering desire to put the Sightless to the sword… is that who I am? It feels so real, and yet…'

'*Does it matter?*'

'All I wanted was to survive. I thought that was enough.'

'*This war is the only way any of us survive. Ferra gave you your life, Dirk gave you power, I gave you purpose. We are nothing if not our connections.*'

Caelan closed his too-blue eyes. Kuyt. Addie. Danni. 'We are nothing if not our connections…'

A clunking, gasping sound rang from the ladder behind. Caelan spun, fingers darting to the bloody-tipped knife at his waist, just in time to see Kuyt's face emerge over the lip of the wall.

Blood sheeted down a gash in his forehead. Wide-eyes stabbed at Caelan.

'They found us.'

The foundry was deserted but the scars of battle remained. Silver-edged gouges in the floor. Dusted coals from spilled braziers. Fallen weapons. Blood. Ashes.

Three bodies soaking into the stone. One Walker. Two Austelli.

'They came first thing.' Kuyt's voice was faraway. Soft. 'To capture. The first executions for the new scaffold.'

'Addie?' Caelan asked.

'She'll be the first.' He closed his eyes. 'They knew her by name.'

'How did you survive?'

'I… hid.' Kuyt gestured at the stone walls. 'They're spidered with cracks. Some just a hair, but others are enough to fit a grown man.' He touched the sticky blood on his forehead. 'Almost. That's where the Walkers came from. Burst from the walls, there must be caverns we don't know about. There were just so many of them.'

Kuyt drew his sketchpad from his jacket and knelt beside the corpses. 'Rasha. Ari. You deserved better than this.'

'You coward.'

The word leapt like an ember from Caelan's tongue. He could wish that Reilo said it first, that it was the poison influence of the madman inside his skull.

But it wasn't.

'Excuse me?' Kuyt stood slowly.

'How could you let them do this to us?' Caelan pushed his knuckles into his palm until he heard them crack.

'Let them?' Kuyt's face twisted with a paroxysm of rage. His voice shook the cavern. 'You think I let them? What good would it have done to fling my corpse at the Walker's feet? What about you? Brave fucking hero, where were you this morning *Silverspine*?' How his voice dripped with venom on that word.

'Up on the wall. I can't be expected to baby you lot all day.'

'Doing what?' Kuyt's voice was acid.

An image flickered. Blue fire around his wrist, fingertips dribbling blood. Colour burst in Caelan's cheeks.

'Just as I thought. Never trust a man who doesn't know his own mind.'

'Oh off your high horse old man! You have no idea what I…'

'*I* have no idea? You arrogant little shit. I've known you as long as you've known yourself. Longer! Because I don't forget who you *really* are.'

'I don't forget what's important, Kuyt. I remember you, I remember Addie, I remember those I've killed.'

'Is that all life is for you? A litany of the dead?'

Caelan threw his arms out. 'How are you any different? With your pathetic little pictures, you think a corpse cares if you drew it? Those bodies there were relying on you and you let them die!'

'What do you want from me?' Kuyt's eyes sparkled. 'I know my limitations. I found a crack and crawled inside and wept until the last boot left. And I will have to live with that for the rest of my life. But that's *good*! Good that I'm ashamed. Because I will never leave anyone behind again. Not even you, you little shit.'

'I can take care of myself.'

'Really? Because I remember dragging you from thoughts of the endless waves the last time you lost your mind.'

Caelan snapped his jaw shut. Kuyt was right. The day they met.

It was a cold, quiet day when Caelan decided to kill himself.

The grimy waves of the Mucro lapped at his boots. The factories downriver, long abandoned husks of brick and broken glass, still drained their old poisons into the water. Smog blotted the weeping sky overhead like ink on paper, dirtied the wind with the stink of rust and salt. A gust cut through Caelan's coat like an ice-sharpened razor.

He shivered as he placed the knife against his throat. Death was so final. But he couldn't do it anymore. The cycle was endless. With no past left to forget, he sacrificed all that remained. His memories of emptiness burned away in Dirk's fire. Felt the relief, the rightness it brought. Then the fade. Feeling shame for the very first time, like an ice-pick through his heart. Returning to those blue-fire, violet eyes. Without memory there was no past, no future. Just the endless now.

Caelan steeled himself. Better this way. He took a deep, final breath.

'Want a hand with that?'

Caelan juddered at the slap of a voice beside his ear. He turned to the old man suddenly at his elbow. 'What are you...?'

'Here. I'll start you off.' His leathery hands gripped Caelan's fist, kept his hand wrapped around the hilt of the knife, the blade against his throat. Began to push.

'Stop.' Caelan's eyes widened, but the old man was implacable.

'This is what you were about to do, wasn't it?'

Blood beaded bright on the sparkling blade. 'I wasn't...'

'Wasn't what? Ready? Because you don't come back from that, kid.' His arms bunched, ground the knife closer into a widening gash. 'So if you want it done, best to get it over with.'

'What the fuck is *wrong* with you?' Caelan launched himself backwards, blood sheeting down his chest. Something ignited inside him. A new sensation. An emotion, felt for the very first time.

Anger.

He crunched his fist into the ancient idiot's cheek. The bastard went down with a squawk and a splatter of mud.

'That's going to leave a shitter of a bruise, you ass.' The old man pressed a handkerchief against his face. His face was already purpling. He stumbled back to his feet with all the dignity of a frail bloke who'd just been punched in the face. 'What, you feel better now?'

'No.' The rage subsided like the tide, left him beached in the apathy that had drawn him to the river's edge. 'But I will when you're gone.'

The old man hawked and spat. 'I'll leave soon as you tell me why you're doing this.'

A moment passed, silent but for the whistle of the wind. 'I don't remember.'

'If you don't remember, then why would you ever think that feeding yourself to the fishes was a good idea?'

'If there is a single fish alive down there, I'll eat my left bollock.' The stink of the water was like a chemical cleanse of his nose. 'Besides, I already told you. I don't remember.'

He turned to the old man. Forced him to meet his eyes. The bloke's faced paled in an instant.

'What have you lost?'

'I don't know. I have the basics. I can walk, eat, breathe, shit and piss. I can tell you the days of the week, how many copper coins can be broken from silver, what cards make a winning hand in Veritas. Perhaps there are some fragments of history hidden in the darkness, all jumbled up like shards of glass in a clear bowl. But beyond that, I am just a body and a name. Existence is so intense.' Those last words came out in a spray of bitterness and suddenly he didn't feel like talking anymore.

The wind picked up and Caelan wrapped his arms around himself. Dabbed the blood from his throat. Fingertips to ears he shivered. But he couldn't bring himself to move. He just stood there and watched the water.

'Let me ask you something old man.'

'Not "old man". Kuyt.'

'Kuyt. Why did you come to me today? Do I know you?'

Kuyt snorted something close to a chuckle. 'You should be so lucky. No kid, I was just walking by. Saw what you were going to do. Figured I should step in.'

'No one else stopped.'

'Their loss.' Kuyt grinned, then winced and brought a hand to his bruised cheek.

'Sorry. About your face. I haven't felt anger before.' Caelan closed his eyes and blew out a breath. 'But I think I'm ready now.'

'We are none of us ready for that.'

'You ever tried to tell an emotion that it's lying to you?'

'Emotions are easy, I could make you feel again.' Kuyt rubbed his chin. 'A speech perhaps? I was an actor, I know the best ones. Andi Aranesci from *A Tale of Branded Gentlemen*? He bemoans the cruelty of passing on one's pain to those left behind, those who don't deserve it. But that might not convince a man who can barely remember his name.'

Caelan blinked slowly.

'Perhaps Madam Akali's soliloquy from *In the Chamber of Smoke*. I doubt you'd appreciate the meter, but her lamentation on no longer greeting the sun made me weep the first time I heard it. But then, I paid my dues in tights and dresses long ago. It sounds much better at the right pitch.' He sighed. 'Truth be told, there are countless words written to stave off the void. Some insightful, some ludicrous. But words are cheap, so how about we make a trade. A year of my life. For the rest of yours.'

'What does that mean?'

'Come stay with me. For a year. And a day, for good luck. Afterwards, if I fail, then I swear on my heart and mind that you will have the chance to end it. By your hand, or mine.'

It was a good offer. Far better than he deserved.

He reached out his palm. 'By your hand or mine.'

Kuyt grinned and gripped his wrist.

'But you failed, Kuyt. Six, seven months in and what have we got to show for it? Bodies and blood. I'm so sick of it.' Caelan rubbed his eyes. It would be so much easier to stop. To fade away and let the blue fire take him to bliss.

'Who have you become, Caelan?' The pain in Kuyt's voice was worse than the anger had been. 'I knew who you were when I found you. I've seen that lost kid before. I've *been* that lost kid before. But now... sometimes you are drowning in apathy, ready to hurl yourself in the river just to hide from your own eyes. Other times, you're so desperate to mutilate and murder your way across the city just so the Austelli would know your name.'

'You wanted me to fight. You could have helped me.'

'What the fuck do you think I've been doing for all this time?' Kuyt's voice was truly hurt this time. 'After the Sightless cut you, I watched you *die*. Then you took a breath and I wept for you. You came back to me and I thought, I *thought* you'd found a reason to keep breathing. But that's the problem with your bloody magic.' His indignation split the air. 'You cut connection with the real world and no wonder things get difficult.'

'What do you want, Kuyt?'

'I...' He slumped to his knees. 'I want Addie home safe. I want you off the blue fire for good. I want the Austelli to be able to live their lives again.' He buried his head in his hands. 'I never wanted all of this.'

Caelan looked at him. And deep down, beneath the shadows and the apathy and the anger, he felt something. Not a fire, not this time. Roots. The ties that bind.

'Okay old man.'

Kuyt sniffled. 'What?'

'Okay. You want Addie home safe. You want me off the fire. You want the Austelli back. It's time I made good on our deal. You promised me a year of your life for what's left of mine. All I need is one more day.'

Caelan held the pine-pitch torch and let the Fires of Remembrance burn. Smog darted between his lips, flavoured the air. The flames burned bright. Illuminated the shadows, even in the Nest.

'Quill!' Caelan shouted. 'Get out here before I smoke you out!'

Eyes flashing in the torchlight. Bodies scurrying. A wall of metal broke from between the buildings, spears, axes levelled at Caelan. Torches glittered in fists held overhead. Hundreds of grizzled, scarred faces. The Nest had come for war.

Caelan stood before them alone.

'So you did decide to die.' Quill stepped through the line, lash twirling in the dust at his feet. 'Life on your crusade getting tiring? I heard of your defeat on Highdock. And now everyone who stood with you is to be executed. I said you wouldn't like the cost. The things we have to do.' He looked up between two close-clustered rooftops.

Caelan followed his eyes to the body that hung there. Bright green eyes and a three-pronged spear dug through her chest. Suzi.

'Your enemies are my enemies,' Caelan muttered. 'I know the cost.' He closed his eyes. Felt for the torches held aloft. Sucked down a thick lungful of the smog. Blew it out.

Blue flames burst through the alleyway. Torches dropped into the muck, but the flames grew higher, brighter. The line buckled as people dodged the fire licking at their throats.

He stepped towards Quill as he shielded his eyes, swung the whip. It curled around Caelan's arm, bit deep into his skin. 'You are looking for open war. I will give it to you.' He stepped closer, dragging the spikes deeper into his flesh. 'A city burning, isn't that what you wanted?'

'We won't die for your bleeding heart, Silverspine.'

Caelan hissed another breath, sent the gouts of blue flame higher. 'The Walkers are already attacking. With us gone, how long before they decide to end you? It's coming.'

The look on Quill's face told him he knew.

'One more fight. And I will hand you the ashes of a dying city. What you do with them, is up to you.'

'And what would that cost us?' Greed sparkled in Quill's eyes.

'Blood and fire.' Caelan lifted his arm, watched the blood drip from his elbow. 'When has it ever been anything else?'

CHAPTER 23

Ruairi wiped the rain from his face with manacled hands. The pitter patter made the street sound like it were pissing. Thick, rolling smog soured his breath.

Grimy prisoners packed Highdock, wound together like a nest of eels. Walkers stalked around small groups of chained-up bodies. Ruairi's own coffle were seven-strong, with him slumped right at the back.

He'd heard the fighting from his cell. Despite the rain, the mud were still tinged with pink. The weight of ended lives sucked at his feet.

Some Walker lass moved down the line, winding a chain around them.

'You'll burn for this.' The lass locked in front of him held herself tall. Her eyes were different colours, one red and one green. A thick, jagged scar ripped across her throat.

'That'd be something. Least I'd be warm.'

A stumbling clank of chains rattled beside the line of prisoners. And for some reason, they all went just a little quiet and watched. A lass in leather armour were marched down the road, hood cinched around her neck and chains thick between her wrists, ankles and throat. Scabs and half-healed cuts darted down her arms. Three Walkers stood in tight formation around her.

'Addie...' the prisoner said.

'Turncoat,' the Walker lass said.

'She made the right choice.'

'Reckon she'll agree when the axe falls?' The Walker shook her head and moved on down the line.

The chain jerked. Icy water ripped at his ankle and his neck sent a vicious little sting right down his back. Every tug felt like his bones were scraping together. Nose leaked like a tap in the sharp air.

One last bit of agony then. Before the end.

He'd thought about it. A lot. Not much else to do in a cell. Figured exactly how it would go. Useless legs will shake. Slobbery lips will quiver. Eyes will leak and piss will stream down his legs. He were gonna beg and bawl and screech for a Ma who weren't there.

And then he would die. Strange how that thought were always so... empty.

The Walkers yanked them up before a row of barges, six gleaming buckets filling with rain. One already slushed across the choppy river. The others were cramped full of waiting Walkers. The chain had no sympathy. It dragged them in.

As soon as the barge got going, one prisoner near the front bent and emptied his guts against the deck with a juicy splatter. The river surged, every icy-spike of spray piercing down Ruairi's back. Pins-and-needles the size of blades.

The rock of water against the hull made him think of Pa.

The barge thudded soft against the opposite bank. Chain tugged and Ruairi crept forwards, duckling after Mama. Almost slipped on his face when they yanked him over the lip and into the muck of the street. A vine of pain strangled his hips.

Ruairi kept his head down. Watched his toes squish and squelch against the muck, did his best to dodge the pebbles and rocks and shards of glass. Tried not to think about the last time he'd walked these broken streets. How he'd done this to hisself by opening his stupid mouth.

A gob of spittle splattered near his feet. He lifted his eyes.

People crowded the street, silent and staring. Hundreds of them, clustered between buildings, in alleyways, even kiddies cramped together on the rooftops.

'You bastards!' Some bloke with a burn-scarred arm lobbed a rock at one of the blackcloaks, missed by a whisker.

The Walker levelled his blade at the would-be-attacker.

'Gonna kill me?' the bloke snarled. 'Was Highdock not enough for you lot? Or would you rather wait for me to starve to death like our Nattie did?'

The prisoner lass in front of Ruairi bared her teeth like a wolf. 'We grow hungry together. But there is one man who stands between us and starvation. One man who murdered that traitor Jace DeSané. One man who ran Highdock slick with Walker blood. One man who brought me back from death itself.' She threw her head back, defiant. 'One man who will burn Arx again and return the smoke and ashes that have always been ours.'

A murmur in the crowd. Then a shout. An outpouring of noise.

'*Silverspine!*'

'Guy, blade down,' The Captain ordered. 'All of you, get them to the scaffold, you're not here to talk!'

The pace picked up and Ruairi were stumbling just to say in line. Sweat boiled from his armpits, felt like he were chipping at his bones with every step.

The chain fell slack and the line stopped, so sudden that Ruairi had to slap his hand against a nearby building to keep from smacking into the lass in front.

The scaffold were burning.

A bonfire blazed in the middle of some mud-soaked square. Yellow flames licked across varnished wood, a heavy crash as planks clattered to the muck. Three bodies hung from the platform. Flames seared their black cloaks. The smell of charring flesh curled through the smog-soaked sky. Rain sizzled against the blaze.

'Captain. What do we do?' The Walker lass' voice shook.

'Adira Signasti's body isn't here. Fuck. Fuck!' The Captain kicked a brick down an alleyway. 'We go back. There aren't enough of us for this.'

They turned. But the road behind them were blocked. The grim-faced, rain-soaked folks stood en-masse behind them.

'These are our streets, Walker.' The burned bloke's voice were firm.

'Blades down!' the Captain shouted as a Walker went for his sword. 'No chance with that many. We go around.'

'Where?' one of the walkers asked.

The captain rubbed his palms down his face. 'Nest.'

'Captain, with all respect have you lost your fucking mind?'

'I'm not dying out here like a dog. Do you see a better option?'

No one spoke.

'Then get these fuckers moving!'

Ruairi weren't quite sure how to feel. Couldn't pretend he were upset that the chopping block were blazing away. But the sweet smoke of burning bodies rankled something fierce. And he didn't reckon being ripped apart by the mob would be a more pleasant way to go.

Truth was, he were just terrified. Didn't leave much space for anything else.

The chain dragged tight again. Ruairi stumbled through the streets, rain pelting like icicles. Roads blocked off by folks lobbing rocks, bottles. The pace picked up until all of a sudden, the light vanished. Buildings clustered overhead, so tight it were like the shadows reached out to grab them. They scuttled over a tiny bridge, river water lashing below.

'You took your time.'

A new voice. Ruairi peered through the darkness.

A man stood before the Walkers. His shirt were tight to his chest, but sommat were off about it. Didn't sit normal. He held his arms out in welcome, then turned.

The back of his shirt were missing. It tucked around his waist and left his spine open to the elements.

A metal pillar shone where his backbone were supposed to be.

CHAPTER 24

'You!' The Captain stood tall, blade in hand, but there was no hiding the quaver in his voice. Fear *seeped* out of him.

Caelan flicked his dagger with a flourish taken straight from Reilo's memories. A simple threat. Confidence poured from Reilo and he drank it down like medicine. Yes. This was right. Certainty. Power. Silverspine was a danger so let them see it.

'You are brave, aren't you?' Caelan stepped forwards. 'I wonder if the others are just as brave? Listen.'

The sound was faint, but unmistakable. Metal crashing. Screaming. Fires crackling. The sound of death.

Caelan grinned. Rain drizzled down his hair. He could taste the liquid smog on his cheeks.

'Guy, Dart. Citadel. Warn DeKeita.' The Captain gave a wave of his hand and a pair of Walkers ran. 'You know I'll have to kill you. Obviously.' He held his blade level. Rain pinged off the copper surface.

Caelan weighed the tip of the dagger between his fingers. 'I already died. Twice. It didn't stop me.'

He threw the blade. Right through the Captain's throat. The man dropped without a word.

'Drawing Walker blood in the Nest again. It has been far too long.'

Caelan found his lips drawn into a smile. Sweetly maddening, images of so many dead blackcloaks rolled through his veins. He knelt and pulled his knife free from the dying captain.

Without a thought, he threw himself at the Walkers.

CHAPTER 25

Ruairi huddled against the wall. The sound of clashing metal burst in his ears.

The line of prisoners stretched across a broken building, thick stone digging into Ruairi's back. Three Walkers charged to engage, but that lass who had fastened the chains still stood firm. The final guard, her sword were plenty big enough to keep order.

At his side, the prisoner with the mismatched eyes grinned like her teeth were dripping poison. 'I knew he'd come for us.'

'So what?' The Walker tried a grin right back, but her face were tight and her eyes glittered with panic. 'Three-on-one and we've got swords. The man is already dead.' She raised her blade. 'You are one of his. I should do my part too.'

In an instant, she swung.

Ruairi watched the blade. Everything slowed. The Walker's muscles bunched, a cold competency on her rain-soaked face. Raindrops split against the cutting edge. A tiny mote of light soaked through the copper like liquid heat.

In that timeless moment, he saw what would happen. The blade piercing the lass' throat. Layer after layer of flesh peeling apart in an instant. Bone and gristle crunching beneath the weight of the sword. Hot blood steaming in the cold air.

He couldn't bear it.

'Stop it!' Ruairi pulled the chain between his manacles taut. With the feeling of broken bones grinding together, he threw himself in front of the blade. The sword struck in a shower of sparks, inches from his face. 'Please.'

'Get. Off.' The Walker grunted. She tried to pull her blade back, but it were caught fast. All she did were drag Ruairi closer. Not enough space between them for even the rain to find.

He tried to scrabble back, but the floor were soggy and his ankles were stiff. They went down with a squeal and dragged the whole chain with him.

The world flashed around him. Black and brown and red. Dark edges. Faded light. Twisted limbs. Kicking and screaming. A rock smashed into his face, sliced the inside of his nose. Rain soaked his vision until he swiped the soggy muck from his face.

That lass prisoner sat astraddle the Walker, manacle chains wrapped tight around her throat. Her blade just out of reach, no matter how her fingers twitched.

Ruairi couldn't move. The bunched-up chain locked him so close he could feel the heat from the Walker's skin. Her eyes bulged. Her face turned red, purple.

'Don't do this. Please...' Ruairi whimpered.

'Shut it, you don't get it.' The prisoner growled. The veins in her neck twitched with effort.

She began to twist.

The chain tightened and Ruairi were dragged even closer. The Walker's eyes were desperate. But there were nothing he could do.

CHAPTER 26

Caelan's arms burned.

He grimaced, leaking blood. The trio of blades whipped closer. Lashes of fire in the freezing rain. Reilo was skilled, but three on one was bastard odds.

'I don't suppose you fancy facing me one at a time?' He dodged a strike and flung his knife.

It missed. The blade clunked, hilt first, into the wall. So much for that. He was running out of options. Only the narrow street was keeping him alive.

A flicker. The blade leapt at his throat. Caelan slammed his back into the wall to avoid the cut. Another blade swept at his legs. He skittered back. Further away from his knife.

The trio of Walkers advanced.

'Help me!' Caelan hissed.

'Why would you throw the fucking knife? Find a weapon!'

A Walker slipped and Caelan lunged. He ripped forwards, curled his fingers around the hilt of the Walker's blade. Sweat froze on his forehead. Blood pounded inside his skull.

The Walker's fist slammed into Caelan's stomach.

He careened backwards, spittle dribbling down his lips, falling on to his arse.

Bollocks.

Sweat dripped with the rain into his eyes. If he ran, those blades would be through his heart before it had the chance to beat again. Something was going on behind the Walkers, some struggle between the prisoners, but the trio didn't even turn.

'Fuck this.' He'd done his best, but no weapon against three swords was impossible. 'Kuyt! Quill! Hurry the fuck up!'

A window shattered overhead. Quill leant out, bow gripped tight. An oily cloth wrapped beneath the copper head of the arrow. Kuyt knelt beside him and struck a spark against the rag. It filled the alley with orange light.

Quill drew back the bowstring and fired. The arrow thumped into Caelan's chest.

Blood bubbled down his lips but behind that curtain of liquid rust, Caelan smiled. He sucked in a deep, blood-soaked breath. Smog slipped into his lips and he blew it out gently.

Blue fire blazed around him.

CHAPTER 27

On his knees, Ruairi wept.

The Walker were dead. The other prisoners were busy freeing themselves, but Ruairi clung to his chains.

Felt like he belonged in 'em.

Blue fire roared through the alleyway. People screamed. A man laughed.

The Walker lady were still warm. Blood soaked Ruairi's sleeves.

'Kuyt!' The lass prisoner grinned.

An old bloke scuttled over. Whiskers cuddled up across his face and white hair were crusted to his scalp with sooty rain. 'In the flesh. Sorry I let them take you, Danni. Never again. Let's get you lot somewhere safe.' He looked down to Ruairi. 'And you lad. Come on. There is nothing more to be done here.'

The Walker's dead eyes shone. Burnt brown and lifeless.

'He's not right.' The lass glared at him. 'Head's gone. It happens. Leave him.'

'He saved you,' one of the others mumbled. Bloke with a small fringe of hair rubbed his wrists.

Ruairi stared at the blood on his hands.

'Don't you worry about him,' the old bloke said. 'You lot, go to ground for a few days. Find somewhere safe. We'll find you when this dies down.'

The lass shrugged. 'We won't be hiding much longer. These are not flames that will die so easily.' Her eyes trained on Silverspine for a long time. That smile were filled with longing. 'With me!' She gestured and led the other prisoners away.

The old man knelt beside Ruairi and slung an arm around his shoulders. 'It hurts, doesn't it? Men like us, we aren't made for a life of blood. No shame in that lad. But you gotta get up again. Else it's all for naught.'

For a moment, the old bloke sounded so much like Pa that everything stopped. The thumping. The fire. For a single moment, everything were gonna be okay.

Then a burst of that phantom blue fire incinerated the wall beside them.

Ruairi snapped his head up. Silverspine stood in the middle of the alleyway. Bursts of fire streamed from his hands, ribbons of burning, boiling, bloody flame. It lanced through the buildings, the walls, the bridges. Ash and rubble fell like hollow seeds from a dying tree.

'Silverspine, that's enough!' A short bloke leapt from a window out in front and marched up to the blood-soaked fire-singed murderer.

'Quill. I thought you were willing to pay the cost?' Silverspine's voice were off. Words flickered through his lips, like each one were said by someone different. A huge hole pierced the middle of his shirt, blood dribbling across the cloth. But the skin underneath were unbroken. Just a huge knot of a scar.

'The Nest is burning!'

Silverspine curled a fist. Blue flames leapt through the buildings behind him.

'I didn't kill them. Does fire count?' Silverspine's voice twisted. Soft. He were talking to hisself.

At his feet, the three Walkers began to move. Ruairi blinked away the rain. Their eyes were gone. Blue-fog licked from the empty sockets.

'What are you talking about?' Quill said.

Silverspine blinked. Came back to himself. 'I promised you blood and fire. This is what you wanted.'

'You have no fucking idea!' Quill tore a whip from his belt. Vicious thing, silver spikes and lashing leather. 'You've done more damage than the Walkers ever managed!'

'A hatchet in my spine couldn't kill me. An arrow to the heart didn't do it. You think you can?' The fire rose over Silverspine's shoulder. 'Run away Quill. Scrabble here in the muck and filth. That, I give to you. But the rest of Arx is mine.'

Their eyes locked for a moment, Quill's whip quivered in his fist. 'This ain't done.' He turned and left him there.

Silverspine watched him go. He turned his terrible eyes on Ruairi. 'What's going on Kuyt?'

'This one just needs a moment. Help me with him.' Kuyt grunted and heaved Ruairi to his feet.

Ruairi gurgled. Fire and irons through his body. Snorted snotty breath. Even with Kuyt at his elbow, he shook with effort.

'You alright kid?' Kuyt asked.

'No.' The world were an ocean of pain and he were drowning in it. 'Just gimme a moment.'

'We don't have a moment!' Silverspine's voice were right by his ear.

'Balls to it Caelan, just get going.' Kuyt shook his head. 'It's not like you need the help of an old coward. Addie is waiting for you.'

'Oh come the fuck on Kuyt.' Silverspine scratched at the back of his neck. First time the bloke had looked human, despite his soul-blue eyes. 'What if there are still Walkers around?'

'I can't leave him.' Kuyt just shrugged. 'Guess I've got a soft spot for kids who can't save themselves.'

Silverspine gestured, moved his lips but not much came out. 'Fine,' he eventually managed.

'Fine,' Kuyt said.

The broken-plate silence held for a moment.

'Fine.' This time, Silverspine spat it. He spun on his heel, no looking back, turned a corner and vanished.

'Just us now.' Kuyt jammed hisself into the space under Ruairi's armpit. 'One step at a time, eh?'

They passed through the alleyways. Every now and then, the old man took a scrap of paper from his shirt and squinted at it. 'Blackened stars, but the kid doesn't draw pretty. So this one leads to our foundry,' he muttered. 'This one near Ferriway...'

'That's where your Silverspine bloke were going, right?' Ruairi asked.

'Aye...' Kuyt chewed his cheek. 'I kept him alive, once. Caelan could have been a good man. But Silverspine...' The old man scratched his neck. 'I followed the Ant once, and we lost everything to this fight. I won't let Caelan go the same way.'

Ruairi laughed. 'The Ant! Now he were a real hero, I wouldn't even be here if he hadn't saved my Pa. I always wanted a piece of that. Turns out, that hero occupation is a mite too dangerous for my liking. Figure I'll be much happier back home. Just point the way.'

Kuyt scanned his bit of paper. 'It's not far.' He gestured at one of the more sizable bridges. 'Follow that to the end, two alleys down to the left, then back around on yourself. You'll see the gate.'

'I can make it.' Ruairi tested his ankle. 'I reckon he's gonna need your help more'n I do.'

The old man looked at him for a moment. 'Just make sure you hurry.' He gripped Ruairi's wrist. 'Thanks lad.'

Ruairi nodded and the old man raised a hand in farewell.

Cold, tired and sore, Ruairi put one leg in front of the other. Time to get home.

CHAPTER 28

Caelan slipped on the sludge of the Ferriway. 'Addie? Addie are you...'

He found her amidst a circle of corpses. Hatchets, Kuyt had kept them hidden when she was taken, dripped with blood. Rain soaked her hair.

'How many people have died today, Caelan?' Addie's face was slack. Her eyes were lost.

Thunder boomed overhead. For a moment, the Ferriway was lit with pure, white light.

'People die in rebellion, Addie.'

Her eyes pierced him. 'People *die*? What happened to you? The first time you saw an execution it almost broke you. Even with no memories, you knew the weight of a life. Where did that go?'

On impulse, Caelan's hand fell to the pouch of bloodmetal at his waist.

'Of fucking course.' Addie's scorn was sour.

'You weren't complaining when I killed those Walkers to save *your* life.' Caelan's jaw clicked.

'But you didn't kill them, did you?' Addie's voice was sharp. 'The fire did. You just took their eyes.'

Shame speared through Caelan's chest. 'For you.'

'I never asked for that.' She looked off over the water.

'Then what do you suggest? We give up? We're winning!'

'You think this is a *victory*? First Highdock, then the foundry, now the Nest. This isn't rebellion. It's self-inflicted genocide. Everyone who followed us is dead, captured or worse.'

'This is what you wanted.' Caelan fixed his eyes on her. 'You led the Austelli whilst I was dying on a slab. You bloodied the Walkers to save me. You got captured!'

'I made a mistake!' Addie's voice stole the strength of the wind. 'We were wrong, Caelan. The Flame Protests fought for something. For food and iron and a city broken by industry. We are nothing but violence. A legacy of ash.'

'The Flame Protests didn't go far enough!' Caelan tore through Reilo's memories. 'The Ant was soft. He let them talk and lie and lure him over the river. Bleeding hearts lead to bleeding bodies. You can't play the system that's designed to control you. You have to break it open and start again. If we stop now, then all that death will be for nothing.' A rumble growled through the sky and moments later, a flash illuminated the Mucro like the river was on fire. 'If the memory of what this cost hurts you, then destroy it.'

He grabbed Addie's wrist and slipped the dagger from his belt.

'Get off me.' Addie tried to yank her hand away, but Caelan squeezed her wrist.

'Get a fire going.' He placed the edge of the blade against her index finger and pushed. A bright bead of blood welled beneath her fingernail.

'Caelan, stop it!' Addie crunched her forearm into his hand and broke from his grip. 'What the fuck is wrong with you?'

'With me?' Caelan shook his head. 'Don't be so fucking precious, you've sacrificed to the mists before.'

'Once! And it wasn't my choice. My old captain tried to shove his fingers inside me at parade inspection. I resigned, took a barge across the river. He followed. Smashed my face in with a brick. I managed to kill him before I bled to death.' Addie rubbed the scars on her cheeks. 'It was only luck that a Mindbreaker found me.'

'Who? Dirk?' Caelan asked. Something like jealousy swirled in his heart.

'It was me.'

Ferra's voice was almost lost in the storm. The coal around her throat spat puffs of smoke against the rain.

'You never told me,' Caelan said.

'You're not owed my past just because you sacrificed your own,' Addie said.

Caelan grimaced.

'I am assuming you called me here for something a little more important than your little spat?' Ferra said.

'Do you still stand by what you told me, the day we met? That I could come and find you when I realise that...'

'Pain alone cannot fill that void in your head.'

'Exactly. But Arx can. My people can.'

'*The blood of every Walker can.*' Reilo's voice quenched steel inside his mind.

'I need your help. Both of you.'

'What else is there?' Addie said.

'The river. So long as the barges run, we'll never be free of the Walkers.' He gestured to the links of cast iron that glittered on the banks. 'These chains span the river. We have a hammer, an axe and fire. If we break them...'

'Then the only way across will be the Nest,' Addie said.

'And Quill is hunkered down there like a tick in livestock. I made sure he's angry.'

'Why would I help you?' Ferra asked.

Caelan almost bit his tongue clean off before repeating Dirk's words. 'Because your enemies are my enemies. And because I control the Fires of Remembrance same as you. You won't be alone here.'

A lazy smirk flitted across her lips. 'I've heard that before. But I do so enjoy being lied to. If you have a plan, we better hurry.' Ferra pointed across the river. On the other side, black-cloaked figures were piling through the smog. 'Best way to break a chain is to snap the solder. Impossible when the things start moving.'

'Ferra. Can I use your fire?'

She took a long time to nod.

Addie held her hatchet over the chain. Ferra squinted through the rain, adjusted the angle a touch. She looked at Caelan.

He sucked in a breath of the smog. Filled himself with emptiness and blew smoke between his lips.

'*Reality burns. Inhale the memory.*'

A coil of blue fire leapt from the coal around Ferra's throat and wound around Caelan's arms, cupped in his hands. He held them against the chain. Felt the bite of hot metal.

'Now.'

Ferra brought her hammer down on the back of Addie's hatchet. The vibrations bit into Caelan's hands as the chain link shattered in a single blow.

One down.

The three of them moved through the chains. The crunch of metal, the ice-sharp snap, the warming, teasing flame. Chains snapped one after another. But it was slow going.

With just one chain left, a barge began to move across the river.

Ferra groaned and stepped back. 'Damn it.'

Caelan glanced up at the barge. He wiped the sweat from his forehead. 'Just one. Even if they've packed it full, we're talking ten, fifteen Walkers. We can do this. Together.' He looked at Addie.

She met his eyes. Her face was unreadable. She tossed one of her hatchets into the river. Breaking the chains had mangled the edge. The other flickered between her hands. 'One last fight.'

Ferra stepped forward. 'I'm fighting too.'

'Why?'

She glanced at Addie, then back to Caelan. 'Because before I was a Mindbreaker, I was born on this side of the river. I had a name that's long been lost and there were people who knew me. If I fight with you perhaps I can be known again.'

They spread out along the bank and watched the barge draw closer. Caelan felt his heart beating in his chest. Slow. Methodical. Reilo's advice whispered to him and he drank it in. Strategies for taking more than one enemy. His memories made it seem easy.

Caelan pierced his fingertips with his knife. The coal around Ferra's throat flickered blue and he sucked in the smoke. Threads of blood pooled in his palm, cooled into bloodmetal. The fear of facing three blades in the Nest, the certainty of his outnumbered defeat, excised. He slipped the bloodmetal into his pouch.

Confidence roared loud in the back of his skull. A lazy smile drained across his lips.

Oblivion replaced fear for all of a single, blissful heartbeat.

The barge squelched into the muck. The back ramp descended in a groan of rusted metal. Thunder speared the sky overhead and illuminated the Iactura, far in the distance.

The ramp splashed into the dirt and Caelan's spine burned. A single figure stepped free of the barge. Blue-silver armour shone beneath the rain.

CHAPTER 29

Ruairi were sodding lost.

He limped slowly. Felt like his legs were encased in ice. Every breath came with a sharp stab of cold air. The big street were odd quiet around him. Well, except for that damn thunder. Every boom had him jumping half to heaven. At least there were no one around to see him twitching like a toddler.

'Hopalong! There you are.'

Ruairi turned. 'Fetch! No, you get away from me.' He stepped back, palms outstretched.

The bloke heaved a heavy breath. 'Solder my arsecheeks lad, how does a kid with legs like yours move so fast? I was following you up until that Silverspine nutter started getting stabby, didn't figure it'd take all that long to free you once he was done!'

'Well, it don't matter now, does it?' Ruairi said.

'Maybe not, but if you keep going that way you're dead.'

The words fell from Fetch's mouth. The soot-soaked rain dribbled black down the meagre fuzz of fine hair at his temples and his shirt were skewiff. There were blood on his arms. Didn't look like he'd had the best of days.

'What d'you mean?'

'You're on your way to Warmarch Street, back on the other side of the river.'

'This bloody place! I just want out.' Ruairi would have kicked the sodding wall, if it wouldn't have felt like breaking his arse open like an egg.

'Why do you think I'm here?' Fetch grinned.

'Why?'

'To get you out you moron!' Fetch slapped him on the back.

'Bugger my arse Fetch, don't *do* that!' Ruairi felt jelly-tears punch his eyes, like his whole body were being gnawed on. 'Why would I trust you? Only reason I got locked up is because of you.'

'It's a good question.' Fetch's face lost its smile. 'I've done and will do worse. But I'm here. I found you. And I promised you wouldn't die.'

'I just wanna go home…' Ruairi murmured.

Fetch shrugged. 'Well you can try and find the road on your own it if you want lad. Nothing wrong with that. But you'll be killed. Sure as the sun rises in the morning.'

Ruairi twisted his neck. Thunder stabbed in the distance. Lightning boomed overhead

'I can help you.' Fetch held out his hand.

Ruairi slapped his hand away. 'You better.'

CHAPTER 30

'This is futile.'

'Try something helpful!' Caelan shouted at himself. The Sightless' axe whipped out, just missing his side and sending sludge flying.

'Focus!' Addie slammed her hatchet into the Sightless' wrist. He shrugged her attack off. 'Ferra, how do we fight that fuck-off axe??'

'Only the head is Callisteel,' Ferra shouted. She swung, but the Sightless stepped contemptuously around the strike. 'Parry the haft. Or it'll cut through your blade as easy as it does your mind.'

The Sightlesss spun. Caelan threw himself out of the way. He wracked his brain, but there was no way he saw them breaking through that armour. Even Reilo was at a loss.

'The fucker killed me. If I could have beaten him, he'd already be dead.'

The Sightless lunged for Addie but she danced aside, her hatchet a blur of metal. Ferra stepped in and met the shaft of the Sightless' axe with her hammer. The impact sent her sprawling away.

Caelan burst forwards. His knife wouldn't do much, but momentum on the other hand...

He crashed into the Sightless' back and forced it off a step. A shockwave smashed through his arms. The Sightless shoved back and Caelan was thrown aside. The giant stepped in and swung its axe down.

The haft smashed into a hatchet. Addie stood over him, weapon across her shoulders to hold back the blow. Blood dripped down her arms.

'Addie get clear!' Caelan shouted.

She threw the Sightless' axe back and yanked Caelan to his feet. 'No heroics, idiot. We take him together.'

Caelan nodded, an instant before the Sightless' gauntleted hand smashed him away.

It charged at Addie. Mud flew from the armoured boots. Its axe flashed and Addie ducked. She swung. The Sightless caught her blade in an armoured hand. Tore the weapon from her hands. The shaft of its axe lashed out and crunched into her. She flew back, her leg slamming into the broken wall of a nearby building with a sickening *crack*. Her eyes rolled back.

'Addie!' Caelan roared and pounded at the Sightless.

The giant dropped its axe and grabbed him. Metal fingers clamped shut around his neck. Lifted his from the sludge and held him, helpless as a doll, over the Mucro.

Caelan panicked.

He scrabbled his fingernails against the Sightless' hand, but it was like a mechanical vice. His knife clashed harmlessly off the metal fist. No escape. Already breath was hard. A noose around his neck.

Ferra raced forwards, her hammer held over her head and aimed right at the Sightless' arm. That much weight behind her attack and even armour wouldn't stop her.

The Sightless twisted and slammed a fist into her chin. The gilded cage around her throat tore open and the coal fell to the mud. Ferra smashed down in a spray of slime. Her hammer spun from her grip and blood bubbled between her lips.

The Sightless squeezed.

Caelan's heartbeat rushed in his ears. Vision began to fade. Red dots swarmed in his eyes, dancing around the sight of Ferra's coal slowly extinguishing in the muck. A thread of smoke rose with one final sizzle. The rain was warm.

He sucked barely an echo of a breath through purple lips. The fading smoke laced his tongue, the taste of an ember down his throat.

Memoria formed for a moment. A twilight sky pierced by the Iactura. Sat atop it, feet dangling like a boy sat by the docks, Dirk looked down on him. Watched him die.

'*Reilo, he learned from your escape last time. Best way to end a Mindbreaker. Stop their breath. I can't save you again.*'

'*You. Promised. Me. Vengeance.*' Reilo's thought boomed through the fog.

In reality, the Sightless squeezed tighter. No breath. Darkness flickered.

'*Without salvation, what else is there…? Perhaps I can give you just one last breath. Let us see what you do with it.*'

Dirk stood atop the Iactura and raised his arms. An endless sky of silver orbs boiled around him.

'*Reality burns.*'

The manifest memories slammed into the Callisteel pillar. The mist vanished.

Thunder struck the Iactura. The sound of an angry god slamming its fist against the world. Blood dripped from Caelan's ears as fire burned the sky open. Blue flames boiled across the sky and a blanket of smoke poured across Arx. Spears of lightning crashed through the smoke.

In the cloud of falling ash, Caelan glimpsed a pair of violet eyes.

The Sightless' grip slackened, just for a moment, and Caelan sucked in a life-giving breath. A tiny scrap of smog dribbled down his throat.

'*Attack!*'

It was ugly. He smeared his sodden hands against the Sightless' mask. No clasps, no buckles. His wet fingers slipped across the metal.

Caught on the chip in its onyx eye. The one from Addie's hatchet, that day on the scaffold. Almost invisible in the rain.

But it was loose.

Caelan dug in with his fingernail. Twisted against the fracture, pulled and prayed. His nail cracked and bled. Fresh scabs opened up on his fingertips. The gemstone shifted by a hair.

Steel fingers tightened around his throat.

He scratched, scrabbled against the stone. Felt it twist and squirm as another fingernail ripped open. The gemstone broke free.

The eye beneath was blue as his. Frozen smoke.

Sightless.

In a bolt of self-loathing, Caelan rammed his knife into the soulless eye. The giant roared in pain.

Then he was flying through the air, flopping and spinning. Caelan slammed into the ground, winded but alive. Breathing hurt. He rubbed his throat with a wince.

A maelstrom of fire swirled in the sky above him. Acrid smoke stained the rain. Blasts of thunder ripped the clouds.

He wobbled to his feet.

With twitching fingers, the Sightless ripped Caelan's knife free and flung it to the sludge. The bloody mess of an eyeball swirled with smoke as the wound closed.

'Impossible,' Caelan said. 'Even for a Mindbreaker. I pierced your fucking brain.' He forced the words his torn throat.

The Sightless lifted a gauntleted hand to its face. Something *clicked*. The mask fell to the blood and slime of the dock.

A young man. Ashen hair. And ice-blue eyes.

'What are you?' Caelan shuddered.

'I am what you are becoming. A metal body, an empty mind. You are a crude copy, driven by madness and emptiness, but beneath it all we are the same. Men who sacrificed who we were so we could kill.' The Sightless lifted its axe from the mud and shook the muck free. Flames burned the sky overhead. Thunder leapt between the clouds.

Caelan's bloody hands swept over his ridiculous costume, but his knife was gone. He cast about in the mud for something, anything.

The handle of Ferra's hammer glinted in the smudge. Just out of reach. It might as well have been across the ocean.

That terrible axe rose once more.

'Fucking die!' Addie screamed. One leg was crooked behind her, blood sheeting from her knee, but she leant against it all the same. She sliced the storm, hair whipping through the wind, and smashed her hatchet into the back of the giant's arm.

It did nothing. The Sightless turned to her and slammed an armoured boot into her broken leg.

Addie screamed, loud and terrible. Her hands clutched at air.

The Sightless pushed down. Harder.

Caelan filled his lungs. The smog oozed down his throat, his nose, filled his chest until it felt ready to burst open and reveal his shaking heart. He filled himself with aching, endless emptiness.

Blood dribbled from his fingertips. Blue fire burned the sky.

Caelan ran forwards in a cloak of ashes. He pulled Ferra's hammer from the slime and swung it with everything he had at the Sightless' face. His muscles tore. He burned through the memory of the pain.

The hammer sank into flesh and bone with a sickening pop. The Sightless' nose caved into a black cavern of gurgling blood, its cheeks split down to the bone. Its eyes leaked milky white.

'I. Will never. Become you.' Caelan swung again.

The Sightless roared in wordless agony, stumbled back.

Towards the Mucro. An armoured boot slipped on the edge of the river.

Caelan grinned. 'You don't get to burn.'

He slammed Ferra's hammer into the Sightless' chest. Metal crashed against metal and the Sightless fell, dragged into the waves by the weight of that blue-silver armour. Its legs sucked into the swirling waters of the Mucro, arms flailing against the bloodslick bank.

Caelan lifted the hammer. 'Are you afraid to die?'

'I am afraid...' the Sightless mumbled through mangled lips, 'for those I leave behind.'

Caelan swung the hammer to the sound of thunder.

It slammed into the broken nose, the pulped-open cheek. The Sightless' grasping hands slipped free from the bank and the armoured giant sank like a stone beneath those endless waves.

It was over.

Rain, cold as life, fell on Caelan's face. Smog wisped around his lips. His throat was sore and his back a scrabbled mess of pain, grit, slime and blood.

He threw back his head and laughed.

'Don't laugh, Caelan. I don't want to remember you like this.' Addie's face was pained. She limped with a clearly broken leg dragging behind her.

'What do you mean?' Caelan asked.

'That. mine.' Ferra's voice broke through the smog. A black ball of broken bone and blood swelled against her jaw. She held out her palm.

Caelan handed her hammer back.

The Mucro burst in a welter of froth and filth. A pillar of flame blazed from the riverbed, split the water and seared the air. Icy water sliced Caelan's skin.

Ferra breathed deep. Bruises, cuts, blood all faded and disappeared. Her jaw snapped back into place. The smog swarmed her and when it vanished, her wounds were gone. She held her hammer in one hand once more. Easy.

'What was that?' Caelan tried to suck the smog down himself, but his torn and blood throat rebelled. He hawked a cough instead.

'The Sightless. Perhaps that is how long it takes to drown?'

Caelan chewed his lips. Maybe. But then why, in that glimpse of the riverbed, had he not caught sight of the creature's armour?

'You won,' she said. 'I did warn you.'

Her hammer leapt for Caelan.

He dodged aside, rolled through the muck. 'Come the fuck on, you think I'd fall for that. I've been waiting for you to turn. Only Dirk would bother saving me just before ordering me dead.'

'*It wasn't you he saved.*' Reilo's voice was triumphant.

'Not even the Sightless could kill me,' Caelan roared at Reilo, at Ferra. 'It will take more than a lonely apprentice Mindbreaker and a long-dead madman inside my head.'

'I know.' Ferra cocked her head.

The cold metal of a hatchet sliced through the back of his leg.

Caelan howled. The snap of his muscles tearing followed him down into the mud. Water from the Mucro splashed around his shoulders.

'I'm sorry, Caelan.' Addie spoke softly. A burst of light, Ferra's hand on her shoulder. Her leg straightened and snapped back straight. The scrape on her elbow vanished.

No.

Caelan scrabbled back. His leg was agony. Even small movements sent spears of light through him. His breath came so quick, he couldn't hold it. The smog danced from his lips, tantalisingly out of reach. 'Addie. Not you.' Stupid tears formed in his eyes. 'We could have turned the tide today. We won! Those bastards over the river would have listened to us, they would have...'

'This was never about victory Caelan. It was about survival. You could have died a hero, the man you so almost were.'

'There is no heroism in death. I saved your life!'

'And I yours. Now I have other people to save. Your fire is too hot, Caelan. When you set fire to the past, you incinerate the future.'

'You'd rather work with Dirk?' Fuck how it hurt. His leg throbbed.

'It was never about him. It was about you. What you could have made from the life he left you with. I can't trust you Caelan. No one can.'

Ferra stepped in. 'You should be proud. You killed the Sightless. Don't worry. We'll let everyone know it was you that ended the beast. Isn't that what you wanted? To be remembered? Your name will live on. Even if you won't.'

She smashed her hammer into his stomach. Pain clawed at his insides. It screamed through his body. Ribs shattered. Organs burst.

A pink tear rolled down Caelan's nose. Blood splattered between his lips. Black rain fell across his face. The sky overhead boiled with soot-soaked clouds.

'Fire destroys. That's all it can do.' Addie's voice was soft. 'I want to save more than just ashes.'

'Addie. Please,' Caelan whispered.

She turned and left him there.

Dying alone again.

CHAPTER 31

The Iactura shimmered under the winking eye of the moon, high over the Citadel. Smog scoured its unblemished surface. Light flickered across the metal and the brand on the back of Sam's hand burned. She went to scratch it.

'You'll scar.' Mira snatched her hand away.

'I can't help it.' Sam's shoes slipped on the gravel path but she couldn't tear her eyes from the sky. A thunderstorm that struck the Iactura and set the sky on fire. Sod knows what could happen next.

'Yes you can.' Mira frowned as they made their way towards the gates.

Something was wrong with her, even if Mira refused to talk about it. The worry line over the bridge of her nose was etched permanent now and it had been an age since she'd last spouted some election nonsense. Cynicism didn't suit her. It made her seem… smaller, somehow.

The Citadel courtyard clustered with black brick buildings. Some of the old lessons barked in the back of Sam's skull as she tried to put names to them. The Hall of Laws, with a domed roof and a single door. Ardent of History, the low-rise with amber-tint windows.

The Midnight Chamber, where the Governors met under the shadow of the Iactura that broke from the roof.

'They should have invited us. Father was…' Sam began, cut herself off with a grimace.

'At least it's a public funeral.' Mira shoved open the gilt-chased door.

Five chairs arranged around a table. Soft wood and dyed leather seat covers, the air smelled like the wings of long-dead moths. Stained glass windows reflected the moonlight across a carpet rich as blood.

Behind the chairs, the Iactura rose from far below the ground. A knife through the heart of government. Bolts of blue skittered beneath the silver surface. It flickered with stolen lightning.

They approached the wooden railing. A small gate held them back from the Viceroys. Four chairs were filled, but the fifth was empty. They didn't so much as look over.

'Us next,' Walter DeWhit spoke around a thick cigar poking free from a wild, orange beard. 'Unless we do something now.'

'There *is* nothing. DeSané was...' Leanne DeSüle leant across the table, her iron curls quivering. 'For all his flaws, he was an excellent accountant. The ledgers are pristine, and very clear. We don't have the supplies to feed those across the river and the Walkers.'

'Then we let some go,' DeWhit said. 'The barracks are fit to bursting, it's...'

'We cannot weaken the Walkers. Not now,' she snapped.

'Then what happens next?' DeWhit held out his hands.

'People will starve,' DeSüle said. 'And because of that, next winter will be easier. There is no alternative.'

Silence fell on the room. Was this really how they thought? Sam looked over at Mira. Her nails dug into the wood of the railing. Usually placid eyes burned behind her glasses.

'We're playing into their hands, these new Austelli.' Var DeKeita spoke softly. His hair was grey, but despite his age his arms were thick with muscle. 'You've all heard of that Silverspine lad, what he did on Highdock.'

'You told me you had his people captured, Var.' DeSüle spun on him. 'I sent the Sightless.'

'I saw their chains myself this morning,' DeKeita said.

'You can't execute an idea.' Andross DeGaya spoke up for the first time. 'It doesn't matter who leads them. The people will fight if the only other option is to starve. And we deserve it.' DeGaya rubbed his temples. 'How did it ever come to this?'

'Then what do you suggest, Ant?' DeKeita's voice dripped with venom on that last word, but DeGaya didn't even seem to hear it.

'Open the gates, open the ports! We were a trading city once. We still have the forges, in a fashion. Let us work metals as we once did, and maybe...'

'For such an old man, your history is dire.' DeSüle's voice was like a storm. 'We built those walls to keep Dirk's influence contained. I will not let you break that now. I would rather bury this city than leave it to him.'

'We know exactly what *influence* Dirk had on you,' DeWhit spat. 'You and your Sightless.'

DeSüle glared at him.

'Who are they talking about?' Sam whispered to Mira.

'No idea. Just another fucking secret.' Her own whisper was remarkably less quiet. Unfortunately, that meant the Viceroys' eyes were drawn firmly over to the pair of them.

'We are in mourning!' DeWhit's voice blustered. 'What do you think you are doing here?'

'Viceroys of the Upper Senate, my name is Mira Iudex and this is Samantha Acarris.'

'Girls, it's really not the…' DeKeita began.

'No.' Mira's voice was sharp as a slap. 'Don't even start. Not girls, women. And not just women, but Arxian women with all the rights of citizenship. Section three, article eight B of the Ashen Accords states that any voting member of the citizenry might prevail upon a member of the Upper Senate to hear a petition relating to emergency action. Such action includes, but is not limited to, death, arson, treason and memory theft.'

When she was finished, her chest was heaving. Sam goggled at her. What was going on?

'Don't quote statutes at us.' DeSüle's amber eyes glowed in the reflected light of the Iactura. Steel-haired, she was bedecked in ugly, iron jewellery. Chunky bangles and heavy earrings. 'We don't have time for this.'

'Then you will make the time!' Mira's voice broke on the shout. 'My request is fair and lawful, which is more than can be said for those seats you've conned your backsides into.' She reached into a pocket and drew out a slip of paper. Sam glanced over her shoulder. Was that a map? It was an odd one. Thin as a snake and covered with X's.

'What is this?' DeGaya looked nonplussed. He picked up the paper and studied it.

'This is how you never lose the little kingdoms you've drawn your-selves across our city. Impossible to vote out councillors when you just re-draw the map to keep them in power.'

'Leanne, is this true?'

She snarled at him. 'You think an old War Criminal with no heart left to fight would remain here without some…finesse? They might hate you across the river now, but they hate us more.'

'Change the system from the inside… People bled to get me here.'

Despite everything, the look on his face smote her, just a little. Sam was nothing on politics compared to Mira, but she knew how deadly a crack in the façade could be. Andross DeGaya, hero of the Flame Protests, had spent his life on a lie.

It was a pain she recognised well.

'And unless you want me to share these with every family in this city, to litter the streets across the river with proof of your lies, you'll lis-ten to my friend and help her get her Father's mind back!' She scrubbed her face with her hands.

'I… am sorry, Miss.' DeKeita flicked his eyes at the others. 'But it doesn't work like that. Some of my Walkers were afflicted as well. When the memories are gone…'

'The mind collapses.' DeSüle's tone was all business. 'There is noth-ing to "get back". When did he succumb?'

Sam tried to take a breath, but it was difficult. She'd known. Of course, she'd known there was no going back. But that scrap of hope was all she'd had for so long. When it tore, she felt it. 'He was… a councillor. He lost his eyes protecting DeSané.'

'Oh miss.' The shared grief in DeGaya's voice was genuine. 'What was his name?'

Sam snapped her head up. The taste of acid burned across her tongue. 'You should know it. You all should! He worked for you! You should be mourning him as much as his boss.' Her teeth clicked together. 'He wasn't a great man, but he deserved so much better than to work for people like you.'

'I am surprised that you are both so comfortable speaking to us like that,' DeSüle said. 'Having come all this way. Alone.'

'Petty threats?' Mira slapped her hand on the railing. 'Is this what you've become? No. No of course not. You always have been. Little petty rulers of little petty houses so afraid of losing that meagre scrap of power that you've put us all on the pyre to keep it!'

DeSüle stood up. She gripped the candle on the table beside her like a knife.

A Walker burst into the Midnight Chamber. He was drenched and the stink of smoke and rust followed him like a cloud of flies. Blood ran down his arm. His stomach dripped black and his face twisted in pain.

'Apologies, my lords, my lady.' The Walker's voice was tight. He leant against the railing, blood spilling on the polished wood.

Sam and Mira leapt out of his way.

'Don't be stupid.' Var DeKeita scurried over, opened the small gate. 'Sit, sit down. Dart, isn't it? What's going on?'

'Head Captain, I will stand.' The Walker cradled his hand. His fingers were broken and crushed into a swollen fist. His whole body radiated exhaustion, but his legs did not waver. 'The river is lost.'

Silence fell on the room like a blanket of snow.

'What do you mean lad?' DeKeita asked.

'From the start.' The Walker gulped a breath. A splatter of blood leaked from his stomach. 'My squad met Silverspine. Captain Ramsey sent Guy and me back for reinforcements but we were betrayed. A Walker. He knew the words, but as soon as we turned our backs his blade was through Guy's throat, my stomach. I crawled to the river. There was a body there. Metal spine. I don't know if he was breathing. Took the last barge across.'

Sam could hear the blood pounding in her ears.

'What of the Sightless?' DeSüle's voice shook between the attempted neutrality.

'I found...' The Walker took a step and crumpled. He fell over the railing and splattered it with his blood.

Var touched the Walker's wrist. 'Dead.'

Then something began to glow, deep within the ruins of the Walker's hand. His eyes burst into flame and smoke replaced them.

The dead man smiled and stood back up.

'*The Midnight Chamber. Such an honour.*' The voice grated from his throat. Heavier than before. Unnatural. '*Walter. Var. Ant. Leanne.*'

Var DeKeita took a step back. 'What... who are you?'

The Walker turned to Var and smiled. Blue fire flickered from his lips. '*Dirk.*'

Andross DeGaya shook his head. His eyes were wide and white.

'*Truly, I apologise for the gruesome necessity.*' The Walker-corpse reached under his shirt and drew back a hand shining with gore. He shook his head. '*The Walkers fought well. A credit to you, DeKeita. But that is over now.*' The corpse clasped its hands behind its back, strolled towards the table. Blood leaked like spilled wine down to the carpet. '*Have no fear. I've no desire for your little chairs. Simply remain here and do nothing. That is all I ask. If you do, you have my word that you will survive this.*'

DeGaya's eyes were tight. 'I look forward to seeing you executed.'

'*I'm afraid that might be more difficult than you imagine.*' The blue-fire corpse opened its crushed hand.

The Sightless' mask fell from its nerveless grip.

Leanne DeSüle threw herself from her chair, scrabbled over to the mask. 'No. *No!*' Her voice tore open like a fracture in stone. 'How could you do this to him? He still remembered you!'

'*Since when has that ever stopped me?*'

Everything happened in a blur. The Walker leapt forwards. His hand jumped towards DeSüle's throat. She didn't have time to move.

DeGaya did.

From somewhere he produced a short-sword and leapt at the Walker. His strike was so fierce it separated the head from the body. As soon as the cut connected, the blue fire eyes faded. The Walker's head rolled to the carpet.

Sam fell to her knees. Hot bile stung her throat. The headless body branded against her mind. So much she didn't understand. But the blood and scent of death speared her. Her limbs were heavy, aching. She grabbed for Mira's hand.

'Guards! Guards!' DeWhit shouted, like a child seeking his mother, but no guards were coming.

'Andross...' DeSüle said in a shaken voice. 'Thank you.'

DeGaya flicked the blood from his blade with a practised flourish. 'Come. We need to get to the Mucro. Var, with us. Your people need you.'

'You'd fight with the Walkers?' DeKeita asked.

'I'd fight for Arx. For my people. Dirk cannot be allowed to hold the river. His Fog-Eyes fought in the Flame Protests... Whatever evils you've done in my name, he would do worse.'

Var DeKeita took a deep, shuddering breath. 'You're right.' Together the pair pushed through the doors. For a moment, they looked like young men. Leanne DeSüle followed close behind. Her eyes burned.

Walter DeWhit looked with wide eyes at the empty chairs around him. He jumped to his feet, stumbled over the corpse and barged past Mira, muttering to himself.

'Do nothing it said. Do nothing. Fine. Fine.'

'Sam.' Mira grabbed her sleeve. 'We need to get out of here. Who knows if it will... get up again.'

Sam nodded. Except... the Sightless' mask. It lay against the carpet. Light reflected off the surface.

Blue-silver. Callisteel. She raced over, scooped it up.

'Come on!' Mira hissed.

Out in the courtyard, the cold wind slapped some sense into her and some red in her cheeks.

Thick, oily smoke rose in the distance. Flashes of blue light lit the night. Black fog boiled through the sky and ash fell like snowflakes.

CHAPTER 32

The air in the foundry were burning. Ruairi held his hands to his ears as a column of liquid fire roared up from a pit dug deep into the stone, ignited in the air and sent gouts of flame ripping through the night.

'It's not right being here, Fetch.' He wiped sweaty palms down his sides. 'What is that stuff?'

Fetch leant on a balcony made of sheet metal, peering off into the caverns. 'Heartfire. Hotter than a blast furnace. I'd stay away. Warms a bloke up though.' Rubbed his hands together. 'Relax kid. He always knows where I am. Shouldn't be too long.' Fetch took a big gulp from a flask. 'Want some? Firewhisky, all the way from Narisé. The bloke cut me a deal, I've got a whole bottle of it back home.'

'Come on Fetch, what're you doin'? I gotta get home. I gotta tell Pa and Ma'll need my help with the preserves. Weather's already turned. And I don't have no more clothes, and Abi will...'

'Kid. You're babbling.' Fetch capped the flask and tucked it away. 'You should really enjoy the time before he gets here. Wish I had.'

Fetch snapped his jaw closed. Smoke, thick and black, rolled from the pit of heartfire and a silhouette wavered through the ash.

A change in the air. Like reality were catching up to itself in a shift.

A man stepped through the haze, dressed in black'n gold. Tall, close-blonde hair and expressionless there were an... aura that surrounded him. A presence that drew the eye. Like at the single stationary point in the sky, when all else were moving. A gilded cage hung around his neck, coal burning orange inside.

His eyes were violet as the sunset.

'It's you.' Ruairi's voice wavered. 'The rider from the woods. Dirk, right? They almost killed me just for knowing you. Last I saw you were on fire. Reckon it'd be better for us all if you'da stayed ablaze.' He whirled on Fetch, failed to ignore the creak in his back. 'This is who you brought me to see?'

Fetch's eyes were downcast. He didn't speak.

Dirk gave a lazy smile. 'I swore I would remember you.'

Heartfire crashed like waves into the air. A column ignited and azure flames seared the smog.

Ruairi's dry tongue stuck to the inside of his cheek. 'The blue stuff, is this you? You planning on melting anyone else?' Throw the catch back, but the rabid dogs of terror were chewing through his tailbone. Didn't realise he'd crept on back until he banged into the railing. Nice little pebble of agony ground between his hips.

'Such a question. Yes Ruairi. This is all me,' Dirk said.

Footsteps. A lass clomped down the stairs cut into the rock. Thick ponytail stuck to her back with rain and a wicked-sharp hatchet gleamed at her waist. Ruairi rubbed his head. Figured he recognised her from somewhere, but he couldn't quite drag it out.

'Addie. I am glad you made it.'

'Adira,' she said.

'What say your people?'

'They were never mine. But the Austelli will fight. I told them… told them Silverspine died fighting the Sightless. That they ended each other.'

'Silverspine's been killed?' Ruairi whispered to Fetch. Felt weird. The bloke had obviously been short a catch or two, and that arrow in his chest couldn't have helped. He hoped the old fella, Kuyt that was it, were doing okay. Guess he hadn't got there in time.

'So it would seem.' Fetch's voice was quiet.

'Silverspine isn't dead. Not yet.' Dirk's eyes glittered in the firelight.

'Ferra smashed a hammer into his guts. If he's not gone yet, he's only got a few heartbeats left.'

'Oh that heart will beat long beyond tonight. Ferra knew you would never be able to kill him, so I gave her her orders. Silverspine fades. But Reilo remains. And the Austelli will need a new leader.' Dirk offered his hand. 'They followed you once already. I was there at Highdock.'

'And we lost. I'm done fighting. Give it to Danni. She'll kill whoever you point at, so long as you tell her Caelan wanted it.'

'Why surrender now?'

'Because things have to change. Silverspine's legacy is my legacy. The city needs re-making, I won't help it burn.'

'Think of the lives you can protect.' Dirk's eyes glittered. A small blue flame flickered on his palm.

'No.'

'Would you die because of him?' Dirk's voice changed. The high-brow lilt melted and steel shone beneath. 'Because of guilt?'

'What do you know about guilt?' She gripped her forearms with white fingers. 'You're the same as he was. You've forgotten what it means to be human.'

'No, Adira. I have not.'

The coal flickered blue and Dirk sucked in a mouthful of smog. He blew it into her throat.

Ruairi felt his chest go cold. Instinctively, he held his breath. Memories of a burning clearing and smoke forcing its way into his throat boiled up like a lobster pot. Weren't going through that again. What were she seeing, trapped in the smoke?

Adira blinked past blue-flecks in her eyes.

'The voices. How do you stand it?' She took a step back.

'I could never forget them. The will of those who have died is what guides me. Their sacrifice. You see it too, don't you? The weight of all of those lives.'

'I don't…' She gnawed at her lips. 'It hurts.'

'Guilt is powerful. I can teach you how to wield it. What it takes to truly mend what is broken. A mind. A body. A city.'

She scratched a fingernail down the edge of her hatchet. 'I'll fight. The Austelli have earned my blood ten times over. But it will be as me. My guilt, my failure. Those are who I am. I won't lose that.'

'We are all as we are remembered. I will see you again.'

She left.

Dirk whipped back to Ruairi. 'So sorry for the interruption. I have a gift for you.'

'What d'you mean?' Ruairi tried real hard to clamp down on the shudder in his voice.

Dirk's violet eyes glittered. 'I am a Mindbreaker. I can cut away memories of pain. When a memory is gone, the physical effect of that memory disappears.' He lifted his trouser to show off an unscarred knee that had once held a soot-soaked arrowhead. The same arrowhead that had almost got him killed. 'You have seen what I can do.'

'What's that got to do with me?'

'I can take your pain away.'

Ruairi licked his lips. Sweat poured down his arms. The room were sweltering. He took a breath and a sliver of hurt slashed at his arse.

Pain.

His constant companion. A knife beneath the fingernails. A screw turning in his feet. Breathing, moving, eating... it were always there. Sure, he could force it aside. Do his best to ignore it. But that were near impossible when even sommat as small as tripping over made it feel like his bones were made of broken glass. To be free of that.

Sommat sharp clicked near the top of Ruairi's shoulders. 'You're not the first to offer. Few years back, some travelling surgeon come to visit the house. She'd just stopped that outbreak of ribsnap fever in Vos and were doing house calls on her way back. And she looks at me. Pulls out this whacking sharp knife and says she's seen bodies like mine before. Big book, size of a boulder, she flicks through and shows me some bones and red strings that are apparently what we all look like inside. Says if she cuts here and here, then I'll be able to walk straight. Couldn't get rid of the pain the whole way, but would'a eased it something major.' He shook his head slow. 'All it would cost was my ability to go for a shit on my own terms. She showed me this bag they'd stitch into my side, that someone would have to help me empty.'

Fire whipped from the pit, hotter'n hot. Ruairi watched the drops fall.

'Pa were furious when I said no. Even Ma wouldn't look at me proper for weeks. They thought I were scared. And they were right. But not of the cutting. I were scared of losing one of the few things I could control. I didn't want more help than I already needed. It weren't even about the bag, one of Pa's mates has one and he's a bloody riot with a beer down him. Besides, it hurts like fire to squat for a shit as it is! But you can hide a bag under a shirt. And other folk don't have to see it. And that's me.'

He scratched at the knot on his back. Didn't like touching it. The thick, chewy flesh, wet and clammy skin. 'Sucks I were born like this. No bones about it. But I'm not alive just so folk can pity me, or change me. I'm here cause I deserve to be, same as you, same as everyone whose legs work proper. Walking fine ain't worth it if it ain't me doing it. Keep your fire to yesself. I'm going home. And I'm gonna fight with Pa, and let Ma tut at me, and tell Abi she's gotta set the table.'

The bloke looked at Ruairi for a long moment. 'A pity.'

He lashed out and gripped Ruairi's shirt front, dragged him to the pit of heartfire.

'Come on,' Fetch said. 'He doesn't…'

'Would you rather take his place?' Dirk pulled a knife from his belt. No, not a knife. It were that arrowhead, lashed to a knife handle.

Fetch looked at Ruairi. His eyes were full of fear. He shook his head.

'I sa… saved you. Why are you doin' this?' Ruairi blubbered. The fire boiled beneath him.

'You were born beyond these walls. The Iactura barely knows you. With the Sightless dead, we have a straight shot at Aer and I need an untainted mind to do it. I'll put your pain to a far more productive use.'

Ruairi groaned. He could feel the heat under his skin. Crisp and sharp. 'Fetch, help me! You promised.'

The bloke didn't look at him. 'I promised you wouldn't die. And you won't. I'm sorry kid.'

'Our healing relies on forgetting, but not for you. I can't heal something that has always been there. You'd become a Fog-Eye. But I can help you remember.' Smoke began to pour out of a pouch at Dirk's waist. He ripped it open, a chunk of black-red metal steaming into mist inside. 'Aer keeps every memory she's taken from generations of Walkers that have come through the flames. You have no idea what I risked to steal this for you.'

The mist formed into a familiar figure. Younger than he'd ever seen him, but the resemblance was uncanny. The thick hair, the curling shoulders.

Pa.

'Your Father's memory. His Walker training. For as long as you fight, your pain will be gone.'

The metal chunk melted beneath Dirk's fingers, wound around his wrist, the edge of that arrowhead knife.

'Reality burns, Ruairi. Will you inhale its memory?'

Dirk plunged his knife into Ruairi's chest. He screamed and liquid metal poured down his throat.

CHAPTER 33

Caelan shivered in a puddle of blood and rainwater. Everything hurt.

'You're dead.'

A tongue of flame roared down his spine and something shifted. Caelan felt himself sinking. Not into darkness, but into himself. Shadow hands tugged at him, pulled him back.

Someone else blinked Caelan's eyes.

'Reilo? What are you doing?' Caelan tried to speak, but his lips were no longer his to control.

'When Dirk removed the gap between us, I knew this is how it would end.' Reilo's voice spoke from Caelan's lips. 'You were never worthy of our fire, of my knife. We are all forgotten in the end. It is time you found the oblivion you are so desperate for.' He grabbed the corner of the building behind them and pulled Caelan's body forwards.

It felt like a comet struck him. If he had eyes, he would have wept. If he had a body, he would have bled.

As it was, he just hurt.

Blinding, mindless agony thrashed through him with every movement. Inch by inch, Reilo dragged Caelan's body across the Ferriway. Fingered his needle-sharp blade from the filth. A river of blood spread out behind him.

Reilo placed the blade against Caelan's throat. 'Either rid this body of your tiny scraps of memory. Or we die here.'

'Reilo. Don't do this. It will destroy me. Think of yourself! How long can you survive with a madman inside your head?'

Reilo curled his fingers around the hilt. 'You know what this blade is called? Misericorde. A merciful death. Isn't that what you've been looking for since the moment you woke up with those empty eyes?'

Yes. It was.

'No! Not again. Put the knife down, son.'

The power of a memory. Caelan saw Kuyt's face, mirrored inside his mind. The riverbank, that urge, that hope. It gave him his body back. Pulled the knife from his throat one final time.

Reilo bellowed his frustration. He faded, but not far. A dark, serpentine presence coiled around Caelan's heart.

'Caelan… Caelan!' Kuyt splashed through the mud towards him, a tight-gripped torch throwing shadows across the walls.

Caelan blinked. The corpse of a smile slumped across his lips. 'Kuyt. Glad you are here. So I can die. As myself.'

He watched Kuyt's mouth move, watched the tears fall, but the words vanished into the void. It was just as well. There was nothing to say to a dead man.

Caelan turned to the sky. Black clouds hung overhead, reaching out to claim him. He counted his heartbeats. When his final breath came, he savoured it. The taste of Arx, sweet soot and a salt-tinged sky. Cold, crisp wind and the muted tang of rust. The sharpness of the smog down his torn throat.

'We burn. Reality remains.'

He spoke to the city itself. To the Iactura and the foundries. To the dead. To Addie and Ferra and Dirk and Kuyt. To himself.

Caelan's eyes rolled shut and that last breath rattled from his throat. The torch in Kuyt's hand burned blue.

Caelan crossed over into Memoria. The Iactura rose beside him. He stood on solid fog beneath the faint light from a handful of silver stars in the twilight sky.

'*You failed Caelan!*'

A body rose to confront him. A shadow with a familiar face. Reilo's jaw was cleft with fury.

'*You think I want to be bleeding out in a gutter?*' Caelan spat his sour thought like a mouthful of fire. '*You were supposed to help me.*'

'*I held back the void!*' Reilo raised his hands. Tiny threads of shadow sparkled on his fingertips.

He ripped his hands down like claws.

The twilight sky tore open and a web of gold blazed overhead. Threads and quivering tendrils connecting the silver orbs, impossibly fine. A surging, breathing network of spiderlight connections. '*My life, my memories, that anger you so despise, it's me. It's all that is keeping you from falling into a Fog-Eye. And I did it despite you ripping holes in your own mind! Did you never wonder why Dirk shoved my dying breath inside your head? Only a Mindbreaker could have done this. Only me!*'

Inside the golden threads, faces formed. Caelan recognised them from Reilo's memories. Revolutionaries. Warriors. The Ant. The thickest thread, the one that was bound to the Iactura itself, reflected Lara's eyes.

The child Reilo lost. The reason he became who he was. And the reason he had to die. Madness is easy. Grief is so, so much harder.

'*Ferra knows metal. Ignis' soul is fire. Aer commands the breath in our lungs. Dirk speaks with the Iactura. And I... I know connections. What it means to be part of something so much larger than yourself. The only Mindbreaker to truly fight for this city. The only one to die for it. I was the only person who could save you.*'

He sliced his hand through the mist. Overhead, one golden thread cut and a single silver orb began to spin away from the others. For a moment, Caelan could see the memory it held. Danni grinning at him, her knife pressed against his flesh as they sparred. That ember he felt.

And then it was gone. The silver orb faded into the darkness and the memory was lost.

'*So it ends with emptiness. I thought it would.*' Fear turned the sky red.

'*I will not end with you.*' Reilo drew so close their noses were almost touching. '*I want your body.*' Shadow fingers gripped Caelan's throat.

His touch was the burn of ice against naked skin. Caelan struggled, but it was useless. The pain had finally caught up with him. The agony from his body, the searing weight of Reilo's shadow, it was too much.

'*You will forget yourself,*' Reilo projected. '*I will take your body. And you will fall silent.*'

Reilo dragged him to the Iactura. The bridge between reality and the mists. A golden thread lashed out from high overhead and snapped around Caelan's neck, lifting his feet from the fog. He hung before that impossible pillar. In its reflection, he saw his body back in reality. Skin leaking like a wineskin. Leg torn like tissue paper.

Kuyt cradled him and wept.

'*This is what comes from saving me.*' Caelan reached out to wipe the tears from the old man's face.

He touched the Iactura and a silver orb darted from the sky. The Ferriway. The knife against his throat, that desperate desire to end it. The warmth of Kuyt's intervention. That smallest of reasons to take another breath.

A glimpse of kindness at the end. The gift of a few more months of life. Gratitude swept through him like a cold wave.

Reilo's hand pierced through his back and into the Iactura. Caelan screamed, wordless. Skin held to a burning brand, a needle through his eyes.

Back in reality, his spine began to glow.

Caelan almost let it end. It was so tempting. He had fought and lost and failed. It would be so much easier to just let go.

But what had Reilo done to him? All that anger. All that blood. Yes he had a purpose, but with this cost…

Kuyt would never forgive him for letting Reilo take his body. For giving up.

'*Then the old man will die.*'

And they would both be forgotten.

'*You never understood the emptiness. Even when you lived in it. But I do.*' Caelan drew the memory of the riverbank over his palm. No matter how much time passed, it was always there. A rotting corpse beneath the waves of his mind.

Kuyt had given him something that day. Call it hope. It alloyed with his pain. Hope is what made it hurt.

The Fires of Remembrance burned cold beneath the silver orb.

Caelan ripped the memory from his own mind and slammed it into Reilo.

The orb blazed against the shadow's arm with the sound of hot metal and Reilo yanked his hand out with a scream. Shadows distorted his face and he flung himself back through the mist. The golden rope around Caelan's neck faded.

'*Pain alone cannot kill.*' Reilo's hands burned blue and he ripped flaming fingers through his throat. They gashed out silver, pieces of memory.

Caelan felt it vanish. Kuyt's intervention, the deal they made. The pain and the hope. It almost broke him. Standing on spiderwebs atop an endless chasm waiting to fall. A piece of his heart torn out.

Then it was gone. Forgotten. But Caelan felt weaker. Oblivion usually bought respite, forgotten fear lashed back as strength, the rightness of reality connected. This time, he just felt... numb.

Reilo stalked through the mist once again.

'*When we cut our memories, we have to re-live them. Let's see just how much you can take.*' Caelan summoned another memory from the sky. Fresh and dripping, the feeling of Addie's hatchet through his leg, the slam of Ferra's hammer through his stomach. The betrayal that burned beyond any physical agony. The Iactura *pulsed* as the orb shot out and dug into Reilo's chest.

He howled and the mist parted for it. Blood dripped from Reilo's eyes as Caelan forced him to relieve the agony.

'*Not. Enough!*' He tore a flaming hand through his chest and yanked free the shadow-scabbed silver. With a roar, he crushed it between his flaming fingers. Forgotten.

'*Thank you.*' Caelan found a grin. '*That was what killed me. I wouldn't have survived the memory long enough to cut it out. But now it's gone, I...*' Caelan turned back to the Iactura.

Back in reality, his body was still not moving. His stomach still oozed. His leg still bled.

'*When you gave me your memories, you gave me your body. You didn't forget this body's pain. I did.*' Reilo launched himself through the mist and into the Iactura.

He melted into the silver.

Back in reality, the cuts closed. The blood vessels re-attached. Organs healed.

Reilo was stealing his body. Silver orbs overhead began to wink out of existence. Memories of pain, drained and discarded for strength.

He felt his eyes begin to burn.

Caelan's body grew stronger around Reilo, his flesh warped around the mind of the long dead rebel. No. *No!* This couldn't be how it ended, his soul discarded in shards of bloodmetal…

Bloodmetal. Like his spine. That was a part of him still.

Silverspine.

A manifest memory formed in Caelan's hand. Inside the silver orb, the Sightless' face crushed a thousand times. His pain forgotten, this was what remained. He fixed the idea in his mind.

Forced the memory into the Iactura. Back into his body. His spine.

The mist screamed and the sky warped a tempest of blood. But the Iactura was a bridge, and what could pass one way could pass another. The memory boiled into Caelan's body, stored in that gleaming metal spine. Whispered lies to his flesh.

Back in Arx, his body fell still. Reilo's fury simmered through the Iactura. Caelan grinned.

Manifest memories gathered around him. Every moment of power, of survival, of rebellion and violence, he forced into the Iactura. The metal spike shone almost to blinding.

He felt his body again. Just a hint, the shadow of a shadow. Almost enough to twitch his fingers.

But seven months do not make a life.

All too quickly, the memories dwindled. '*Why? What more do I need?*' Caelan could see the body through the Iactura. His body. But he had nothing more to give.

'*CAELAN!*' Reilo's projection was like a roar. The sky shuddered with the strength of his triumph. The mist began to fade into the darkness that would become his existence. It swept through the edges of his mind, ate through the smoke and the steam until only a puddle of light around the Iactura remained.

Back in Arx, Caelan watched Reilo curl his hands into fists. Kuyt looked down, his face crushed with confusion and hurt.

At his side, the discarded torch smouldered azure sparks.

'*Kuyt! Please. I need you. The blue fire, breathe the smoke!*'

Caelan's scream melted into the Iactura and he watched, transfixed, as his body opened its lips and spoke the words. The last word burst free just before Reilo snapped his jaw shut, teeth almost sawing through his tongue.

Kuyt frowned and shook his head. Rain stuck his grey hair to his face.

Reilo opened Caelan's too-blue eyes.

Something changed on Kuyt's face. He winced and his jaw twisted. The blue fire at his side flickered in one final burst before it died in sludge and rain.

Kuyt drew the smoke into his lungs.

A shadow burst from the Iactura and Caelan reached out to drag Kuyt into his mind.

'Kid? What's going on?' Kuyt's thoughts were wild and erratic. *'I saw your metal spine start to glow and I swear, you died, but you spoke and those eyes aren't you… Where am I?'* Kuyt's projection glanced down at his shadow form. *'What am I?'*

'No time Kuyt. I need your help.'

Kuyt turned to Caelan. Drawn into the magic despite his hatred for it, forced into a shadow form that he didn't understand, and faced with death creeping in at every moment, he still nodded. *'What can I do?'*

'Let me into your mind Kuyt. I can use your memories of me to come back to my body. Back to my life. We can fight again, finally finish the…

'No.'

The word hung in the air like a stone.

'Kuyt, please. That body in the Iactura, it's a dead man. It isn't me, not anymore.'

'I'll kill him Caelan. Don't worry, I won't let him use you like that. On my honour.'

'Don't kill me. Help me!' Caelan was pleading now.

'I promised my hand would help you end it. I owe you that much. But if we forget what happened here… it'll only happen again.'

'No, that doesn't…'

'It already did! I caved once. Fetched you a Mindbreaker when the Sightless cut you open and death was certain. You forgot in order to survive. And here we are again. All I brought you was pain. Neither of us deserves that. I'm sorry, son.'

And that was it. The end. Caelan's mind was still for a moment.

But then, what did he really owe an old man whose only contribution to his life was to watch him die?

Caelan slammed Kuyt into the Iactura.

Kuyt's projection hit the metal spear like a face held to a branding iron. He screamed and smoke speared his throat. Silver orbs flickered around him. His own manifest memories. An ocean of lived experience. There were so many.

Caelan sorted frantically. Every memory Kuyt had of Silverspine, of their rebellion, of their fight, was forced into the Iactura. Kuyt was a good man. He saw his friends as so much more than they were. His memories were like triple distilled brandy. The strength of an optimist.

Kuyt screamed as his mind was flayed, but he was helpless. Caelan drained him of memories like emptying a water jug.

More.

The faces of the dead burst from Kuyt's mind. Pages of an endless book, the sketches he'd held of all those who had been executed. Forty years of bravery, of sorrow, of fury earned and sacrificed. They flowed into Caelan like blood beneath his veins.

When he was done, Kuyt's shadow vanished with a wisp of black smoke.

Caelan's sky was filed with silver and the mist boiled. Covered the darkness in endless fog. Reilo's shadow was thrown back from the Iactura.

Caelan focused his will. Conviction flowed through him. Memoria was his. He seized Reilo's shadow with his hand. Why had he ever been afraid of this?

He squeezed and Reilo burst into a stream of silver orbs.

Caelan drew the memories into himself and Reilo's past became his.

Strength coursed through his mind. Caelan. Kuyt. Reilo. He could remember *so much*! The darkness fled and he turned to the Iactura, stepped through like it was a doorway, back into his body.

AD INTERIM

TWO

FETCH

Fetch hadn't been bored in a long while. Weren't fair. He *liked* being bored. Just sitting there and… well, not watching the grass grow. Arx didn't do grass, best it had were those thorny little bushes that had never heard of the colour green. Watching the clouds maybe? Once, he'd been hidden with an eye on the Walker barracks up Northamber Close after it had just been whitewashed. And just watching it dry… Now that had been a top day.

Today, too many people were talking to him.

He sat, cross-legged despite the fact he was no longer a teenager and his thighs were now made of concrete, at the lip of the Rustscrape foundry crater. He played with the broken stone on the edge. One grace he'd given himself was that every time that blue fire belched up and into the sky, he wouldn't look at it. Heat soaking his ancient cart-arse, fine. But he wouldn't give it the satisfaction of actually turning around.

Wished he could tune out the beatific screams just as easy.

Some lass scuttled between a pair of broken refineries nearby. Ratty scarf left nothing but a black fringe and some watery eyes peeping through, like anyone was watching. She did what kiddos might call sneaking and made her way over to him.

'Is this the place?' she asked.

'Certainly is a place. Though in fairness, most places are.'

Another *whump* of wind and a muted roar sucked sweat from his pits. Not fair. He didn't turn, but the lass' wide-eyed stare reflected the blasted stuff like a tainted mirror.

'I'm here to join.'

'Join what?' Fetch tossed a shard-snapped rock between his hands until his thumb caught the corner. Sharp little bugger, he lobbed it down the hole behind.

Look out below.

'Silverspine's Martyrs.'

Fetch snorted. Would'a given it a good old belly laugh if it weren't so tragic. 'Never heard them called that before. Doesn't really make sense. Silverspine was the martyr. Those who survived him would be... his supplicants maybe?'

'Could you... this is it, right? I heard they feed you if you fight.'

Smash his gonads but it was hard hearing that so often. Sabotaging the Salt Ponies had been one of the less-bloody orders he'd followed, but the deaths that came from it...

Still, Dirk demanded it. It's not like he had a choice.

'Aye, this is it.' He jerked his head over his shoulder. 'Follow the eyebrow-eating fire down the stairs.'

She nodded, moved to step past.

'Hold on. You got a blade?' Fetch asked.

'I heard they arm you here.' Worry creased that scrap of face she was showing.

'They do. But only after. Here, let me.' Fetch wobbled up to his feet. Slice a scrotum when did his knees die? Not fair he was still lugging their corpses around. He drew the sword from his waist. 'Look off into the distance and give me your hand.'

He rammed the tip into each of her fingers. Thick, bright blood spotted into the dried puddle from those who came before her.

'Keep it bleeding 'til the folk down there get a look. They'll turn your blood to metal, nick your doubt for good measure. Then you're all signed up.'

She sucked a breath between her teeth. 'Thank you.'

'Don't thank me. I stabbed you.'

Her eyes narrowed. 'You're Fetch right?'

'No.'

'Yes you are. Everyone knows you. Dirk's voice. His right hand.'

'His throbbing member? Aren't you here to see him? Wait around much longer and you'll see me become his shitting arse. Off you bugger.'

She scuttled down the steps behind him.

Fetch flipped open the satchel he had, until moments ago, been using as a cushion and wiped his blade clean on the blackcloak hidden inside. His soot-stained, ex-foundry clothes bundled tight underneath.'

It felt wrong, sitting out so open. A lifetime of turning his cloak, of spying for Dirk, and suddenly people knew him. And they weren't trying to kill him for it. Some of them even *bowed*. To him! He couldn't stand it. Their grovelling respect, that admiration, just brought into focus how much he hated himself.

He leant back on his palms and watched the folk nearby at work. Some massive wooden structure was taking shape down the road aways. On Dirk's orders as per. He paid and fed them, so folk were flocking to see what else he wanted. Been at it for a week now, already levelled a massive foundation. How big was it gonna be? Fetch scratched his fingers against the stone on the lip of the foundry. Been a long time since he worked with his hands.

Couldn't remember when it had started, the self-loathing. But then again, that was kinda the point. He didn't reach for the pouch of bloodmetal strapped above his heart. He was far too long in the tooth for such an obvious tell. But he flexed the withering muscles on his chest. A lifetime of service to keep just one person out of mind.

The worst part was, he'd never know if it had been worth it.

'Do you pay attention? Or do you just sit here to pretend you're doing something?'

Adira Signasti leapt up the last few stairs. General Adira as they called her now. Though how anyone could claim to be a 'general' of Dirk's rabble was anybody's guess.

'Come off it, we both did the Walker training. You should know the importance of sitting.'

'I left before the end of training. That way, when *I* stabbed my former colleagues, it was from the front.'

Oh, it was gonna be like that was it? Suddenly, all that boiling loathing that muddled around in his ancient head had a new target. 'Aye, that so? Well thank fuck you did, else we'd never have been rid of Silverspine. Stabbed him in the front did you? Not how I heard it. I wonder if all your little followers would be so keen to kiss your arse if they knew what you'd done to their venerated corpse.'

Her cheeks burned and she gripped the hatchet at her waist hard enough that it shook through her belt. 'Do you think your little farmer boy would be the same if he knew you'd led him to this? That it was never bad luck, it was a bad man. Would Ruairi bleed for you?'

'You keep his fucking name out of your mouth.' Fetch's blade leapt into his hand. 'Outta your mind as well. I swore he'd survive. I don't give a shit what it takes, and you are far, far down on the list of people I wouldn't kill.'

Adira sneered at him. 'Because we all know what a promise from you is worth.' She swept past him, elbows sharp.

'Be careful lass. He only has one tie to me and look what I've become. That training you're doing in the mists... you're binding yourself close.'

'How many times, Fetch? When I want your advice, I'll give you the signal. Which is me having my head caved in and being left to rot for a few weeks.' She stalked off down the street, shouted something at the workers to get them moving faster.

Fetch slumped back to the floor, huddled in on himself with his chin on his knees.

Blackened stars, he missed being bored.

DANNI

Danni drove the copper-tip of her spear through the Nestling's spine, just over the tailbone, and listened for the crunch.

'You and your master... can go and fuck yourselves,' the dying man managed from his spot pinned like a butterfly beneath her boots.

'Surprised you can still speak. That takes some doing, you have my compliments.' She twisted the spear, slowly. Ground the metal against the bone. 'But my master is dead.'

His scream was sharp. 'Adira...'

'...is not my master.' She leant against the spear and this time the words vanished. Didn't have the breath left to form them. She drew her weapon out with a thick *pop*.

It didn't help. None of it did.

She marked her circuit around the edge of the Nest. Alone. She had no interest in listening to another of Addie's sanctimonious whinges. And she certainly didn't need anyone's help killing.

Besides, the Nest had turned on Silverspine when he needed them. They retreated, hid in their smoking hovels and watched him bleed out alone. It was their fault he died. Them and the Walkers. And Adira.

She'd kill them all eventually. Payment, for bringing her back.

Danni clicked her jaw and felt the thick scar twist around her throat. She'd wondered about it every day since it happened. Why her? So many Austelli died on Highdock, and yet Silverspine saved her alone. Sometimes, she taunted herself with the idea that it meant something.

But Dirk dictated the legacy of his fire. Addie had stolen the Austelli. What was left for her?

She shivered a little. Bloody cold tonight.

Ferra helped, a little. Danni visited every night. She'd never sacrifice a memory of Silverspine, but all else was fair game. She needed the strength. And every time, she almost felt... conviction. There was a reason she'd survived even him, there had to be. She just had to find it.

'You're very skilled.'

She whirled around, spear held low. Some bloke with a creased face and white-hair flowing down to his shoulders bobbled around a broken-walled storage shed. As usual, she watched his hands. Unarmed, but the calluses were familiar. He knew how to fight.

'Come closer, old Nestling, and I'll show you just how skilled I am.'

'I'm not from the Nest. We're just... people with similar goals. I'm not one of anyone anymore.' He gripped his hands together and stared at his thumbs.

'Who are you?' Danni took two steps forward, her spear spiking through the smog by his feet.

'My parents used to call me Andi. But my baby sister couldn't pronounce it right, so for the four years she was with us, I was always Ant-ee.'

'Andross De-fucking-Gaya. You're the Ant.'

'Not for a very long time now.' He shrugged. 'It's a name I was sad to lose.'

'Why come back? You're not as popular these days.' Danni favoured him with a grin. 'And we don't look all that fond on you lot still acting like you own us.'

'You said "we." I hear you call yourselves Austelli? Same as we did. I was wondering if I might be able to convince you to stop?'

'Stop what?'

He gestured to the corpse behind her. 'This mindless killing solves nothing.'

She spat at his feet. 'What solution is needed? It shows our anger.'

'That's why I'm here. I know all about anger. My second died of it. Reilo Sandrasova. He was so filled with rage it broke him. To kill is a grave thing, but to enjoy it... He made sport of murder, counting his killings into the hundreds. It was his wife who turned him in, in the end.' He took a step closer.

Danni raised her spear and levelled it at him.

The Ant raised his hands, one scarred palm. 'Their daughter died. Terrible consumption, couldn't keep anything down. And he went out slaughtering Walkers. It shouldn't have been me who helped her dig the grave beyond the city walls. And the bloody trophies he brought back with him... no one in grief should have to see that. The Sightless was waiting for him outside their house that night. I found his corpse on the scaffold the next morning. He went un-mourned. Is that what you want?'

Danni looked down at the bloody tip of her spear. 'I'm not a monster.'

Saying it aloud, it sounded weak.

'It only takes a moment. We all have a point we can't come back from.'

'So what, you're here to save me?' Danni looked around. At the smog and the mud, the broken buildings and empty roads. The winter moonlight was icy. 'I don't have anything else. With Silverspine gone. Without... Caelan.'

She hadn't said his name since the last time he'd saved her.

'It is better this way.' The Ant approached again, and this time she let her spear droop. 'The anger is all he left you. Cut it out.'

The anger...

Danni nodded. She held her spear in shaking hands as the Ant moved to take it from her.

With a twist, she rammed it through his side, the wooden shaft piercing deep into his spongy flesh.

The Ant fell.

'Thank you, Viceroy DeGaya.' Danni leant over his ancient face. 'For your help. My anger is his. *That* is his legacy.'

She left her spear in him and made her way through the frost-soaked night.

DIRK

'I hear you.'

Dirk raised his palms to the Iactura. The cavern carved in Arx's bedrock, hidden deep beneath the Midnight Chamber, this was where it came sharpest. The point at which rock gave way to metal and the smog was thickest. Its taste was rich, foam flecks from the Saltiron sea, the echo of bladerust, smooth as polished stone.

It stirred the voices.

'He won't raise his fuckin' hand...'

'The river's so cold, but the soil is colder...'

'Death before mutilation...'

'Let me sleep again...'

'I hear you,' he said again, his palms inches from the metal. But he didn't touch it, not yet.

Blue fire flickered from around his throat and he drew in a mouthful of smoke. Didn't swallow, he didn't need Memoria for this. Just held it on his tongue and let the memory seep to the surface.

Made it much easier to tell which ones were his.

The mist inside his mind coalesced into images. A young man with violet eyes circled an obelisk no bigger than he was tall. Driven underground by guilt that his Father died and he'd been across the sea, studying an artefact from a civilisation long extinct. Grief was a ripping tide, dragging him beneath the waves. An infinitesimal speck of black smog rose from the metal in response. The sweet promise of oblivion. All he had to do was touch.

The mist flickered. A handprint on the obelisk. The earth shook, rocks cracked and boiled open to a stream of molten iron. Every iron

230

deposit for miles around, exhausted in an instant to feed. The pillar grew. Burst through the ground as the young man cowered in its shadow.

A blue flame flickered in the air and brought with it a whisper of the name *Iactura*.

Dirk blew out the smoke carefully and the images faded.

The Iactura wasn't alive, not really. There was no consciousness achieved by a lump of metal. But it was filled with lost memories. And to those silent screams, it gave voice.

Dirk took a pouch of bloodmetal from his belt. It was easier now. The spectre of death always gave one a chance to learn.

He stepped back from the Iactura, took himself to a small crack in the rock nearby. A slow river of heartfire bubbled far beneath. He emptied the bloodmetal into the liquid flame.

Smoke filled the cavern. Dirk breathed it in, lungful after lungful of sweet, sour, burning memory. He held his breath. The guilt of a young man whose woodaxe had killed his scabby-fisted father. A woman with three dead children and nowhere to bury them. A warrior who'd lost her arm and her will to fight. The faces of Walkers, killed by an ex-colleague who couldn't bear to dream about them anymore.

The Iactura *gleamed*. He felt it beneath the ground, arterial magma feeding into the metal spike.

Dirk blew a breath of smog and the Fires of Remembrance burst from the coal around his throat. A darting needle, it pierced the Iactura.

Mist swallowed the cavern and took Dirk with it. Memoria was familiar as breath by now, but as the smog escaped his lips, shadows leapt from it and melted into the Iactura. Those still felt achingly new.

The Iactura lit the sky with silver orbs. Overlapping, bursting, fighting for their place. He remembered too much.

'*You never taught me this.*'

Dirk smiled as Aer materialised in the mist, far out of reach. It was not entirely unexpected. Her steel-grey hair hung loose around her shoulders and her amber eyes were swollen.

'*I did not teach you how to eavesdrop either.*'

'*The Iactura is a simple bridge to follow. The Midnight Chamber is empty, no one knows I'm here.*' The mist puffed up around her feet as she walked. '*Besides, I knew you'd be here. I could never forget you. Or what you taught me.*'

'*Healers together.*' Dirk lifted his palm and a manifest memory crashed against the mist.

The man with violet eyes knelt beside a young woman with curling hair and skilful fingers. Together, they held a coal above the body of a blood-soaked infant. Blew out their breath and watched it spark blue. The blood vanished and the child's chest began to move.

The memory vanished.

'*Heal is not the word for what we did, but we kept people alive. The least you could do.*'

The mist shifted again. Burned blood red though bodies and corpses that hacked and died.

'*The Flame Protests were inevitable. Iron is a finite resource, I just accelerated things. The number of deaths went down, but the fighting got worse. It's easy to bleed when you don't remember how much it hurts.*' Dirk plucked the arrowhead knife from his belt. The same here as it was in reality. '*And then they discovered Callisteel. Why kill someone when you can melt their mind? Slit a Walker's throat and watch her stand with you as rebel. It was endless.*'

'*Only because we took different sides…*'

They watched as bodies stabbed and bled and rose again with blue fire eyes. Callisteel spread from hand to hand until the city was gripped in an undying war.

'*The Iactura should never have awakened.*' Aer's voice was sharp. '*We raised walls to keep the rest of the world from discovering what we birthed here. I used to pretend we were noble back then. A heroic sacrifice, to hide from the world and keep Callisteel contained. Keep us contained. But all that did was increase the pressure. Boil the city and bring it to the brink of ruin. We had to do something.*'

Her memory pierced the mists.

The young woman knelt beside the Iactura. A man held her hand, tight. Tall, striking, his eyes were so deep a brown they were almost black. Lips pressed tightly, tears like jewels rolling down their cheeks. Together, they looked back, expecting a third. But the cavern was empty. The man nodded, once. She pressed him to the Iactura. His mouth burst open as dense, blue fog burned out his eyes. Metal crawled across his body. A liquid skin that melted into his flesh. Sightless.

'We should have matched his sacrifice. That axe was forged for you and I. Our magic could have died then. Should have. And yet you ran. Trained new apprentices. Let the poison fester.'

'People deserve to live without pain. Agony does not make us stronger, it just makes us scarred. In all this time, I have never met someone who would not be happier with something forgotten. Not even you. How often do you force yourself to think of him only as The Sightless? Lucianus' name is a burden. It'll kill you, one day.'

'You loved him as much as I.'

'I loved you as well.'

An image, unbidden. Three bodies in a bed, hands squeezed tight, heart pounding like a drumbeat. Love like shining veins of silver.

It burned away in the blue fire.

Aer's eyes flickered. For just a moment, she looked like the woman she'd once been. Then it was gone. Her face a mask tightly bound as her Sightless' had once been. 'What do you want, Dirk?'

'To heal. As we always have.'

'Heal what?'

'Everything.' He lifted his hands and tendrils of shadow burst from his fingertips, skewered through the Iactura.

Those who had lost their memories, even those at a distance. He felt them. Their connection to the Iactura. He whispered a breath and sent a pulse of fire through the shadows on his fingertips. One by one, the four shadows he had connected to the Iactura… forgot. Just a hair, an eyeblink of memory that was connected to something lost.

Their voices screamed inside his head.

Dirk was flung from the mists. Aer vanished as the Iactura boiled bright.

He slumped to his knees, blood streaming from his ears, his nose. Smog lapped against the crimson stains down his face.

But it had worked. The link was stronger this time.

It would all be over soon.

PART 3

VIVERE

CHAPTER 34

Rank-sour sweat stuffed Sam's nose and sharp needles of hunger jabbed through her stomach like a sparrow's beak through a rusted cage. But that was nothing new.

She held her hands out to the cold marble of the fireplace and tried to pretend it still held a shadow of heat. Sat there alone, the empty house felt so much bigger.

She poked through the ashes. Their last fire had been a hysterical one. Default contracts, bonds, trade agreements, debt readjustments, all up in smoke. Mistress Ignis' displeasure was public and merciless. Sam scratched the brand on the back of her hand until the edges began to bleed.

Her legs ached, how long had it been since she last stood up? She forced herself to unsteady feet, stumbled and slapped her palm against the wall. The off-cream paint was brighter. A gap. Something must have hung there, but she couldn't remember what. Must have sat in the living room thousands of times, but never took a moment to remember it properly. When she closed her eyes, all she saw were the insides of her eyelids.

Sam crept downstairs, ears alert. Technically she was trespassing. But sod it all if the Walkers didn't have better things to do. She made her way down into the forge. The muted whistle of the winter winds outside followed her down.

If she hadn't known better, she might have pretended that the basement was just as she left it. Weight had saved most of their equipment. No-one wanted to drag an anvil up a flight of stairs, let alone a pair of them. The forge and furnace were built into the walls.

But her hammer was gone. Jak's too. The little box of tat under his workbench, the drawer of knives. The Walkers had stolen a lifetime of her anger.

Worst was the chill. The forge was always cold in the morning, but this was different. Settled. Only the scars of life remained. Chips in the blast-furnace, a silk-line of scratches on the floor from when Jak got a nail stuck in his boot, a crack in the wall from an ill-timed, ill-tempered swing. It was like standing in an open grave waiting for the rain.

But she hadn't come for a grave. She'd come for a pyre.

Sam shook a pile of loose wood shavings on the dead firepit, a flint spark and she had a curl of smoke. Too clean. Without the coke and ashes of the previous day it just smelled like burning. She added more scraps, coated the fire in old coals, worked the bellows – wait for the air to shimmer. Ripples over the fire, that'll do it.

Sam untied the pouch from her belt. Felt grandiose calling it a purse with no money or iron inside. She threw it on the fire.

The Sightless' mask, swept up in the Midnight Chamber three weeks ago, poked through the smouldering leather. Blue-silver. Callisteel, obviously.

She watched it burn. The fire flickered. Orange tongues of flame licked through the empty eyehole and burst into blue sparks. Just as she'd expected. The same as Ignis, the same as the corpse in the Midnight Chamber. The same as those gouts of flame that burned every night across the river.

The puddle of blue light was small enough to trap her from the darkness creeping in at the edges. Not hot enough. Not yet.

The bellows were stiff, but she threw herself at them. Out of practice, her arms throbbed but she forced herself to move. She pictured those muscles she'd spent years cultivating tearing and twisting from the force of the sweat-damp wooden handles. The fire grew higher, grew hotter, the air in the forge thickened into a cloud of asphyxiating heat. Her lungs rebelled but she filled them anyway.

If heat hotter than fire could make Callisteel, perhaps it could destroy it as well.

Blue fire chewed across the mask. The remaining onyx eye cracked and fell from the socket. Heat shimmered like a mirage over the flames and smoke poured from the mask.

A shadow rose behind those ashen clouds.

Sam dropped the bellows. It looked like… it was moving. Walking, no running at her. Her back slammed against the wall. Stupidly, she sucked down a panicked breath.

And the shadow lunged down her throat.

An axe weighs more than the deaths it causes. Don't weep.
The blacksmiths have to die. Dirk has to die. Aer has to die.
I have to die.
Emptiness is better than knowing who I could have been.

Sam crumpled to her knees, spat up stomach acid laced with black smoke. By the blackened stars, she could *feel* it inside her chest. That voice, that memory. Like the one Ignis had shown her. The axe in her hands, the blood at her feet, the weight of so many dead. Countless bodies.

And… sorrow. The Sightless had still felt their loss. The mask had purged him of his grief, but for just a moment each time the axe fell, he'd felt the weight of that life. Fresh each time, like tearing off an infant's eyelids at birth.

Sam stumbled over to the fire, sweat dripping down her fringe and into her eyes. The mask boiled with heat, shimmered silver as the smoke grew thicker. A memory of Ignis' forge rose to the fore. Blue fire didn't hurt. It just felt warm. She grabbed the mask.

Her hand exploded in a bloom of searing, sizzling, stabbing pain. She threw herself from the forge with a screech, the mask stuck to the skin of her fingers, flesh bubbling and blistering against the metal. It peeled a long, wet strip from her thumb and forefinger, then clattered to the stone floor.

Sam rammed her forearm between her teeth, drummed her heels against the floor. Tears spiked down her cheeks, the heat trapped beneath her skin felt like her flesh was molten, churning around her bones. Breath rattled like jagged ore down her throat.

She threw herself at the quenching barrel, rammed her hand into the icy water. It was almost a surprise she didn't hiss, but it soothed the edges of the fire. She could have melted into it herself.

Eventually, she managed to draw her wrinkled hand free. She soaked a pair of gloves in the cold water and slid them over her hands. First Ignis' brand, now this.

She'd never burned herself under Jak's watch.

The mask stared from the floor. Something was wrong. The prints from her thumb and index finger remained, embedded in the blue-silver. A swirling pattern, picked out like ash mirrored on either cheek.

For a long time, she just stared. Urged herself to leave it behind. But it was an odd vulnerability. Who knows what someone like Ignis could do with her fingerprints?

With tentative fingers, Sam scooped the thankfully cool mask up and into the lining of her boot. Not like she had a pouch for it anymore. The burn on her hand pulsed beneath the wet woollen glove.

She left the forge and the house behind. Memories of a life she no longer lived were a dangerous trap.

Outside, the wind bit into her exposed arms. Her rotten shirt flapped about her like a flag on the empty street. No one left their houses anymore, not unless they had to.

Shouting rumbled down the street. The clash of blades.

A single warrior. No. A child. Seventeen at the most, his hairless cheeks crusted with half-dried blood. He darted between a knot of seven Walkers. They had him surrounded, but when he lunged they moved with him. Kept him fighting, even as myriad slashes bled down his arms, his eyebrows, his chest. Blood-soaked shirt and sword-scored trousers were a sharp contrast to the Walker's polished leather and velvet cloaks.

They baited him like hounds tearing into a fox.

'Come Nestling, don't they teach you how to swing?' A salt-and-pepper Walker darted forwards and ran his blade, gently, across the back of the lad's thigh.

He squawked, stumbled to one knee.

'Parry, and thrust!' Another leapt forwards, her blade clashing against his, once, twice and then…

Sam hid in her elbow so she wouldn't see the blade pierce his throat. At least he didn't scream. The only confirmation she had of his death was the raucous laughter. She didn't look at his corpse. Just stumbled around the spreading pool of blood soaking between the stones of the walkway.

Despite it all, she still felt guilty. Like she should have thrown herself at them, begged them to stop. But what good would it do? The Walkers were a shadow of their former selves. Ever since they lost.

The uprising south of the river was a complete success. DeKeita's Walkers were outmatched and outfought, even as DeGaya led the countercharge himself. Rumour varied, but most agreed that the moment the soldiers stepped off that single barge, they were met with blue fire and enemy soldiers that would not bleed. The Walkers were humiliated. DeGaya lost, presumed dead. Desertions in the hundreds, DeKeita barely had a skeleton force left. The only ones still fighting were in the Nest. They bled against Walkers and Austelli both. They wouldn't last long.

A gust of wind forced smog into her face and Sam coughed. Ever since that first night, rolling banks of soot the colour of coal were ever present in the sky. Her breath was heavy with it.

The temple rose from behind the smog bank. Sam took the stone steps two at a time and yanked open the door. Forced herself to leave thoughts of war and loss outside.

The wedding was starting soon.

CHAPTER 35

The temple was ugly as sin. A water-damaged roof held up by gold-flaking pillars. Moth-eaten rugs led through the entrance hall and down towards a corridor at the back. A few occupied benches near the walls. Rich cloaks torn with fire, blouses bled through. No one spoke. Most just watched their feet. One wept.

'May I help you?' One of the Scelus approached her, a priest with a face soft and round as a Winternight pudding. His dusky robes were stained with hard use.

'I'm an Acarris.'

'Then shall we?' He bowed.

Sam followed down the empty corridor at the back. Torches lit ancient wood, soot and spiderwebs stained the sconces. Alcoves broke up the walls with nameless statues, their heads bowed and hands pressed in prayer.

Except for two. Their eyes were carved like smoke and their hands bound by chains over the lintel of a door stained with blood. Sam stopped outside.

'Our hospital,' the Scelus explained.

'I know. I've visited. Reckon they'd take another patient?' Sam peeled the now-dry glove from her burned hand, winced as another scrap of skin scraped away in the wool.

The Scelus grimaced. 'Fortunately, we have all become well versed with burns.' He led her through the door.

Someone was screaming, a bubbling stump where his shoulder used to be. Lots of bloody people clustered the beds. Reminded her of the dead soldier in the Midnight Chamber. Would any of these stand up again? The thought made her stomach ache.

'Sit, sit.' The Scelus ushered her towards the edge of a bed. It was occupied, a huge fellow snored fitfully beneath the sheets, but the room was packed and there was nowhere else. Wadded bandages coated his side, but pink specks still broke through.

The Scelus ducked away for a moment before returning with a small, ceramic pot. He dipped his fingers in and slathered the salve over Sam's hand.

Oh that was *so much better*. From the feeling of heartfire being injected into her fingers, down to a dull throb. It smelled familiar, honey and those spikey plants Jak used to grow in the back garden. The Scelus wrapped her hand in a clean, greasy bandage and handed her the pot. 'Twice a day,' he told her. 'Keep it clean and covered at all times. Now, shall we?'

'Not yet. Father should know what day it is.' Sam stood up and pushed past the scurrying Scelus, towards the ever-familiar dividing curtain in the middle of the room. She ducked through. A thin cloth, it still cut the noise. On this side, the patients were silent.

Fog boiled in every eye. This was where they kept Father now. He sat up in bed, next to a bubbled window that was impossible to see through. Someone had cut his hair too short and dressed him in white pyjamas.

'Da?' Sam bent over to meet his empty eye sockets. 'Do you remember me today?'

'Miss please, don't upset him.' The Scelus scuttled after her.

Father's hand hovered in the empty air. Sam gripped it. Tight.

'Da, Vicky's getting married. Remember Vicky? She'd want you there.'

The fog in his eyes boiled and swirled. He dropped her hand and stared off into the distance.

Sam didn't weep. This time. She closed her eyes and took a deep breath.

'I'm ready now.'

She followed the Scelus out of the room and down the corridor to a pair of gold-chased doors.

A little chapel cramped inside, with rows of pews set out like a schoolroom. Ancient altar stained with mildew. The Scelus did an admirable job at ignoring her disgust and led her to a screen in the back corner, a faded frieze of sod-knows-what.

Vicky sat ensconced behind. Even after everything, she still managed to look good. Midnight hair pinned around her shoulders. No necklace. She looked oddly naked without one, though her face was painted with a casual perfection that Sam doubted she could achieve in fifty years. Her dress was immaculate. Deep blue, almost black. It clung to Vicky's shoulders like gossamer. A night without stars.

'Samantha. So glad you could make it.' The acid in Vicky's voice could have etched steel.

'Wouldn't have missed it. Look, I know today might not be how you pictured this day, but...'

'Oh I've been prepared for this for a long time. Sold off to settle my sister's debts. My only regret is that they won't be handing you a sack filled with coins. All promises and paper. Very gauche. But it's no great loss. After all, I get to spend the morning with *you*.'

Sam sat on the bench behind her sister. There was nothing for her to say.

'Why me?' Vicky ran some rabbit-fur brush across the top of her tits.

'What?'

'You're the eldest. Why can't you get put up like some brood mare that can't gallop anymore?' She smeared something black on her fingertip and dabbed it at her eyelids. 'Do you know why we never got on Samantha?'

'What a lovely conversation to have on your wedding day.'

'We both had the same education, the same advantages, the same expectations. And yet you got to spend your life underground with your fingers in your ears.'

'You think I wanted to be such a colossal disappointment? I'm not made for your world. I can't...' She shook her head.

'Can't what? Fuck?'

Sam blinked. Did nothing, so she blinked again. 'What?'

'You think we didn't know? So you don't want to open your legs. So what? That doesn't mean you have to spend your life in a cave underground. You could've still had friends, been a part of the family. It's not all or nothing. No excuse to push us away and turn into a bitch about it.'

'But...' How had it possibly happened that Vicky knew? Did it matter? It felt like it did. Sam flushed to her ears, but she had no idea why. 'I didn't want any of those things. Why do I have to be a good daughter or sister or friend? I just wanted to be a blacksmith. To do something that made me happy.'

'What about my happiness? Or Father? You think he's happy now?'

'I... don't know.' Those boiling blue eyes. 'I don't think he's anything anymore. But Mother was. At the end.'

'Excuse me?'

She pushed her knuckles into her eyes. Ever since that day at Ignis' forge, it was harder to forget and the mask had ripped it open like the skin between her fingers. 'I was in the room when you were born. The day she died.' Grey sky outside a cold room. Surgeons whispered, tools ground through flesh. 'She was so pale. Couldn't even lift her head to cough. And yet, in that final breath she leant forwards and kissed your forehead.' Didn't glance at Sam in the doorway. Four years old and terribly, terribly alone. 'Father always said she was beautiful. Fair that you got that from her.'

Vicky was quiet for a long time. She chewed the end of her brush a moment. 'I don't know what you think telling me that achieves.'

'Nothing. But you should know. Since she's not here, and Father... well, I'm going to stand beside you and be your sister. First time for everything.'

'And the last. My final moments as an Acarris. Shame we didn't get here quicker.' Vicky tapped her lips. She wrapped an old shawl around Sam's shoulders. It hid most of the tears on her shirt. 'Don't want them distracted by your shivering.'

'Of course.'

'Ahem.' That pudding-faced Scelus was back. 'We are ready for you.'

Vicky took a deep breath.

'Ready?' Sam asked.

'Don't ask stupid questions.' Vicky marched from behind the screen.

After the ceremony, Sam sat beside the liquor and watched Vicky. 'Dance' would be a kind word for it. She was lumped around the floor like a bag of turnips. Lance Schär, her brand-new husband, wiped his sweaty forehead on a napkin. At least the boy wasn't hideous. A little meat at his waist, watery eyes, but a fashionable beard and well-trimmed hair. Handsome, maybe? Besides, his face was still split by his smile. Truly obsessed.

The music cut off in a final wail and Vicky curtseyed. Muted applause at best, most guests had left long ago. Vicky patted her new husband's arm, then scuttled over to Sam.

'You look like you're having fun.'

'Would you believe I actually miss it?' Vicky shook her head. 'The dancing, the conversation. Marriage as the city burns. Dear lord, I've lost my mind.'

'What little you had in the first place.'

'So lovely. Anyway. We're leaving. It's late.'

'So?'

Vicky just looked at her.

'Oh. Right.' Sam felt a stone pressing against her throat, liquid edges.

'Yes, duty calls. Still, they say this is the worst one. All expectation, no technique. Good to get it over with.' She barked a laugh devoid of humour.

'Vicky. I'm sorry.'

'It's too late for that now.' She looked over at her new husband. 'For all of us. So you should have this.' Vicky handed her a scrap of paper.

'What's this?' It unfolded along well-creased lines. Sam, five years old or so, with baby Vicky in her arms. The artist had been honest. Scowls, scrubbed faces and squalling tears. The pair of them were so petulant.

'Why would you want this?' Sam found the edges of a smile.

'Father gave it to me. He told me, whenever I got angry with you, I should look at it and remember we were sisters.'

Sam blinked past the image of a drawer full of hand-made knives. 'I can't take this…' She tried to hand the thing back, but Vicky closed her fingers around it.

'I have a new family now. Time I got used to it.' Vicky straightened her back, tilted her chin.

Despite herself, Sam felt a warm curl of pride. Vicky was made of stronger stuff than she had credited. She raised her hand in farewell and Sam returned the gesture.

'Goodbye, Victoria Acarris.'

The door closed. Vicky was gone. And Sam was alone.

Wasn't this what she had always wanted? No responsibilities. No one to let down. No one to prove herself to. She could do whatever she wanted, free of expectation, of family and failure. The thread tying her to the past had been well and truly cut. The freedom to forge her own path.

So then why did it hurt?

She wandered through the temple alone, back outside and into the cold night. Mira had been letting her sleep on her floor, but Sam couldn't face the company of the living right then.

She made for the graveyard instead.

There was no path between the graves, but her route was well-trodden. An older corner of the cemetery. Moss and mildew clustered on white-stone slabs that burst like teeth from the overgrown lawn.

Sam stopped at a familiar grave.

'I never know what to say,' Sam whispered. She cleared her throat. This was ridiculous. 'I know I don't visit often enough. I probably owe you an apology for that. Not sure how many times I'm supposed to turn up. I guess just enough not to feel guilty.

'You missed Vicky's wedding. Thankfully. Dreadful ceremony, be glad you didn't see it. Though, being fair, if you were still around then I don't suppose she'd have had to get married in the first place.

'Ah, this is so stupid. At least Father is still *there*. I can look him in the... space where his eyes used to be. This is just, why am I speaking to the worms?' She stared at her bandaged palm. 'I could get one of those priests to pray for you, would you want that? Do prayers mean anything when you're dead? I wouldn't want them. But then, I'd be dead, so who cares?

'Things have changed, Ma. Everything is worse and I know it's not your fault but I can't help but think it would have been better if you were still here. I don't know why. I barely remember you, I... I can't keep doing this.'

247

The words dried up and she just sat beside her mother's grave for a long time.

'You're dead.' Sam unfolded the miniature from Vicky. Set it on the limestone grave. 'And you always will be.'

She made it back to her feet and wandered through the headstones. A lantern bobbed in the darkness, gravedigger working on an open plot, empty graves and a pile of wooden markers, ready for engraving.

'Who are they for?' Sam asked.

The gravedigger didn't look up. 'Whoever needs them. Only reason that last ferry still runs is to bring the corpses over to us for burial.'

'Everyone gets buried here?'

He leant back from his hole, cricked his back and wiped a hand over his forehead. 'Not everyone. Some folk still get dumped in the river like always. Others'll have friends take them beyond the city. But most are my responsibility now. Way it should be.'

'What do you do for the dead that don't show up here?'

He shrugged, left his spade in the soil. 'Not much, usually. Some folk go to the temple to pray. Others get a marker made up so they have somewhere to mourn.'

Somewhere to mourn. The mask lay heavy against her ankle. At least she still had her grief.

'Can I request one?' she asked.

The gravedigger turned to face her for the first time. 'I've got a lot of work to do...'

There was something familiar about his face. The way he spoke, with his tongue touching his lips.

'Jonas.' Sam stepped forwards. 'Jonas Karrin.'

'Miss? How'd you know my name?'

'Samantha Acarris. I'm a... We spoke, one time.' The memory of a fake Callisteel blade cut through her mind, bent and discarded.

'A fine profession.' He grinned. 'Spent a lot of my time in the forges. Before this.'

'Don't you remember me?'

'I... He cocked his head, like he was listening to something faint and far away. A blue fleck swirled through his eyes. 'I'm sorry Ma'am, can't say I do.'

Something lurched in the pit of Sam's stomach. 'Why did you stop working as a blacksmith, Jonas?'

'Oh that.' He paused again, frowned. Blue flecks darted through his eyes, one after another. He turned back to the grave he was digging.

'Jonas?'

'Yes?' He turned back again, smile brittle on his face. 'Right! The headboard. Who's it for?'

Sam swallowed. It was better this way. 'Jak Mendy.'

'Ah now that's a kick.' Jonas removed his cap and held it to his chest. 'Jak was a fine fellow. You know he made the chains that span the Mucro? When did he die?'

'Didn't make them alone,' Sam muttered. 'And I don't know when. He died across the river, sometime in the last few months.'

Jonas' face creased. 'What are you talking about? He was a Forgemaster.'

'So?'

'They aren't killing Forgemasters.'

Sam's heart thumped against a stone lodged in her chest. 'What do you mean?'

His mouth moved, but nothing came out. A blizzard of blue flecks across his eyes.

'Jonas. Why aren't they killing Forgemasters?'

Blood dripped from his ear. His neck began to twitch. Then all of a sudden… nothing. He blinked, eyes clear, and he turned back to his shovel.

For all the world, like he had forgotten she was even there.

Sam's heart tumbled around her chest. Sparks of iron and fire. It was thin, so thin. The word of a proven liar, a bridge of blown glass. But she couldn't ignore it. A faint hope burst into flame.

Jak was still alive.

CHAPTER 36

Ruairi ran around the top of the Patriae Wall circling Arx. Not away from anyone, not because he had to.

But because he could.

Three weeks. Three weeks, and it still hadn't lost its lustre. The feeling of his legs thundering out in front of him, the cold snap of air darting in and outta his lungs with each bellowful. The straight line of his spine shifting beneath his shoulders when he pumped his arms.

He leapt over a pile of dust-pattered bricks, then darted around the crack they'd been hauled up to patch. Everything looked brighter from up here. Black stone that clicked beneath his boots, sapphire spray from the Saltiron far below, white mountain peaks catching sunlight off in the distance.

And the Iactura rising from the heart of the city like a ripple-shining blade.

Ruairi wiped his forehead on the back of his sleeve. Dirk had given him this. The memory of his Pa's body, trained and healthy. It wrapped his limbs.

It took away the pain. Free. Free at last from the wincing, shuffling agony.

Maybe now he'd be the son Pa always wanted. Now he could run.

'Course the real question were why he didn't keep running. All the way outta Arx and off back home. But the answer were dead simple. Same reason he'd come to Arx in the first place.

Dirk knew him now. Knew his name, knew his *mind*. Weren't no escape. So he could stay close and keep him sweet. Or he could flee back home, and watch as a man who'd stab a weeping farmer through the heart set fire to his family, his home and everything he ever knew.

No. That life were over now. Ruairi the broken boy were gone. Disappeared, or maybe even killed far beneath the foundry. He were a new man now. One of Dirk's. Time he got used to it.

Circuit completed, he slowed to a jog and made for one of the ladders. Rusty things gave his heebies the jeebies every time he felt them wobble against the stone. He gripped the rungs tight and felt his shoulders tense. Slid his arse down into Arx. No. Into Austellus.

It were healing.

Folk took to the streets in their numbers. But the rush were gone. Ain't no head-down, eyes forward no more. People meandered. They strolled. Stopped for a smile and a chat. Admittedly, the two lads Ruairi marched past seemed to have focused their entire conversation on who could piss the furthest, but it were a far cry from the grit-soaked eyeballs he'd clocked when he'd first wandered up and through those gates.

''Ere, Running Man. I found your sword.' Fetch steamed towards him. Fella were always just around the damn corner. Weren't fair. Ruairi were half convinced he listened out for the 'plop' every time he took a shit, just so he didn't spend too long squatting.

'How'd you always know where I am?'

'I've got a good ear for dipshittery. Like someone's smashing bells together right in my ear every time you do something moronic. Getting sodding tinnitus.' Fetch thrust a, thankfully sheathed, copper sword into Ruairi's hands. 'What have I told you about pissing around unarmed? Some Nestling is gonna ram her fist down your throat if you don't start taking it more seriously.'

Ruairi rubbed his scalp. 'You used to be nice.'

'No I didn't, I arrested you and you almost died,' Fetch said. 'Then I delivered you to Dirk and let him break you.'

'I ain't broken.' Ruairi still weren't sure how he felt about Fetch no more.

He could still see it, in the back of his mind. Fetch holding back, tears in his ancient eyes as Dirk violated his mind and forced his body to work. But he didn't hate the bastard. Not proper, anyway.

'Besides, you can't run with a sword. Goes flapping between your legs. Rather not slice a bollock off, just so you can mother my hens.'

'You keep this up and I'm gonna get Ferra to hammer up a nice beartrap and see how you like it hanging from your jaw. Speaking of, she's clicked her fingers so we're off. Open Kitchen will be packed soon and I don't fancy sharpening my elbows just so that woman can rip me a new arsehole. And put your sword on!'

The back of Fetch's shiny head bounced with sunlight when he did his angry walk. Ruairi pulled a face, but he slipped the scabbard through his belt and buckled it in place nonetheless. Followed the spirit of baldness through Firesale.

Firesale were one of the new districts opened up. A little market with bright-ribboned stalls and dusty heirlooms for sale. Dirk had transformed a sludge-soaked, road-to-nowhere into... well, a sludgy market where people swapped coins for sommat else. Cracked shopfronts played home to fresh-painted carts and the smell of sawdust mingled with the rust in the air.

'Sirs, sirs! See anything you fancy?' A weasel-faced bloke wiped his hands down his thick apron, rubbed them together. 'Just made this, sirs, what do you think?'

Ruairi let another bloke shove a sword at him, be juggling the bloody things before the day was out. The blade didn't feel right. Too light, and there were a bunch of chips down the cutting edge. Discoloured copper the colour of earwax.

'Didn't reckon I'd remember it all so well, ain't been in the forges since my Pappy died and I chucked the apprenticeship in, but that's a right blade that is.' The bloke grinned. Two of his teeth were missing.

'How much?' Fetch asked.

The blacksmith's eyes widened. 'Master Fetch! For you there is no charge, consider it a donation to the cause. The least I could do.' Bloke bowed so low he almost smacked his nose on the anvil.

'You know, you lot don't have to...' Fetch rubbed the bridge of his nose. 'What does it matter? Cheers then.'

They left the bloke to his grinning.

'Thought Arx were famous for its swords,' Ruairi said. 'This looks...'

'Shite. We were good at it.' Fetch barked a laugh. 'We. Like I've ever held a damned hammer. Dirk gathered all the Forgemasters he could when he came back. Demanded access to their minds, something about Callisteel fragments caught between memories. But the night we took the river, the lot of them just… vanished. And this time it ain't us. So we're making do with old apprentices, barely-trained journeymen and any bugger who looks big enough to swing a hammer'

'Where did they go?' Ruairi asked.

'Oh the bells, the bells.' Fetch dug a finger in his ear. 'I don't know. That's why I said "vanished".' He plucked the sword from Ruairi's fingers and lobbed It into a nearby alleyway. It cracked when it hit the cobblestones. 'Come on.'

Fetch led 'em over a makeshift bridge that spanned a whacking great puddle of brown water. Stank like rotten veggies and old meat, but at least they didn't have to trudge through it no more. Over the other side, fresh as a lick of paint, the Open Kitchen towered over the lot of them. Three-storeys tall, glass windows and a real, brick chimney.

Winter hit Arx hard and there weren't a lot of grub to go round. Things got real hairy for a while, then Dirk stepped in. Sent some raiding parties across the river, nabbed supplies from the Walker ration stockpiles. Got the thing built, stocked and opened the doors for anyone who needed a meal.

Best of all, it were free. Almost.

Inside, wooden tables clustered with gaunt faces. The smell of unwashed bodies mingled with leathery salt-pork. Couple of blokes at trenchers stopped gnawing when Fetch went by. Almost dipped their chins into the apple sauce as a sign of respect.

Fetch ignored 'em. Always did, got a right scowl on his face when people started minding the old Ps and Qs around him. He led Ruairi to the back room.

Some short bloke burst out, face split in a blissful smile. Blue flecks flickered in his dark eyes. Were a familiar sight, nowadays. The bloke barely looked at the pair of 'em when he wandered past.

Ferra poked her head out after him. Folded her arms tight enough to make her apron creak when she saw Fetch waiting. The sweat on her arms dripped down her tattoos like dew on grass in the candlelight. 'Oh good. It's you two.'

'In the flesh, you lucky so and so. How's work?' Fetch leant against the wall, spoke close by her ear.

'Oh marvellous. Been in the mists more than my own bed these last few weeks. Won't be a single mind this side of the river that isn't scarred before too long.' She gestured at the candle-coated room behind her. A pile of bloodmetal glittered on the floor.

'Well, you're the Mindbreaker. Isn't this just a regular week for you lot?' Fetch scratched his chin.

Ferra peeled some errant candlewax from the edge of her thumbnail. 'Preferred it when we were a badly kept secret. People have the right to live without poison between their ears. But Dirk's arrangement to trade memories for food is just… off.'

'No one forces them to come here.'

Ruairi tried to lean against the wall like Fetch did and almost fell on his arse. Bloody sword, how did people wear one of these?

'Hunger is a bitch of a motivator.' For the first time, Ferra looked at Ruairi. 'Stop shifting like you've got crabs. Stand up straight.'

Ruairi set his palms down his legs and beanpoled up his back. The two of them nattered on, sommat about stock levels of grain and the price of beer kegs, and he felt his eyelids giving it the drifties.

Snorted, blinked sommat fierce and slapped his cheeks. Pay attention, he were supposed to be on the lookout. Kept his peepers on the folk eating. A good handful sat together around long tables, chatted quiet in the candlelight. Some lad were laying on what sounded like poetry for the bloke next to him. Weren't working all that well, far as Ruairi could tell.

With so many jaws moving, it were easy to see who wasn't. Some bloke loomed like a shadow across the back wall, a whacking great hood hiding his face. Didn't touch the plate in front of him. Just sat there. Watching.

Ruairi twisted his neck, tried to look inside the shadow of the hood, but the fella clocked him peering. Stood up and made for the door sharpish.

'Hold on.' Ruairi started for the bloke, just as his cloak wisped outta the door. 'What's the deal leaving…'

The door swung back at him. Outside, the hooded fella were gone. In his place, a handful of bodies clustered by the doorway. Some wore black cloaks. Others…

Fog misted where their eyes should be.

'Fog-Eyes!' Ruairi shouted and lugged back as blue-misted folk stormed the building. The blackcloaks followed close, blades bare and eyes like coals.

One of the Fog-Eyes lifted a hand and pointed at Ferra.

'Austelli, to me!' Fetch whipped out his sword and dragged Ruairi back as the folk by the tables levered to their feet. Knives flashed, swords clattered free, an axe thumped the floorboards. 'Reckon it's time we see all that training come in handy, eh kid?' Fetch whispered to Ruairi. 'Thank fuck you got a sword.'

With fumbling hands, Ruairi managed to draw his blade.

Then chaos swallowed the room.

Fetch roared, pounded towards one of the tables and smashed into it with his shoulder. The thing flipped, whacked a Fog-Eye face and spilled candlewax like blood. A nearby Austelli gripped a Walker's wrist as he tried to swing his sword, the two of them dizzy around the place like a pair of drunken dancers.

Someone stabbed someone else. Folk died. Smoke hissed from drowning candles, people shouted and screamed and grunted that solid thud that came with the final breath. Hot copper and salty smoke flavoured the air.

Ruairi darted back, a shard of sommat flying at him and drawing a sour scratch down the side of his face. He ducked behind the upturned table, felt someone thud into it and throw splinters into his face. He scrabbled back as a Fog-Eye clawed its way over the table, hands clenched towards his throat.

'Oh please.' Ferra blew a breath at the coal around her throat.

The fire flickered. Sapphire flame licked across the coal but then... broke. Two sparks hovered over the fire. Blue and white folded over and over like crashing waves inside a pair of glass orbs. Like the fire were trying to swallow itself.

Ferra cocked an eyebrow. 'Never seen that before.' She shrugged, then gestured at the Fog-Eye. A coil of white smoke lashed towards its mouth.

'Fight for me.' Her voice was a searing order, shrouded in smoke.

Something shimmered between the Fog-Eye's teeth. Smog, thick and black. Ferra's smoke faded like fog in the sunlight.

'Never seen that either,' she muttered. 'Fuck you Aer. Still, there's an easy way.'

The Fog-Eye crawled close to Ruairi. She swung her hammer down on the top of the Fog-Eye's head. It… squelched. A crimson puddle splashing gore and sharp fragments of bone into Ruairi's watery eyes. He felt sick. He felt weak. He felt…

The copper blade shook in his hands. Fetch's lessons were mute, the buzz of a far-off fly. He could barely move. No chance of getting to his feet.

People died around him.

It ended slow. Fog-Eyed fell to the clatter and slice of blade after blade through the neck, through their skulls. New floorboards were slick with Austelli and Walker blood alike. Bodies piled in the corners. The attackers were dead, but far more Austelli had fallen alongside. Fetch, knee freshly gashed, shouted and ordered for the corpse carts to come take the bodies to the Mucro. Ferra sent smoke chasing after the survivors' injuries. The only one who turned her down were Fetch.

Eventually, he looked at Ruairi. The look of disappointment on his face weren't vanquished swiftly enough.

'Easy does it.' Fetch knelt and hefted Ruairi to his feet.

For some reason, the blade didn't stop shaking. It rattled between his fingers until Fetch plucked it from him.

'Now now. You'll take someone's eye out,' he said.

'Not if Aer gets to them first.' Ferra wiped the sweat and dirt from her forehead. Blood flecked her forearms. 'Those Fog-Eyed must be hers. We Mindbreakers can control them, in a fashion. Their minds are so empty they'll hold on to anything. But these ones… smog captured in their throats to keep them loyal. As much as a mindless hunk of meat *can* be loyal.'

Ruairi swallowed. Aer. The Mindbreaker Dirk needed him to kill.

'This is the price of your hesitation, boy.' Ferra swept her eyes over the dead Austelli.

Hesitation. That were one word for it.

He turned to Fetch. 'We need to go see Dirk.'

Fetch gave him the side eye. 'Guess we're headed down foundry then. Come on kid, I'll get you some… I don't know, some fucking tea or something on the way.' He wrapped an arm around Ruairi's shoulders, then looked back at Ferra. 'Take care of yourself. You're a target here.'

Ferra snorted. She hefted the hammer over her shoulders. 'I'll be fine.'

Fetch led Ruairi from the room. Ferra's eyes tracked him as he left.

CHAPTER 37

Down in the foundry, Ruairi broiled under his shirt. Big juicy drops rolled down his arsecrack. Fetch were melting besides, head shiny as a half-sucked sweet.

Austelli wound around the cavern, half-spiral like a snake trying to gum on to its rattling tail. Waiting for their turn at the heartfire.

The pit in the middle of the room slushed and scalded. A young lass with scabby eyebrows and bony shoulders lobbed a chunk into the liquid fire. Smoke boiled around her face, wisped between her lips. Her coal-black eyes flickered with blue specks as the cavern rumbled beneath her feet.

'What're they doing?' Ruairi asked.

'Feeding,' Fetch said. 'Listen.'

Ruairi closed his eyes and really focused. The rumbling, groaning noise between his feet. He could hear it, boiling off… somewhere. Like a boulder rolling slowly out of sight.

The next Austelli stepped up and lobbed their offering down into the heartfire. A handful of bloodmetal this time, the rumbling that followed was louder.

'Feeding what?'

'The Iactura. So Dirk says.' Fetch led Ruairi deeper into the cavern, following the constant *shwick-schwing* of blade on whetstone. Scraped the edges of any good humour clean from his mind like nails down sandpaper.

General Adira didn't look over as they approached. Despite the heat, she was dressed for battle, thick leather armour and metal-toed boots. The glass-sharp edge of the hatchet gripped between her knees sparkled in the orange light. Austelli gave her a wide berth.

'Dirk's busy.' She didn't so much as look up.

'Oh thank fuck, I was worried he'd be sat with his feet up whacking one out before noon.'

'You born an arsehole, or do you really have to work at it?'

'I only shit on the lazy.' Fetch rested a hand on the hilt of his blade. 'Now get up and do your job.'

'My job is to keep the Austelli safe.'

'Really? And hiding down here whilst they die is keeping them safe is it? Guarding Dirk whilst our people get hacked to bits. You're the real hero.'

General Adira rolled to her feet, hatchets swinging. 'You're right. I should be doing more. Perhaps I'll start by cutting out the traitor in their midst.'

'Suicide is never the answer.' Fetch slid half his sword blade free.

'Reckon you'll be so glib when I start cutting strips off you?'

'Woah, easy now.' Ruairi stuck his feet right between the two angry buggers. 'Let's not let the fire get to us all, eh? General, thanks for seeing us, much appreciated. We gotta go find Dirk. Aer attacked the Open Kitchen. It's past time we... dealt with her.'

Addie narrowed her eyes, spat a breath between her teeth. 'Alright. We can agree on that.'

She jerked her head and led them over to a grey platform near the rusted balcony. At a look from her some worker leapt and yanked at the chain with a three-fingered hand. The screech of churning metal stabbed the cavern as they were thumped down to the lower level.

The cavern were filled with fighting. Swords, daggers, some sort of spiky ball-on-a-stick Ruairi had never seen before. The smell of fresh sweat and rusty scabs.

A small bloke with cuts over his eyes danced around a lass with short hair, flung out a lazy cut at her legs. She reversed her spear, knocked his blow aside and drove her weapon through his chest with a thick *plorp*. The spearhead squelched out the other side covered in blood and meat.

'Clean kill Danni.' Adira stopped.

'Don't need your praise,' Danni muttered. Loud enough, but Adira ignored it.

The bloke's eyes flickered closed.

'What in the fuck are you do-?' Ruairi started, but Fetch's kick were not subtle.

The torches around the cavern burst with sapphire light, like the whole cavern blinked. When the glow were gone, the bloke stood up and fingered the hole in his shirt. A piece of bloodmetal tumbled to the floor. Underneath, the skin were smooth.

The bloke didn't so much as blink. Just handed off the bloodmetal to Adira and lifted his sword. 'Again?'

'Why? You're no challenge.' Danni went to heft her spear, then her gaze caught on Ruairi. She pinned him with her eyes. One red, one green. 'You.'

'Me.' Ruairi rattled his fingertips down his chest. Tried to meet her eyes, but couldn't quite manage.

She advanced on him, spear held ready. 'Silverspine died because of you.'

'Danni.' Adira's voice were firm.

'*You* slowed me down. *You* kept us in the Nest. *You* let the Sightless get across the river and fight him alone.' She spun the spear in her fingers.

'Stand *down.*' Adira stepped forwards, gripped the woman's wrist and slammed her boot on the shaft of the spear. It cracked, the head spinning off into the dirt.

'Get your fucking hands off me.' Danni yanked her hand free.

'Next time I'll break more than your weapon. Dirk wants this kid alive. Besides, he didn't kill anyone. Silverspine died because of… who he was.'

For all of an instant, Ruairi reckoned he saw a cloud pass over her usual firebright eyes. She blinked and it were gone.

Adira glanced around to the forming crowd, weapons lowered. 'All of you, get back to it! If anyone is unscarred after today, I'll douse the fires then kill you myself.'

She didn't wait to see if they obeyed. It took 'em a long time to listen. Weapons started clacking again, but only slowly. Danni just watched her walk away.

Ruairi followed to the back of the cavern. Cracks spiderwebbed the rock wall, fissures wide enough that the light got lost in the darkness.

'Hurry up.' Adira pressed herself into the rock and slipped on through. Ruairi scuttled after her, Fetch in tow.

The tunnels twisted like veins beneath the skin of a pig. Hot too. Worse than in the foundry. Cracks and pits of heartfire broke open the rocks at their feet. The rumbling were fiercer down here, like the throes of a dying beastie. Ruairi watched the bubbles rise and pop far below. A shudder gripped hold of his legs.

'You still with us, kid?' Fetch clamped a hand on his shoulder. 'You know she'll leave you here.'

'Aye. I'm alive.'

'Both of you, keep it down,' Adira snapped over her shoulder.

Fetch mimed sewing his lips together and they shuffled on through the caverns. Eventually the pathway opened up. Ruairi traced the wall with his fingers. Harsh rock made way for stone steps and granite that opened out into an enormous antechamber.

The Iactura speared through the cavern.

No matter how many times he saw it, the metal spire broke through Ruairi's eyeballs and lodged right in the back of his head. Smooth as silk, a pillar of blue and silver. Despite the heat, it made him shiver.

Dirk turned from the metal. His black shirt were tight with sweat, ageless violet eyes glittered in the reflected light.

'Dirk.' Adira's voice was sharp. 'Fetch and the kid to see you. Aer attacked. She sent Fog-Eyes this time.'

'No surprise. They are potent weapons, if you're desperate. As you will Addie.'

'Adira. General. Since that's the rank you gave me.' She turned to leave.

'I'd expected longer.' Dirk's voice froze her feet. 'Before the regret began in earnest.'

'Is that a fucking joke?' Adira turned slow. Her hand gripped the air just over her weapon. 'You promised the will of the dead would be remembered, that we would put a stop to all this. And now I sit up there, all day, and watch people's memories melt. Caelan was a liar, but at least the only mind he destroyed was his own.' She slammed a fist against the wall.

'It is necessary.' The corners of Dirk's mouth twitched.

'So you say.' She turned and left without a glance.

'You know she'll turn,' Fetch said when Adira had vanished back down the tunnels.

'She won't. She can't. Her commitment is far more solid than your own. Adira and I walk the mist together. She's not a Mindbreaker, but I am teaching her how to fight. Besides, where else would she go? Don't worry about her.' Dirk dismissed the retreating general with a wave of his hand. 'What's this about Aer?'

Fetch plunged into the whole thing. Ruairi left them to it. No point listening in, he'd lived it. Besides, all that talk of blood and foggy eyes… made him remember sitting there against the wall and shaking half to pissing. He wandered over to the Iactura instead, went to trace his reflection in the burnished surface. As if he could wipe away his cowardly eyes like dust from a shelf.

'Don't!' Someone slapped his arm.

Ruairi grunted and turned around only to see the prettiest lass he'd ever managed to gawp at. Eyes red as a burning sunrise, tattoos painted a sunset scar across her scalp. And cleavage by the bucket load did no harm neither, he weren't no priest.

'Children burn themselves by trying to catch fire.' She looked at Ruairi and suddenly he felt about six inches tall. 'How old are you?'

Ruairi flushed.

'Ignis, glad you could join us.' Dirk waved her over, then turned back to Fetch. 'You're right. It was Aer. An attack on Ferra is worrying, what happened to make her so bold? But I don't want to kill her.' He blinked, almost like the words surprised him. 'Even after all this, I still don't want her dead.'

'Dirk.' Ignis' voice were boiling honey. 'She has to die.'

'Else we stop this,' Fetch added. 'Fog-Eyes and Walkers won't lie down just because we ask. She wins.'

'Neither of you are listening to me. She has to die. I just don't want her to.' Dirk flipped the knife from his belt. 'Memory is easy, but emotions are far harder.'

Ruairi felt a twinge. Little ache building up right around his leg. He crushed his palm into his thigh and kneaded until it buggered off. The middle of his chest itched fierce.

He remembered how Dirk stabbed him. Dangling over that heart-fire. Pain gone in an instant. Should'a been ecstatic, but instead he just felt a little stronger and a little… less.

Dirk took a deep breath. 'Sentiment is human. This should be easier. Fetch?' He held out his palm and Fetch dutifully stabbed each of his fingertips.

With a strained breath, Dirk held his hand over a crack in the rock nearby. The heat and hiss of heartfire boiled below.

'They keep a piece. No matter how we wish they didn't.' Dirk gripped his shirt, right around his chest. Left five bloody fingerprints behind.

He rammed the arrowhead into the back of his hand.

Dirk's head snapped backwards, his mouth open, but no sound burst free. Blue flecks rippled across his violet eyes as bloodmetal fell, piece by piece, into the waiting heartfire.

The rumble was deafening. Behind Dirk, the Iactura shone almost to blinding and thick smog poured around it. The breath of the city itself. A splash of heartfire leapt from the broken rock and licked towards Dirk's wrist.

He jerked his hand back with a grin. 'You'll get all of me soon enough.' Dirk sheathed the knife at his waist.

When he turned back to them, his violet eyes were dull. 'So. Aer has to die.'

'Yes!' Ignis whispered a breath at the coal around her throat. Just like Ferra, it burst into two flame-filled orbs. She cocked an eyebrow. 'These twin sparks… is it the Iactura? Because of what you do?'

The corner of Dirk's mouth curled up. 'No. I'd tell you not to trust the flames, but what else do you have?'

Ignis' eyes smouldered. 'I am stronger than Aer, stronger than Ferra. Stronger even than your pet Reilo was.'

'Where did you hear that name?' Dirk turned on her.

Ignis just looked at him. She flipped a weapon from her belt and tossed it between her hands. What were that? Sharp on one end, but splayed out on the other. Like a funnel made from metal feathers. Little swirlies cut through the metal like irrigation channels. 'I can do this. I can kill her.'

Dirk grinned at her. 'It would appear your plan is much more than to simply kill her. I thought Aer had destroyed the last of our lancets. No, Ignis, you won't win that fight alone.' He glanced at Ruairi. 'Ruairi is the only one who can withstand her storm.'

'What do you mean?' Ruairi swallowed a hot breath.

'The shadow of your Father's past protects you. It shrouds your memories, not a silver orb of its own but a cloud that keeps your pain hidden. She'd have no idea where to look. She could drain your mind and you'd fight until your eyes melted. Of course, it also means we can't heal you. You'll die easy. And Aer is surrounded by Walkers.'

His throat were dry and his leg were twitching. Must'a pulled sommat on the run earlier, felt his muscles cramp like a fist were squeezing them around his bones.

Ruairi swallowed past a pebble lodged in his throat. 'I'm not brave like you lot. I don't have... whatever it is. That drive to go cutting folks who don't see things the way I do. I used to say...' He stopped hisself, blinked a couple of times. 'Pa used to say that the only bloodletting worth a damn came from a pig, 'cause even a murderer can eat the bacon. When I was there and watching those Fog-Eyes, I couldn't raise a hand to them.'

'It'll come in time, kid,' Fetch said.

'No. It won't.' Ruairi chewed his lip. 'Because Fog-Eyed folk are innocent, aren't they? Can't call it their fault, they got less between their ears than I do. But this Aer...' He knit his fingers together, tore the skin from the side of his thumbnail. 'She's someone needs stopping, no bones about it. So then... why does the thought of it make me feel so hollow?'

'One death to save thousands. What you do is a mercy.' Dirk gripped his forearm, pinned him with those violet eyes.

'Mercy?' Ruairi asked.

'This is why you are here. Why walk, when you can run? Why stay silent when you can speak? Why stay your hand when you can save countless lives? We need you, Ruairi.' Dirk's eyes shone.

To be needed. Not a burden, but something useful. Someone who mattered. A life were more than just existence, and this were sacrifice worth making. Aer were responsible for those deaths. She'd ordered the killings. With her gone, the city could find peace.

Ruairi drew on the memory of hisself, quivering and quaking beneath the weight of violence.

One death. That's all it would take.

'I'll do it.' He swallowed. 'I'll kill her.'

As soon as the words fell free, he felt cold. An instant, anxious pulse. Like plunging through a black lake in the middle of the night.

CHAPTER 38

'I know you're desperate Sam, but this is batshit.' Mira glanced around the empty alleyway, eyes wide.

'Just keep watch.' Sam tossed her old clothes into a pile for the rats and squeezed into the rough uniform. Jonas hadn't noticed her steal the shirts as she left the graveyard. Or at least, if he had, the memory didn't stick around long enough for him to give chase.

'They'll kill us Sam.' Mira gripped her thumbs in her fists. 'They'll take our *eyes*.'

'Like father like daughter...' Sam cinched her boots, felt the Sightless' mask dig into her ankle. Carrying it still felt wrong, but she couldn't bring herself to throw it away.

'This isn't a joke! We both saw that Walker, they'll... ' Mira caught herself. Stopped. 'But you know that. Of course you do. Sod me Sam, do you really hate yourself this much?'

'Have you ever used a Mindbreaker?' Sam spoke quietly. Mira shook her head. 'Me neither. Not properly. But when I went with Ignis into those mists, I felt what it meant to truly lose who I am.' The feeling of the lancet against her fingers, the shattering of memory. 'And it was better than this.' She pulled thick gloves over the brand, a slimy trail of salve from the blistered burn on her palm. 'If this is all "Sam" is, then better she vanished.'

'And what about me?' Mira's voice was small. 'I've visited your Father with you. You don't cry in front of anyone else. What do I do when my best friend can't remember me? Can't even look at me?'

Sam turned away. 'You sound like Vicky.' She wasn't being selfish. She was... 'Don't guilt me.'

'Jak wouldn't want you to sacrifice your name.'

'When I find him, I'll apologise.'

'Find him? Sam, Jak's dead.'

She didn't shout it. Mira didn't shout. But the words cracked like concrete beneath a hammer.

Sam stared at the handkerchief in her hands. 'You don't know that.'

Mira caught her sleeve. 'He's been missing for months. The Austelli fight hardest against those who crossed the river. You're not thinking about this.'

Sam paused. 'You're right.' She wound the handkerchief across her hair. 'And doesn't that make it easier.'

Out from the alleyway, Highdock was quiet. The Mucro hushed against the bank. Only one barge was still operational. Despite everything, the sight of their chains just piled up and rusting on the bank cut deep.

The last thing they'd worked on together.

She stalked over to the Walker standing guard by the waterwheel.

'You the one that runs this thing?' Sam tried to disguise her voice with a cough.

'I am.'

'Can I get across?

'Why?'

'Bodies.' Mira's voice very nearly caused Sam to leap into the river. 'We're here for a pick up.' She tucked an errant curl into her headband.

'We?' Sam asked. '*We* aren't here for anything. It's just me.'

'Not unless you intend to kneecap me and leave me here,' Mira said. Her face was pale, pinched, and she quivered just for standing. But her jaw was firm.

The Walker snorted and pushed his hair back from his face with thick fingers. 'Don't care how many of you there are, you ain't here for the bodies. I know the blokes. They bring a cart along too, unless you figure you'll just drag them one at a time from here to the graveyards?'

'Uhh...'

'It isn't worth it. Whatever you're looking for across there.' He scratched his stubble, the skin pinched against a thick white scar down his cheek.

'You never met him,' Sam said.

The Walker held up his hand. 'Don't want to hear it. Not here to argue. You want across, get in the bucket.'

'You said you didn't believe us.'

'I don't. But it's no business of mine. I just wanna make it home to the little one later.'

'You're not much of a guard,' Mira said.

The Walker shrugged. 'Only two kinds of folk want across the river nowadays. Either you're off to fight the Austelli, which means you're good as dead. Or you are one of them, which ain't worth my life to check. So. You want across? Get in the bucket.'

Mira met Sam's eye and shrugged. Together they stepped across the wet gap and into the rocking barge.

Even under the stink of chemical cleaning, the red-stained metal stank. Copper and ammonia burned the hairs in Sam's nose. The chain heaved and sent them sawing through the water.

'Couldn't have made these a bit... softer?' Mira's face was almost green.

'Tuck your head between your legs. Try to keep your mouth closed and just... swallow what comes up.'

Mira sank to her heels. 'I can't believe I'm here.'

'You shouldn't be,' Sam said.

'Neither should you.'

The retching silence stretched on for an eternity before the barge shuddered and *squelch*-ed into the Ferriway bank.

Immediately, they were met by a wall of black cloaks and copper swords. The only Walkers still allowed on this side of the river. To guard the corpses.

'Who are you?' the Captain asked. Cold eyes, her hair was stuck to her scalp with pitch.

'Uh, we're here for the corpses,' Mira said, less convincing than on Highdock.

The Captain's eyes narrowed, nostrils flared with a half-shake of her head. But she didn't comment, just looked over her shoulder.

On the far end of the street, a group piled bodies in heaps. Homespun, silk, black cloaks, all tumbled into the slime. Old blood congealed thick.

'Today them, tomorrow us. Try to show them some respect.' The Captain held up an arm and Walkers corralled Sam and Mira towards the bodies. They stopped a few feet away. Those loading the corpses stopped too.

'Kairi. You're very close to the end of my street.' A woman propped up a ramshackle doorway, picked her fingernails with the tip of a copper-bladed spear. Handful of people clustered around her, heavy weapons slumped in the muck. They looked at the Walkers like starving animals. No. Starvation was understandable. This was more than hunger. It felt heavy. The desire to hurt. To break something, just because they could.

'The corpse rats are here Danni.' The Captain jerked her head at Sam and Mira. 'Are you going to let them do their job?'

'Why ever not?' The woman grinned. Her eyes fell on Sam. One green, one red, both burned with something raw and barely hidden.

Sam knelt to grab a corpse. Revulsion vomited milk down her stomach. He'd been a young man, peach fuzz on his cheeks.

Mira whimpered at her side.

Heads down, they dragged the body up the Ferriway. No one stopped to help. They just stood facing one another. The edge of violence cut the smog.

'What are we going to do?' Mira whispered.

'Keep loading bodies until someone looks away. Then we make a run for it.' Sweat trickled down Sam's sides. The corpse was heavy.

'Sam.' Mira's whisper danced so softly. 'What are we doing here? I can't handle this.'

'Try not to think about it.'

'That's not...!' Mira shook her head. Tears spilled beneath her glasses.

Sam felt a piece of her heart break off in her chest. She opened her mouth, but what could she say?

They heaved the body into the barge. Mira shuddered, belched into her forearm. Sam gave her what privacy she could. Returned to the corpses. Tried not to look at who she was grabbing. Grip. Drag. Ignore the smell.

Sam's forge-strengthened muscles burned and the musty smell of rot clung to her hands. She grabbed another corpse.

Its eyes opened.

Sam screamed, loud and sharp. She scrambled back but the corpse moved so *fast*. It gripped her ankle, dragged her to the floor. Blue fog boiled in its eyes.

'Sam!' Mira shouted.

Sam kicked out, twisted back as her foot slammed into the corpse's face. Her heel sunk into its nose, but it clung to her other leg like a vice. She shook her foot free of her boot and yanked herself away. Mira dragged her back to her feet.

'Fog-Eye!' The woman with mismatched eyes leapt and pinned the corpse to the floor with her spear through its neck. It opened its mouth and a dense, black smoke whirled inside.

Instantly, weapons thudded into the flesh. Clubs and knives and arrows slammed into the once-again corpse. The body puddled against the floor like molten steel.

'Figured.' Danni twisted and sliced the head free. The Fog-Eye stopped kicking.

The dam finally burst and Mira was very noisily sick.

'I knew you two were green, but don't they train you anymore? Blokes yesterday had swords with them.' She pulled her spear free. Not much blood on the blade. Like it had all stuck to the inside.

'No one... told us...' Sam just shook her head. Felt like her heart was trying to break out of her chest and swim back across the Mucro.

'You've got massive feet.' The woman plucked Sam's discarded shoe from the hands of the still-again corpse. She went to hand it back, then stopped. 'What's this?'

She drew the Sightless' mask from the lining of the boot. Sam's mouth was dry.

'You were there.' The woman held the Sightless' mask in shaking fingers. 'You were *there*.'

'I wasn'...' Sam began, but a gag snapped around her mouth and suffocated her words into howling silence.

CHAPTER 39

Sam sat in a dank corridor, surrounded by candles. Her saliva had dried on the rag between her teeth and her jaw ached. Mira shuddered beside her.

A woman leant against the wall, arms folded. Axe-handle shoulders, tattoos that spiralled down one arm and a chain around her neck. A coal inside a gilded cage glowed against her throat. Just like Ignis.

'Danni. Why'd you bring them here?'

'They had this on them.' The woman with the eyes, Danni, held out the Sightless' mask.

Her tattoos shifted as she plucked the mask from Danni's unwilling fingers. She rubbed a thumb across the fingerprints scored in the cheeks. 'That's new. How is that possible?'

'I intend to find out.'

'Danni. This isn't healthy, what you're doing.'

Something cold dripped down the back of Sam's throat.

'Are you going to stop me, Ferra?'

The woman, Ferra, looked at her, but didn't speak.

'Exactly. Now move.'

Danni shoved past, crooked a finger and Sam and Mira were dragged down the corridor, forced against the wall beside a pink-tinged door.

Inside, a single chair was bolted to the floor. Reds and browns stained the floorboards and the air tasted like old skin and fingernails. Sam's gag was pulled down to hang around her throat, Mira's too, and they were shoved against the wall.

'Who wants to go first?' Danni asked.

'Please don't,' Mira whispered at her.

Danni grabbed her arm.

'No, wait! I found the mask, I'll tell you whatever you want. Don't hurt her,' Sam said.

'Never let people like me know what you are trying to protect.' Danni dragged Mira into the room and slammed the door shut.

'Let her go!' Sam thrashed against the manacles. 'Or I'll...' What? What was she going to do? Piss herself at them? Even that would be a stretch. Her guard kicked her in the back of the leg and she slumped to the floor as the door closed.

The guard rammed her gag back between her lips, the taste of an oily rag, then shoved two balls of wax into her ears. A hood slammed around her neck, plunged her into darkness.

All she could do was wait.

Her breath was hot inside the hood and snot dribbled from her nose and over her top lip. Bruised knees shuddered.

Mira. Oh sod it, *Mira*. What were they doing to her in there? Sam tried to blink past the darkness, to will her eyes to burn through the hood and let her see... what? Her friend being tortured?

The only person who had ever stuck by her, bleeding because Sam was so stupid, selfish, stubborn.

Vicky was right about her. She did deserve to be alone.

It was impossible to tell how long she quaked there. By the time the guard tore the hood from her head, her scratchy shirt was soaked to her back with sweat.

Sam blinked and the room came back to her. Mira was shoved up beside her. Her face white as a skull, she wept like a waterfall. Two words bubbled from her tortured throat, over and over again.

'My hands. My hands.'

Bile tore the roof of Sam's mouth.

The skin on the back of Mira's hands had been peeled away. It hung from her wrist, translucent strips of shredded flesh. The red and purple viscera *pulsed* with blood. Her arms shook uncontrollably and splashed crimson down her trousers. Sam couldn't turn away. The inner workings of the hand were exposed like a meat-puppet.

'Your turn.' Danni's voice was calm. But her face...

Sam had expected it to be empty. A blank mask. But the woman looked... pleased. Something seethed behind those eyes, something unchained.

The guard dragged Sam into the room and her panic won out. She thrashed against him, but he crushed her arms to her side and slammed her into the chair. Wires fastened her wrists to the arms and her feet were manacled to the floor.

Danni stepped close. 'Did you see your friend?'

'Aren't you human?' Sam shook.

'That's why I'm so good at this.' She pointed a weapon at Sam. A thin horseshoe with a handle attached. The inner curve was pierced with spikes and hooks and razor spines that dripped with red.

Mira's blood.

Danni stepped over and set her weapon over Sam's wrist. 'I'm glad you're wearing gloves. It'll make this last longer. What is your name?'

'Samantha Acarris.' The answer burst free like a leak from a wine-glass. She shook. All her desperate desire to remain silent melted like gold in the furnace.

'Why are you here?'

Sam swallowed a breath. Images of Mira's hand burst through her mind. 'To find my Forgemaster.'

'Two for two. You did get your stories straight.' Danni tapped her lips and left an off-pink fingerprint on her cheek. 'Why did you have that mask?'

'It's... Callisteel.'

'Callisteel. And he still killed it.' A blue fleck swept across Danni's pupils and for an instant, her lips curled into a beatific smile. It was soon crushed. 'Before he died.'

'Who died?' Sam's voice shook.

'Silverspine.' Danni hooked the skinning tool around the cuff of her glove. Spikes dug into Sam's wrist. 'Tell me what they did to him.'

'I don't know.' Sam's hand began to shake.

'That's not very convincing.' Without warning, Danni backhanded her.

Sam's head snapped back, her mouth filled with hot blood. The chair rocked beneath her and a thick line tore through her glove and into her skin.

273

'They didn't leave me his body. Tell me how they killed him. Tell me what they did!' Danni's eyes were white and wild.

'I wasn't there,' Sam whimpered.

'You had its mask! Did they tie rocks and throw him in the river? Did they burn his bones to ashes? Did they bury him outside of the city? What? What happened? Why did they take his body from me? Tell me!' Danni's free hand wrapped around Sam's throat. 'Your friend already said that you knew. She told me you'd seen him die. She swore it on her eyes.'

'No!' Sam dribbled blood. 'She just said what you told her to! You were *skinning her hands!*'

The spikes began to scrape down Sam's wrist. 'He wouldn't have begged the likes of you.'

Sam screamed.

The door banged open.

'Danni, enough!' The woman bellowed from the doorway. Ferra, the one from the corridor.

Danni didn't turn.

'Wait, wait, please!' Sam squirmed. She looked at the woman stood behind Danni. The coal around her throat sparked. 'Ignis, I know Ignis! I am… hers. She marked my hand.'

'Danni. Stop.' Ferra threw something at her. The Sightless mask. 'Stop torturing the girl and take this to the General. Dirk will want it.'

Danni snatched the mask out of her air. Her eyes bored into Sam's. Something was broken. Inside her head, Sam could see it. A thin trickle of blood dripped, click-splat down the arm of the chair.

Danni stepped back. Clean, precise, like a sweeping dance. She drew a knife from her belt and slashed it across her own wrists.

Blood spewed into the air, squirting, splattering crimson. Danni turned her back on Sam and held her bloody wrist to Ferra.

'Do it,' she said.

Ferra blew out a breath and the coal around her neck sparked blue. Moments later, Danni's wrist was bloodless and she held a chunk of metal between her fingers.

'You can't keep doing this,' Ferra said.

'I will find his body. He deserves that much.' Danni chewed her words and spat them before marching out of the room.

Sam sagged against the restraints. Cold sweat rolled off her like a river.

'I don't think an apology would help.' Ferra glanced down at Sam's trapped hand. 'That's Ignis' mark. But you're hardly the first to work for her. What did she want from you?'

'Callisteel.'

'Makes sense. The mask…' Ferra knelt beside the chair and undid the restraints keeping Sam's wrist lashed down. Just the one. She peeled the shredded glove and blood-spotted bandage away and ran a thumb across the burned flesh. Oddly tender. 'What did you do with it?'

'I…' Why start lying now? 'I tried to melt the thing. I didn't think your fancy blue fire could burn people.'

'It comes down to intent. Memoria awaits, but fire is still fire. You worked with Ignis, you should know all about the Fires of Remembrance.'

'She was not the most forthcoming patron,' Sam said.

'No surprise. She's powerful though. Ignis been trying to bring back Callisteel since Dirk first vanished. To impress him, perhaps. Or to show that she could surpass him. I don't even think Dirk truly remembers how to make it anymore. Maybe Aer does. Did. It was her Sightless, after all.' Ferra shook her head. 'Still, to do that to the Forgemasters… I might be a Mindbreaker, but I'm also a smith.'

Sam sat up. 'What about the Forgemasters? What did she do?'

Ferra cocked an eyebrow. 'You are not a subtle creature. I'm doing the questions here. When Ignis marked you, what memories did she take?'

'Nothing. I… I didn't let her.'

'You know she and I speak? I'll know if you're lying to me.'

'I swear it.'

'If that is the case, then yours is the only mind in the city that is unbroken and still retains some understanding of Callisteel. I can use you.' Ferra knelt to untie the restraints from Sam's other hand.

'I will not be used again.' Sam was surprised by the vehemence in her voice.

'I thought you wanted to know what happened to the Forgemasters?' Ferra raised an eyebrow.

Sam narrowed her eyes. 'What do you want?'

'Callisteel, what else? If you help me, then I will tell you where the Forgemasters are.'

Sam's heart pounded at her ribs. 'And if I don't?'

'Then you will wish I let Danni finish skinning you alive.'

CHAPTER 40

'When Dirk said we were going to a party, I figured it'd be more exciting than this.' Ruairi rolled his shoulders. The stolen Walker leathers were tight as turnip skin. Felt wrong. Last Walker he'd seen had been a dead one, pinned to the ground of the Open Kitchen by a pair of knives through his chest. And yet here he were, playing dress up like a kiddie in Mama's best frock.

'We aren't missing out.' Fetch stifled a yawn.

The mansion behind radiated bad taste. The size of five barns stacked atop each other, red brick walls and everything chased with gold. Window frames, chimney brackets, door trim, even the eaves. Like some god had just dribbled piss around the edges.

'You've done this before?' Ruairi asked.

'Loads of times. I… was a Walker, remember? Well, sort of. Guard duty was the worst of it, I never mind playing messenger. I miss leaving this place. I miss Ro.'

'Your horse? What happened to her?'

'They fucking *ate* her.' Fetch's words were cold as the wind. 'When Dirk sent people to rob the Walkers, what do you think they replaced their supplies with? The stables have been empty for weeks.'

Ruairi cleared his throat. How were he supposed to respond to *that*? Ignore it completely seemed the smart thing. 'So, uh, what now?'

'We wait. Ignis clears the room, then we rush in and stab Aer when she's not looking.' Fetch folded his arms and leant against the doorframe.

'Not very… heroic.' Ruairi shuddered. He pictured the blade fastened at his hip squishing through meat and bone.

'It never is. Just wait for the signal. Blue fire up through the chimney. You'll see it.'

Ruairi watched his feet. 'How can I be pissing myself scared, and bored all at the same time? Not fair, should be one or the other.'

'Count your blessings.' Fetch wiped his nose on the back of his hand. 'Boredom is the best part.'

They watched the night together.

'Fetch,' Ruairi said eventually, 'how long have you known Dirk?'

'Too long.'

'What did he do for you?'

'He… Aw bugger it, he took the memory of someone close to me away.' Fetch tugged his collar, revealing a leather pouch strapped around his throat. 'I don't know what happened to him. All I know is it made things duller and easier. My turn. You gonna kill her?'

Something swooped through Ruairi's stomach, like he'd swallowed a chick fighting and clawing for its life. 'I have to.'

'That's not what I asked.'

Ruairi tapped his teeth together. 'I know.'

'Ah kid. "No" just isn't an option for folk like us, is it?'

'What do you…?'

Fetch uncurled, suddenly alert. 'There's someone out there.'

Ruairi gripped his sword.

'Easy lad, don't give the game away. Just look up to that building on the left and tell me if you see anyone.'

Ruairi flicked a glance to the guardhouse. 'That's the guy!' A hooded figure darted past an alcove, slinked around the chimney. 'From the Open Kitchen. The bloke who'd vanished when the Fog-Eyed arrived. The one who…'

Who let him prove what a coward he was.

Not this time.

'Kid, what are you doing?' Fetch hissed.

The guardhouse walls were smooth, but a few paces away an old stable roof bowed with age. Ruairi spat on his hands. 'Sommat stupid.'

He hefted himself up, splintered wood flaked around his fingers as he shuffled up to the flat roof. Smog were thicker up here. He could taste it.

'You're gonna break your idiot neck!'

'I know.' Ruairi walked to the back of the stable roof to get a better run up. 'I'm a bleeding lunatic.'

He took off. Wood crunched under his too-big Walker boots and the lip of the stable approached awful quick...

'Ruairi!' Fetch shouted.

He landed on the roof of the guardhouse, shoulder first. The Walker leather scraped down his arm like sandpaper.

Ruairi wobbled to his feet and looked down to the street.

'Fetch, your head is right shiny from up here.'

'I swear on my fuckin' arse...!'

'Eyes out. I ain't pissin' into the wind up here for you to miss it if they decide to run.' Ruairi walked up the slope of the guardhouse roof and on to the outcropping half-roof of DeWhit's mansion. Went looking for a window. Luckily it were a muggy night. Enough of them were thrown open at a pretence of getting some chill. Beyond the windows, the roof dropped off sharpish. Either the bloke had wings like a woodpecker under that dramatic little robe, or he'd snuck inside.

Ruairi pushed past the gauze curtain and thumped into the house.

Wood panel hallway led to a pair of stairs down the back. He took them two at a time, slipped his fingers down the burnished gold banister. The noise of the party broke through the double doors at the base of the stairs.

Ignis were gonna be so pissed at him.

Marble everywhere. Who had fountains inside? Larger than life statues of blokes pissing in unison gushed all about the place. Made the room feel like a massive toilet. Candles festooned the walls, dripping and guttering, the smell of tallow and acetic smoke. Trencher tables sank under the weight of what might'a been a feast? It were certainly displayed like one, but the food itself... grey porridge and anaemic chicken done up like it were going courting. Fetch's horse would'a been more appetising.

'What are you *doing* here?' Ignis bore down like a stallion-mid charge. Dress red as a sunset, rich as spider-silk. A mask hid most of her face, orange and blue painted like a parrot. Languid feathers curled all the way around her head, keeping the tattoos a secret, and traced around her neck. Hid the tiny coal beneath. She'd have been more than gorgeous if she weren't so pissy with him.

'Ignis, I...'

'I'll rip your tongue out and make you taste your own eyeballs if you use that name again. What's the matter with you?'

'Right.' Ruairi clamped his jaw tight shut, scanned the room. Problem were, all the sodding masks made a sea of fake-faces. Not to mention enough folk had whipped out a hood to complete their 'look.' Where was the bastard?

The *tink-tink-tink* of knife-on-wineglass. All the masked folk, dressed rich and smelling like flowers no one had ever heard of, shushed themselves to pay attention. Ignis thumped Ruairi's arm, then clamped her jaw shut.

Some massive bloke, copper hair and curling beard, stumbled up to a little platform at the top of the room. Sagged under the weight of his wineglass, smile too wide to be genuine.

Viceroy Walter DeWhit, Lord Treasurer. Dirk had drilled their names in 'til Ruairi could'a recited them in his sleep.

'Friends and voters all, welcome!' Sounded like he were trying to talk with a frog hopping off his tongue. Bright spots of colour bloomed in his cheeks. 'I am so glad you could make it.'

He paused like he were expecting applause. Didn't get it. Ruairi had half a mind to cough, just to distract him from the awkwardness.

'The war that rent our streets has reached its final close, and I am delighted to have you here to celebrate the victory. We can finally get Arx back to the way she should be. A toast!' He raised a glass.

'Toast to what?' A bloke launched from his chair. No mask, his salt-and-pepper moustaches twitched.

Var DeKeita. Head Captain of the Walkers.

'A war is won...!'

'... but not by us.' DeKeita cut him off. 'What celebration is there for our blood? We lost, Walter.' His steel eyes were cold. 'We lost.'

'Dirk told us to do nothing.' Bloodshot eyes twitched over sunset cheeks. 'That's all I'm doing. Bringing normalcy back. Maybe if you'd have done the same, the Ant would still be with us. Maybe more Walkers would have survived. Maybe...!'

'Never reason with a drunk.' New voice, a woman with an owl mask peering through a tumble of grey curls. She hefted a gilded brazier, tipped out the coals.

Smacked the sodden ginger bastard with the base and sent him tumbling off the stage and into one of the tables with the sound of shattered crockery.

Murmurs, voices raised. Someone swore, a couple even made it to their feet.

'Remain where you are!' The woman threw off her mask.

Amber eyes. Leanne DeSüle.

Aer.

Ignis drew her long fingernails slowly down her forearm. Red runnels speckled across her pale skin.

'You will hear us.' Aer's voice was not raised, but it wailed like a squalling wind. Ruairi felt it against his shoulders, almost shoved him back a step. Windows banged on shutters, wineglasses toppled and guests were thrown back to their seats.

Except one. A bloke leant against the wall, hood twitching in the gale. There's the bastard. He plucked a broken wineglass stem from a nearby table and slunk through the candles' shadow towards the stage.

Ruairi mirrored the bloke's movements. Tried to make it seem natural, like he were patrolling or sommat. There were real Walkers all over the gaff, he fit right in.

'Where are you *going*?' Ignis snarled, but Ruairi just gestured.

'The smoke of the present buys peace in the future. I urge you to remember that. DeKeita?' Aer stepped aside.

Var DeKeita bound forwards, massive moustache bristling. 'For over a month now, you have heard me beg for your assistance in re-taking the city, and for over a month now, most of you have turned a blind eye.'

The grumbling increased, but DeKeita forged on regardless.

'Why would you not? What was once the Nest still holds and only one barge can cross the Mucro. Why should we do anything to take a reborn Austellus from that blue-fire cult? Doubtless we will *eventually* starve, but I realise the futility of trying to tell you to think about the future.' DeKeita shook his head. 'Bring it in.'

A team of Walkers slammed open the front door, surrounding a captain. The lead blackcloak Walker thrust a sodden bag into DeKeita's arms, stood back with a sad salute.

DeKeita tore open the bag and yanked out a severed head by the hair. The stink oozed off it, like an abattoir a couple of days after cleaning. The smell of death is not so easily cleansed.

Ruairi's stomach folded in on itself. He didn't recognise the bloke, but he knew those eyes. Or rather, he recognised the lack. Scorched flesh puckered around the empty eye sockets.

A dead Fog-Eye. 'Cept it weren't just the eyes. A corpse looks empty, but this were sommat else. The skin were drawn, teeth exposed by leathery lips, like the inside had been scooped clean out. Drained of everything it didn't even look human.

'Some still fight. Mindless, they wage war on our behalf.' DeKeita's eyes flickered at Aer. 'But it all ends the same way.' His voice faded. Soft as human. 'Who amongst you wants this future?'

The room lapsed into silence.

'This is not our future.' A deep voice, pitched to carry. 'This is our reality. It cannot be stopped.'

The figure in the hood darted from the crowd and leapt up beside Var. Ruairi swore, and shouldered past to try and get up there hisself.

'Who the fuck are you?' DeKeita whirled on the interruption. His hand fell to the blade at his hip and the Walkers started barging towards the stage proper.

Some lass screamed and flipped a plate over, but no one paid her much mind. All eyes were transfixed on the stage.

'The Fog-Eyed are a stopgap. Blunt instruments, if effective. Our fate is far more insidious. Everyone who has engaged a Mindbreaker is a target now. Your memories exposed. They can be sliced at will. You won't even know it's happened. Until one day you wake up and there is a stranger snoring next to you. You'll plunge a knife through their throat, because the lives you shared together no longer happened.' The hooded bloke cast out his arms, broken wine stem levelled like a knife towards the crowd. 'You'll see an infant you don't recognise living in your house and you'll feel nothing as you let it starve. You won't even question it. *That* is what is at stake here.'

Ruairi felt a shudder boil down his shoulders. A memory hit him. Danni's spear plunging through an Austelli chest. A burst of blue flame and the bloke stood back up, ready to die again.

'Alright, this is lunacy.' DeKeita drew his sword.

In the pit before the stage, Ruairi mirrored him.

DeKeita placed the tip against the hooded bloke's chest. 'Who *are* you?'

'What, Var, you don't recognise me?' They threw back their hood.

An older face, but youthful eyes. He gestured at the blade, hands up. A thick scar ate through the palm of his hand.

CHAPTER 41

Andross DeGaya. The Ant. Hero of the Flame Protests, saviour of Pa. A wash of gratitude rattled through him. The echo of an echo.

Pa's memory. The Ant had saved his life. He were the reason Ruairi even got to exist at all.

'Andross! Step down.' DeKeita gestured at the Walkers. One by one, they sheathed their blades. 'We have nothing to fear from this man.'

Speak for yourself. Ruairi kept his blade bare, just let the tip rest against the polished floorboards.

'They told me you died,' DeKeita said.

'I don't blame them.' The Ant lifted his shirt, revealing a starburst scar across his side. When he turned, the exit wound spidered across his back. 'Fortunately, my mates in the Nest found me before I bled out. But then, I've always been far luckier than I have any right to be.'

'A necessary deceit.' Aer gripped the Ant's forearm. 'He has been leading sorties against Dirk for us. Things were... simpler, when he was reported dead. The Fog-Eyes can be manipulated, drawn to broken minds. That kitchen is a beacon.'

'Then why are you here?'

'We had agents watching Dirk. Last night, we found their bodies pinned like puppets through the Nest. Quill is spitting blood, sweeping the place. There is no way Dirk could have known. But he did. Which means there is no hiding anymore.' He looked over the crowd, flipped the sharpened glass in his fingers. 'For any of us.'

Ruairi felt his blood get right nippy. He tried to shuffle back, but the crowd were blocking him in tight.

DeGaya hurled the jagged dart. Not at Ruairi.

At Ignis.

The wine stem flew past her cheek, carved through her mask. Blood dripped from her chin with a soft tap.

'Mindbreaker,' the Ant growled. 'You are not welcome here.'

DeKeita leapt from the stage, blade bare and held in readiness. He gripped Ruairi's shoulder and squeezed. 'Good lad. Walkers, blades out!'

The squad gathered up close. And Ruairi really began to sweat.

'Hypocrite.' Ignis raised a hand. The coal around her throat ignited, burst with a line of blue flame. It wound around her arm and leapt from her fingers.

Fire slashed across DeSüle's skirt. Cloth smouldered away and her left leg were exposed. Tattoos swept around her thigh. Grey as ashes and infinitely intricate, they leapt and swirled across her skin like swallows in an updraft.

Aer sniffed. She held out her arms. The air around her shimmered and smoke poured from the candles that scattered the room. Thick and grey, it soaked the air like a veil. She turned to the crowd. 'I do hope you will all consider what you have witnessed here this evening.'

The smoke lashed through the room, a tempest of ash and soot. Guests covered their faces, leapt up screeching and hollering at the filthy air that chased them outta the door. They barged past Ruairi and the Walkers, cloud of smoke close behind. It ripped the skin like beestings.

'You've had the bottle,' a young Walker lad whispered. 'You've had the bottle now. There isn't anything else, stop crying, please stop crying...'

A lass beside him held her arms around herself and shuddered. 'Let me be, Da. I'll be good, I'll be so good...'

'They're just memories. They can't hurt you.' DeKeita's words were firm, but his voice wavered. Just a hair. What were he seeing beyond the mist?

Ruairi blinked past the dust. An image of a young man in Walker leathers, striding powerful and standing tall. So much pride, so much potential. But he knew... he knew it weren't him.

His leg twinged.

When the smoke faded, the guests were gone. Only the Walkers and DeKeita remained, alongside Aer and DeGaya. Blades were drawn. All focused on Ignis.

Her mouth quirked. 'You are weak, Aer.'

'I am kind.' The smoke gathered about Aer, bolts of energy leaping and twisting through the ash.

DeKeita spoke quietly. 'We need the half-bald one. Captured, if possible. Dead if not. Charge quick. Keep her away from the fire. Be brave, be certain. Ready yourselves.'

Ignis narrowed her eyes at the lazy smile on Aer's face. Sweat poured down Ruairi's neck. What were he supposed to do? His blade were out, but he weren't taking seven Walkers on his own.

Someone shouted from outside, and from nowhere a body came flying across the room. It hit the base of the pissing fountains with a *thud* and crumpled at the bottom. Blood leaked down a familiar face.

Fetch.

Behind him, a boot clanked through the doorway. A figure emerged from the murk outside. A giant. Clad in blue-silver armour.

Ruairi's legs wobbled. They'd spoke about this. He'd *seen* it in the mist. The Sightless. Except it were different from Dirk's memories. The armour were chipped and dull. And the mask were gone.

The severed head had looked more alive. Its eyes were missing. Fog in one socket, but the other... a black-scarred clump of flesh, jagged and twisted flaps of skin. Blue-tinged, sunken cheeks ripped and torn, hollow to the bone beneath. Lips scarred and twisted open, cheeks hollow to the bone beneath. When it opened its mouth to breathe, blood dripped down its chin. It were chewing its tongue.

Ignis' eyes were wide and wild. 'Ferra told me that thing was dead!'

'Life is air and blood.' Aer's smile was brittle as ice. 'Lucianus drowned for me.' The way she spoke were so... tender.

The giant jerked its head around at the sound. Looked past her. Drew its axe.

'Fetch!' DeKeita snarled. 'You dare show your face here after what you've done?'

'Head Captain.' Fetch wobbled on his feet. He twitched his cloak. 'Don't suspect you'd let me turn this thing one more time? For old time's sake?'

'You making jokes?' DeKeita's voice was tired.

'S'all I've got. My Captain, you were the one who taught me to laugh when things look their worst. We doing this?' Fetch drew his sword.

'Enough of this.' Ignis tore a torch from the wall and dashed it against the floor. 'This city has long since bent knee to the flames!'

A spiral of azure fire spread from her feet. Ruairi sprinted free of the Walkers as the flames *burst* outwards in a blaze of terrible heat.

'*Reality burns. Inhale the memory.*'

So hot. A curtain of flame. It licked at the pile of copper blades and bent, melted their honed surface. Ruairi's saliva boiled in his throat. Tears sizzled unshed from his eyes.

Beyond the wall, a pair of sapphire orbs hung overhead. Crashing, boiling flame that scorched the ceiling.

Eyes of fire.

'What kind of idiocy woman? We're trapped! Do you have a plan?' Fetch growled.

'The edges of…' she began.

'A pretty trick.' A voice broke through the crackle and spit of the flames. Aer wore a cloak of ash, an empty void that shrouded her. The fire left her untouched.

Ignis turned to face her. 'You use our power even as you decry it.'

'I will turn the blade Dirk placed in my hands against both you and him. And then I will turn it on myself. That was always what we planned.' Aer gestured to her side.

The Sightless stepped through the flames. Like a mountain given movement, his armour boiled. Living silver. Blue sparks shot from his shoulders, reflected on the edge of his axe.

'You drained the memories from a rotting lump of flesh to bring your Sightless back.' Spiral flames curled around Ignis' waist, up to her arms, pulsing and churning.

'It took far more than that.' Smoke *burst* between Aer's lips as she spoke. 'You cannot imagine how it burns. But we swore to exterminate this foul magic and everyone it has touched. Dirk. You. Ferra. Then me. Lucianus will survive us all. Immortal, he will stand guard of the Iactura from here until Arx is dust.'

'How could you do that to him?' Ignis' voice faltered. 'What did he do to be punished like that?'

'He loved us. And we him. He could never master our flames, but he was the only person strong enough to carry Arx's burdens on his back. I have spent forty years mourning him as dead. Because I cannot face what I have done to him living.'

For the first time, Aer looked old.

'For what it is worth, I'm sorry Ignis. If I had been braver all those years ago, Dirk would be dead and this never would have happened. It is my responsibility. But I loved him too. I never forgot.'

'You talk as if you've won! Silverspine killed the Sightless once, and there are three of us against two of you. You...'

'Not quite.'

Ruairi looked up. Somehow, the Ant had stacked a bunch of tables atop each other and were standing, somewhat unsteadily, on the top one. With a grunt, he flung himself over the top of the flames and smashed into the floor beside Aer. The tables beyond the fire fell with a crash.

'Var and the Walkers are formed up beyond the flames. More are on their way. As soon as the fire is gone, they are surrounded.' The Ant drew a sword.

'It dies when she does.' Aer gestured at Ignis.

'Very well.'

He looked down at his scarred, vein-crossed hands for a long time. The sword jabbed into his palms. Drops of blood beaded on his hands.

'What are you doing?' Aer asked.

'I want to forget.' Blood dribbled down the Ant's sleeves. 'I fought for this city. Despite my every attempt, it still bleeds. The legacy of the Flame Protests is nothing but an empty title and an uncomfortable chair. Give me my youth. Give me my rage. Make me a hero again.'

'You'll lose your eyes. No one could sacrifice that much.'

'These last forty years are empty. It would be no great loss.'

Aer looked at him for all of a heartbeat. Then she crooked a finger.

Smoke billowed towards the Ant. Drew him into the air, feet dangling, blood dribbling from the holes in his hands. Ash poured into him, through his nose, his mouth, his ears, the bleeding gashes through his palms. The storm swallowed him, a hurricane beneath the ceiling, the sound of shattered windows. A chunk of brickwork tore from the wall and smashed through a fountain, spraying white chips stinging through the air.

Light blazed from within.

'Any ideas?' Ruairi shouted through the storm at Fetch.

'Not a one. How'd you fight the wind? Reckon we're fucked.' He gripped tight to his blade like it were threatening to rip outta his hands.

The tempest slowed, then broke in a wave of ash and soot. Ruairi covered his eyes, wiped them clear.

The Ant stood beside the Sightless. Thick arms almost split the sleeves of his shirt. Clean, beardless face and a tousle of brown hair.

His eyes were so pale blue they were almost white. But they still remained.

'You can't,' Ignis breathed. 'We are not gods!'

Aer just smiled. 'He never let you reach to what we became.' Smoke curled around her wrist, raced forwards and wrapped around Ignis, binding her arms, her chest. Her mouth opened slack. Aer clenched her fist and the chain of smoke tightened. Sweat beaded on her forehead.

The Ant bolted at Ruairi and Fetch, the speed of youth and fire. Fetch leapt forwards to clatter his strike aside but the Ant just forced Fetch back. He flicked the bald bloke's blade outta the way and scored a deep cut across his ribs.

Which left Ruairi alone before the Sightless. Before he could blink, that axe were swinging.

Ruairi leapt back. He'd seen what Dirk's little spit of Callisteel could do. No bugger's way he were touching a whacking great axe of the stuff. Relentless, the Sightless came again with a deadly arc that bit into the floorboards.

Ruairi's sword flickered, useless as a gnat. Every strike made his hands hurt, his shoulders shudder in their sockets.

He weren't gonna win this.

The Sightless pressed him back, no rush. Heat, intense, roared into his back. Ruairi spared a glance over his shoulder. He were right against the fire. Close enough to start cooking his arse.

The Sightless reached for his throat. Burned-out eyes narrow in that mangled face.

With a roar, Fetch barrelled into the side of the Sightless, pushed him off a step. The Ant's blade whistled round and licked a deep line down his side. Fetch screeched. The Sightless' axe came crashing back. Ruairi leapt up on the splintered remains of a table and just about managed to fling himself away.

Fetch kicked the Ant in the stomach and launched himself at the Sightless. Ruairi raced to help, their swords flickered across the armour, but there were no gaps. No clasps or joints. The metal had been melted to the bloke's flesh.

The axe came cleaving at Ruairi. Fetch grabbed his collar and shoved him outta the way, the wind of the strike passing inches from his face.

Behind them, the Ant rammed his sword through Fetch's shoulder.

'Fetch!' Ruairi leapt over, but the hilt of the Sightless' axe slammed into his legs and he went sprawling on to his face.

'*The pair of you-!*' Ignis' voice pierced the soupy air. Blood speckled her lips, the smoke tight around her throat, but she had an arm outstretched. Not towards Aer.

Towards the wall of flame.

'*Exhale the truth.*'

The air shuddered.

Meteors of blue fire rained from the blaze. Craters boomed into existence across the polished floor. The Ant and the Sightless were forced back.

The flames hurtled at Aer.

The Sightless turned and pounded towards her. With a grunt, he wrapped her in his arms and blue fire burst against his armoured back. The smell of cooking flesh, the sizzle of fat. He didn't scream.

The smoke faded from Ignis' arms. She took a deep breath, like she were bursting outta water.

Ruairi raced over, grabbed her wrist. 'You okay?'

She shook free of him and pointed. 'Behind you!'

Ruairi turned. The Sightless, neck clustered with weeping blisters, thumped over at him. Ignis threw out her hand, a rope of flame slamming into the Sightless' broken face.

The fire vanished.

Aer's laugh were bitter. 'What do you think he has left to forget?'

The Sightless swung at Ruairi. He danced back, held his blade up to parry. A metal fist ripped the sword from his fingers and slammed it into the floor at his feet.

'Not now!' Fetch bolted across the floor, one useless arm streaming out behind him. The Ant's blade licked out across his legs, but he ignored it like it weren't nothing. He leapt at the Sightless and shoved his sword through the back of its head.

The Sightless stumbled back. Armoured fingers lifted to its face. Touched the blade of the sword sticking out beside its ruin of a nose. But it didn't wobble. Didn't fall. Didn't die.

'You're fucking kidding me,' Fetch said.

'Lucianus.' Aer's voice were a whisper, a promise. A cloud of ash buzzed from the flames, swirled around the Sightless' face, hid them both in shadow.

From behind the smoke, the Ant leapt at them. Fetch ran forwards. His shoulder were still a ruin of blood, but he drew a dagger with his off hand. The Ant spun, almost contemptuous. He were inhuman fast. The blade flickered and Fetch bled, the dagger flung from his bloody fingers.

The Ant's white eyes shone. His fist crunched into Fetch's face and his blade flashed at Ruairi.

Ruairi screamed. A trench of white-cold fire burst across his chest and he collapsed.

'Leave him!' Fetch shouted. Weapons forgotten, he wrapped his arms around the Ant's waist and threw them both into the splinters and rubble.

Ruairi picked himself up. His chest burned, his lungs were tight with smoke and blood dripped down his shirt.

The Sightless stepped outta the storm of ash. Fetch's sword were gone, the Sightless' face clean of blood. Smoke swirled between Aer's fingers.

'He has nothing left to forget.' Ignis dragged her nails through her hair. 'How can she...' She stopped. Her eyes bulged from her head. 'Callisteel! He has nothing left to forget. But that armour is filled with forty years of mindless execution. He can't forget. But his armour remembers everything.'

She lifted her arms and clawed through the air. The fire *pulsed* and rushed towards her. Every spark, every flame, the candles, the torches, a firestorm wound around Ignis' body. Fury of avenging flame, it swallowed her in a raging inferno. Her red eyes broke through the blue-white flame.

Overhead, the flaming eyes remained. Unmoved.

Ignis threw her hands out and twin bolts of flame roared at the Sightless. 'Remember!'

The armour lit up like the sun.

'You dare!' Aer clenched her fist and smoke gathered around the Sightless. The glow in its armour faded. It picked up its axe.

The Sightless walked towards Ignis. Flames rippled from her hands, splashed into the metal, but the smoke and dust shrouded it. It pushed through the heat. Drew close. Inexorable.

'*Kill her!*' Ignis screamed at Ruairi.

She sounded afraid.

Ruairi rushed at Aer. Without thinking, he wrapped his fingers around her throat.

As soon as he touched her flesh, his back began to ache.

Her amber eyes pierced him. Sweat dribbled down her cheeks. 'You don't want this.' Smoke lashed from her fingers, boiled around the Sightless. But its heavy footsteps had come to a stop. That broken face twisted from Ruairi to Ignis and back again. Paralysed by indecision.

'Stop this,' Ruairi shouted. 'Surrender and...' He swallowed. 'And we'll let you live.'

'Dirk would never allow that.' Her voice was calm.

'He's not gonna have a choice.' Ruairi forced his fingers tighter. Felt the bone of her windpipe against his palm. 'Call off your monster. Let the smoke die. It's over.'

'Can you...' She drew a desperate breath, wheezed down her throat like sludge through a straw. 'Can you do it?' she croaked.

'I don't know.' Ruairi's hand shook. His eyes hurt. He squeezed harder. 'I really don't want to have to find out.'

A long, slow breath burst from Aer. Her cheeks began to purple.

A tear trickled down Ruairi's cheek. 'Please don't make me do this. Don't make me kill you in front of him. You said he drowned for you. Ain't it time you two stopped having to die for one another?'

Aer's eyes darted to the Sightless. They filled, wide and wet. Her head sank and she gave an infinitesimal nod.

The smoke died.

Ruairi dropped her throat like a serpent's tail.

She stumbled a step, rubbed her throat. 'Dirk wins. We will all regret this.' Her voice scratchy, tired.

'Fire is power.' Ignis' eyes blazed. 'It burns.'

Another bolt of fire slammed into the Sightless. The armour began to shimmer. To sear and cook beneath the onslaught of flame.

'Ignis what are you doing?' Ruairi shouted over the flames. 'It's over!'

Fire poured into the Sightless' expressionless eyes. The armour shaped and spiked and bubbled around it. The heat were so intense. Ruairi felt it beneath its skin, inside its mouth. The stink of burning hair. Flesh fell from the Sightless' face, eyebrows crisped and sizzled.

'Lucianus!' Aer sprinted towards him.

Armour erupted in an enormous spray. Fragments blasted outwards from the slop of meat and blood. Ruairi threw himself to the floor under the deadly hail of metal. Aer slammed backwards, a massive shard embedded in her stomach.

'Fetch!' Ruairi spun around. Where were he? There! Huddled on the floor. Blood leaked from countless wounds, like juice pulped from an orange. The bald idiot twisted his head and stood up with a grin.

'Good thing you remembered your sword, eh kid?' Despite the bravado, his whole body shook. A couple of steps, then he sank to his knees again.

'Easy Fetch, easy. Bugger me, what happened to you?' Ruairi gripped Fetch by the shoulders and gently levered him back to his feet.

'He was distracted trying to keep you alive. I was better.'

Ruairi spun. The Ant propped up a splintered table, his head nodding over his chest. A piece of broken armour pierced deep through his leg, pinned it to the floor. 'Time my luck ran out.' He winced and shifted. 'My leg's gone. That's me done. This is... how it should have happened. Dying for my city.' He looked up. 'I can't remember a day beyond when they offered me that fancy chair. But I should have turned it down. Should have kept fighting. Finish me. I've earned that much.' The Ant tilted his head back, bared his throat.

Ruairi looked at Fetch. He just sorta... shrugged. Gestured to the hilt of his sword.

Fury bit at Ruairi like a hound tearing through his open, steaming chest. 'I'm bloody not! What is it with you bastards and dying? Nothing heroic about the sodding grave. To think I looked up to you...' He knelt beside the Ant, just like he had Dirk all that time ago, and ripped the blue-silver metal free from the bloke's flesh. It plorped and burbled blood down his side.

The Ant's white eyes flickered. He shoved his hand against the wound. 'You're so green. Why won't you kill me?'

'Wanna die so bad?' Ruairi drew the Ant's knife from his belt and slapped it, hilt first, into the bloke's palm. 'Do it yesself. Or focus on getting up and keeping those leaking bits inside you. You saved my Pa.' Instantly, the twinge in his hips began to throb, like someone chained a belt of steel right around his waist.

Ruairi stood up, left the Ant to his blood. Looked over at Fetch. The bloke's face were carefully neutral.

'What?' Ruairi asked.

Fetch's face broke open into an ear-splitting grin. 'I'm proud of you, kid.'

Well. Bugger that. Little bit of warmth inside, who cared? No need to flush the way he did, he weren't no child.

Still though.

Together, they hobbled over to Ignis.

Ignis' hands were charred. Thick, ashen lines cut her skin like razorscars, but she were nothing on Aer. A thick wedge of metal in her stomach dug deep. She were dying, no two ways about it.

Ignis tore that lancet-spike from her belt and pressed it to Aer's chest.

Aer's amber eyes flickered. 'A crucible lancet. I thought we had destroyed those after Reilo. To capture a person's dying breath, the memories that flash before their eyes at the end... our evils weigh heaviest at the end. Souls trapped in metal... but you will not forge Callisteel from me. It cannot come from a broken mind. So simply watch. My final memories.'

Ignis shoved the spike into Aer's chest.

Blood drained from the lancet-blade, slipped through the channels engraved on those metal feathers, red and silver like threads of silk. The patterns in the metal began to glow. To smoke. Aer's final breath fell from her throat in a cloud of smog.

Despite himself, Ruairi sucked down a breath and fell into memory.

'Dirk. This has to end.' Aer's voice were torn, fury and disappointment. Her eyes were dry, but beside her Lucianus' beard was wet with his own tears.

In the cavern beneath Arx, Dirk's violet eyes glittered. His teeth split his lips and he stared at the Iactura.

It rippled around his wrist. His hand was gone, disappeared inside the metal. Smog spiralled around him, drew him closer to the pillar.

'I've destroyed the memory of Callisteel.' Dirk's voice was pained, but proud. 'Every broken mind in the city has forgotten how to make it in an instant.'

'How?' Aer's voice was sad.

'The Iactura connects us all. Every broken mind. I can control it. I can control Arx.' Blood dribbled down his ear. 'Callisteel, flesh and fire. I have all three. The Iactura. I can...'

'... you can what? Dirk, the Flame Protests are burning the city. We can't keep this up. Every time we use that fire, we make things worse!'

'Not now!' Dirk shouted. He turned over his shoulder, face vicious. 'We've come so far. Anyone with a memory lost will listen to me. I can alter their memories, I *know* I can. Everyone will forget this war, forget the hatred. I can stop them here!'

'You'll steal their humanity!' Even broken, Lucianus' voice was deep. 'Have you seen what happens to those who keep visiting you two? Those who have died over and over in this war? Their eyes...' He gulped a desperate breath. 'You can't do this Dirk. It's monstrous. Please. Come back to us.'

'I am responsible!' Dirk's face contorted. 'This war is *my fault*! I stole their iron, I awoke the Iactura, I broke open their minds. I need to do this. I need to stop them. They will listen to me.'

'And what about us?' Aer blinked. 'Will we become your obedient vessels as well?'

'Not you.' Dirk hung his head. 'This won't work on a Mindbreaker. The Fires of Remembrance keep you immune.'

'So then...?'

'Don't fight me,' Dirk whispered.

Silence cracked the cavern.

Aer clenched her fist. The coal around her throat sparked blue.

'Is this what we've come to?' Dirk's voice ached.

Lucianus drew the woodcutter axe from the sheath across his back. His hands tightened white against the hilt. 'I love you, Dirk. But I can't let you do this.'

'Lucianus is right. I can't love a man who sees himself as a god.' Smoke began to pour from the coal around Aer's throat. 'I'm sorry...'

Flame spluttered from the coal around Dirk's throat. He drew his hand from the Iactura and faced them both.

Fire raced into his palms.

'But we couldn't kill him.' Aer's voice pierced the memory as it faded into empty white fog. *'Lucianus' axe against his throat, Dirk's fire long burned out and yet... we couldn't do it.'*

'Why not?' Ignis' voice was flame and fury.

'I...' Aer's voice faded. *'I didn't want to remember him like that...'*

A flicker. Dirk, a young man with life behind those violet eyes. His arms around Aer's shoulders. The smell of ash and soot and blood on his shirt. Their bodies held back from exhaustion by Lucianus. His chest a stable pillar against which the whole world could batter itself and leave him unmoved. The only man who could stand before the storm and come out unscathed.

The trio leant into each other.

The memory faded into ash.

Aer's breath faded from her throat.

Ruairi sat back, beside the corpse. He hadn't killed her. It weren't her blood on his hands.

So then why did he feel so guilty?

'This is all we were to him? He wanted us to kill each other because we know how to resist his fire.' Ignis' voice were fury itself, her lips twisted so fierce with rage they tore and blood oozed down her chin. She ripped the lancet from Aer's chest in a spray of crimson. A couple chunks of bloodmetal rattled on the floorboards at her feet. 'Aer couldn't do it, but I can! I can stop him. I won't die for his apotheosis.' Ignis turned on Ruairi. 'And you're going to help me.'

'No. I won't.' Ruairi were so tired. Half-tempted to let his eyes sink shut and nap right there. 'How many times do I gotta prove it? I ain't killing nobody.'

'I'm not asking!' A coil of fire burned around Ignis' arm. 'You heard Aer. You can't make Callisteel from a broken mind.'

'Leave it, Ignis.' Fetch grabbed her elbow. 'The kid said no.'

Ignis' lips curled. Cruel. 'You know, when we cut a mind it never *wants* to lose the memory. So it implants a subtle urge to keep hold of the bloodmetal produced. For most people, the memory is small enough that they barely notice. They don't want to give it to us, but they can be convinced. But for those who forget something major, something connected to so much of who they are, that urge is much stronger.' Fire burned in her palm. She gripped Fetch's shirtfront. 'Strong enough to make you do something as stupid as bringing your own bloodmetal into a fight with Mindbreakers. Did you never wonder? That phrase that calls the fire.' Blue flames reflected in her eyes. '*Inhale the memory.*'

Fetch's shirt burst into flame. A hole near his heart, that leather pouch incinerated and a thick chunk of metal fell into Ignis' palm. The fire boiled and bubbled around it. Melted the metal into a black puddle in her palm.

She shoved it down Fetch's throat.

The bloke tried to scrabble back, tried to scream. Ruairi just watched, frozen. Fetch threw hisself back, scrabbled away.

Tears dribbled from his eyes.

'No. No, *no!*' Fetch writhed against the floor like he were struck by bolts of lightning.

'You're next!' Ignis threw out her arms. The flame wall roared, tightened around the pair of them, a searing pillar

'Your magic ain't do shit to me,' Ruairi spat. 'What did you do to Fetch?'

'Nothing is immune to fire.'

Ruairi couldn't move. So hot. Sweat poured down his face. Beyond the fire, he could hear the Walkers. 'Ignis, you gotta stop this...' He blinked, wobbled.

She clenched her fists and the fire slammed into the floor. Singeing, burning wood creaked and clattered and then something below them *snapped*.

Ruairi's foot slipped as the ground gave way beneath him. Ignis' vengeful eyes followed him down.

Overhead, those two blue spheres winked out. He smacked his head on something and crumpled into the dark.

CHAPTER 42

The Ferriway stank of smog and rot and the corpses they hadn't managed to shift. Ferra's friends, the self-styled 'Austelli', marched Sam and Mira down the winding road of sludge. Mira's steps were unsteady. Muck sucked the slipper from her foot, but she just left it there.

She stared at her hands.

The grimy bandage already stained with red. The dog-leech that had taken a needle to her wasn't hopeful they would ever heal. Amputation was talked about. Gangrene. Hopefully the temple healers would have some better ideas. A slim hope.

The Walkers were gone, the Ferriway abandoned. That single barge waited by the bank. An Austelli hand on Sam's shoulder kept her from moving further.

'I'll tell someone you're here.' Mira blinked a few times.

'It's okay.' Sam tried to force the corners of her lips upwards. 'Whatever happens now is on me. I'm just… sorry you got caught up in this.'

'So am I.' Mira didn't look at her. She took the barge, sank to her knees beside the waiting corpses. The back panel rose with a clank and a hiss. Mira disappeared and the barge clanked back across the river in a screech of chains.

'I let you have a goodbye.' Ferra rolled her hammer across her shoulders. 'We need to move.'

Ferra dismissed her soldiers and led Sam down a side-path between two houses. Sounds of families squabbling filtered through the walls, the windows. The path widened out at the end, down towards a cluster of buildings near the wall. Smithies, picked out by their sandstone chimneys, clustered like grapes on the stem. Girders, dropforges, fire-stacks and even a blast forge.

'Where are we?'

'Just off Rustscrape. Where Callisteel died, and the forges with it.'

A long building stretched off down the street. The wooden door was polished to shine, but the walls and roof were stone.

'My home,' Ferra said.

Sam glanced through the window. Candles cramped the space inside, but a comfortable chair and a well-used kettle gave it a homely feel.

'Come on. The forge is waiting.'

The open forge beside the house was clean and well put together. Forge oven freshly swept and the anvil was carved to resemble a bull. Beside it was a rack of hammers and six brass-bound quenching barrels. Competent, understated. Reminded her of back home.

'Set up.'

Sam lit the forge and stoked it until the flame burned white gold. The smell of scorched stone and charred metal filled her lungs. She threw on an apron and a pair of gloves. Took her time in selecting a hammer. A blacksmith's hammer was an extension of her arm and each option deserved proper consideration. She ran her finger across the cool metal and a thrill sparked down her back.

Eventually, she settled on an Abies design. The shaft was a little shorter than she was used to, but the oval curve to the head made it a far more effective 'all-rounder'. It was nothing on the Salix that Jak made for her, but it would serve.

'Good.' Ferra nodded. She threw a lump of metal at Sam.

'Iron?' Sam rubbed the grey surface. 'Is this real? Got a lodestone?'

'It's real. A test. Make me a sword. And remember, if you fuck this up then I'll send you back across the river in pieces.'

Sam sighed. 'How wonderfully threatening.'

The quenching barrel *hissed* with steam.

Sam picked up a pair of tongs and, very slowly, began to draw the blade free.

Oh yes.

The blade was perfect. A ripple of metal, it folded like waves against the shore. True, it was missing a handle and some work needed to go into polishing and sharpening the thing, but for a base piece, it would serve.

Sam flipped the blade up and, for the first time, realised she was alone.

She set the weapon on the flat of the anvil and scuttled over to the opening of the tent. Soft voices carried through the smog. Back towards the other side of the tent, by a pile of boxes and old crates, Ferra was talking to someone. Someone familiar.

Ignis looked terrible. Her hair was scorched, her hands blistered. Scabs and cuts scattered across her face. 'See it sister.' She grabbed Ferra's wrist, pressed a lump of metal into her hand and a coal sparked into life. Twinned blue flame.

For an instant, Ferra's eyes flickered closed. When they opened, her face was fury. 'He knew all this time we'd have to die. Keeping us apart, not teaching us everything... it made us less of a threat.'

'We are *still* a threat.' Ignis flexed her fingers. 'We can still create Callisteel, if we figure out how. I won't die powerless and pathetic on his orders. I *can't.*' She cast a glance around and Sam jerked her head back. Her breath caught and unspoken prayers whispered through her mind. Please don't have seen me. She scratched the brand on the back of her hand.

She poked her head out again. Slowly.

'So what, we try to take him by surprise? He'll kill us before we even get close.'

'We need a new weapon because he won't turn on Dirk.' Ignis gestured.

For the first time, Sam noticed Danni loitering in the shadows. She held someone by the shoulders. Impossible to tell who. A black sack cinched around their head, manacles locked their hands behind their back. They struggled. Weakly.

Ferra sucked her teeth. 'He never taught us Callisteel. My last attempt... metal from living flesh... It didn't go so well.'

'Silverspine is dead,' Ignis said. 'But you still saved him. No one else could have done what you did.'

Danni snarled, her hands tight around the spear.

'But Silverspine would never have worked. Aer admitted it. Callisteel can't be made from a broken mind. That's why we need him.' She nodded to the captive.

'I don't know if I can do it, Ignis. We worked together, me and the boy. He's weak, but he doesn't deserve…'

'Use him. Or we die. And the rest of this wretched city along with us. Is he really worth more than that?'

Ferra winced. 'We still don't know what to do.'

Ignis tapped her chest. 'Fire.' She jabbed a finger at Ferra. 'Iron.' Her nails tightened around that piece of bloodmetal. 'Air. There is a reason Dirk named us as he did. We are Callisteel. The Fires of Remembrance.'

Heat hotter than fire.

'Bloodmetal as your base.'

Unmined iron.

'Alloyed with the dying breath of an unbroken mind.' She slapped something into Ferra's palm.

Sam felt her throat squeeze around the back of her neck. Her crucible lancet. Razor-edged, the symbols carved into the spout reflected the spiral waves tattooed on Ferra's arms.

Quenched in blood.

Ferra scratched her neck. She looked at the sackcloth prisoner. Something muffled came from beneath the hood. 'I'm sorry kid. If we had any other options…' She shook her head. 'Who am I making excuses for? I've sacrificed more than this in the past.' She turned to Danni, cleared her throat. 'Why are you here?'

'You need the Austelli. I will lead them against the Walkers, one final time. We'll burn the city and salt the ash to draw Dirk's eye.'

'Addie wouldn't go for it. Dirk's been training her. Not as a Mindbreaker, but to walk the mists. Anything she knows, he knows,' Ferra said.

'I will deal with Addie.' Danni folded her arms.

'For what?' Ferra's eye twitched. 'What do you want?'

'I want the truth. How did Silverspine die?'

Ferra met Ignis' eye. 'Addie killed him.'

Danni's mismatched eyes blazed. 'He saved her.'

'She slashed his leg. Then… smashed his stomach in. I don't know what she did to the body.' Ferra spoke to the floor.

Danni clenched her fists. Her mouth twitched, twisted.

She drew a knife from her belt and ripped it across her throat.

Sam shrank back, her stomach boiling. Blood spewed from the gash in Danni's neck.

'Take my memories of her.' Her voice was cracked, jagged. Desperate breath. 'My memories of the Austelli, the companionship, the hope. Leave my anger. Leave me Silverspine. Nothing else.'

Together, Ignis and Ferra touched Danni's neck. A twin blaze of blue fire and the gash closed, a scar mirrored against the one already there, an X across her throat.

'I'll kill her. The Austelli will fight for Silverspine as we always have,' Danni said.

Ferra's face twitched. She clenched her fists, once, twice. Then sighed. 'It's all pointless. Dirk will kill us.'

'I know. But what other hope do we have?' Ignis said.

Ferra rolled her shoulders. 'True. Just let me sort something first, I've got…' She turned back to the tent.

Sam scuttled back inside and grabbed her sword blade with a pair of tongs. Mimed dragging it free of the quenching barrel, just in time for Ferra to re-emerge.

'This it then? The best you could do?' Ferra asked.

Sam ignored the footsteps that clomped past the entrance of the tent. 'You asked for a sword.'

Ferra lifted the blade to the late-afternoon light. 'That blood channel is straight and the double-edge style is certainly an effective design.' She lowered her eyes. 'There is talent there, but you need more patience. See those swirling imperfections? They're a sign that the steel isn't fully tempered. It'll break, eventually.'

'Everything breaks eventually.'

'Not everything…' Ferra's fingers twitched towards the lancet Sam knew was hidden beneath her belt.

'You know why Mistress Ignis marked me?' Sam dragged the heavy forge glove from her hand. 'It's because I refused to work on Callisteel. That's what I signed the contract for. And I was excited to sign as well.

Until someone attacked my Father with a Callisteel blade. Someone with violet eyes.'

Ferra's hammer stopped.

'I *hate* the person who did that. But for a long time, I didn't realise why. Yes, he snuffed my Father's mind out like an errant candle, but… selfishly, there was more to it than that. I hate him, because he stole my dream from me. Callisteel. To make Jak proud. I wouldn't wish what he did on anyone else. I could stay. With the forge. You know I'm good. I could help you.'

'I thought I saw you eavesdropping.' Ferra hefted her hammer.

'You can't expect me to believe you'd rather do this on your own.' Sam refused to step back. She straightened her spine as Ferra's face loomed dangerously close. 'I can learn from you. You're not the monster you think you are.'

Ferra looked at her. 'I'm not a monster. A monster is blameless. Instinct and emotion. I know exactly what I am doing. That makes me far worse.' Her eyes glittered.

'Ignis said she gave you the memories of every blacksmith who got close to Callisteel. She gave you my lancet too. I carried that for years. I know it, better than anyone else. It even…' She winced. The broken trail of memories, the loss of who she was in a heartbeat. 'I've felt its power. Let me help you. If a blade is going to carve Dirk from this world, then I want it to be one of mine.'

For Father's broken mind. For Vicky's forced marriage. For Mira's hands.

For Jak.

Ferra looked at her for a long time. 'You know there is no guarantee? All I know are the rumours.'

'Me too.' Sam knelt to lift her hammer, shoulder's firm. 'But that's not stopped me before.'

'Me neither. Very well. Tomorrow.' She looked up to the darkening sky. 'Tomorrow.'

CHAPTER 43

Sam sat awkwardly at Ferra's table and watched her cook. Candles dotted every free surface, but it was remarkably... clean. The wax was wiped away, the table polished, small curtains neatly set against the windows. The smell of spice and salt warmed her. A pot of soup bubbled over the stove.

Ferra caught her gawking. 'What?'

'It's just... not what I expected,' Sam said. Though really, what had she thought a Mindbreaker's home would be? Something... big. And on fire. And misty.

'Well, we can't all lounge in the mansions you lot built over the river. Sit.' Ferra plonked a bottle in the middle of the table.

'What is it?' Sam tried to disguise the desperation in her voice. But sod it, real wine! From a bottle and everything.

Ferra pulled the cork with her teeth and sniffed. 'Red.' She splashed wine into a pair of battered tin cups and slid one to Sam. 'Cheers?'

Sam clinked her glass with Ferra and took a sip. Coughed. Vinegar and furniture polish, but Ferra knocked hers back easily enough.

Ferra turned back to the pot. Sam watched. Her movements were oddly delicate. Touches, pinches, measured cups. It was an odd side to see. Ferra the Mindbreaker, one of the most powerful women in the city.

Ferra the human, just cooking a meal at the end of a long day.

'Stop staring.' Ferra spun around and spooned up two bowls of soup. 'Eat.'

'Do you communicate exclusively in barks?' Sam lifted the spoon to her lips.

It was good. Rich broth, chased with a silky puree and seared chunks of tender meat running through. The spoonful disappeared fast, and the next followed swift. She only paused to tip a mouthful of wine down.

'Warm,' she mumbled through the broth.

'Mm, there is too much pepper. A habit, you never know what meat you end up with this side of the river. Does wonders to disguise the facts.'

That slowed Sam's chewing somewhat. What *was* the taste? Game, rabbit maybe? Though it was a bit tougher than that. She ran the fibres between her teeth.

'Stop it.' Ferra frowned at her.

Sam shrugged. She'd had worse, Vicky liked to insist on 'flavour of the month' meals that made rotten meat seem appealing. Besides, hunger was a great amnesiac. She attacked the rest of the bowl until she was certain droplets were flying over her shoulders.

When the last drop was spooned up, Sam set her bowl aside and drew her wine back. The cup was emptied. As was the next one. Then another bottle appeared from under the table and that disappeared quite swiftly as well.

Sam snorted. 'Can't remember the last time someone spotted me a meal and a glass. Well, except for Mira. And I suspect that won't be happening again anytime soon.'

'I think I'm sorry about that.' A remarkable honest apology. 'I'm not happy her hands were hurt, but we had to...'

Sam just shook her head. 'What does it matter? No matter what decision I make these days, it's the wrong one.' The words poured from her throat. 'Jak vanished, Father lost his mind, Vicky got married and Mira got mutilated. I'm meant to be alone.'

'No one is meant to be alone.' Ferra's voice was far older than it had any right to be. 'Surely there is someone waiting back home. A partner or a pen pal or a favoured prostitute or something?'

Sam spat a laugh into her wine. 'Not for me. I'm not... into that.' She spun the liquid in her glass. 'There was one girl, a while back. Mira introduced us, but I'm not sure if she knew or not. She was like me, we used to laugh about the thought of the others grunting and sweating and... expelling all those fluids. But when I asked her to hold me, she pulled away. Which, okay, fine, that's fine. But it brought it home. I don't want to fuck, but that doesn't mean I'm not allowed to be…' She downed her wine. 'Sod me, I was going to say "loved." How strong is this stuff?' She held her glass up.

'For what it's worth, I know what it's like to feel that way. Not the fucking, I'm up for that, but the loneliness. Dirk saved my life when I was younger, and in payment I lived it for him. I've served as his Mindbreaker for as long as I can remember. Obviously I'd rather that than my death, but… no one wants to be close to someone who could steal their eyes. Reilo died before my time, Aer was an enemy, Ignis can't see anyone but as a rival and Dirk vanished soon after my training finished. There wasn't anyone else. And now, it turns out, it was all just so I could die on the pyre he's lit to clear the way for… whatever perfect world the Iactura whispers in the corners of his mind.' Ferra's head sunk. She stared at the bunched muscles of her arms. 'I always wondered, why the tattoos? Dirk insisted on them. I used to think it was camaraderie. He even had Ignis and I calling each other 'sister.' But now. Well, you brand a cow so you know which ones to slaughter.' She shrugged and raised a glass. 'To sleeping alone.'

The empty glasses clicked together.

Ferra set her glass down, then frowned at Sam. 'How drunk are you?'

'Not drunk enough to follow you to a whorehouse, if that's where your mind is going.'

'That's not…'

'But I'll come to bed with you,' Sam said.

Ferra's frown deepened. 'What?'

'I assumed you were heading there after your dramatic little toast. It's late and I'm tipsy. I don't want to have sex with you. But that doesn't mean I don't want to be held.'

Ferra laughed. She stood up and took Sam's hand. Her fingers were calloused, rough, but her touch was oddly… gentle.

'You better keep your damn elbows to yourself. And I warn you, I've got cold feet.'

307

The next morning, Sam woke alone. The curtains were open to the cold, bright morning.

She sat up and gasped. Held her fingers to her temples. It felt like a horse was kicking her in the head. She could hear her blood thumping in her ears. She did not so much as walk to the kitchen, but crash through the door.

'Here.' Ferra was already up and dressed. She held out a cup.

Water. Precious water. Had grit and slime ever tasted so good?

'Drink quick. It's time.'

'Time for what?' Sam asked.

'Callisteel.'

The word fell like a china plate on the pavement.

'Do you... know what to do?' Sam asked.

'The lancet, you said you felt its power?'

'I touched its blade when Ignis took me into the mist. My memories... separated. I lost myself, every single one of those silver orbs broke from the sky and threatened to vanish. It was only with Ignis' help I kept my mind together.'

'A lancet is for bloodletting... can it be that simple?'

'Could it be a touch simpler? I've got no idea what you are talking about.'

'Come with me.' Ferra led her out of the house and into the cold. It was early, the streets were quiet.

Sam followed Ferra down a road. It didn't curve like the others, straight as an ingot. Buildings drooped over either side, the threat of collapse ever-present. Ferra moved a stack of sheet metal and revealed a small building with metal walls. She unlocked the door and led them inside.

Ferra produced a small oil lamp, but it barely pierced the inky blackness. Something groaned overhead and Sam shivered. An anvil gleamed in the darkness at the heart of the room. The cast-iron was so dark it stole the light of the lantern.

'Stay here.' Ferra's tone had changed. Back to the cold, commanding tone of when Sam had first met her. She returned with her hammer and a single, silver-red nugget of unrefined metal. 'This is bloodmetal. The iron in human blood given form. It can store Manifest Memories. Those are...'

'The memories that define us.' Sam remembered that much from Ignis.

'This is our metal.' Ferra pulled a sack from her waist and produced four small pieces of coal. She set them in a square atop the anvil, then placed the bloodmetal inside. Five dull rocks on a black platform.

'Does… does it matter what kind of memory they hold?' Sam asked.

'I have no idea. I've been operating on 'stronger is better' but that could just be ego.' She gestured at the metal. 'This piece contains one of mine. When I was little, my mother used to send me out picking purses on busy days. One time, a man with quicker hands than mine took exception to my work, and hit me so hard with his cane my jaw came clean off. Everyone just left me to drown on my own blood. Except one. That was the first day I met Dirk. He removed this memory from me, so that I could heal. This is why I owe him. It's long past time that connection was cut.'

'But, you just told me what happened. How can that be, when this memory has been cut away?' Sam asked.

'It's just a fact. I know what happens, but there is no connection to it. I don't see it when I close my eyes. Facts are easy. Emotion is hard.'

How could she explain that so calmly?

Ferra drew a flint and steel from her belt and got a few orange sparks to dance over the coals. 'There are only two sources that are hot enough to forge Callisteel. The first is heartfire, the magma that roils far below the city. The second,' she rolled up her sleeves, 'is our fire. The Fire of Remembrance.'

Ferra closed her eyes. She took a breath and blew it out.

Reality burns. Inhale the memory.

The words came like a whisper from the darkness.

Orange sparks shot with a pulsating blue light. A column of blue fire raced upwards, the blinding after-image searing into Sam's eyes. Two glassy orbs swirled lazily in the darkness overhead. The fire inside followed their movements.

'Now on to the last part.' Ferra's face fell. 'This was the other reason I wanted you here. To share the guilt. Two hands on the blade.'

She stepped into the darkness and tugged a lever. The harsh clank of chains sounded from above and Sam squinted into the darkness. Something was being drawn towards her. A lump. No. A body.

He coughed and Sam leapt back. It was still alive! Lank hair hung over closed eyes and a half-healed scar ran across his chest.

'Ferra.' Sam choked back some sick. 'What have you done?'

'Ruairi doesn't deserve this. But he is all we've got.'

'Got to do *what?*'

'To forge Callisteel, we are going to need to kill him.'

Silence fell like a noose.

'Callisteel is quenched in blood. It is the only hope we have. I will use the Fires of Remembrance to melt the bloodmetal. You will use the lancet to drain Ruairi of his dying breath, and in his blood a blade will be forged.'

'This is madness,' Sam began. She cast about for the controls. 'I'm letting him down.'

'No. You aren't.' Ferra grabbed her wrist.

'Let go of me.'

'Sam, you're not thinking this...'

'Let *go!*' Sam lashed out and slapped Ferra square in the jaw.

Ferra's fist crunched into Sam's nose and she smacked the stone floor with her face. 'I knew this would happen.'

She plucked her hammer from Sam's fingers.

'Wait.' Sam spat pink saliva onto the floor, her lips salty with the taste dripping from her bloody nose. '*Wait*! Ferra, you don't have to do this.'

'Dirk will find you if I let you go.' She lifted the hammer. 'He can't know what we are planning.'

'You don't have to kill me!' Sam held up her arm. 'I won't say anything. Please. I don't want to die.'

Ferra paused. Considered. Then nodded. The coal around her neck burned blue. Mist oozed from the fire, swamped the room, coating everything in a featureless field of white. Overhead, endless silver orbs danced in the false twilight sky.

Two azure bright eyes burned beside those memories.

'*Then surrender your memories to me. That's enough to buy your life.*'

'I can't give you that!'

'*I am not asking.*' Ferra held out her hand. Her hammer materialised between her fingers. '*Your memories. Or your life.*'

Sam's eyes were wet. Mira had said this was what she wanted. But now… She shook her head and sent tears spinning into the mist. 'I don't want to lose them. Jak, and Father and Vicky and Mira. The way they were… that only exists in my memories. I can't let you take them.'

'*Then I am sorry, girl who was once called Samantha.*' Ferra readied her hammer. She held a hand out to the sky.

But the silver orbs didn't move. Instead, those blue spheres of flame roared like comets through the mist. They floated before Ferra.

A voice echoed in the mist.

'*We speak between the cracks in your mind.*'

'No…' Ferra glanced at Sam. '*How can he…*'

A knife burst from her chest. Smoke and flame and ash. A cruel voice boomed through the mist.

'*Pain is no substitute for experience. But damned if it isn't satisfying. Do you know how long I've waited for this?*'

Smoke burst from the phantom wound. It wound around those two blue orbs of flame and formed into a figure. A man. His body materialised and with a wave of his hand he dismissed the mist.

Ferra's body slumped to the floor with a gurgle.

The new figure looked down at Sam. She caught a glimpse of his eyes in the lamplight.

Blue as frozen fire.

CHAPTER 44

Silverspine's heart thundered with that familiar rage. Ferra was dead. Sure, she'd saved his life one time, but she'd also tried to kill him. On balance, this was fair.

The twin voices, as always, disagreed.

She needed to die.

She saved you.

She killed you.

She gave you your life back.

They whispered and whimpered and drawled like nails caught in a tempest around the inside of his skull. Silverspine twisted his thumb on the tip of the bloodslick misericorde. After all this time, he trusted no weapon better. The thing had served him well since the Flame Protests. Like pulping a fruit, the never-healed scar on his thumb opened up once more.

The oil lamp guttered on the anvil, clean orange to murky blue. Smog. Spark. Smoke. Fingernails of bloodmetal clattered down the side of his leg, fell to the floor by his feet as he purged the guilt and anger of their latest argument. The voices faded again. He felt the doubt recede, the fog slip away. The mist gave him clarity, gave him purpose, gave him sweet silence.

Now he could smile.

'What did you do?' The girl's eyes were wide, trained on him. Overhead, the young lad hung from the ceiling like a side of beef, wrists shackled to some mechanism high above. Something familiar about the face. Plain, ugly if he was being fair, rugged if he wasn't, and dense as sod.

'Ruairi. That's twice I've saved you now.'

'Who are you?' The lad's voice sounded like someone had taken a sheet of sandpaper to his throat.

Silverspine turned and lifted his shirt.

The smoke from the candles, the thread of smog that lingered in the air, swirled around the bloodmetal connection that rattled down his back.

'I've heard of you,' the girl whispered.

'Your voice.' The inside of his chest was cold and he flipped the misericorde over in his fingers. 'You're not Austelli.'

The girl scrabbled back, slammed into the wall. 'I'm just a blacksmith.'

'I know. I've been watching.'

Ever since Ferriway, he could *feel* the Fires of Remembrance. They drew him like a lodestone, waypoints on a map. His eyes of frozen fire opened with every spark. Death in the Open Kitchen. Dirk feeding the Iactura. Ignis' fight with Aer. Ferra's Callisteel failure. He had watched them all.

He took the lancet from her dead fingers, keeping clear of the saw-sharp edge. The spiral inlay carved into the stylised feather spout curled against his fingertips.

The final piece.

'She knew I was waiting for her. Twin flaming eyes in the mist, every time they summoned our fire. She'd been avoiding Memoria since the Open Kitchen. I want to thank you for trying to get her to break you. Now we're even.'

She isn't Austelli. She should die.

She's innocent. We saved her for a reason.

Silverspine dragged his thumb down the tip of his blade again.

'Even if...' The girl's eyes fell to Ferra's corpse. 'That doesn't make you a good man.'

'Good men change nothing. Some are born innocent.' Lara. His daughter. Soft brown eyes, so wide they could swallow the world.

Blood on her blankets. Skin sloughed down her chest, pink tears on porcelain cheeks.

The ripping, screaming tear of Walker scalps cut free with the tip of the misericorde. Slice the tendons, pierce the armpits, leave them immobilised but alive when he started.

'Some have to die to end their corruption.' The kid, bloody and bleeding out on a slab, his spine severed and his lifeblood draining slowly beneath the skin.

Burning blue fire every night to forget his own misery.

Blade at his throat on the Ferriway, broken and breathless.

'I have died so many times.' The chill of certainty iced his words to the cold, stone floor.

'What do you want?' Sam's voice shook a little, but she clenched her jaw.

He cocked his head.

The blood of the Walkers.

Freedom for the Austelli.

And a tiny voice. Hidden beneath.

To remember. And be remembered.

Silverspine growled and rammed the misericorde into each of his fingers, deep and hot enough to pierce through his fingerprint and up out of the nail on the back. He spat out smog, the candles flickered, blood boiling down his hand, the sting and split of his own flesh.

Smoke coiled around his fist. The wounds closed and bloodmetal dropped like rain.

'Revenge.' He shoved the knife through his belt. 'On the violet-eyed maniac who poisoned this city.'

Master.

Mindbreaker.

'Dirk drew out the Iactura. Dirk created Callisteel. Dirk caused the Flame Protests, the Sightless Executions, the massacres of Highdock and the Nest.'

And yet, for all of that he keeps his life.

Now, for the mind of the man who became Silverspine, he would bleed.

Silverspine shook his head, opened wide his too-blue eyes. 'Which is why you are both coming with me.'

'Why?' Ruairi called down with a wheeze, his lungs taut beneath the chains.

'You, because your mind is protected. The memory of your Father, ripped from his head, keeps you safe.' Silverspine turned on Sam. 'And you, because Ferra just taught you Callisteel. I can use you both.' He cast about. A winch-system was set up beside a lever and he yanked the handle.

Ruairi clanked down from the ceiling, flopped against the anvil. The chains slid loose from his arms.

'Thank you. For not agreeing to off me,' he said to Samantha.

'Let's get you out of here.' Samantha lifted Ruairi to his feet.

Silverspine grabbed the lamp and followed them out. Mist rode the wind and a fine drizzle had everything as slick as slaughter. The smog was thick, he could practically chew it.

Ruairi huddled in on himself. Shirtless, the wind tearing into him. 'Ferra would'a killed me. Killed me proper. I'm glad it were you there, lass.' He looked up, held out a hand.

'Samantha, not lass.' She heaved him back up.

He groaned. 'Samantha. Sorry, got it.' Then he turned on Silverspine, brown eyes fierce. 'We ain't coming with you.' Difficult to do "intimidating" when shirtless, bloody and weeping, but he gave it a decent scowl. 'Not how I'm repaying her. We're buggering off back across the river. You can do what you like over here, but I ain't being no part. Less it's to put a stop to this.'

'Is that a threat?' Anger and laughter tore at his lips, set his jaw twitching.

'No, this is.'

Ruairi lashed forwards and ripped the misericorde free. Without pause, he rammed it into Silverspine's thigh.

Agony. Sweet, merciful *fucking* agony.

Something new to forget.

His thigh burned cold. Warm liquid dripped down his sock. He yanked the knife free. Needles, thousands of needles pierced him over and over. Breath cut short. Each gasp felt like a slap.

He gripped the lamp tight. Closed his eyes and blew a breath of smog.

Everything slowed. He watched Ruairi run, feet pounding on the sludge. Watched him shout for Samantha. Watched her falter, slip.

Mist poured from Silverspine's leg. Drops of blood rose towards the palm of his hand. Solidified into bloodmetal. Still warm.

He blinked. The wound was closed. And his hand curled around Samantha's throat.

Ruairi stopped, half-way gone. His turned, face pained. 'She didn't let Ferra kill me. Let her go.'

'I won't kill her.'

'How'd I know that?'

'You don't. But you'd have to kill me. Reckon you could do it? Far, far better than you have tried.' Silverspine grinned, showed all his teeth.

'I 'ain't no killer.' Still, he stepped forwards and raised an untrained fist. It would have been amusing, had it not been so pathetic.

'Oh would you just sod off!' Samantha squeaked from Silverspine's fist. 'Don't try and punch the lunatic, he's letting you go. Send help, find the Walkers, don't just bleed out in a gutter here for some bizarre version of honour.'

'She's trying to save you again,' Silverspine smirked. 'But she's right. Blood is all there is down here.'

'*All there has ever been.*'

'I know!' Something like anger bubbled from Ruairi's lips. His fists drooped. 'All I'm real good for. Being saved. Someone'll… I'll find you again, Miss Samantha. I swear it.'

He didn't say another word. Just turned and left. Didn't run. Limped.

'Move.' Silverspine grabbed Samantha's shoulder and forced her to march in front of him, his knife pressed between her shoulder blades.

They wound through empty streets. For a long time, he had wondered where was best to hide in Arx. It was a simple enough realisation. Where would Addie avoid?

Eventually, when a tiny fragment of afternoon sun pierced the smog, they made it back to the Ferriway. To the gutted husk that had once been the home they'd shared. Truth be told, once he'd recovered from Ferra's attack and come back from Memoria, he hadn't the strength to walk far.

He fumbled a key from his belt and opened the main door. The upper level was still deserted, Silverspine's legacy had been enough to attract a couple of eyes in the beginning. But even those had faded long since.

He locked the door behind. Samantha twitched, but he gripped her forearm and shoved her down towards the stairs at the back of the room.

The Forgemasters looked up when he entered. Ignis had rounded them up the moment Dirk gave the call. They had two choices. Sacrifice their memories of Callisteel. Or sacrifice their tongue and their freedom, working indebted to her until their body gave out. So many empty eyes. He spent the last two months tracking them down.

Working on a weapon.

'I have it.' He flung lancet at the nearest smith.

The smith nodded. His white hair was burned down almost to his scalp and a huge, sweeping scar threatened the corner of his mouth. He held out an arm and gestured to the metal slab at the back of the room.

For a moment, he saw double. Kuyt's body lay where he once had. Blue smoke swirled in his eye sockets. The sight like a flensing knife against his soul.

How could you do this to me?

Silverspine's finger's twitched towards his belt, but he tore them way. He didn't feel guilty. He barely remembered the old man.

You can't burn me out of your soul.

Silverspine rammed his hand into the misericorde and blue flame gouted from the torches nearby. A thick chunk of bloodmetal slipped from his hand.

'Let's get this started.'

The blacksmith drove the lancet into Kuyt's chest. Six candles burned around the body and Silverspine burned them blue. Smoke danced across his body. Blue sparks danced from the lancet.

Blood pooled in the feather-like runnels, engraved the swirling, spiralling patterns.

No mind. No eyes. But he still twitched. His mouth curled in... fuck it, in pain he couldn't scream out.

The lancet unfolded against his chest, like a flower slicing open. Those feathers spiralled against his flesh. Smoke bubbled through the hole, warped across the feathers.

Silverspine rammed the misericorde through the centre of the lancet and into Kuyt's heart.

The needle-blade plunged deep and held there. Blue flame roared. Sparks circled Kuyt, the taste of ash. A whorl of blue flame burst from the old man's chest.

When the fire died out, the knife was changed.

Wrong.

The blade was black, not blue-silver. Steam leapt from the edge. Silverspine pulled it free. It slid out without a drop of blood.

'This isn't Callisteel.' He whirled on the blacksmiths. 'What the fuck is this?'

The nearest one shrugged.

The old man was empty.

My soul is in you, boy. Not in that knife. All you've kept is my emptiness. An emptiness you know all too well.

'Oh, you don't know?' Without warning, Silverspine rammed the knife into the blacksmith's throat.

And felt his mind… expand. The blacksmith's body fell back, but his memories coursed into Silverspine. Nori. Forgemaster. Knowledge assailed him. He'd *known* this wouldn't work. A man with no mind could never temper Callisteel. But he could make something else. Callisteel sliced clean through memory, cut the links between the mind and the experience.

A knife from an empty mind drank the memories of those it cut. Fed them to the wielder.

'*Perfect,*' Silverspine said as Nori's final memories filtered into his mind. The last ones were tinged with rank vitriol for the man who had imprisoned him.

He drank the self-hatred down like bile, thick and bitter.

CHAPTER 45

Silverspine leapt up to the rooftop.

Memories blew lazily through his mind like dandelion seeds. Sitting on the roof of an old factory. Talking to himself. Leaping down to kill his first Walker and save some woman who didn't speak. Had he ever been so innocent? So wise?

He wasn't insane. He knew the memories hadn't always been his. Each tinged with a somber fondness. Reilo, Kuyt and the dead rebels, Nori. So many faces clustered for space inside his skull.

Day by day, the memories kept him going, kept him alive. But at night, when quiet hit, the voices burned. The echo of their lives made his own so empty. Every night he pared more away. Lost some of that spark that animated him – but that was what kept the breath in his lungs.

Silverspine threw himself from the slats and on to a flat, stone roof on the outskirts of Rotheart. Despite the growing drizzle, the streets were still packed. The Austelli were no longer confined, not crawling through the muck. Beneath his feet, gaps in the rooftiles were boarded over. Sometimes, laughter and the odd burst of heat from a cookfire warmed his feet.

The Austelli. He loved them now in a way he'd never managed before. The faces of dead rebels, Kuyt's whispering pride inside his head. Patriotism wasn't fighting for a name, Arx meant nothing, and Austellus was barely a whisper. No, it was the people. The wonderful complexity of each life lived. A shared connection between those whose experience overlapped. The rage he had stolen from Reilo burned brighter now he embraced it.

The Walkers must die.

The Austelli have to survive this.

The city burns.

The ashes in the hands of its people.

The whispers warred inside his head. He peeled the scab from his thumbnail and let it bleed. It was too wet for a fire. He'd have to use pain.

And today was going to hurt.

Silverspine crouched on the edge of the rooftop. The plaza was packed, bodies clustered close around the scaffold, but this was no execution. A pair of burning sconces lit the slats of long-burned wood. Puffs of steam sizzled in the rain.

Addie.

The sight of her sent a twinge through his whole body. The familiar scars on her jaw. The battle leathers. The tired eyes. He strained his ears to pick out what she was saying.

'-without our blood! Well no longer. Today, we take the fight to them. The Nest joins with us – and together, we will take back what they stole!'

Her diction had improved. Kuyt was... would have been proud.

I always was.

Addie gestured, and a figure bumbled up beside her.

Quill, safe to say, had seen better days. The small gut he'd been growing was emaciated, his rain-soaked shirt clung to his ribs. Burned flesh poked free of the bandages wrapped down his arm and a huge valley of a scar clove his face, from forehead to cheek.

Deep as a hatchet swung in anger.

'The Ant has fallen.' Even his voice was muted, fire extinguished by the ceaseless rain. 'But the Walkers still fight. Something pissed them off, they don't retreat anymore. They fight until they die. We can't take you both. And at least...' The water dripped from his hair when he shook his head. 'At least some of you remember what Austelli means. The Nest bows to Dirk.' His voice was jagged, bitter on those final words. Like someone had ripped them from his chest.

Dirk. The name was like a flensing knife. Silverspine's fists clenched, blood trickled between white knuckles. Dirk had stolen everything from him. His past, his body, his Austelli. Even Addie.

There would be a reckoning. That man would not control his future. No one would.

Addie lifted an axe. 'We fight for a city that grew fat on our labour, then cast us aside. The Austelli will rule in Arx. It is our blood that made these streets, our fire that burns the sky.'

The crowd began to ripple. Something close, elastic pulled taut. They just needed a final push.

'This is what Silverspine died for! We will take Arx in his name. For the honour of our valiant dead.'

That did it. The roar from the crowd was loud enough to rock the rooftop that Silverspine was crouching on. Apparently he was far more popular dead than he ever had been alive.

Time to test that.

'Don't I get to decide what I died for?' He pitched his voice to carry and leaped from the rooftop.

The crowd turned silently. Eerie. Like a wall of corpses.

He drew his shirt over his head and let it fall to the rain-soaked ground.

Blackened rain drizzled down his bloodmetal spine.

'You're alive. Your body, I thought… *you're alive!*' A woman shoved out from the crowd, the haft of her spear slamming between bodies to carve her a path.

She fell to her knees at his side. Slowly, she lifted a hand and touched the metal of his back.

Tears fell with the rain from one green eye, and one red.

'Danni. I've returned.'

She grabbed his wrist, sobbed against his sleeve. 'I thought you were dead.'

He ran soft fingers across her neck. She'd been scarred again, another thick line crossing the one he'd burned shut on Highdock. 'You should know that death is no end for people like us.'

'I wanted to believe you were alive. Even after Dirk showed me, I wanted… Never again.' Blue flecks flickered across her eyes. 'I am yours.'

'And I am yours.' He turned to the crowd. 'I am all of yours. My Austelli. What has Dirk done to you?'

He saved them! Reilo's voice slavered.

But this time, it was all too easy to ignore.

'Your blood spent to keep Walkers at bay. Memories sacrificed for food. I know too well the pain of having your past ripped from your head.'

The crowd rippled. Silverspine walked through them and those he passed fell to their knees.

'If we truly want to forget this agony, the starvation, the silence, the sorrow, we won't do so by mewling to a man who would salt the city with our ashes. The Austelli do not exist simply to be ruled. Dirk would force his version of the future on all of you. I will give you the means to take that future for yourselves.'

Even Quill, after turning his head and looking for what Silverspine could only assume was an escape route, managed to make it to his ragged arse. He knew the tide had turned. Bow or die, it wasn't a difficult call.

The only one left standing, was Addie.

'She did it!' Danni snarled from his side. 'General Adira turned on Silverspine, she killed him!'

The Austelli rumbled. A few hands fell to weapons, but Silverspine waved them down.

'Ferra is dead,' he said to Addie. 'There is no help coming. Stand down. It's over.'

'What did you do to Kuyt?'

Silverspine frowned. 'That's it? I return from the dead, and that's your question?'

'I had hoped...' She turned her head, twisted her jaw. 'I had hoped you were dead. But without a corpse I knew you'd come back. What I can't figure out, is where Kuyt went. He disappeared on the same day as you.' Her eyes blazed. 'You killed him, didn't you?'

'Kuyt is still alive.' Silverspine sucked down a wet breath of smog and sent it out towards the sconces steaming behind Addie. They sputtered into the azure Fires of Remembrance. Smoke roiled beneath the rain.

An image carried in the ash. Kuyt's body on a slab. His eyes burned out.

I am sorry, Adira.

'What did you do to him?' Addie's voice was empty.

'I survived.'

'What did you *do*?' Addie's voice tore like ripping flesh. 'Kuyt hated the Mindbreakers. I'd rather you killed him. After all he did for you...'

She pierced him with her eyes. 'You're worse than a Fog-Eye. I promised you an end if you ever became that empty.'

'Hold on to that hatred, Addie. It won't be yours for much longer.' Silverspine drew his black knife.

'I have learned to hate far more than you can imagine.' She drew something from the belt of her trousers.

A gut-burning rage poured through him.

The Sightless mask.

Addie pressed it to her face and it held there. She touched a nearby brazier, fire burning blue. 'Reality burns.'

Rotheart plaza faded into the mist. Buildings disappeared into the endless smoke. This wasn't possible. Silverspine leapt back. Addie was no Mindbreaker.

The Iactura rose like the hand of a vengeful god from the smoke behind Addie. And overhead, a pair of eyes broke open the twilight sky.

Violet as a dying sunset.

'I can fight you here now.' Addie's voice boomed through the mist from behind the mask. Silver orbs exploded out of her, danced around her body. She blinked behind the mask, and when she opened her eyes they were as blue as his.

Memories sacrificed for power. But her mind was still intact. Silver orbs clustered like raindrops beneath Dirk's violet eyes. He held her together just as easily as he had ripped Silverspine apart.

A hatchet appeared in her hands. She launched through the mist.

Silverspine braced himself for the strike.

Her weapon vanished into smoke.

Silverspine watched as the axe re-formed inside his guard. Addie slashed at his chest and her blade bit deep.

He roared, the gash burned hot then cold and Silverspine threw himself back. The mist rose to claim his blood. A silver orb spun beside him, the memory of this newest scar. He lashed out and the orb vanished, along with the cut on his chest.

'You would turn on me, yet fight for him?'

'I'm fighting for Kuyt.' Addie rushed at him.

A silver orb leapt from the sky and burst into Silverspine's chest.

He was in the warehouse. A lifetime ago. He saw himself through Addie's eyes. Weak. Untrained. A muted dagger, lazy in his hand.

A kick lashed towards his face.

Back in the mist, Silverspine's nose burst with blood. He flung his hands to his face, screeched between bloody fingers. *'What did you do to me?'*

'Just because you don't remember it, doesn't mean I don't!' Another silver orb hurled towards him.

Silverspine threw himself aside and the orb burst in the mist. The image of a Fog-Eye's hand, gripped tight around his throat.

'Remember, Silverspine. Remember who you really are. Remember Caelan!' Addie rushed through the mist. Manifest memories swirled around her, a tempest of silver. She pointed her hand and they slammed into him.

A blade in a Walker's throat.

A man falling into heartfire.

The Sightless, broken and bleeding.

The bodies of the dead.

The cyclone of memory tore at him, over and over. He watched them all. Those he had killed.

'It still hurts! Caelan. You're still in there.'

He fell to his knees, tore at his hair, clawed down the side of his face. *'I'm still... me.'*

Pain is not a weakness.

The grave is not the last.

We fight beyond death.

We fight beyond life.

Kill her.

Kill yourself.

Let it end.

'Remember what it is to be human.' Addie's voice whispered in his ear.

'Everyone just shut up!' Silverspine, no *Caelan* screamed and the mist boiled around him. He felt it. The guilt. The pain. The life he'd tossed aside. The memories burned, boiled like tar in open wounds.

He tried to hold them. For a heartbeat, he really tried. But like a breath trapped too long, it burst from his throat and drowned his resolve. The sweetness of oblivion was just too strong.

He lashed out, weeping, panicking, his black knife slammed into Addie's memories.

They slipped into his mind like sweet poison down his throat. Tears dried, his mind fell silent. He drew on the death he had wrought. Addie's fear of him, her disgust. The horror deep in her soul that no training could ever eliminate.

The fact that even after all of this, she still thought there was something in him worth saving.

The screams of the dead were his strength. He raced forwards. Addie charged to meet him. He grabbed her wrists.

A shockwave blew through the mist around them. He gripped her arms and strained. It was more than just strength. He could feel her bend her mind to fight him, fuelled by memory. Addie's eyes flashed and the blue-silver mask burned like starlight. What memories was she losing to stay so strong?

Addie's hatchet twitched an inch closer to his flesh and he began to panic. His will was strong, but Addie had always been stubborn. He just didn't have the memories.

At least… not to fight her with.

He forced his mind back and dragged the scrap of an old memory from the depths of his consciousness.

A memory of the banks of the Mucro. The sight of her walking away as he bled to death. The silver orb melted into her. It touched Addie's mind.

She was better than him. She still felt guilt. Addie twitched.

'*You deserved it! I had no choice. You were lost. Caelan died on Highdock and Silverspine was…*'

'*Silverspine was born in Rotheart. I died to save you.*'

A final memory. Long ago. The Sightless, wreathed in flame on a smouldering scaffold. A hatchet in its hand. Aimed at Addie.

Caelan's hand in her back, forcing her out of the way.

'*You did this.*'

Addie blinked past the memory. Her strength faltered.

Silverspine ducked under her arm. The black knife danced over his fingers.

He rammed it into her stomach.

Her scream crackled like thunder. Silver orbs vanished. Mist whipped around in a frenzy.

It faded into the blue fire back in Rotheart.

People popped into existence and the wooden boards of the scaffold phased in behind his head. Buildings and muck splattered into the world. The crowd appeared once more. Confused and cold in silence.

Addie's mind held firm. For now. The last vestiges of Dirk's power still held her together but her strength was leaking from the black knife dug deep into her stomach. Her mind was his. She just didn't know it yet.

'I knew... this would happen. Dirk trained me. But you've lived in those mists for far too long.' Addie tried to sit up, but her strength was spent. The Sightless' mask clattered from her face. 'You know what's weird? I almost feel like I deserve this.'

'Addie.' Her name twisted something inside his chest.

'At the end... I'm glad I got to see you. The real you, hidden in those mists. I turned on Silverspine, I want him dead. But Caelan, you were my friend.'

She touched the corner of his jaw.

'Thank you. For saving me, all that time ago. I'm sorry you lost your way. We would have helped you find it, if only you'd let us.'

His hands shook around the hilt of the knife. He could feel her mind begin to break, like an overburdened bridge, moments from snapping under the pressure.

Kill her.

Reilo spat strength into his mind, conviction that steeled his arms. He was so loud.

But he still couldn't stop the whisper, hidden beneath the patchwork of corpses.

It's Addie.

He drew his knife from her stomach. As soon as it slid free, the flesh closed behind it. A wound of the mind, not the body.

Addie blinked. Her eyes were still her own. 'What are you doing?'

'You were right. I really was soft. I can't kill you, Addie. You remember... that I was human.' He spoke to his hands. 'Fuck, what a mess I've made of it all.'

'Caelan. I can finally hear you.' Addie found a small smile for him. 'It's been so long.'

A shadow thumped on to the scaffold, a worshipping hand soft on his shoulder.

Then Danni shoved her speadhead through Addie's neck and pinned her to the Scaffold.

Addie struggled, black blood bubbling down her lips, kicked out once. Then fell still.

Her open eyes gazed sightlessly at the weeping sky.

No.

No!

NO!

The whisper became a scream, became a riptide of grief, dragging him in, dragging him back into his mind. Addie was dead. His stomach felt hollow, his chest tight as a fist squeezing his pumping heart. Breath shot like arrows from his lungs, sickness scoured liquid bile through his nose.

He couldn't stand it. The Sightless mask stared up at him.

He slammed it against his face.

Take her from me.

Unlike Addie, he didn't have Dirk's power to protect him. Callisteel against his flesh. Connections severed in a heartbeat, fierce waves of grief dragging smooth the broken edges of his mind. One by one, his memories of Addie faded into nothing. The shift of her scar when she smiled. The cruel edge of her laughter. The words they had shared.

She had seen him as human. It was time he lost that weakness.

His eyes hurt. He could feel them, churning, swirling inside his face. The edges tore, flickered, so close to the mist.

Remained. For now.

Silverspine blinked. He stood up from the corpse of the old Austelli leader. Danni gripped his wrist, and he grinned for her.

He turned to the crowd. The Sightless' mask made it so clear. Their eyes. All flecked with blue. All of them broken, all of them with something so human torn from their minds.

These were his people.

CHAPTER 46

The caverns beneath Arx were dead quiet. Weren't a soul around for miles. 'Course that'd been his hope, but it still felt off. Couple of weeks ago they'd been packed with bodies and soldiers. Now, there were nothing. No-one.

'Cept for him.

Ruairi skirted a pit of heartfire, held his arms close to his chest. Back at the foundry, he'd managed to find an old shirt to wrap around his shoulders, another one ripped up made for some decent makeshift bandages. A catalogue of injuries. The cut across his chest from the Ant's sword. Burns and blisters all the way up his arsehole. The sores around the manacles still fastened to his wrists. It would be quicker to make a list of all the places he weren't leaking from.

Worst of all, he were limping. Couldn't remember anyone doing much to his legs, but the ache in his back were piercing.

Ruairi sniffled. Couldn't stop shivering. Nothing to do with the heat. Sommat felt broken inside, like rusty teeth chewing through his skull. The feeling of death waiting for him… he couldn't shake it. Memories of the chains tearing, Ignis threatening, even of stabbing Silverspine. They choked him.

Though they weren't the worst.

Tried not to close his eyes too long. Sleep didn't come easy at the best of times, but now all he saw were the people he'd abandoned. Fetch, that molten memory forced down his throat. The Ant, still breathing. That Samantha girl's scream.

No. That one, he could still do sommat about. There would be Walkers he could find. They could save her.

Walkers. Against Silverspine.

Ruairi scrubbed his eyes on his sleeve. Delusion were a vice, but one he weren't letting go of yet. Turned around a corner and things got real dark. Stank like mould. The walls were slick with condensation and his boots slipped on the slimy floor. At the end of the cavern, he reached a metal ladder built into the wall.

'Where the shit is this?' Took a grip. Rust flaked around his hand and he almost slipped off.

He pulled himself up. Slowly, slobbering and scowling. His chest sheeted blood clean through the bandages before he managed to get the trapdoor. Smell were clear, he found himself right near the Highdock. The wind were really giving it a go. Almost forced him back down by the strength of the gust.

The strength of the smog.

Whacking banks of dust and grit rolled low through the sky. Hid his face in his sleeve just to keep from swallowing. Black and red, it tainted the air. Shrouded the sun. The whole world locked in bleeding twilight.

The Iactura rippled like a tongue of fire, right at its heart.

Ruairi walked through Arx in grey silence. The streets were empty. Occasional lamplight flickered between shuttered windows as folk hunkered down. Couldn't blame 'em. Only the morons would be out in this.

He made for the citadel. If there were any Walkers left, that's where they'd be. The closer he got, the thicker the ash taste were on his tongue. By the time he reached the pathway up to the front gates, he had to duck his head and push through the gale.

Ruairi wandered through the deserted courtyard. This close, the Iactura *burned*. It broke out from the top of some building, the door engraved with all the phases of the moon. There were noise coming from inside. He pushed the door open.

The Iactura shone fit to blinding. The room were trapped in its shadow, like the fangs of some great demon pierced the bloodred carpet. Six chairs clustered around a long, wooden table. Four were empty.

Dirk sat at the back of the room. He didn't look up when Ruairi entered. Just flipped that arrowhead knife over and over in his fingers.

Beside him, a bloke wobbled at the side of the table. Ginger beard, thick hair curling down the back of his neck. Mist gathering where his eyes used to be.

Walter DeWhit. Lord Treasurer. The latest Fog-Eye.

'I promised they would survive if they did nothing. DeWhit was the only one who listened.' Dirk's voice had lost its heat. He flicked his head up and stared at Ruairi. Lord those eyes were tired. 'I am glad you survived as well, Ruairi.'

'Don't reckon I'd call what you did to him "survival." Don't reckon I'd...' Ruairi took a step towards the table and his leg buckled under him. Just about managed to grab the polished edge, hissed hisself back upright. 'Don't reckon I'd call what you did to me "survival" neither.'

'A necessity. I needed you to kill Aer.'

'But I didn't.'

'Ignis would have died without you. I never thought she had it in her. Taking out Aer with Lucianus. I know I should feel sad about that.' He tapped his feet against the floor. 'And then she turned on me. Ferra too. Perhaps I should weep for that as well.'

'Ferra's dead,' Ruairi said. 'Silverspine...'

'I know. Easy, Ruairi. You don't have to worry.'

'Then Ignis...?'

'See for yourself.' Dirk gestured behind the chairs. To the Iactura.

Ignis were pressed against the metal. Her back half-melted into the blue-silver. Blood globbed down her sides, and her eyes burst with fits and spurts of fog. Half her face were burned, boiling into the metal.

Ruairi's stomach roiled. 'Dirk, this ain't right.'

'She's already dead.'

The weight of Dirk's words landed heavy. The truth that couldn't be ignored. 'I can't save anyone.'

'What did Arx make of you, boy?'

'A coward,' he whispered.

'And you say it with such shame! Aer was brave. Ferra was brave. Ignis was brave. Adira was brave. And look what it brought them. Cowardice keeps you alive. For a little longer.' Dirk turned to watch Ignis. Her hair had tangled in the Iactura. It dragged the back of her scalp into the metal.

'Dirk. What are you gonna do?'

'The Iactura connects us. Every cracked mind in Arx. From inside, I can cut. I will force peace on this city. Cut out memories of hatred, memories of war, of evils done in service to some long-forgotten, impossible past.' He scratched his cheek. The gesture made him look... smaller. 'It's easy to fear a bogeyman. Evil Dirk wants to get you drowning babies. No he doesn't. He just wants to take your suffering and force you into peace. Nothing wrong with that. Is there?'

That final question almost sounded genuine.

'I learned from Silverspine. You can't take that many memories and expect the host to survive unbroken. But you... I gave you exactly what you wanted.'

'No Dirk.' Ruairi's voice were firm. 'You just gave me some shadow of how my Pa saw the world so I could walk straight. I said no, that day you offered. And I stand by it.' He gripped his aching side with firm fingers, tried to massage out a knot. 'Rather be the broken boy I was than the man you made me.'

Dirk stood up. A breath licked across the coal around his throat and a tiny wire of smoke pierced Ruairi's nose. He tried to hold his breath, but the thing made him sneeze, made him drag it down into his lungs.

Dirk's eyes flickered, blue then violet, then white. 'It was just a shadow. A living mind, new experiences echoing the old. You are... reverting. To the boy I met on the road to Arx.' He blinked and the smoke faded. 'It was a slim hope. A long time ago, I used the Iactura to purge the memory of Callisteel from this city. But I didn't stay connected. I fled. And now Callisteel is returning. If I leave again, they'll all remember that desperate urge to hate eventually. I have to stay.'

'You can't do this Dirk. It's madness, that kind of control... it's just fancy Fog-Eyes. Yeah, folk are messy and stupid and complicated, but that don't mean we give up on 'em.'

Dirk's smile were sad. 'I was naive once too.'

The ground shook. Felt like the world were cracking apart. The Iactura burst with light. Ignis eyes boiled bright. Her arms shook, head twitched. She screamed. A raw, wet sound.

'*No!*' She tried to rip her head free. '*What...?*'

Another pulse of light Another scream.

'*Help me.*' She strained and blood poured from her back. '*Dirk, please!*'

'I'm surprised you still remember me at this point. Your mind is strong, Ignis. I never suspected you had such power. Unfortunately, that just means this is going to hurt even more.' Dirk folded his arms.

That terrible blue fire burst from the Iactura, whipped around Ignis' body. Flesh fell off in chunks. Fire crisped her flesh. *'DIRK!'*

Her head snapped back, mouth opened wide in an undulated scream. Blue fire burst from her eyes and raced down her body.

When it vanished, there were nothing but a pile of charred bones at the foot of the Iactura.

'Fascinating, that it wouldn't take all of her...' Dirk knelt to stir the bones.

Ruairi stepped back to the Fog-Eye on the chairs, ripped the fancy knife from his belt Levelled it at Dirk. 'You can't do this Dirk. It ain't right.'

'Are you going to stop me? Truly?' He didn't sound angry. Curious, maybe. He unbuttoned the top of his shirt. Pulled it open, bared his flesh. 'Can you kill me, Ruairi?'

Ruairi's hands shook around the hilt of the knife. He had to do it. This were the right thing. Kill Dirk. Don't let his poison spread. Don't let him steal what makes folk human.

Footsteps outside. Heavy boots. A lot of them.

'Time to choose, Ruairi. Who are you?'

Sweat ran down the side of his face. The knife were the heaviest thing in the world. How easy would it be to slam it home. To be done with it. It were all he could think. He had to. Had to. Had to!

But it just weren't him. The shadow in his mind. Pa's memory. It echoed his own.

Better coward than killer.

The knife drooped. Dirk plucked it from him.

'You did this.' He slid the copper knife into the Fog-Eyed throat. Walter DeWhit spluttered, spurted blood between his lips. Died, eyeless and empty. 'The end of the old order. I hate lying.' Dirk pressed his back to the Iactura. Grimaced. 'My advice is to flee. Aer is dead. Go home. You might be safe.' He drove that Callisteel knife deep through the palm of his hand and into the Iactura. Dirk's body wavered, like a reflection over the water. His lips spread in a deathly smile, his skin flashing silver. Then he poured into the metal, leaving nothing behind.

Ruairi just stood there. Couldn't say how long. A squad of Walkers burst in. Their blades formed a copper wall. They were shouting, but he didn't hear it. Didn't hear nothing but the rushing blood in his ears.

When they came for him, he didn't resist.

CHAPTER 47

The Austelli marched from the Nest with Silverspine at their head. Through the Sightless' masked eyes, he watched smog scar the sky. Ripples of energy like lightning pulsed through the haze. Light drowned into the spreading shadow.

'The last time we fought them here was at the end of the Flame Protests. The Sightless broke through our lines and sent us scurrying.' Quill rubbed a hand across his head and pulled his palm away covered in loose hair. 'I can't believe I'm back here again.'

'Your belief is not necessary.' Danni rolled her shoulder, spearhead flickering. 'Find your courage or flee. This ends today.'

Silverspine glanced over his shoulder. Bodies marched behind, but he could see so much more. Austelli, minds broken open for Dirk's vision of an impossible past. Nestlings, desperate to die for some indefinable freedom. Ex-Walkers offered a simple choice. Join or die. Idealism melted quickly with a dagger in your face.

He turned back. Beyond the Nest, across the river, an open plaza stretched out before them. Razed during the Flame Protests, it was left as an empty killing field. A buffer, between civilization and the Nest.

Rows and rows of Walkers hunkered down across the way. Had to be all those who were left. A final stand for the blackcloaks.

He lit a torch and approached them alone. 'No one needs to die today. You can run, if you want.'

He hadn't expected much. Where would they run to? Still, it did no harm to appear magnanimous.

A line of Walkers stepped free from the others. Archers, bowstrings taut.

A man with white hair and thick moustaches lifted his hand. Var DeKeita. The Head Captain was here to see his Walkers die.

Silverspine lifted his torch. 'More blood is nothing when you have already drowned in it. Do what you must.'

DeKeita chopped his hand down and the twang of bowstrings cracked through the air. A handful skipped across the stones at Silverspine's feet.

The greater number slammed into his chest, legs, groin and arms.

Silverspine sighed a breath behind the metal of the mask. It came out with a dribble of greasy blood and a curl of darkened smog. Flames burst blue from his torch and the arrows fell from his scarred skin.

One archer stood up. Tall, his bow was twice the size of the others. He drew back a single arrow.

The bowstring whipped and the arrow crunched into his chest.

Without the splitting of skin. Without the crunch of bone. And still Silverspine smashed into the ground. The torch in his hand screamed with blue fire, but nothing happened. He felt... hollow. A drooling, drawing sensation from his ears. The arrowhead burrowed in his chest, just about where his heart was. Blue-silver.

Callisteel.

'Bastards!' Silverspine wavered to his feet. His fingers were slick with soot and ash and he couldn't pull the arrow out. He stumbled back to the Austelli line, weak, forgetting.

Blood and ash...

Peace before death...

Mindless existence is torture.

The voices broke apart in his head, words swirling together like a blizzard of snow and ash and fire. They whipped at his mind, scratching gouges behind his eyelids, gnawing teeth through the wet inside of his head.

Silverspine stumbled, threw an arm around Danni's shoulders to keep upright. 'Pull the arrow when I say,' he whispered to her.

Danni's eyes blazed. She gripped him tight.

'Quill, prep the firebombs.'

Quill winced. 'That's my home, Silverspine...'

He fell silent when Danni's spearhead levelled just beneath his chin.

'I'm not asking. I won't die here.' Silverspine lifted his head.

He turned to the Austelli.

Off in the distance, the Walkers charged.

'People of Austellus, hear me!' Fuck but shouting took it out of him. The sound of boots on the cobblestones behind him. Fear in Austelli eyes.

'Today I want you to remember the boot on our necks, because the boot itself sure doesn't.'

Kuyt. A good man.

The Walkers were closer now. Close enough that he could make out the individual snarls in that sea of black.

'Forget your fear. Oblivion is freedom.'

Reilo. The strength of righteous anger.

'So leave a memory of yourselves today. Ash survives the flame and today we burn!'

Silverspine. A symbol. No longer a man.

And then quieter, so much quieter, right at the back of his head.

'Remember me. Because I can't.'

He held out his hand. Someone slapped a bottle into it, a rag crammed down the neck. Flint spark and it smouldered, caught. Silverspine flung it into the Nest.

It crunched against a building, tongues of flame lashing out across old wood. Down the line and countless other bottles smashed and shattered and burned.

He took a deep breath. 'Reality burns!'

The words broke from his lips, soaked in smog. It rumbled towards the Nest. Orange flame flickered.

'Danni. Now.'

The arrowhead *sucked* free from his chest.

'Inhale the memory.'

The Nest exploded in a conflagration of perfect, azure heat. The Walker charge stumbled. Fire washed across Warmarch. An angry spirit of flame, cloaked by roiling, choking smoke. Bolts of blue skittered through the smog. It pulsed with energy.

Silverspine drew the power into his lungs.

The voices in his head burned to ashes in the Fires of Remembrance. For strength. For power. For glory.

Silverspine leapt to meet the Walkers. The Austelli charged with him.

The two sides met in a crash of bodies and blood.

Silverspine sheared through the neck of a Walker. The black blade faced no resistance. The Walker's memories drained into Silverspine, forgotten in an instant as each stolen memory was sacrificed to the flames for strength.

Beside him, Danni's spear darted, flickered like a razor whirlwind. Walkers fell in hot sprays of blood, the taste of silk rust wound through the smog.

Chaos boiled. Blades and bone and blood. A hammer shattered a Walker's face. A blade carved out someone's jaw. Boots slipped on that too-red gore and bodies tripped the living.

A blade slashed into Silverspine's cheek. The smog swept around the dripping line of red and the cut vanished. He turned and slashed the throat of the Walker who held the blade.

It was almost too easy.

At his side, the Austelli line buckled. A group of Walkers burst through, their faces tight and focused. Two Austelli died in a spray of blood and copper. A handful turned and ran. They made it as far as the wall of fire that had once been the Nest. The Walkers were on them in a heartbeat.

Silverspine roared. His black knife slid under the guard of the closest Walker and boiled the eyes from his face. He tore through the squad like a scythe through wheat. Every swing he felt his muscles crack. He drank the death and got drunk on it.

All too quickly, there was just one left. A tall man with a giant bow strapped over his shoulders.

Then he fled.

Silverspine gave chase, Danni close behind. They broke from the melee and into a side street.

Fear gave the bloke speed, but Silverspine was faster. A barricade rose across the abandoned street. Stone and wire, it was clearly set up to halt an Austelli advance. No way through.

The Walker turned with a shudder. He held his blade in shivering hands.

'What is your name?' Silverspine asked.

'Sebastian.'

'Are you afraid, Sebastian?'

The Walker nodded.

'You should be.' Silverspine held out his arms, dagger pointed down. 'The only time a man can be brave is when he is scared.'

The Walker's eyes narrowed and he slashed Silverspine's outstretched arm. Skin and muscle sliced open. Bone crunched against the metal. Black knife fell from nerveless fingers.

Danni stepped forwards and plunged her spear deep into the Walker's side. Nicked something vital.

Smoke and flame ripped across Silverspine's arm and left him another scar. Danni wiped the blood from her spear and leant against the haft.

At their feet, the Walker choked on his tears.

'Please help me,' he whispered over and over.

'Would you forget?' Silverspine held up his palm, azure flame flickering over his flesh. 'I could heal you. I could take your death.'

Sebastian met his Callisteel-masked eyes. For the first time, something steeled beyond his gaze. 'Every Walker forgets something when they join. I lost a part of myself that day. I was so angry. Went to see the Mistress of the Ropes personally. Told her I'd rather die than use that magic again. She offered me the chance to end it for good. If I were a better shot, Dirk would be dead. If I were a better shot... Choke on it, Silverspine. I'd rather die as me than live like you.'

He turned his head and closed his eyes. Breath juddered in and out of heaving lungs.

The Walker died slow.

Danni kicked the corpse. 'Took his fucking time.' She grinned. 'One more dead Walker. Arx is falling.'

'It's not Arx I'm worried about.' Silverspine wiped dried blood from his newest scar.

The dead Walker's eyes boiled with blue smoke and he stood up.

'Dirk. I was wondering when you would make an appearance.'

'*Your little knife is quite frustrating. I can't speak through those whose minds you steal. Congratulations Silverspine. The city is yours.*'

'As soon as you're gone.'

'*The world of the flesh is no longer my concern. You can return to Warmarch. The Walkers will fall. DeKeita will die. And the city will be yours.*'

'We never needed your permission, Dirk!' Danni growled.

The corpse laughed, a grating sound.

'Hey,' Danni tugged Silverspine's sleeve.

He turned. The alleyways nearby were filled with Fog-Eyes. Some in Walker cloaks, others dressed as Austelli. They circled the pair. Cut them off.

'You would never let me hold Arx.'

'*Oh but I would. The peace I seek, it cannot be achieved with a Mindbreaker still alive, still... present. So keep it. Hold Arx. Do good for the people. Live well.*'

Silverspine's tongue darted across his lips. Sweat down the rivets in his metal back.

Dirk's puppeted corpse flung out a hand and the cloud of smog that surrounded Silverspine blew away. '*Or come to the Iactura. And forget your emptiness.*'

Silverspine looked over his shoulder. Past Dirk's Fog-Eyes encircling them, the Walkers beyond had surrounded the Austelli line. Their training was beginning to show. He could see it like it was written before him. The Austelli would break. They would spill from the battleground and into the streets.

A trio of Austelli went down to a crush of Walkers. Blue fire roared through the Nest behind them.

His people needed him.

But before him, behind Dirk's puppet, the Iactura blazed through the smog.

To fight or to forget. For such a long time, he had believed those were the only two options.

But beneath it all, that quiet voice still whispered.

Before Addie. Before Ferra. Before the Sightless. Before Silverspine. Before Kuyt. That voice had always been there. The single question around which his entire life had turned.

Caelan whispered.

Who am I?

The Fog-Eyed parted for Silverspine. Closed rank behind him. Surrounded Danni.

'Wait, what are you doing?'

The dead warriors advanced on her.

'You can't leave us here!'

She flipped her spear, jammed it through a Fog-Eye's stomach. The corpse didn't pause. It tore the spear from her hands. She ripped a knife from her belt, slashed a throat that bled fog.

The Fog-Eyed didn't pause. One stepped up, gripped Danni's wrist and snapped her arm with a sharp *crack*. Her knife stuck, held in a bloodless chest.

'We fought for you. You brought me back! Why? Just to die for you here?'

Silverspine turned back to her. For the first time, his face beneath the mask reflected what was carved into the steel. Emotionless. Empty. 'What else?'

A fist into her mouth, fingers grabbing, tearing at her lips. Danni screamed as they fell on her.

Silverspine didn't turn back a second time.

CHAPTER 48

Ruairi sat in a temple infirmary. A nippy morning, windows spilled shadow across the floor, picked out blades on blackcloak hips. They marched through the hospital, scaring the priestly Scelus and patients alike.

Ruairi hid in his silence. He'd tried to mention Samantha, tried to get someone to go for her. But they ignored him. Left her to whatever fate Silverspine could mete out. Same as he had.

Ruairi shifted his shoulder. Least they'd patched him up. Difficult to question a corpse. Their proper bandages and tinctures put his grubby ripped shirt out to pasture. The memory of his night with the sawbones and that bastard needle-and-thread could bugger off soon as it pleased. How were it fair that the cure for being stabbed were to get stabbed a bunch more times? Still, not like he had the worst of it.

Patients groaned throughout the hospital. Wounded Walkers, bloody civvies. The girl one bed over had spent most of her time in and outta bandages. White mittens on either hand, she wept when they changed her dressings. Ruairi had been minded to join her. Skin scraped all the way from the back of her hand like rushes swept from a barn floor, a mess of scabs and scars. The doctors said sommat about how she'd kept the fatty layers, and how lucky she were that they might save her hands.

'Stop staring at me.'

Ruairi blinked, realised he'd been gawking at the poor lass. 'Sorry, I didn't mean...'

'If you didn't mean it then look away.' She glared at him, reached one of her enormous gauze fists for a cup of water and knocked it over. 'Oh sod me sideways.'

'Here, let me.' Ruairi grabbed his own tin cup and jumped from the bed to hand it her.

A Walker blade flickered to touch the base of his throat.

'Alright, I don't gotta do it if you don't wanna.' He swallowed. Felt like he were shaving his Adam's apple. 'Here, why don't you give it her?'

The Walker smacked the cup outta Ruairi's hands and sent a luke-warm spray down his chest.

'Get up again and I'll gut you.'

'That's clear.' Ruairi slid back to his bed.

The girl huffed at him. 'Gallantry is dead.'

'I tried.'

'Not very hard.' She pushed her blankets around with a heel. 'What did you do to earn the personal attention of all these lovely Walkers that are stopping me from sleeping?'

'That'd be a long-arse yarn.'

'You going somewhere?'

Ruairi almost smiled. 'Got me there. But if it's all the same to you, I'm keeping schtum. This is Arx. No-one remembers anything.'

''Ere, Hopalong, so you were listening.'

Ruairi whirled around, tempted to pluck off his own ears and accuse them of fibbing to him, but there he *were*!

'Fetch!' He leapt from his bed. Some Walker lass bellowed sommat and there were all sorts of blade-loosening commotion, but by the time those copper points were pressed up against his back he had Fetch in a skin-tearing bear hug.

'Easy you lot, can't the lad have one moment of homoeroticism before you get to cutting? Not my fault I'm so bastard handsome.'

If anything, the blades just pressed tighter.

'Fetch. You're alive.'

'You sure about that? 'Cause some days I doubt it. You want to get off me?'

Ruairi held Fetch out at arm's length. He'd looked better, being kind. There weren't much of him that were free of bandages, beyond his face and one of his elbows. Thick wodge of padding around his shoulder and his cheeks were hollowed out like someone had gone digging with a soup spoon. Mucky five o'clock shadow sprouted from his shiny pate.

'You shave your head?'

'What? Yes. Or, I did. Harder to hold the razor with a hole in my shoulder.'

'I always figured you were just bald. Who chooses to look like that?'

Fetch snorted. 'Great to see you've got your priorities in order, kid. Come on, take a pew. My arse is aching and Captain headrush over here is about to have a paroxysm if we let her keep that blade out much longer.'

The Captain ground her teeth, the few she had left. Squash-flat nose and bumpy jaw gave the impression of someone who'd been walloped in the face one-too-many times. Her blade shook, like it took everything she had not to ram it home when Fetch hobbled on over to sit at the edge of Ruairi's bed.

'How come I ain't seen you before now?' Ruairi asked.

'I… didn't exactly announce myself when I saw you got here. Though you gotta believe that I was happy to see you survived.'

'Why didn't you come over?' Sommat ugly flickered in Ruairi's chest. 'I thought you were dead.'

'Oh you know, had a lot on my plate.' He sighed. 'I didn't come over 'cause I didn't want you to hate me.'

'You saved my life. More'n once.'

'You're only here 'cause of me.'

'Dirk's the one that stabbed me.' Ruairi shifted his arse. Felt like someone had wrapped a vine of thorns around his hips and started to pull.

'I led you to him.'

'Aye, you did. You massive prick.' Ruairi made a fist and gently bumped it against Fetch's shoulder. 'There. Now we're even.'

'That's not… you can't just forgive someone like that.'

'Can do whatsoever the fuck I please, I reckon.' Ruairi grinned. 'Not gonna turn my back on the one bastard stupid enough to bleed for me. Besides, it's what you wanted. You really thought I'd hate you, then why come over?'

'Following orders. All I've ever bloody done.'

'What?' Ruairi felt cold. 'Orders from who, Dirk? Have you heard from him?'

'It wasn't him,' Fetch said. 'Cuts a man from taint to toenails and still expects they'll do as they're told…'

Two Scelus shuffled across the well-scuffed floor, some bloke held up between them. His youthful face hung gaunt, clothes trailed from his shoulders like a scarecrow. A blood-soaked bandage wadded thick where his leg used to be. Eyes so pale blue they were almost white.

The Ant.

'Just leave me here.' His voice were faint, like it took all he had just to get enough breath in his lungs.

'Viceory, this is not...' One of the Scelus shifted her weight to keep him upright.

'I'm no Viceroy.' He eased himself out of their arms and almost immediately went careening to his face. The Scelus moved to help, but the Walkers got there first. The Captain were gentle, but firm. Dragged out a chair and sat him in it.

'Walker... scum. You shouldn't be helping me.' The Ant closed his eyes, took a deep breath, then opened them again. He caught Ruairi staring at his stump. 'It's Ruairi, isn't it? You know, when someone gets stabbed it is usually best to leave the blade in place until you can get them to someone who knows what they're doing. I was bleeding to death thanks to you. Had to cauterize the wound myself. Mindless agony, I pissed myself until my bladder hurt. Never thought I could scream so loud.'

The nearby Walkers crept closer, hands flickering to blades.

'But.' The Ant held up a hand. 'The Scelus say that if you'd left that Callisteel stuck in my knee, the last vestiges of my mind would have snapped. I owe you my life. So I will execute you myself.'

'What?' Ruairi's chest were cold.

'You betrayed Arx. What did you think would happen?'

Ruairi swallowed.

'Murder is not an execution. It's illegal without a trial. Technically its outlawed now, since only the Sightless was permitted to mete our sentences...' the bandaged girl muttered, and not that quiet neither.

The Ant leant back in his chair. 'And you are?'

She scowled. 'Mira Iudex. Don't you remember me?'

'I remember all the pretty girls, but you...'

'Do you sodding mind? It's enough that your bandages are stinking up the place. If you try to insult-compliment me then I'll smack you even if it does mean my fingers will fall off.'

343

She cleared her throat. Fetch barked a laugh.

'You can't just decide to execute someone in a hospital. If you are questioning this man, then you need a councillor or Viceroy to bring the charges, I suppose that's you...'

'I'm no fucking Viceroy,' he grumped.

'Yes Viceroy. You'll also need a witness on behalf of the accused...'

'Dibs.' Fetch folded his arms.

'...and a neutral party to sit as Chair.'

'Congratulations Mira Iudex,' the Ant said. 'You're now a chair. Fuck it, you can be a whole bench.'

'You're worse than period cramps.' She shuffled to the end of her bed.

The Ant cleared his throat, shifted in his chair. Wobbled a bit and blinked one too many times. 'It appears we have a quorum. Now. What do you have to say for yourself, Ruairi?'

Ruairi sighed. Second time he'd had to babble his bullshit out in this place. And they didn't much care for it last time. Still, what other choice did he have? Weren't hoping to take an axe through the neck. 'It all started on the road to Arx, when I saw some bloke fall off his horse...'

He dredged his way through. From flaming skulls to seeing the Ant speak, to letting Fetch trick him into prison. The march to the Nest, Silverspine. That night beneath the city with Dirk's knife through his chest.

The pain in his hips strangled tighter.

He were about halfway through Aer's party when the lass, Mira, gestured for him to stop.

'I think we can pause here,' she said.

The Ant were asleep. Fits and starts shuddered through his stick-thin frame and a line of slobber dribbled from the sides of his mouth.

'When do we...?' Ruairi asked.

'When he's awake,' the nearby Walker said.

'If he ever wakes up,' Fetch mumbled.

'Are you trying to get yourself killed?'

'Oh leave off Golli, you've seen him right? Amputation and infection, coupled with a Callisteel wound. The Ant is not long for this world.'

No-one said much of anything for a little while after that. Couple of Scelus rattled over and tipped a flask into the Ant's slumbering mouth.

'For the pain,' one of them told the clearly agitated Captain.

'Any more of that going?' Fetch scratched at a bandaged arm. 'He was the one that decided I'd look better covered in scars.'

'I am sure you deserved it.' The Scelus sniffed, made a point of corking the bottle, then turned on her heel.

'Charming.' Fetch folded his arms. 'Thought it might get me through the rest of your gabbled story.'

'I were remembering the best I could,' Ruairi said.

'Aye, but who can trust what you have to say?'

'You're one to talk. I remember everything, I just don't always… figure how it should feel. But you, I heard what Ignis said. You forgot sommat to their little flickery fire ways. Mind like maggoty cheese.'

Fetch's grin fell. 'Aye. I did forget. Once. 'Til Ignis forced it back.' He looked up at Ruairi.

Eyes were just a little misty.

'What was it?' Ruairi asked.

'Does it matter?' Fetch picked his fingernails. 'We've all forgotten stuff before. It's not like it'll be anything new.'

'Don't care. If it's got you close to blubbering, then you can crack that bald egg of yours on my shoulder and let the salty yolk dribble out 'til you feel better.'

Fetch snorted, wiped his nose on the back of his hand. 'I had a brother. He fought in the Flame Protests. He died.' His laugh was wet. 'Told you it wasn't anything new. Hundreds of us have the same memory. But I was… proud. At the start. That he went to fight. I didn't. Wasn't brave enough. Except I saw what bravery brought him. He didn't die a hero, he wasn't holding the line, wasn't screaming defiance. He died from an arrow in the back. Whoever fired it… I bet they've no idea they actually killed him. I found his body two days later. It was so cold; the blood and muck of the street had frozen him face-down. When I peeled him up, I almost couldn't tell… but he was still… my brother…'

Fetch's face disappeared into his hands.

Ruairi gripped his shoulder and let him breathe.

Eventually, Fetch's face emerged, red-rimmed eyes wiped against spotted hands. 'Dirk was there with the rest of us. Waiting for us to find the ones we lost. A whole generation, we should have known better than any the cost of blood. But he helped us to forget. He stole my brother from me. Stole his name. But left me that pride. Left me my anger. I picked up a sword the moment he asked for volunteers… stained my hands so red I could never see beyond them. Guilt is the most effective cage.'

Fetch fell silent after that.

'What were his name?' Ruairi asked.

'Hm?'

'Your brother. What were he called?'

Fetch found the tiny edges of a rugged grin. 'Steff. My brother. Fuck me, it's been a lifetime since I said it. Steff. He laughed like a saw through old branches and baked a tray of biscuits every year for my birthday. They always tasted like shit.' He turned to Ruairi. 'Thanks kid.'

Ruairi opened his mouth to respond, but sommat sharp smashed outside.

Broken window, maybe. Another crash, a shatter and then a *whoosh*. Someone screamed off in the distance. One of the Walker's leapt up and the Captain nodded him outta the room.

A heartbeat later the Walker rushed back in, face white. 'We need to move. The temple is burning.'

CHAPTER 49

Ruairi spat out the taste of smoke as he stumbled out the temple doors with the fleeing Scelus. Flames licked the woodwork, spat sparks across his arms. The cuff of his trousers smouldered until he stamped it out. Fetch careened through the blaze beside him, hawking up black spit.

Outside, the smog were thicker'n breath. Tasted like blood in the back of his throat. Smoke boiled around smog-soaked clouds.

The Walkers burst from the temple behind them. Some held the injured, the infirm, the Fog-Eyed. Others had their blades bare. Captain Golli supported a blinking Ant out into the filth. Mira were crammed under his other armpit. They were whispering together.

'ANT!'

The scream burst from the bottom of the temple steps. Ruairi squinted. A group clustered together at the bottom, ten, fifteen maybe. A couple held bottles with handkerchiefs stuffed down the neck.

A wave of Walkers surrounded them. The arsonists must have been outnumbered three, four to one. Why were the blackcloaks just standing there?

'Here, kid.' Fetch nudged him with an elbow, and slid a knife into his hand.

'Wha... Where did you get these?'

'The Walkers were preoccupied. Don't flash the buggers, just... keep it close, eh?'

'Andross DeGaya. We've come to make a deal!' the bloke shouted up again. Looked to be their leader. Short-arse, he spun some nasty looking whip in one hand, all metal spikes and cutting leather.

347

Ruairi tossed a glance over his shoulder. A handful of Scelus were lobbing buckets of sand through broken windows. The others rushed about, bandaging old wounds, salving fresh burns. Amidst the chaos, DeGaya took a breath, opened his mouth to speak and then collapsed in a welter of wheezing. He nudged the Mira girl. She shook her head, eyes wide. He nudged her again.

'State your name and your terms.' Impossible to hide the fear in her screech, but the words certainly carried.

'He knows my name. It's Quill, Lord of the *fucking* Nest. I kept the bloodsoaked fucker alive and now I'm here for what he owes me.' Bravado in his words, but his eyes darted from blade to flame and his tone were far too high.

A wash of flame burst from the door. Some Scelus jumped back and two others lobbed sand through the doorway. Sommat creaked and crashed inside.

The Ant whispered. Mira cleared her throat.

'Mr, uh, Ant acknowledges your prior acquaintance, Quill. He asks for further details of your proposal.'

'Mr twatting Ant wasn't too high and mighty to speak with me himself when he begged the Nest to bleed for him against Dirk. We've come for what we're owed. And in return, he gets his friend back.' Quill gestured at one of his mob and a man were dragged through the middle by a rope around his neck. The Walkers drew closer like an intake of breath.

Ruairi recognised the bloke being led through the smog. Var DeKeita. One eye were crusted shut and old blood dried on his arms.

'I told you disobedient bastards to attack!' Var shouted at the nearby Walkers. 'One life is worth nothing.'

'Your mate talks a big game,' Quill shouted. His whip began to whirl. He kicked DeKeita to his knees. 'Shall we see how he keeps it up when I start to take his skin?'

The Ant stumbled a step forward. Mira held him up, listened close. Ruairi's ears twitched.

'You have to do this. I've burned so many memories…'

'I'm not elected! I can't speak on your…'

'You talk. Or so much blood is spilled. It's your call.'

Mira cleared her throat. Her eyes shifted. 'Viceroy DeGaya acknowledges your original agreement and shares your desire that those terms be met. However, he regrets that he cannot treat with anyone over the threat of bodily harm.'

'The Ant promised me freedom if I followed him into the foundries. Andross DeGaya promised me freedom if I fought against bluefire demons. Silverspine promised me freedom if I went to war with the Walkers. You're all the same! Only man who keeps me free is me. Tell the Walkers to stand down or I'll start cutting.' Quill's whip cracked to punctuate his point. 'You've got until three. One!'

The Walkers drew closer. A spark over a firebomb fuse. Fetch held his knife tight.

'High Governor DeGaya asks that...'

'No more fucking talking! Two!'

Quill's whip snapped through the smog, sliced it into air.

'Thr...'

A Scelus slipped back and his heel kicked one of the metal buckets they'd had filled with sand. It went crashing down the steps of the Temple, one agonising thump at a time. At the bottom, it spun against the cobblestones by Quill's feet. The metal whirled and whirled until it finally came to a scraping stop.

Ruairi couldn't help himself. He burst out laughing. Big, meaty giggles that threatened to turn his bladder tap and soak his trousers. Couldn't stop it, slurped up smog-soaked breath just to get more outta his throat.

'Stop fucking laughing!' Quill snarled.

'Viceroy DeGaya insists that you stop being such a mindless moron and...'

'What does it matter!' Ruairi held his arms out. A Walker approached, blade out. 'Oh go on then, cut me down if you like, it's all going that way anyway. Here, I robbed a knife to fight back with, you can have it.'

Ruairi chucked the knife at the Walker's feet.

'You gotta know Mr Ant won't do anything so long as you're threatening to kill his mate,' Ruairi shouted at Quill. 'Can you imagine it? Oh, good job you let me go since I flayed your bestie, fancy leaving me be for the rest of the time?' He shook his head. 'And Ant, you were my absolute hero growing up, but if all you can figure is more blood and misery then you're thicker'n I am!'

'Kid, I'm not sure...'

'Oh shove a sock in it Fetch. It's all crap, the whole pissing lot of it! We're standing here, ready to die, just so no one has to *fucking talk to each other!* If you could all believe for just one crab-fucking moment that no one actually wants to kill you then this whole damn thing would be over and I could leave you all to burn this city down on your own time. But no chance of that, is there? So go on then. Who wants me life? Mr Whip down there, or Blackcloak Betty here with the face like a squashed tomato? Or do I just stand around until the fire back there burns my bollocks off instead?'

Sometimes, Ruairi would admit, he would really prefer if he knew when to shut up.

'Nice speech, dipshit.' Fetch shook his head.

'He's right, Quill.' The Ant's voice were strong, if breathy. 'I deserve your anger. But blood only begets more blood.' He gestured for a sword and leant on the blade like a crutch. Captain Golli stepped up to help him, but he waved her away.

'You swore that once before.'

'Did I? Those memories aren't mine anymore. But the fact I'm stood amongst Blackcloaks with snitty little women...' - he wobbled as Mira shoved him off her shoulders - 'calling me "Viceroy" it would appear I failed. I failed you. I failed Arx. I am sorry.' His words were heavy, unfeigned. 'The Flame Protests were never to get me a throne. It was to break the yoke of the system that took everything from us. Well the city is in ashes. Looks like we finally managed it. So now we re-build. And if that takes my life, then so be it. I won't resist.'

With agonizing slowness, he hopped down the steps of the temple. Slow. Struggling. Felt like everyone held their breath.

Quill looked over his shoulder. The men and women behind him were panting, exhausted. The Walkers were so close, sweat and smoke-stained skin. So many were bloody, bandaged, injured.

'Var. You fought well.' The Ant panted like a hound, exhausted from the steps.

'No, I didn't.' Var's moustache bristled.

The pair looked at Quill. His hand were curled tight around the handle. The whip whirled faster, faster, lashing through the smog.

Then fell still.

'It's hard to threaten with a whip. My shoulder is killing me. We're all going to starve anyway, might as well see if you're full of shit first.'

CHAPTER 50

Silverspine melted into the Iactura. A single touch and it welcomed him like a pair of open arms. A doorway, left open.

It felt familiar, passing through the pillar. A memory he'd held on to. Watching a shadow once called Reilo thrown back inside his mind. Using it to take his body back.

Silverspine broke into Memoria. A twilight sky flickered with endless silver stars, mist impossibly solid beneath his boots. It billowed out to eternity, an endless snowscape of white.

With a single figure cloaked in shadow, waiting for him.

Dirk strode the mists. It licked his boots, washed out before him. Master of his domain. Shadows crawled from his feet, dozens of them. Drawn towards the light of the Iactura.

Silverspine flipped his knife between his fingers and lunged. Dirk just smiled, held up his palm.

'Unwise, but not unexpected.'

The mist rose as ropes, bound Silverspine's ankles and dragged him down to his knees.

Beneath the fog, something stirred. A silver river. It crashed around the base of the Iactura, ocean spray on salt-slick rocks.

'What is that?' He strained to try and force his way from the mist, but it held tight as a steel trap around his legs.

'Bloodmetal, melted into heartfire. So much pain, so much lost, so much better left forgotten. The arterial magma that bleeds beneath the city has become our collective unconsciousness, the angry howling spirit of Arx itself.'

Silverspine glanced down. The silver crashed towards the Iactura, but there was something else. Something hidden in those hoary depths.

Hands. Faces captured in screaming masks.

Just like his. His fingers twitched to the Sightless' mask fused to his face. No escape. Not anymore.

'This is your war. The Flame Protests, Silverspine's rebellion, death, injury, loss. They define us. Can't you hear?' Dirk cocked his head, closed his eyes.

A silver wave poured into the Iactura. Something, like the crash of a mountain of ice into boiling tar. The scream of broken rock. Weeping tears of iron.

Silverspine gasped a breath into his rebelling lungs.

The Iactura burst with light, shadows crawling through the metal surface, silver orbs budding from the tip. Countless memories made manifest.

Dirk lifted a hand and silver orbs raced to meet him. He dragged his fingers through them. *'So many memories. So many minds, cracked open to lance the poison of reality.'*

Silverspine tried to move his feet, but the mist held tight.

'I will open their eyes. Here, I can cut. I will slice the bitter hate from this city and we will find an endless harmony.'

'A mindless one.' Silverspine strained his legs until his ankle popped. *'Fighting doesn't come from hate. It comes from need. Food, shelter, a place to sleep with the promise that you won't wake up waiting for the axe. You can't force peace on people, Dirk.'*

'Oh but I can. I just need your help.' Dirk curled his fingers.

Silverspine flew through the mist and slammed his back into the Iactura. The metal spear groaned. Countless lines of blue fire raced from the tip of the Iactura and connected the stars.

'Did you ever wonder why I captured Reilo's mind inside your skull? He walked the broken connections in your empty mind. Created consciousness from a handful of disparate memories. The Iactura amplifies these connections, not between the memories of one mind but between us all. We are one.'

An image flashed in Silverspine's mind. Reilo's shadow, crawling between manifest memories. A net of gold.

'*Wait.*' Something warm and wet dripped down his back. He turned his head. His bloodmetal spine boiled across his skin. Fused and melted with the Iactura. Painless. Eternal. It locked him in place. '*Who... was I?*'

'*You were a Fog-Eye, Caelan.*'

'*Before that!*'

'*You never understood. There was no "you" before that. Mindbreakers change the mind, change the body. Your body had a past, but that body is not you. It was never you. This consciousness didn't exist until I forced Reilo between your ears and he stitched together some errant fragments of your Fog-Eyed mind. That was your birth. Caelan, the man, the individual, is simply this. Memory makes the man. It was never about who you were. It was always about who you could have been.*'

He knew. Somehow, he'd always known. The past that had been stolen... it didn't belong to him.

All he had. Was this.

Shadows poured from the Iactura. Scores of them, mouths and faces moving, distorted.

Memories. His memories. He recognised them like seeing an ex-lover across a crowded room. Fused with the Iactura, they were not forgotten. Not lost. Not anymore.

He knelt at an execution and wept in the rain...

He felt the crunch of a foot that broke his nose...

He took an axe through his spine and bled out on a slab...

He dropped a man in heartfire and smiled to watch him fall...

He burned blue fire and raised a woman from the dead...

He died by the river in the arms of the man who had saved him...

'*So many different people you could have been. I can hear them scream, Caelan.*'

The shadows leapt at Silverspine, curled around his arms, his legs. Pinned him tight to the Iactura.

Wordless whispers burst in his ears.

'*I will shroud this city in a smog that smothers protest, passion and pain. War will suffocate on peace. The fighting will end. And I will watch over them all.*'

'*Apathy. That's all you can imagine?*' Silverspine's throat was burning, smoke and smog ripped through his lips. '*The memories of a city inside your head, and that is all you can see. You have been in control for far too long.'*

Something pulsed down the remains of his silver spine.

'The Iactura has been shouting for all this time but you've never really heard it. How could you? You don't understand it. But I do. The hunger of a mindless city, of everyone who sought oblivion rather than face this vile, twisted world. Screaming eternally for something, anything to fill the endless empty void.'

Mist rose from Silverspine's feet.

'No!' Dirk lifted a hand. *'The Iactura belongs to me. I created it, I fed it iron, the mists formed at my command.'*

'You created me too. Stole Reilo's soul with that lancet and shoved it inside a Fog-Eye. Both the Iactura and I... we were created so you wouldn't have to face your failures. So you could hide from your shame. For all your power, you have always just been a child refusing to accept the truth.'

Tendrils of fog snarled across the mist, snapped around Dirk's arms, legs, throat.

'Memoria is mine. You are no longer required.'

Dirk tried to step back, but the smog tightened around his body. Drew him face-to-face with Silverspine.

'We are all forgotten in the end.'

He plunged the black knife into Dirk's heart.

The last Mindbreaker gasped. He jerked over the knife, glanced down. Violet eyes wisped from his face.

And his memories swarmed into Silverspine.

Knowledge boiled like acid. He screamed, laughed, wept as Dirk's mind melted into his own. His hands were shaking. Shuddering. Dirk's corpse fell to the silver ocean far below. He could finally hear.

It hurt.

He thought he had known emptiness before this, but now... The voices of Arx were beyond empty. Memories of children who had never had cause to dream. Adults whose hope was burned in the heartfire of the empty forges. Walkers whose lives were forfeit to a broken system. They numbed their minds to their own slaughter so they could still sleep. Austelli, forced into endless war in desperation to return to an impossible life. The iron was gone, but they burned their lives searching for its echo.

Life without living. Arx was a gaping maw, an endless abyss without hope, without a future, the eternal *now*. It would never change. It could never change.

It broke him.

He fumbled his knife with shaking fingers. The emptiness was too much.

He slammed it through his throat and into the Iactura.

Trails of fire burned from the fog in his eyes. Silverspine was ripped from the weeping prison of flesh, ascended as something *more*. God of the Mist.

Ice blue eyes opened beneath the twilight sky. The Iactura pulsed, a new heartbeat. The mist curled around it like blood through his veins.

With a pulse of unimaginable power, the consciousness exercised its will. Arx the eternal. All would be forgotten.

Deep beneath the city, heartfire burned blue. The silver stars blazed in a web of cosmic flame. Every cracked mind bound to the mists, bound to Silverspine, bound to endless oblivion.

Their memories drained into the Iactura.

CHAPTER 51

Ruairi sat in his assigned spot and kicked his feet under the table, waiting for sommat to go wrong.

Their little gazebo right in the courtyard of the Citadel did nothing to keep the smog away. He could feel it like a second skin. Needed a bath. Needed six or seven to peel the grime off. The wind had picked up, felt like being attacked by sandpaper. The Iactura overhead were swallowed in thick, black smog.

'I really don't know if this is lawful,' Mira said. 'We should have some Councillors look it over... the language feels so ugly.'

'Please, Miss Iudex, it really is fine.' The Scelus Mira had chosen as scribe rubbed his eyes with ink-stained hands. 'And we should really have someone look at your bandages...'

Fetch picked his fingernails with his stolen knife and ran his hand over his freshly-shaven skull. 'I ain't listening to you dictate a fourth one of these. Call it done. Besides, all fancy language is ugly.'

'Not liking things doesn't make you interesting. It just makes you miserable.' Mira didn't even look up.

'Now, come on that's not fair,' Ruairi said. 'Fetch does way more than just not like stuff to be as grouchy as he is.'

'You count as many years as I have you'd realise why I'm not always a ray of sunshine for mewling idiots who still don't know how to hold a sword right.'

'*Can* you count as many years as you've had? I didn't think numbers went that high.'

'Would you two shut up?' Mira scowled at them.

Despite Mira's evident disapproval, Ruairi still felt good. The fighting had stopped. No one had bled since morning, least no one who weren't already gushing. Runners from the Walkers and those folk left from the Nest had spread out through Arx, from the Citadel all the way down to the gate in Austellus that he'd first hauled his arse through what felt like the rough length of eight lifetimes ago.

Little campfires dotted around the streets. Closest one were just 'round the corner from the courtyard. Packed with the folk who were still breathing, it were an easy enough lure. Big pots of stew, supplies from the Walkers mixed with Dirk's Open Kitchen grub, drew folk like butterflies to buddleia. Hard to argue with your gob full.

'Course it hadn't all been smooth. Standing too close to the Ant and DeKeita, he'd heard enough of it. The Austelli's final stand had broken both sides. Walkers and Austelli both had fled. Not so much a war as a brawl that broke out through the city. Streets packed with bodies, scrawny kids slumped in corners, Walkers crushed like leaves underfoot. Worst were the stories of the houses. Most of the rich folk had barricaded themselves indoors when the fighting spilled over, but a locked door ain't always that effective. Especially when folk got desperate. There'd be a reckoning, so DeKeita said. One day.

'Right. Sod it. If they don't like it they can do it themselves. Stay here, you two are witnesses. Scribe Carsi, thank you for your help.' Mira shooed the Scelus away and stalked off.

'Can't believe it's over.' Ruairi shook his head once Mira were out of earshot.

'Not even close. Don't blue sky it, kid, we're gonna be here for a while, listening to all the Billy-big-bollocks negotiating. The look on your face!' Fetch slapped his thigh, then scowled as one of his bandages pulled against his skin. 'Don't get pissy now that things are boring. Boring bits are the best ones, remember?'

Ruairi smirked at that.

'Please rise for High Governor DeGaya, Head Captain DeKeita and Lord of the Nest Quill.' Mira's voice were doing that screechy thing again, clearly desperate to remember what she were supposed to say.

'If we're being official, I believe it was "Lord of the Fucking Nest,"' Fetch murmured.

'An afternoon is all I ask, Fetch,' DeKeita said. His eyes were tired. Well, the one that weren't screwed shut by a whacking purple bruise.

'They get titles. Why shouldn't I?' Quill glared around the table. 'If this is official.'

'It is.' The Ant held tight to a Scelus. He looked worse, like his skin had been melted to his bones. The bandage around his knee stank like the Mucro and no matter how they wrapped it, it still leaked. He went to lean on the table and almost thumped his chin on it.

'Uh, everyone, let us be seated.' Mira's eyes flickered between the Ant and the table like she figured there were a real risk he weren't gonna make it to a signature. 'Witnesses Ruairi... do you have a surname?'

'Whassat?'

'Witnesses Ruairi and Fetch...'

'Marquises of Pissingabout,' Fetch added.

Mira's eyes made a dagger look dull. '*Silent* witnesses Ruairi and Fetch will sign first, to state that this document meets all legal statutes and codes.'

'We will? How we supposed to check that?' Ruairi asked.

'Lad, think it through.' Fetch dragged the paper towards himself and scrawled his name. He thrust the paper at Ruairi.

It were right fancy. Loopy letters and little doodly-things in the margin. Not that he could read it. Looked like a bunch of little worms after a rain, but he got a R scribbled down where he were supposed to.

'Excellent. Next, we shall sign the Articles of Disengagement, which simply state that during the negotiations we are operating under a truce.'

'For now.' Quill scratched that giant scar that swallowed half his face.

Fetch's eyebrows rose at Ruairi in the biggest 'told-you-so' his shiny pate could offer.

'Head Captain DeKeita will sign first.'

The DeKeita dipped a pen and signed with a flourish. 'Second time I've signed for peace. Here's hoping there won't be a third.'

'High Governor DeGaya, if you could?' Mira gestured.

DeGaya just looked at it. For a long time. His eyes blinked slow.

'Uh, sir?'

'I can't sign.' His voice wavered.

'I knew it!' Quill almost threw the table over launching to his feet. His hand ripped that whip from his belt. 'Full of shit!'

'Quill, calm down!' DeKeita held out a hand. 'Andross, this isn't the time for idealism. This has to end.'

DeGaya's jaw creaked into a tiny smile. 'No, I mean I *can't* sign it. I'm no Viceroy. If we get to go again… I never wanted to be one of them. Back then, Reilo's madness made me… rethink some things. But he's not here this time. I will remain the Ant.'

'Memory aside, the legality is…'

'I, the apparent High Governor Andross DeGaya, elected Viceroy of the corrupt and murderous Upper Senate, hereby resign my post effective immediately. I nominate Mira Iudex as my replacement.'

'Second,' DeKeita said. He looked at Quill.

The bloke sat back down and shrugged. 'If it'll get this fucking done.'

'An accord is agreed. Mira DeIudex. Enjoy my chair.'

'What?' Mira's voice were so high it coulda shattered glass. 'You can't do that!' She flushed all the way to her forehead. She looked around the table like she were certain someone were gonna stop her. When they didn't she sighed. Looked like a tear in her eyes as she stared at her hands. 'I'm afraid my ability to sign anything is somewhat limited.'

'The job is never easy. If you want it, then you will find a way,' DeKeita said.

Mira chewed her bottom lip. She glared around the table, as if daring anyone to speak, then lowered her head. She bit the pen between her teeth, bit of spit rolling down her bottom lip. Managed to lift it upright and made a faint scrawl on the paper. Colour in her cheeks only got deeper.

Fetch started clapping like a pillock until DeKeita's glare froze his hands together.

Quill pulled the sheet towards himself and took the pen using his sleeve as a glove, wiped it clean before adding his name.

Peace in Arx. It were finally here.

An earthquake rocked the ground beneath the table.

Ruairi leapt to his feet. Felt like the city were breaking in two. A massive fracture cleft open the courtyard and one of the buildings crumbled into the hole, stone splinters flying everywhere.

Heartfire roared in gouts and spurts from cracks between their feet. Not orange. Blue.

'What is going on?' Fetch roared.

'Look to the Nest!' Quill pointed.

The fire roared in the distance. A massive pillar of light burned a hole in the clouds. Fires ripped from the ground, chewed through buildings, melted cobblestones. Arx burned in the storm.

Overhead, the sky began to twist. Ashen clouds swirled together, a maelstrom of smoke and smog. The clouds ripped from the sky on an unseen wind, dragged towards the Iactura.

The metal glittered black as midnight.

Mist rose from the cracks in the ground. The street were thick with it and yet none of it touched Ruairi. He looked over.

The Ant twitched. The smoke poured into his ears, his mouth. His head slumped forwards.

'Andross, are you okay?' DeKeita ran towards him, felt for breath.

Over the blackened spire, a pair of too-blue eyes opened in the clear sky.

'He's breathi...' DeKeita began.

The Ant's head jerked open like someone had grabbed him by the hair. He opened his eyes.

The sockets boiled with smoke.

The Ant slammed a blade into DeKeita's throat. The Viceroy fell with a gurgle, his blood splattered over their peace agreement.

'What the fuck you doing?' Fetch leapt across the table, his knife lashed out and carved into DeGaya's thumb. Sent his sword clattering to the ground.

The Ant's fist crunched into Fetch's nose. Fetch fell, lumped to the floor like someone had smacked a hammer in his face.

The Ant fell with him, leg gushing blood and puss through soaking bandages, and gripped Fetch's throat. Squeezed. Fetch's eyes bulged out of his head. Mouth open, he couldn't so much as gurgle. His heels drummed against the mist.

Ruairi scooped up the Ant's own sword. Didn't think. Darted forwards.

Lashed a cut through the back of his neck.

The Ant's head fell free of his body and rolled to the side of the table. It hit the leg with a little *click*.

'Kid...' Fetch wiped his hands down his shirt. Cleared his throat half a dozen times.

Ruairi blinked. The Ant's headless corpse slumped to the floor.

'Fuck me, what was that?' Quill's eyes were wide and white. 'He was on the edge of death, how could he...?'

'He sacrificed his memories to Aer to fight us. Dirk said he could cut every broken mind... that's the Austelli. Most of the Nest, all of the Walkers! Any of you used a Mindbreaker before? Are you cracked?' Ruairi asked.

Quill and Mira shook their heads.

'Not anymore,' Fetch touched his eyelids. 'Fuck me.'

'What's happening?' Mira whispered.

'The Iactura, Dirk said it can control people's minds.'

'Those eyes up there, they aren't Dirk's,' Fetch said.

'Silverspine,' Quill hissed.

'What do we do?' Mira asked.

No one had an answer to that. They fell into silence, soon broken by the sound of screaming.

'Bollocks. That's the camp,' Fetch shouted. The others followed behind him as he raced around the corner.

What they saw there were carnage.

The camp were complete chaos, bodies and blood. Greasy soup soaked around the corpses. A small group were pressed up against a building fighting for their lives against the swarm of Fog-Eyed fighters, pinned back by cracks of heartfire.

'We gotta cut through.' Ruairi's hands shook. Blood dribbled down the sword, but there weren't time to think about that now.

'No chance, look!' Fetch dragged his attention away and down the main street towards the Citadel.

It were swarming with bodies. A legion of Fog-Eyes marching through the smog.

'Back!' Fetch barked.

'Fetch, they'll die without us!' Ruairi's voice trembled.

'They'll die just as quick with us there too. Steal their breath and *move*!' Fetch gripped Ruairi's shirt and dragged him back. The four of them crept away, pushed all the way towards the door to the Midnight Chamber. Ruairi's heart slammed against his ribs.

'What now?' Quill asked. His voice were oddly calm. Like a deep breath before plunging into water. He looked at Fetch.

'Depends what your signature was worth. We signed for a new order to shine outta the ashes. As many lives as we can save from here on out,' Fetch said. 'You willing?'

Quill's eyes washed over Ruairi and Mira. He cocked his head. 'I signed for freedom. I'll fight for it again. Just like always.'

The two men nodded.

A curdling screech drowned from the camp. Boots clattered on shattered cobblestones.

'Is this it?' Ruairi wobbled. 'As far as we go?' Jags of light and panic sparkled through his mind.

Fetch tore the sword from his grip. 'Not quite.'

His arm curled around Ruairi's throat and he flung him through the door and into the Midnight Chamber. Mira were hurled in after, she crashed into Ruairi's chest and sent him to his arse. The door slammed behind them.

Ruairi ran at the door, pounded his fist against it. 'Fetch! Let me out!' He smashed his hand until it hurt.

'After all the trouble I went through to trap you in there? Be a right waste.'

'I can't just let you die out there!' Stupid tears welled in his eyes.

'I should never have let Dirk have you that night. Ruairi. My brother, you just wanted to go home.' A pause. 'Besides, you *just* saved my life. And I never liked being in someone's debt.'

'Don't do this.'

''Course, chances are they'll have this door down in next to no time, but when all your options are shit, you gotta swim in it.'

'Fetch! They're coming.' Quill's voice.

'Keep your knickers on, I see them.' A deep breath. 'Fuck I miss Ro. She were a damn good horse. But maybe I can convince myself she's waiting for me somewhere. I'll go riding with Steff. That's a nice thought to end on, ain't it?'

Footsteps. Running. The roar and clash of blades.

'Ruairi, come on!' Mira kicked him. The back of her bandages were prickled with red pinpricks. 'I'm not just standing around to die here.'

'Fetch... he...'

'Fetch is trying to keep you alive a bit longer. So let's repay him by sodding surviving! That or I leave you here.' Her hands trembled. 'Please. I can't cope with this by myself.'

Ruairi blinked the wet from his eyes. He got to his feet. Someone screamed outside.

'Right. What's the plan, Miss Mira?'

The Iactura crackled behind them, pierced right through the heart of the main chamber.

'Sod me, I have no ide-' Mira started, but a groaning smash cut her off.

The floor gave way, sent Ruairi arse-over-tit, whirling and crashing down into the caverns below. White spots punched him in the face as the ground met him, hard.

Darkness burned in the Iactura. Pockets of heartfire boiled around them, walls slick and breaking open. The heat seared into Ruairi's skin, his mouth dry and raspy.

Mira's eyes flooded with tears, face pinched in agony. She stumbled to her feet, one hand drenched in blood.

Ruairi grabbed her shoulder, steered her towards the crack in the wall. She snotted and scrunched her eyes, but her feet moved.

The rocks boiled with heartfire. The heat seared his skin, his mouth dry and raspy. 'Down here, through the caverns, we can...'

Another quake. Boulders loosened, shifted and shuddered like toys hurled about by a giant. The world slammed them into the walls, blood dribbled from Ruairi's nose.

The entrance collapsed. Their only way out, blocked by stone and fire.

CHAPTER 52

Sam huddled in the corner of the empty basement. The burned-out candles hinted at mid-afternoon, but none of the blue-eyed blacksmiths had woken.

For two days they'd slept, collapsing where they stood the moment Silverspine vanished. Their exhaustion pulsed in every breath and thoughts of what he'd put them through rocked Sam's own attempts at sleep. That black knife. Blue eyes. The mindless body whimpering at the back of the room.

Her crucible lancet still stood tall in its barely moving chest.

She couldn't stop looking over. Old, emaciated. Eyes boiled with faint blue smoke. Even the body of the blacksmith Silverspine had murdered, slumped in the corner, didn't haunt her thoughts like the vacant half-corpse did.

Sam shuddered. Was this her fate? As a mindless body, forced to work for Silverspine. No connections to anything. Anyone.

Perhaps it was as much as she deserved.

A groan. Sam looked over. A blacksmith woke up, clicked out his back, wandered over to the little fire-pit kitchen. Soon the smell of porridge filled the room. He glanced over his shoulder, looked to notice her for the first time, and wandered over with two steaming bowls.

'No, thank you.' Sam stared at her feet.

Both bowls shattered against the floor. Boiling porridge splattered her arm.

'What?' Sam scrabbled back into the wall.

The blacksmith knelt beside her. He grabbed her arms. 'Uh.'

'Get off!'

'Um. Ah. Uh.' His glistening stump of a tongue thrashed between his lips, flecked her with spit.

'Sorry! I'm sorry, okay, I'll eat the porridge, I'll do whatever you want.' She shrank back.

The blacksmith shook his head. He rushed to the back of the room, drew the lancet from the body and knelt beside her. He wiggled the metal feather-patterns at her and quirked an eyebrow.

Forced her to meet his eyes. No blue flecks. And something… familiar.

'Um. Ah. Uh.'

The crinkles over the bridge of his nose. The corner of his jaw where the beard didn't quite come through. The skewiff curve of his smile.

She could barely breathe. 'Jak?'

A tear dripped from his nose. He nodded.

Sam threw her arms around his neck.

Everything inside her chest was all jumbled. Her throat was tight but there were tears in her eyes and she couldn't stop laughing.

'I can't believe it. I can't believe I found you. But… do you remember me? The other's, their eyes…' She shuddered at the thought of the endless blue cataracts.

He nodded. Pointed at his eyes.

They were brown. And honest. And unmarked.

'Then… what did they take from you?'

Those very same eyes rolled in an all-too familiar mockery. He gestured at his tongue.

'Right. Oh Jak, I'm so sorry this happened. You'd have never been down here if I hadn't listened to Ignis. I-'

He placed a finger across her lips. His hands slipped around the back of her head and brought her forehead to press against his.

Sam closed her eyes and for a moment, they just knelt there. Forgiven.

Then the earthquake struck.

Jak wrapped her in his arms and held her to his barrel chest as the world tried to flip around her. An enormous, shuddering *crash* shuddered through the building. A chunk of masonry shattered through the wall of the basement, broke a shard of sunlight from outside as a rubble-staircase slid through the rock. A red smear caught underneath it. One of the other smiths.

They were awake now. Fingers pointed and arms waved. Jak uncurled from around her and all of them approached the hole in the wall. Something seeped in from outside. It looked like... mist?

White tendrils crawled through the gap and into the room. Sam glanced down. A small pocket of space surrounded her, an empty gap where the mist would not touch her. The same was true for Jak.

The other smiths froze. Blue flecks raced across their eyes. A legacy of those Mindbreakers.

Then they screamed. Blue fog boiled from their faces.

The closest grabbed a hammer. Without pausing, he swung it at Jak.

'Jak!' Sam shouted.

He twisted around the blow, caught the hilt on his side. Jak grunted, grabbed the haft and tore it from his attacker's grip. He swung and the blacksmith hit the floor with a wet smack. Gobs of blood splattered the wall.

The body twitched. Groaned. And stood up. Blood leaked from the crater in the side of his skull. Sam could see his brain, beating and pulsing in the crack. She swallowed sour spit.

Jak grabbed her hand. Even then, in the midst of the chaos, his warm palm was comfort. He smashed a chunk of masonry from the shattered hole in the wall and dragged her through, up the broken steps and out into the streets. The scrabbling sound of the other blacksmiths followed them.

Cracks rent the ground. Blue-gold whorls of flame ripped through buildings, roads, even the clouds.

'The Mucro!' Sam screamed.

The river was gone. Huge chunks of earth and concrete had pulled apart and water gushed underground. The final barge hung down the Highdock bank like a silver necklace across a slit throat.

Jak yanked her back. He pointed at the wall. A sluice grate was built into the base, but the black stone was crumbling.

The wall around Arx broke open.

An enormous *gush* of water poured into the city, down the empty riverbed. It ripped the barge from its chains, sent the metal meteor slamming into the river's edge, scoured the stone down deep into the bowels of the city.

'What do we do now?' Sam asked.

Jak just shook his head.

At his side, the street exploded with flame. Fog-Eyed, there had to be fifteen of them, shuffled from the fire. Their clothes scorched, skin sloughed off with burns.

Jak barrelled through them, hammer swinging wildly. Hands and fingers tore at them, but Jak pushed on through and Sam rushed behind.

Buildings groaned and collapsed around them. The wall around the city crumbled district by district, ripped apart by flames and heart-fire. Where was safe when the world was burning?

Jak's feet slowed and Sam skidded into his back. Nothing but a hole in the ground.

Her heart was cold. Was this it? The smoke from the fire choked a dirty cough from her lungs. Her shirt was scorched, arm blistered. So hot.

And yet Jak just ran forwards. Towards the pit. Blue light pierced from deep below.

Sam followed Jak down a slippery, sooty staircase dug into the rock. If the streets were a furnace, then the pit was a coke oven. Her tongue was thick in her mouth.

At the bottom, the cavern was filled with forge equipment. Ovens, anvils, an old furnace. Mist crept through the ruins. 'Where are we?'

'Ow. Ry.'

Right. Tongue missing.

'I wish you could talk to me.' Sam wrapped her arms around herself. 'What's happened out there? Fog-Eyes everywhere, the streets on fire, the river just sodding gone.' Her legs wobbled, almost collapsed.

Jak rested his hands on her shoulders. Squeezed tight enough to bruise.

'You're right. You're right,' Sam said. 'But what do we do?'

Jak slipped a hand to his belt and drew the lancet. It gleamed like night, black-iron with wings of silver.

'Callisteel. That's what Silverspine had you captured to make, isn't it? But what good can even Callisteel do against...' she lifted her arms, '...everything?'

Jak just smiled at her. He tapped his nose. A gesture she knew well. Trust me.

Sam took a deep breath. It burned down her throat. 'I do.' She tried a weak smile. Couldn't quite manage it, but the familiarity worked for her. 'But I was... don't we need that blue fire for this to work?'

Jak pointed at a crack in the centre of the cavern and Sam looked down.

Heartfire. The liquid flame beneath the city. Ferra's words flickered through her mind. *There are only two sources that are hot enough to forge Callisteel.* Far hotter than any forge, it boiled blue, lashed at the walls of the stone pit desperate to escape. The liquid fire rose like water, its churning, burning surface bubbling just below the lip of the rock.

Mist raced into the heartfire.

The cavern shuddered. Shadows rose from the heartfire. Memories of violence and loss long sacrificed.

Jak shoved Sam behind him, hammer at the ready.

The shadows tore at him. Claws of red smog vanished between his ears, searing tongues of flame scoured his skin, teeth tore at his arms. Jak slammed his hammer through the shadows, and each one broke into soot that was sucked back into the heartfire.

Slowly, the surface of the heartfire began to cool into an obsidian skin. Impossibly thin. Jak's hands steamed and blistered. Blood stuck his clothes to his skin. A chunk of his ear was missing, and both arms were ribboned with cuts.

Sam wept a scream behind her lips. Oh Jak. What had she done to him?

She was untouched.

The shadows came again and Jak closed his eyes. When they opened, he was smiling.

He stepped on to the heartfire and, as his feet set aflame, he shoved the lancet into his chest.

Delicate feathers unfurled around his heart. Blood lit up in the patterns. And the shadows rushed into his chest.

Jak's body began to glow. His shirt, trousers burned away and the skin beneath...

An impossible pattern of spirals wove across his body. Waves crashing, spiderwebs closing, the trilling notes of a sparrowhawk chiselled into his flesh. They burst with light, orange as a forge fire. The Mindbreaker tattoos were barely a pale imitation. It was beautiful.

And in that instant, she knew what he intended.

Ferra's voice. *To forge true Callisteel we are going to have to kill him.*

'No. Jak, don't you dare!' Sam grabbed his arm. 'I've just found you again. I can't lose you. Not now. Not for this.'

Jak pulled her into a rough embrace. She looked up into his face. Into his deep, honest eyes.

They sparkled for her.

Then Jak grabbed her fist, crushed it around the hilt of the hammer. The head touched the burning symbols in Jak's chest. Impossibly gentle.

Blue-silver liquid rushed the length of the hammer. Jak's memories played out in the mist as his life drained into the metal.

They were memories of her.

Sam wept as she watched herself learning the forge. She watched him forge her hammer, watched that first dagger they ever made together, watched him juggle coin pouches and toss them into a lockbox beneath his desk. They had never done it for the money.

'*I was the only blacksmith to sacrifice his tongue and his freedom. I couldn't lose my memories of Callisteel. They were all memories of you.*'

'But why?' Sam wept. 'Why leave me now, I just found you.'

'*Something is broken in Arx, has been for a long time. You are the only person I'd trust to fix it. You always knew the way of things. It doesn't have to be shaped as a weapon.*'

Jak's voice, smooth as liquid gold, whispered inside her mind. He met her eyes, a smile as wide as the Mucro on his lips.

'*I never had a daughter of my own. But thanks to you, I am luckier than most. Goodbye Samantha.*'

A column of blue flame roared like thunder, blinding bright.

When her vision returned, Jak was gone.

All that was left on the platform of obsidian was his hammer.

Sam took the solid-metal handle. This was not the ratty thing he'd been swinging at Fog-Eyes. An old design, almost unheard of. One side was flat, a pattern etched into the metal, rose thorns and starlight. The other side was drawn into a wedge-spike. Frost gathered on the blue-silver steel.

She lifted it effortlessly, like a breath of wind given form. Jak had finally mastered Callisteel. And it was beautiful.

Sam sobbed into her arm. Her legs gave way and she slumped to the floor. Exhaustion crawled over her. What was she supposed to do now?

A squawk broke her reverie. Sam looked over in time to see a body crash into the ground, pulp and bone and viscera.

More Fog-Eyed crawled around the edge of the pit. They had found her. Some lumbered down the stairs dug into the side. Others slipped, flung themselves into the crater. Their bodies were broken on impact. But the smoke swirled, the fire roared, and they rose to their feet once more.

She leapt to her feet and ran. Breath slapped her cheeks. A crack in the wall, fissures between the rock. Just wide enough for her to squeeze though.

Sam pushed herself into the darkness.

CHAPTER 53

Inside the rock, white mist wisped around Sam. She ran. Countless paths split and curved away from her. Impossible to guess the right one.

Her shoulder thumped against the wall. It was over. The city overrun. Dead, dying, mindless. She was going to die down there. Trapped in a rocky tomb beneath the city.

Alone.

She slumped against the wall, slid down. Mist crawled around her, closer now. Sam closed her eyes. There was no one left. It would be easier if she just slipped into a sleep that didn't end. Perhaps there would be others there, in that ceaseless darkness. Dreams of a memory.

'Jak. You left me. Again.'

It hurt. Like a great weight pressing down on her chest. To find him and lose him again so quickly. It was a pain she couldn't mourn, complex and tender and sharp as broken glass.

Something buzzed.

Sam sniffled, wiped her face. She strained to listen, but it was impossible to pinpoint. It wasn't coming from anywhere. It just… buzzed, like an insect inside her ear.

She traced the pattern on the hammer's head. Did the noise get louder? She pressed her ear to the haft. Nothing.

'Jak?' The mist puffed around her lips.

Something buzzed again. Faint and out of reach.

She licked her lips. There was an idea, gnawing at the back of her mind. Insanity, really, even the thought made her cold. But cowardice is the enemy of progress.

Sam ripped the wedge-spike across the palm of her hand.

Pain like nothing she had ever experienced arrowed through her. Salt in an open wound, boiling tar in her blood, a razorblade through her tongue and she *screamed*. Memories burst before her like jagged stars. But she forgot nothing. Instead, she felt... something new. Something remembered. The shared agony of so many, forgotten in bloodmetal, lost in heartfire. It was impossible to fathom.

The mist began to boil, to swirl and course around her, waves of a violent ocean rising to drown her. And sat there, on a receding island of sanity, surrounded by nothing but pain, Sam could finally see.

Jak's memories flashed before her eyes, melded with countless others. The blinding, golden threads that linked so many lives. Memories, not lost but shared.

It was all connected. The pain, yes, but without it the joy faded as well. To have something and then lose it was the worst kind of agony, but to never have it... It was worse than pain. It was nothingness.

People, isolated by their own numbness. A city, trapped on a peninsula, hiding behind its walls afraid of what it had released. But it was imperfect. Only those who wilfully forgot the past could possibly hope it would last forever.

Arx had a future. She had a future. But it would never be seized alone.

Deep inside her chest, something knit back together and for the first time in her life, Samantha Acarris simply *was*.

Sam rose to her feet. The mist stormed around her now, a translucent blizzard. And she could feel something in that fog. A mirrored heartbeat of the pain from her hammer, amplified thousands of times.

The Iactura.

Memories of those who knew the caverns coalesced and Sam set one foot in front of another. Choices spiderwebbed into action and she followed the twists and turns with certainty, moving through the veins of Arx right towards the heart of the city.

Deeper in and her feet splashed through stagnant water. She sniffed, a familiar foulness in her nose led her to the wall. Rocks ripped out by the quakes gave her handholds and she scrabbled up, finding a tiny leaking hole to peer through.

On the other side, the Mucro rushed through the caverns. Poured into pockets of heartfire in an ear-slicing *hiss*, washed through the rock.

Which fate was kinder, burning or drowning? Her heart tumbled around her chest.

Another quake rocked the ground and Sam grabbed the wall to try and keep on her feet. Rocks cracked and opened, heat poured through the caverns, trickles of water. When the ground stopped jumping, she wiped the dust from her eyes.

The path was blocked. Rocks and rubble piled together. Those faint memories still led her. The Iactura was behind those stones.

As were... voices? Sam crept close. Fog-Eyes didn't speak. She pressed her ear to the stone.

'I can't die here.' The voice was shaky, broken. And familiar. 'Please, we *can't...*'

'Reckon we don't have a choice in the matter.' Another voice. 'Miss Mira, please don't cry. We... we did what we could...'

Wait. Who? 'Mira?' Sam shouted through the rock.

The voices on the other side fell silent.

'Someone there?' the deeper voice shouted back.

'You know my name?'

'Mira! It's me. Sam!' She scrabbled up the rocks, peered through a gap.

Another eye bobbed into view. Tears stained, scratched and undeniably familiar.

'Sam. Sam, no. This is cruel. I didn't think Fog-Eyes could talk...'

'Fog-Eye? Sod off, look at my face.' Sam pulled her eyelid open. 'See any fog there?'

'I can't see shit because of all these rocks.'

'Then stand back.' Sam slid back down. 'You out of the way?'

'Sam, what are you...?'

'Hold on!' She swung the Callisteel hammer at the rocks.

It hewed the rock with ease. What was a solid wall of stone shattered into pebbles and dust and gravel, leaving a half-person sized hole she could just about squeeze through.

The cavern roared. She felt it in her stomach. Heartfire raged from cracks in the rock, the sound of sloshing behind the walls. And two very dirty, very dishevelled people, sat nearby.

Sam dropped her hammer and ran at Mira, her arms tight around her friend's neck. Mira twisted her head to rest it on her shoulder, arms held wide of the embrace. The blood-black bandages smote Sam's heart.

'Could have knocked me out smashing the rubble back there,' Mira sniffled.

'Sorry, we should have used the hammer you brought with you instead.'

Mira gave a wet hiccup. 'Arsehole.' She gestured at the man stood awkward behind them. 'Sam, this is...'

'Ruairi.' Sam shook her head. 'I'm not going to hug you, but I'm glad you survived.'

'Of course I survived. With Silverspine... I left you to die.'

It caught her. The whinging. 'Don't you *sodding* dare.' Her throat was hot and sharp. '*I* rescued you from Ferra. *I* got caught. And *I* survived, same as you. Don't you dare try to take that from me, or I'll chain you back up myself.'

That shut him up.

Sam turned back to Mira. 'I found Jak.'

For a brief moment, Mira's smile was like the sun behind a storm. Then it vanished. 'He's not here.'

Sam clenched her jaw to keep the sob from breaking through. Didn't trust her voice, just shook her head.

'We'll mourn him, Sam. I promise. First, we need to get out of here.' She glanced up to the caved-in floor of the Midnight Chamber. 'The Fog-Eyed are coming.'

'Get out where?'

Mira jerked her head at the hole in the rock.

'Mira, there's nothing back there. Caverns that led to the Rustscrape Foundry. It's overrun.'

'Then what do we do?'

'Reckon there's only one path left.' Ruairi walked up to the Iactura. It pulsed, stained with shadow.

'Did you smack your head on the way down?' Mira asked.

'Aye, and it hurts like a bugger. But this is all we got. Didn't think of it before 'cause I didn't have the tools. But the metal of that hammer you're carrying looks right familiar. Callisteel?'

Sam nodded. 'Jak and I made it.'

'Then that's our way in.'

'Do you two take joy in speaking gibberish?' Mira asked. 'You can't go *into* the Iactura.'

'I wish you were right Miss Mira.' Ruairi walked over to the Iactura. Went to touch it. Dragged his hand back, bit his lip, then forced his palm to make contact.

Nothing happened. He nodded and turned back to them.

'Dirk's in here. Or maybe Silverspine. Or both. Dunno. But I am responsible for this. I could'a killed Dirk once already. I could've stopped him. I need to do this. I need to... Fetch, the Ant, DeGaya, all those Walkers and Austelli and innocent folk whose only crime were being in the wrong place. I gotta do this for them.' His legs shook.

'You're scared.'

'Terrified. But that ain't nobody's problem but mine. 'Sides, my hands are stained now. Not a lot of chances left to make it right. Man's gotta have something to live by.' He blinked, pressed his back to the Iactura and met Sam's eyes. 'Callisteel, through the chest and into the Iactura. I watched Dirk do it. I go in, try to stop... whatever's happening. You stay here. And break this thing.'

'Ruairi, this is insanity. Callisteel through the chest will kill you, and I can't destroy the Iactura, look at it! I don't even know how to...'

'If you've got a better idea, I'm all ears.'

Sam growled. She looked away.

'Sam, you can't seriously be considering this? He's lost his mind.'

'Miss Mira, I'd right appreciate it if you stopped saying that.'

'I'll stop saying it when you start making sense!'

'Enough. Both of you.' Sam stepped forwards. For the first time, the hammer felt heavy. 'What happens if the Iactura breaks and you are still... inside?'

'No idea. But we can't wait no longer.'

Sam chewed her lip. 'Are you ready?'

'Never, but go when you can.'

Sam swallowed sour spit. She braced herself and, before she could think any better of it, she swung. The blade bit effortlessly through his chest and into the Iactura. Ruairi opened his mouth to scream, but nothing came out.

His body melted like quicksilver.

CHAPTER 54

Ruairi fell outta the Iactura and plunged through an endless mist. His arms wail-wobbled out but there weren't nothing to grab on to. Face-first, he plunged into a silver ocean.

It poured into his nose, forced his tongue aside and drained down his throat. Fingers brushed his arms, he kicked out hard. The waves crested high and flung him through the glittering sea. Liquid-pink soaked his eyes, lungs empty and desperate.

'*Breathe. You remember that much.*'

The voice were familiar. Soft, spoke like lips were perched right on his ears. Ruairi gasped a desperate cough, vomited black-silver liquid and pulled a breath right into his aching chest. He tried to speak, but all he managed were bubbles.

'*Brace yourself.*'

Something resolved in the liquid. Images, shadows. Ruairi blinked.

Two kids raced down Rotheart Plaza, the ground blasting stone into their ankles, their sides, tearing with greedy fingers.

A woman with black hair pulled a sword from the hands of her dead husband and lashed out, untrained and ineffective.

Smoke poured into an old man's mouth and fire burst from his eyes. The door was locked, his family huddled in the corner.

'Wha...' Ruairi about managed.

'*This is the extermination of Arx,*' the voice spoke. The words formed inside his head, but they weren't like thoughts. And he couldn't shake the feeling of sommat familiar. Where'd he heard it before?

Ruairi forced another gasp, like trying to breathe with sand in his lungs. He tried to swim, but his body were frozen.

Another image, a shadow that burst through the dark.

Fetch.

He were cornered, blood swimming down his shoulder. Quill gripped his gashed stomach, pressed against the wall. A Fog-Eye slammed an axe between his eyes.

'Bastards!' Fetch ripped his blade right down its chest, deep enough the body almost split in two.

But the mist just poured and the Fog-Eye rose again.

Six others turned around the corner. Fetch whirled his back and, in that instant, Ruairi could feel his exhaustion. The blade in his hands, a red-spike ache in his chest that said sommat were really wrong. The ceaseless sting of countless wounds untreated.

Fetch slammed into the wall. No escape now. His eyes dropped and he took a deep, dry-throat breath.

He charged the Fog-Eyes. His blade took one through the throat and he backhanded a cut into the mouth of one that snuck up at his side. The blade caught in the ruin of the Fog-Eyed cheek.

And the others attacked. Knocked his blade from his fingers, grabbed the bandages, the skin, forced their hands down his throat and tore him open. Fetch didn't even have time to scream.

'Fetch!' The word burst from Ruari's torn throat. A single bubble, it rose through the ocean. Burst.

The weight of the silver ocean beneath the mist pressed down on Ruairi. He struggled, just for a moment. Those fingers wrapped around his arms, his legs.

Pulled him down into the dark.

'*You're giving up.*' It weren't a question.

Ruairi just closed his eyes. Let the liquid swirl around his mouth. Breathing took effort.

'*Are there no more reasons to take another breath?*'

Ruairi were falling. He could almost feel the wind whip around his face. Blue skies overhead, the green grass far below.

'*Never thought you'd get so good at lyin' to yourself, Hopalong.*' Fetch's voice.

'*I thought I was lucky, but you've had more than your fair share.*' The Ant.

The dead spoke to him. He could pay them back. The ground was closer.

'*You think this settles our debt?*' Fetch's voice bit. '*I paid for your life, you think you don't owe me?*'

He had nothing left.

'*You carry our memories.*'

'*And you were always so naïve.*'

Something stirred. An image from the shadow trapped inside his head. He saw Pa as a young man. But there weren't no black cloak this time. Just a head of curly hair and eyes trained far beyond the city. He hadn't left Arx to run away. He'd left for a new beginning. For the future. For the one thing Arx had lost.

Hope. The hope, of those stupid enough to entrust it to a farmer with no skills worth noting, and a conscience bloodied by a stolen blade through his hero's neck.

'The dead ain't want for nothing.' Ruairi opened his eyes and the sky vanished. 'But I'm still here.'

He sucked a breath through the silver. Kicked his legs towards the brightness overhead. Burst from the surface of the quicksilver ocean. A platform of mist formed beneath his feet and he yanked himself free. Breath burst with silver spew right down his chest. Tongue of mist spiralled around Ruairi, lifted him into a twilight sky filled with silver orbs. Ropes of fire burned between the darkness.

Something blinked, high overhead. Ice-blue eyes.

'Silverspine. What have you done?'

'*I have freed Arx from the torment of memory.*' The voice boomed around him, like his heart were bursting in his ears.

'Bullshit.' Ruairi couldn't stop hisself.

'*I can see yours, Ruairi. Your guilt. Their deaths tear at you.*'

'Of course it does! My stomach is crawling with it. But I earned this pain. The Ant, and Fetch and all. I might not have swung the sword at him, but you ain't no way smart if you don't think it weren't on me. Pain is no price to pay for the truth.'

'*The truth breaks us all.*'

A headache began to pulse behind Ruairi's eyes. Like a coil wound, tighter and tighter. Felt like sommat were going on in his head. Like his eyes were being forced from his face and his mind were expanding.

Memories became clear. The smog evaporated from his mind like smoke blown into the open sky.

A shockwave shuddered through his limbs. His muscles twitched and twisted. Painful like. Ruairi gritted his teeth and waited for it to pass.

But it only got worse.

'What… are you doin' to me?' Ruairi gasped. Felt like his back were being trampled. Every inch of his body contracted. Squeezed in on itself, like his blood were trying to strangle him from the inside.

'This is your reality, Ruairi. Without your father's shade.'

Then the real pain began.

Tears squeezed from Ruairi's eyes. The pain came in waves, each one higher than the last. Felt like rusty hooks were trying to pull his spine outta his mouth. His body began to shift. To twist and warp like a cloth wrung out to dry. He bent over, unable to stand straight no more.

He saw Pa. The shake of his old man's head. Ma bending to help him stand up. Abi helping him to the bathroom. Saw that terribly familiar look in their eyes.

Even as his body roared out, it were the shame that hurt the most.

'Don't let it break you…'

Ruairi started. There were that voice again! He looked around and caught the glimpse of sommat fixed to the Iactura.

Every step felt like a bolt of lightning through his eyes. A body were pinned to the metal pillar, black bladed knife dug through its throat. Metal mask clamped to its face, red tears dribbled down steel cheeks.

'Sightless?' Ruairi asked.

He shook his head. The mask fell free, disappeared beneath the mist. The face beneath were bearded and eyeless, with a thick scar against his throat. '… *Caelan.*'

'How are you here? I thought … What happened to you?'

'I just wanted to fill the gap. I have every memory in Arx coursing through my body but I am still so empty.' His head sank.

Ruairi forced himself to his knees. The mist wisped around him. 'You spoke to me, didn't you? In that ocean down there. It was you I were hearing.'

'I can't abandon them.' Caelan's head wavered. *'First it was fear. Then oblivion. Then greed, madness and so much anger. Silverspine was a*

failure. The Austelli. Kuyt. Addie. Even Danni. I owe their memories more than mindless eternity.'

'What do we do?'

Caelan's head snapped back and he groaned. His fingers twitched. *'Did you mean what you said? That pain is no price to pay... for the truth.'*

'I... I reckon so.'

'Then pull the black knife from my throat.'

'That'll kill you.' A memory stirred. Dirk in a forest clearing, arrowhead through his knee.

'I am Silverspine. I am Caelan. Those eyes up there will close when mine do. I want... to do something worthwhile with the life I was given.' He snorted a pink-tinged tear. *'Fuck me, why can I only see it now?'*

Beneath the blue eyes, mist twisted and spiralled. Shadows stormed inside. The blue eyes blinked and those shadows reached for Ruairi.

'It's time to choose, Ruairi. This will hurt. When my connection with the Iactura is severed, the agony of every forgotten memory is about to race through your mind.'

Ruairi gripped the hilt of the knife in Caelan's throat. 'Hold on despite the pain? I've been training for that my whole life.'

The ocean shuddered far below. Waves crashed with the sound of ice on fire. Red bolts pulsed through the eyes overhead.

Liquid silver spiralled through the mist and slammed into Ruairi.

Pain. Singular. Exquisite. Incomprehensible. Iron hooks beneath his fingernails, a spine torn up through his throat, nerve endings burned with liquid fire.

But Ruairi held firm. It were only pain.

He could deal with pain.

Caelan's fog-eyes glowed now. The black knife pulsed in his throat. The Iactura shook behind him. *'I could have been... a good man.'*

Caelan drew a deep breath. Ruairi pulled the knife free. And the silver ocean rose to crash into the Iactura.

CHAPTER 55

Sam passed her hammer between her hands. Couldn't stop looking at the Iactura, the spot where Ruairi had just disappeared. It didn't feel possible. The heartfire lashed just barely beneath the cracks in the ground.

'And now all I have to do is destroy the pissing thing,' she muttered.

'Sam? What are you going to do?' Mira's voice was faint. She sat on a fallen rock, her eyes darting to the doors of the Midnight Chamber high above. Watching for the Fog-Eye.

'Your guess...' Sam just shook her head.

'Sam, get back!'

Mira's voice was all the warning she got before the Iactura blasted light from its midnight surface. Another enormous quake roared through the cavern. Huge chunks of rock fell into blinding cracks and Sam leapt out of the way.

Heartfire boiled from the ground. Mira rushed over and Sam forced her to the back of the cavern, pressed tight against the wall. The molten fire rose like fingers from deep beneath the rock.

With a roar, it poured into the Iactura.

Sam watched, unable to move. The metal burst with light, flickered and flashed and began to bubble. Shadow faces rose and burst across the surface and the rocks shook with unheard screams. Heat like nothing she'd ever experienced throbbed through the cavern. The metal wavered like a mirage, wave after wave, washing over her.

'Impossible.' Her lips dried out.

Heartfire lashed at the Iactura, over and over, slamming and draining into the metal. An image flickered in Sam's mind. An idiot apprentice, stood by a chain-link broken from too high a heat and too cold a quench.

A faint tapping at the wall to her side. Sam looked up. One of the cracks in the wall was leaking. A pile of rocks led to a hairline crack.

'Mira. Stay here.'

'Sam, what are you doing?' Mira tried to grab at her, hissed at her bloody bandages.

'Something stupid. You should be used to that by now.' She scrabbled up the rocks. A wave of heartfire broke from a chasm nearby and she wavered, wobbled and spun her arms to stop from falling deep into that endless fire. 'Proper metalwork needs a clear head and a calm mind,' she muttered.

Sam slammed her hammer into the rock with a grating *crunch*. The wall shuddered at the impact.

The fracture widened.

She struck again. Chunks of rock shattered.

Again. And the wall broke open.

Water from the Mucro poured out of the rock like an arrow from a bow, smashed into the Iactura. This hiss was deafening. It blasted her from the rocks, slammed her into the ground. Steam burst from metal, settled wet into Sam's throat.

She struggled to her feet. Foul-smelling water sucked at her shoes. She blinked past the steam, the spots in her eyes.

The Iactura groaned. The surface was dull, spiderwebbed with cracks. Steam and mist and smog and light poured out. All that blood-metal. It had never properly set. Callisteel was no alloy. It wasn't even *steel*. Just brittle pieces of ruined iron.

Anything made in anger is ugly.

Sam set her feet. Lifted Jak's hammer.

The Callisteel crashed into the pillar with the sound like a great silver bell.

A pulse of light lit the Iactura from the inside. The air was sucked from the cavern and everything stopped.

A tempest of fire, ash and iron burst from the hole in the metal pillar.

And the Iactura shattered into the firestorm.

CHAPTER 56

Sam leant on the back of Mira's chair in the ruins of the Midnight Chamber. Technically, she was sitting in DeMori's seat, DeGaya's had been lost to the heartfire, but no one said anything. Mira said she wanted a new system. Well then, maybe this time around it could just be a chair.

'...he had forgotten so much,' an elderly man was saying. He blinked. His eyes were piercing blue, frozen smoke that had become his pupils. 'My memories returned the same as everyone else. I wonder how many of us remember losing our eyes now.'

'Do you regret it?' Mira asked. 'If you could lose those memories, just picture him as you knew him, would you do it?'

The old man tapped his chin for a moment. Then he shook his head. 'No. No, I wouldn't. It hurts, the boy was closer than a son. I'll never get past that, but I will recover. And I'll cross my fingers we all do the same.' He shuffled to his feet.

'Thank you, Mr Aestere.'

'Please, it's Kuyt. First Minister.' He waved his farewells and scuttled out of the door.

'Don't call me that,' Mira said, but her voice was soft and the remains of a smile kicked the corners of her lips. 'Scribe Carsi, did you get that down?'

The Scelus sat dangerously close to the mismatched scaffolding that spanned the crevasse down into the caverns, nodded and fingered through her sheaf of paper. 'Yes First Minister. It tallies well with what we've learned prior.'

'Good. And how goes the shipbuilding?'

'First Minister, no one has built a ship in decades. We've called in the fisherfolk, but their sloops are vastly different to a seaworthy ship. They've got access to the old designs from the Hall of Records, but progress is slow.'

'I don't care. We need envoys. That last earthquake has done the wall in for good. Arx is open to the world again, and I want someone in audience with Narisé before the end of the month.'

'The end of the month? Narisé is forty leagues away, at least!'

'I've had a titful of you today, what the sodding shit is a league?'

Sam left them to it, wandered over to the window. The destruction was almost total. Arx had been razed. Half of the Citadel was ash, the Nest was gone, the Mucro an empty riverbed and the great walls were rubble.

Yet as she watched, a pair of women outside laughed and set their saws to the stripped back pieces of wood, wiped the sweat from their faces. One wore the tattered remains of a fashionable jacket, the other had a leather smock around her scarred shoulders.

Not three feet below, a chunk of the Iactura was slammed through the wall. No longer blue or black, just dull grey. The surviving pieces were being excavated and hurled into the Saltiron Sea.

It was a curious memory, the destruction of the Iactura. As soon as her hammer connected, the pillar tore open like a hurricane had been released. And she'd felt something in that storm. Strong as a blacksmith's arms around her shoulders. They held her there until the final *pulse* flung her back into the wall, knocked her into darkness.

She'd come to in the Temple hospital, Mira in the bed one over.

The door to the Midnight Chamber slammed and snapped Sam out of her reverie. Scribe Carsi was gone. Mira rolled her eyes behind her brand new, gilt-edged glasses, then winced. She pinned her wrists between her knees. One hand was bandaged, thick and clean. The surgeon, Lincento something, was optimistic she'd regain movement within the month.

The other was missing. Infection and amputation. It was a miracle she'd kept her arm.

'How is it?' Sam walked over.

'It hurts.'

'Mira. I'm sorry.'

'You think a good fight would help to pass the time before my next meeting?'

'I don't want to fight. I just… I should have listened to you.'

'That is always true.'

'You told me I was batshit.'

'You are.'

'And I still dragged you over the river…'

'Oh so you *do* want to fight.' Mira launched to her feet. 'Good. Because the only way to stop thinking about how much it sodding hurts is to take my mind off it. You said this *exact* thing to Ruairi. How dare you try and take away my choices? I followed you. I'd do it again. So bolt your trap or I'll have the Walkers do it for you.'

It was a joke. At least, Sam hoped it was a joke, but it certainly wasn't beyond the realm of Mira's new remit. The Walkers had been gathered around her before she woke. Guard duty they called it, despite her protestations.

First Minister Mira DeIudex was the only surviving Viceroy. Ever since she took her seat, the scribes and small-time councillors, the treasury agents and election officials had swarmed to her.

The old Arx was dead, but those with titles were still clinging, desperately, to the corpse of tradition.

They clearly didn't know Mira at all. You can't patch a crack when a blade breaks. You melt the sword down into something new.

'I still reckon you masterminded all of this,' Sam said. 'First Minister Mira. The world trembles.'

'Oh stop it. First Minister doesn't mean anything. We're starting afresh, all titles are gone. They listen to me for now, but I'll earn a voice or I won't have one. Same as everyone.'

'Yes, watch everyone vote against the Hero of Arx. The woman who single-handedly…'

'Is that a sodding joke?'

Sam grimaced. 'The woman who, by sheer force of will, brought peace to the divided halves of Arx. Rumours abound that you were the one who destroyed the Iactura as well.'

'Why do those rumours abound?'

'Because I keep telling people that you did it.' Sam grinned. Picking on Mira was fun, but the woman was a natural. Sick of the Walkers looming over her, she'd sent them out mining stone. The old riverbed was already half-way filled in. With the Nest razed, the two sides of the city were no more. No Austelli, no Nest, even the Walkers had been threatened with a new name.

Arx was healing. Two sides swallowed into something smaller. Something more… complete.

Not that it was bloodless. Bitter feuds ran deep, and a handful thought it was a great time to settle old debts. But they were in the minority.

Besides, the winter was in full swing. Crops were in short supply, and no one had eaten in days. Austelli, Nestlings, Walkers, Councillors, people with coins and people without were scrambling just to survive.

And they would. Mira would see to that. Sam would have bet her eyes on it.

'Still doesn't feel real. Why me?' she asked.

'Right place, right time. You were always destined for some kind of really dull brilliance. Why do you think I leeched on to you all these years?' Sam said.

'My exceptional arse?'

'Great for sitting,' Sam agreed. 'Especially since that's all you get to do now.'

'Such a tragedy. If only I could hit bits of metal with other bits metal instead. That's the real dream.'

Sam snorted. 'I've got shit to do.'

'Latrines are being dug beyond the walls.' Mira waved her away. 'Go.'

'Such a gracious ruler.' Sam gave the worst curtsey she could manage. 'You coming tomorrow?'

Jak's funeral. They'd reserved a plot for it at the cemetery.

'Wouldn't miss it.'

Outside, the taste of the air was shocking. It was just so clean. Like licking a fluffy cloud. Walkers and workers mingled in the wind, raising buildings and filling cracks in the ground. Despite all the bustle, the city still felt so empty.

After the Iactura fell, all those with memories lost had them returned. And so many had sacrificed injury, death. Most Fog-Eye died the instant their memories flooded back. Some nights, that kept her from sleeping.

Other times, she was just grateful for the ones that survived.

Sam walked to their little hut, just off Steelhammer Row. Old tarpaulin stretched across the wooden bones. It was filled with noise, as ever. Vicky and Lance bustled inside. House-building had not been high on their list of skills she remembered Vicky boasting about, but the self-styled family forewoman went at it with a will.

'Sam!' Vicky called from a hole in the outer wall. 'It's about time. Three orders arrived this morning, where were you?'

'Personal guest of First Minister Mira DeIudex. Why, how did you spend your morning?'

'I carved a lintel.'

'Is that… good?'

'Better than going to see the First Minister in a scraggly old shirt like that. I know Mira is your old drinking buddy, but do *try* and remember a bit of decorum.'

Sam just laughed. 'You hearing this Lance?'

'It really is a poor-quality shirt…' Lance shook his head.

Oh sod it, there were two of them.

'Why are you still loitering? Get to work. You too Lance, hold that beam up. Father, off your backside and help him.'

'Yes Vicky.' Father stood slowly. His blue eyes were haunting, and he didn't speak much anymore, but he was alive. His mind returned and sometimes, he even smiled. He shuffled past the hole in the wall. 'Save me,' he whispered when he passed Sam.

She snorted. 'Later. If I don't get to work, Vicky'll have my kneecaps.'

'I'll have more than that!' she shouted from the back of the room.

Sam made a show of leaving sharpish, moved over to the tent-forge just opposite. The new Acarris family crest was picked out over the opening. Jak's hammer, picked out in silver on a black shield. Steel strong enough to destroy the Iactura.

She pushed open the entrance. The forge was warm, fires burning, metal ready for work.

'Forgemaster.' Jonas Karrin acknowledged her with a nod.

'Not yet.' Sam shook her head at her erstwhile apprentice. Her own legacy, he'd tracked her down in the graveyard. The memories Mistress Ignis had stolen from him… well, she could relate to those.

Sam picked at the faded brand on the back of her hand and pulled on a pair of heavy forge gloves. She walked over to the rack on the wall and took down Jak's hammer. The list of metalwork requests was pinned to the wall.

'First lesson. Axioms are for idiots and those who earn them. Go grab that stack of copper. Not the blade metal, we'll send those back. Stick some more fuel on, we're not making tea here and I'm feeling the chill…'

EPILOGUE

Ruairi groaned. Ground were hard, bloody Arx begrudged him every shifted clod, but he weren't of the mind to give up now. Dirt under his fingernails and sweat wibbling down the crack of his arse, he plunged the spade in and hefted the soil over his shoulder. A tearing ache near his tailbone felt like he'd been paddled but he kept on keeping on, digging past the dark spots that spat in his eyes and eventually had three holes just about the right size.

Wiped his forehead. Sun were sharp beyond the city. Best get to it, they weren't getting any riper. He waddled over to the cart. Rented a mule to drag the thing, and it were a bad-tempered beast. Mangy enough to avoid the cookpots, it went to bite his arm the moment he got too close.

'Bastard thing, I take the harness off and you throw a snit? That's gratitude for you.' He pushed the creature's head away and made for the cart.

Lifted the first of the two bodies held there.

'Fetch.' He daren't peel the shroud free, not after what those Fog-Eyes had done to him. Ruairi swallowed. 'I were too slow to pay you back. Reckon that debt's mine for life now.' He scooped Fetch's body in his arms. He were light, like the loss of his spirit had taken the weight from his bones. 'I hope Ro is over there. Won't hold my breath though. She's gotta end up somewhere nicer than you.'

He knelt beside the grave, heedless of the needle driving into his coccyx, and lowered Fetch's body nice and slow.

Ruairi bowed his head and closed his eyes.

When he were done, he filled the grave and went back to the cart.

The second shroud were more body-like. Some Scelus had popped his head back on his neck, but the shroud were all that kept the two bits together.

'Back to the ants. Sorry about your leg. And your head.' Ruairi lowered his eyes. The sight of his blade through the Ant's neck burned in his mind. A memory he'd never forget. 'You'd have known more about honour than I do. Reckon it'll take me a long time to figure it out.' He lowered the Ant into his grave and covered him up slow, with more'n a little sweating and swearing. Scattered some seeds over both the mounds for good measure.

The last grave he left empty. The hilt of a black-bladed knife stood up as headstone. He sat on the lip of the dirt to catch his breath. His spine twanged like a wire pulled taut, but what were a little pain? He turned to the sky and smiled.

It were blue.

ACKNOWLEDGMENTS

Thank you to Mom and Dad for always making sure I had something to read, and for giving Percy the Parkkeeper a Yorkshire Accent.

Thank you to Kath McKay and Ray French for telling me to stop writing about urine so much, and for their endless patience as I first learned how to write – and then learned how to teach.

Thank you to Martin Goodman and George Biggs. Martin is the reason this book exists – first as a PhD supervisor and then as a publisher whose faith in this manuscript has never wavered. George is one of the finest editors I have worked with and this book would not be what it is without his advice and encouragement. I owe you both more than I can express.

Thank you to all my students, past and present. Your enthusiasm, imagination and mockery has been the finest of inspiration.

Thank you to all the writers I have met, have read, have interviewed, have drunk coffee with, have admired from afar. For not being machines.

Thank you to Alfie, for letting me tell him stories. There is no greater critic, nor more deserving audience.

Thank you to Pickle. He is a dog and can't read. I admire that.

Thank you to Alice for being the reason I became the person that I am. Thank you to Laura for reminding me that the sky is filled with stars. Writing is a labour of love. Which means this book is for the two of you.

Thank you.

BIO

Ed Hurst was born in the misty English lands known as The Midlands. A nerd-of-all-trades, he spent much of his childhood between pages of books, playing video games and of course, writing stories. School was strict, stifling, and saved only through the efforts of Brian Jacques, Paul Stewart & Chris Riddell, and Terry Pratchett. Fortunately, at university he found a lifelong love of education. He worked his way across the UK as a waiter, a bartender and an actor until finally he found the promised lands of Up North.

Ed obtained his Creative Writing PhD at the University of Hull, where he is now Programme Director for Creative Writing. He lectures in Fantasy, Sci-Fi and Horror prose, as well as researching the impact of AI on Higher Education. Fortunately, lengthy debates with AM, GLaDOS and the Geth have thusfar proven to be a fantastic start point.

You can find him online via X @edmund_hurst, and if it is a Wednesday he can often be found livestreaming video games with his Creative Writing students via twitch.tv/edhurst.

Printed in the USA
CPSIA information can be obtained
at www.ICGtesting.com
JSHW010903100824
67891JS00007B/12